CAT
BREAKING
FREE

*Also by Shirley Rousseau Murphy
in Large Print:*

Cat Fear No Evil
Cat Seeing Double

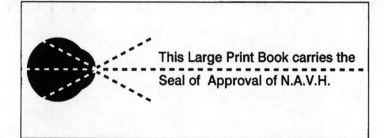

This Large Print Book carries the
Seal of Approval of N.A.V.H.

CAT
BREAKING
FREE

A JOE GREY MYSTERY

Shirley Rousseau Murphy

Thorndike Press • Waterville, Maine

Published in 2006 by arrangement with HarperCollins Publishers.

Thorndike Press® Large Print Americana.

The tree indicium is a trademark of Thorndike Press.

The text of this Large Print edition is unabridged.
Other aspects of the book may vary from the original edition.

Set in 16 pt. Plantin by Christina S. Huff.

Printed in the United States on permanent paper.

Library of Congress Cataloging-in-Publication Data

Murphy, Shirley Rousseau.
    Cat breaking free : a Joe Grey mystery / by Shirley Rousseau Murphy.
        p. cm. — (Thorndike Press large print Americana)
    ISBN 0-7862-8466-8 (lg. print : hc : alk. paper)
    1. Grey, Joe (Fictitious character) — Fiction.   2. Feral cats — Fiction.   3. California — Fiction.   4. Robberies — Fiction.   5. Cats — Fiction.   6. Large type books.
I. Title.   II. Thorndike Press large print Americana series.
PS3563.U7619C313 2006
    813'.54—dc22   2006002266

As the Founder/CEO of NAVH, the only national health agency solely devoted to those who, although not totally blind, have an eye disease which could lead to serious visual impairment, I am pleased to recognize Thorndike Press* as one of the leading publishers in the large print field.

Founded in 1954 in San Francisco to prepare large print textbooks for partially seeing children, NAVH became the pioneer and standard setting agency in the preparation of large type.

Today, those publishers who meet our standards carry the prestigious "Seal of Approval" indicating high quality large print. We are delighted that Thorndike Press is one of the publishers whose titles meet these standards. We are also pleased to recognize the significant contribution Thorndike Press is making in this important and growing field.

Lorraine H. Marchi, L.H.D.
Founder/CEO
NAVH

* Thorndike Press encompasses the following imprints: Thorndike, Wheeler, Walker and Large Print Press.

She possesses an essentially wild soul. Relish her versatility, gentleness, playfulness, adaptability, and capacity for forming loving bonds. But also thrill to hints of that ever present wild creature — her inner wildcat — in all its glory, mystery, and paradox.

— Wendy Christensen, *Outwitting Cats*

Not water nor food can be withheld from the living creature lest it die; nor freedom withheld lest the living spirit wither and give up life.

— Unknown

1

"We don't need that bimbo living next door," the tomcat hissed. "Why would they rent to the likes of her?" His ears were back, his yellow eyes narrowed, his sleek gray body tense with disgust as he paced the top of the long brick barbecue, looking down at his human housemate. He kept his voice low, so not to alarm curious neighbors.

Joe Grey and Clyde had been together since Joe was a kitten, though it was just four years ago this summer that he discovered he could speak. He didn't know whether that revelation had been more shocking to him or to Clyde. For a human, to wake up one morning and find that his cat could argue back couldn't be easy. Joe paused now in his irritable pacing to study Clyde, then glanced toward the high patio wall behind him. Peering as intently as if he could see right through the white plaster barrier to the house next door, he considered the backroom of their neighbors' vacation cottage where Clyde's old flame had taken up residence.

"Bimbo," the tomcat repeated, muttering. "Why did they rent to her?"

"They only just bought the house," Clyde said. "Maybe they need the money."

"But why Chichi? And how did she find you?"

"Leave it, Joe. Don't get worked up." Clyde sat on the back steps with his first cup of coffee, enjoying the early-morning sunshine. He scratched his bare knee and smoothed his dark, neat hair. "Call it coincidence."

The tomcat replied with a hiss. Chichi Barbi was not among his favorite humans; "bimbo" was too polite a word for the thieving little chit. "Maybe they don't know she moved in. Maybe she broke in, a squatter, like that homeless guy who . . ."

"Don't start, Joe. Don't make a federal case. That's so way out, even for your wild imagination!"

"Not at all," Joe said haughtily. "Look around you, that stuff happens. That homeless guy last winter spent three months crashing in other people's houses before anyone noticed. Three months of free bed and board, free food from the cupboards, use of all the facilities — five houses before a neighbor started asking questions, then called the cops. Moved from house to house as innocent as you please and no one . . ."

"Chichi Barbi might be a lot of things, but she's not a housebreaker. That guy was a transient, half-gone on drugs. You knew the Mannings were going to rent the place. Chichi might live a little loose, but she wouldn't . . ."

"Wouldn't what?" Joe's ears were back, his whiskers flat. He showed formidable teeth. "In San Francisco she rips you off for five hundred bucks, but she wouldn't rip off your neighbors? You want to tell me why not?"

Clyde stared at the tomcat and silently sipped his coffee. Clyde's work-hardened hands were permanently stained with traces of grease from his automotive shop. Otherwise, he looked pretty good for a Saturday morning, not his usual ragged cutoffs and stained T-shirt; almost respectable, the tomcat thought. He had showered and shaved before breakfast, blow-dried his short, dark, freshly cut hair, and was dressed in clean tan walking shorts and a good-looking ivory velour shirt. He was even wearing the handsome new Rockports that Ryan had admired in a shop window. "Pretty snazzy," Joe said, looking his housemate over. "Ryan's been a positive influence. She's right, you know — with a little incentive, you clean up pretty good."

"Ryan Flannery has nothing to do with how I look in the morning. I simply felt like showering before I made coffee. There some law against that? And we weren't talking about Ryan, we were talking about Chichi Barbi."

"And I was wondering why Chichi has pushed herself off on you again. Wondering what she has in mind this time."

"You are so suspicious, I never saw a cat so suspicious. Maybe she didn't even know we lived here."

"Right." Joe Grey twitched a whisker.

"Maybe she *is* here for a vacation," Clyde said. "A few weeks at the beach, and to shop, just as she said."

Dropping down from the barbecue to the chaise, Joe stretched out along the green cushion in a shaft of sunshine, and began to indolently wash his white paws, effectively dismissing Clyde. Around man and cat, the early-morning light was cool and golden. Within the patio's high, plastered walls, their little world was private and serene — a far cry from the scruffy, weedy plot this backyard had been some months ago, with its half-dead grass and open to the neighbors' inquisitive stares through the rotting, broken fence.

Above them, sunlight filtered gently down through the new young leaves of the maple tree to the brick paving, and around them, the raised planters were bright with spring flowers, the plastered benches scattered with comfortable cushions. Beyond the trellis roof that shaded the barbecue, they could see only a glimpse of the neighbors' rooftop, which now sheltered Chichi Barbi. Despite his dislike of the woman, Joe Grey had to smile. Chichi's sudden appearance might be innocent or might not, but for the two weeks since she'd moved in, she'd made Clyde's life miserable. He'd started locking the patio gate and kept the draperies pulled on that side of the house. He locked the front door when he was home and he studiously avoided the front yard, slipping around the far side of the house to the driveway, sliding quietly into his yellow Chevy roadster and pulling out with as little noise as he could manage.

"Anyway," Clyde said, "the morning's too nice to waste it thinking about some neighbor. How much damage can one airhead do?"

The gray tomcat's yellow-eyed glance telegraphed a world of ideas on the subject.

"You have a short memory — *and* an amazing tolerance."

"Come on, Joe."

Joe kneaded the chaise pad in a satisfying rhythm. "One airhead bimbo with a big mouth and a nonstop talent for trouble, to say nothing of amazingly sticky fingers. One thieving bimbo who will rip a guy off for five hundred bucks and never once act guilty or ashamed. Who shows up here crawling all over you like she never stole a thing, all smiles and kisses." Joe stretched, enjoying the brightening caress of the sun. The golden morning light gleaming across the tomcat's short gray coat made it shine like velvet and delineated every sleek muscle. Joe's white paws and white chest were washed and immaculate; the white stripe down his nose shone as pristine as new porcelain. There was no stain of blood from last night's hunting, no smallest speck of grime to mar his perfection. Watching Clyde, he yawned with bored contentment — but his yellow eyes were appraising and, looking up again at the patio wall, he imagined Chichi spying on their conversation. He envisioned the brassy blonde climbing up on a ladder to peer over, could almost hear her brash and bubbling "good morning," almost see her flashing, flirty smile.

No, Chichi Barbi hadn't driven down here from San Francisco for an innocent vacation, with no idea that she'd be living next door to Clyde Damen. No way he'd believe that degree of coincidence.

There had been a time when the sight of curvaceous Chichi Barbi had sent Clyde straight to the moon. But now, Joe thought, smiling, Chichi hadn't counted on Ryan Flannery. Ryan had a stake in Clyde Damen that she wouldn't abandon to the likes of that little gold digger; and Ryan Flannery was a fighter.

Clyde had been dating Ryan for nearly a year, since she moved down to Molena Point from San Francisco. Escaping a difficult marriage, she had started life over in her mid-thirties, establishing her own building contracting business in the village.

Ryan had not only brought out the best in Clyde, had not only accomplished marked improvements in Clyde's appearance and attitude, but, with her impressive talents, she had brightened their lives in other ways. She had turned their dull little bachelor pad into a spacious, handsome dwelling, had changed their boxy, single-story Cape Cod cottage into an imaginative two-story residence with a new facade, new kitchen, new upstairs, to say nothing of the handsome and private outdoor living area where they were now enjoying the morning. She had even designed a private cat tower atop the new second-floor master suite, had built for Joe his own retreat, a six-sided glassed house with shingled roof and an unbroken view of the village rooftops and the sea beyond. A singularly private pad with soft cushions, a water dish, and easy access over the roofs to the peaks and upper balconies of the entire village.

"Say you're right about her deliberately finding me," Clyde said, tentatively abandoning the coincidence theory. "Why would she look for me here? I could have moved anywhere when you and I left San Francisco. Palm Springs. Malibu. Cucamunga. I sure as hell never told anyone where I was going. Well, a few close friends, but no one who'd tell Chichi. And how . . . ?"

"The woman can read," Joe said. "She can get on the Web, punch up the directories and cross-references. These days, you can find anyone. A human has no private life — better you should be a cat. Even for us, it's getting harder. Microchips and these new electronic devices . . ." But he licked his paw, thinking with anticipation of cell phones for cats . . .

Though that tempting prospect was a way

off yet, and surely would have its downside. He looked levelly at Clyde. "Easy enough for her to find you, and that's what she did."

"Maybe. Maybe not. This *is* a famous tourist destination, everyone comes to Molena Point. She heads down here for a luxurious vacation, gets settled, and just happens across my address."

"Oh, right. And purely by accident, she rents the house next door."

"She isn't renting, she's working for those people. I told you that. House-sitting's a big deal, to ward off break-ins and burglaries. People want house sitters, someone on the premises. And with rents through the roof, people who can't afford to stay here are eager for the job. Those people who bought next door, they've only owned that house a few months. Living in San Francisco, they don't know anyone here in the village. They hire a friend in the city, someone who wants a free vacation."

Joe snorted.

"Makes sense to me," Clyde said. "Chichi is nothing more than the caretaker."

Joe watched Clyde narrowly, then turned his back, washing diligently. Chichi worried him. Clyde didn't need that little baggage back in his life. Chichi Barbi was still as gorgeous as she had been when she'd dazzled

Clyde years ago, when the buxom blonde had seemed the answer to a bachelor's dreams.

Joe had been just a young cat then, not full grown but not innocent. He'd hated when Chichi made over him with her sickly sweet "Kitty, kitty, kitty," all fake and gushing. And now Clyde couldn't step out the front door without Chichi appearing from nowhere, wearing a tiny little bikini or some equally revealing scrap, prancing out to get something from her car or to change the sprinkler. And she was at their front door at least once a day, simpering at Clyde, wanting to borrow milk, flour, or a hammer and nails to hang a picture — at least Clyde didn't offer to help with her little carpentry ruses. So far, every time she rang the bell, Clyde shut the door in her face while he fetched the required item, left her standing on the porch. That had heartened Joe considerably. But Clyde's rudeness turned Chichi sulky for only a few minutes, then she was all over him again, all smiles and glossy pink lipstick and slick hair spray and enough perfume to gas a platoon of marines — how much of that could a guy take and still keep his hands off her?

"Maybe you're right," Joe said tentatively. "Maybe she isn't after you, maybe she came

18

down to fleece the tourists — or fleece our rich celebrities." Molena Point was crawling with money. "She finds out you're here, thinks you'd make good cover for whatever she's up to.

"Or maybe she reads the want ads looking for a patsy, sees the Mannings' ad for a caretaker, checks the cross-reference to get a line on the Mannings' neighbors."

"Come on, Joe. That's . . ."

"She discovers you live next door, and voilà! Opportunities she hadn't dreamed of. She interviews, gets the job, and moves in. What could be simpler. Set up her little schemes, maybe set up the Mannings for some kind of rip-off, checks their financial ratings . . . And comes on to you at the same time, to set you up as an alibi."

Clyde's usually agreeable square face and brown eyes were dark and foreboding. "What the hell have you been smoking? You've got a whole complicated crime scene going, and she hasn't *done* anything. This snooping into . . ."

"Hasn't done anything *yet*."

"Anyway, she wouldn't believe that she could suck me in again, that I'd fall for a second scam."

"How much did she take you for, the first time? Without a whimper? When you thought she was the love goddess incarnate? Easy as snatching a sparrow from the bird feeder, and in those days, five hundred bucks was like five thousand today — then, you could hardly afford the price of a hamburger!"

"Come on, Joe. I was only a mechanic then, I didn't have my own shop, but I had savings, and if I wanted to . . ."

"If you wanted to be a sucker then, that was your business? Well, whatever you give her this time, Clyde, I swear, if you let her mess up your relationship with Ryan, I'll kill her with my bare claws, then come after you."

Though in fact, Joe thought Ryan had nothing to worry about. Ryan Flannery had everything Chichi didn't. A real, warm beauty. Keen intelligence. Wit. Talent. How many women were excellent carpenters and designers, had a sense of humor, and could cook, too?

Compare that with an artificial size 38C and hair bleached to the color of straw, and it was no contest.

"If Ryan were jealous of Chichi," Clyde said, "it wouldn't say much for Ryan, or for what Ryan thinks of me."

"You're right, there."

"Unless . . ." Clyde looked suddenly

stricken. "That *can't* be why Ryan went off on that pack trip this week with Charlie and Hanni? Not because she's mad at me, because she *is* jealous?"

Charlie Harper, the wife of Molena Point's chief of police, far preferred time on horseback or at her easel to a formal social life. Partly because of this, she and Ryan had hit it off at once. When Ryan's sister, Hanni, moved down from the city, too, to start her own interior design studio, the three women soon became fast friends. The fact that Ryan and Hanni were from a law-enforcement family cemented the bond. Their uncle Dallas worked for the Molena Point Police Department, Dallas and his nieces comprising a family exodus that amused the tomcat. Though why should it? Who wouldn't leave San Francisco with its increasing crime? Molena Point was small, friendly, and comfortable. And the family had had a vacation cottage in the village since the two sisters were children.

Joe said, "If Ryan were worried, you think she'd leave you alone with Chichi for a week? You think she'd go off on horseback, letting Chichi have her way with you?"

"Put that way, you make me sound like a real wimp."

"Anyway," Joe said, "Ryan and Charlie

21

and Hanni have planned for that trip all year, getting their horses in shape, calling the blacksmith, checking their gear . . ."

Clyde smiled. "I'm playing second fiddle to a couple of lady equestrians and a sorrel mare."

Joe yawned. "I'm surprised Chichi keeps pushing you, though, after seeing the chief of police over here two or three times a week." Chief Harper and Clyde had grown up together. Max and one other friend were as close to family as Clyde had. "Unless," Joe said, his yellow eyes narrowing, "unless *that* fits into her plan."

Clyde stared at him. "She's going to pull a scam on Max Harper?"

The tomcat licked his white paws. "Why not? That woman would try to scam anyone. She even tried to make up to Rube, just because he's your dog. Just like she used to baby-talk me in San Francisco."

"She backed off Rube fast enough," Clyde said, smiling. Chichi had been mad as hell when Rube growled at her. In Joe's opinion, the old black Lab was sometimes smarter than Clyde. He looked down at Rube, stretched out across the bricks, his aging black bulk soaking up the sunshine. "Rube knows his women. He should, he's lived with you since he was a pup." Joe watched

22

the elderly Labrador roll over onto a warmer patch of paving.

"Slowing down," Clyde said sadly, setting down his coffee cup and kneeling beside Rube to stroke and talk to the old dog. Rube lifted his head to lick Clyde's hand, his tail flopping on the bricks. But Clyde and the tomcat exchanged a look. Rube hadn't been himself for some time; they were both worried about him. Dr. Firetti had prescribed a heart medication, but he hadn't been encouraging.

Joe was thinking it a blessing that the morning was quiet so the old dog could rest, a silky calm Saturday morning, when their peace was suddenly broken. Loud rock music shattered the silence, jolting all three of them, hard rock coming from next door where they heard a car pulling up the drive on the far side of the neighbors' house. They could hear nothing but the car radio blasting. What ever happened to real music? the tomcat thought. In Clyde's house, the old Basin Street jazz was king; and, since Clyde and Ryan started dating, a certain amount of classical music that even a tomcat could learn to like.

The radio went silent. They heard two car doors slam, then two men's voices, one speaking Spanish as they headed down the drive, to the entry to Chichi's back bedroom. They heard the men knock, heard the door open, heard Chichi's high giggle as the door closed again, then silence. Rising, his ears pressed back with annoyance, the tomcat leaped from the chaise to the barbecue to the top of the plastered wall, where he could see the door and the drive.

An older brown Plymouth coupe stood in the drive. Stretching out along the top of the wall, Joe watched the one bedroom window he could see; the other was around the corner facing a strip of garden and the drive. Inside, Chichi was sitting on the bed facing the two men who sat in straight chairs, their backs to Joe. The three had pulled the night table between them and were studying some kind of papers they had spread out. Frowning, the tomcat dropped from the wall down into the neighbors' scruffy yard. Racing across the rough grass and around the corner, he leaped into the little lemon tree that stood just outside Chichi's other window.

Scorching up into its branches he tried to avoid the tree's nasty little thorns, but one caught him in the paw. Pausing to lick the blood away, he tried to keep his white markings out of sight, hidden among the sparse foliage. What were they looking at? A map?

He climbed higher, stretching out along a brittle limb, peering down.

Yes. A street map of the village. He could see the words "Molena Point" slanted across one corner. One man was Latino, with collar-length black hair. The other was a gringo, with sandy-red hair and short beard. Of what significance were the streets and intersections that the Latino man traced so intently with one stubby finger? Joe could not see the notes Chichi was making, where she had propped a small spiral pad on the corner of the table. He tried to peer around her shoulder but couldn't stretch far enough without risking a fall out of the spindly little tree. He caught a few words, but they were doing more tracing than talking. They seemed to be working out some scenario. It was clear to the tomcat that these three were not, by the wildest stretch, planning a Sunday church picnic.

2

Nothing could be seen on the vast green hills but the three riders, their horses jogging across the rising slopes high above the sea; they were pursued only by swift cloud shadows as ephemeral as ghosts slipping along behind them. Far below them where the hills dropped away, a carpet of fog hung suspended, hiding the cold Pacific. California weather, Charlie thought, loving the swiftly changing contrasts of light and shadow and the damp smell of iodine and salt. The chill wind was refreshing after a good night's sleep and a big breakfast; she was deliciously warm inside her leather jacket; her mass of wild red hair, held back with a leather band, kept her neck warm. She sat the big buckskin easily; she was watching a gull swoop low to disappear below the fog when her attention turned suddenly to the pine forest that followed on her right, deeper inland.

Something moved there, something small and quick. Many somethings, she thought, frowning. Small creatures slipping along fast among the shadows as if secretly following them. In the shifting patterns of sun and shade she tried to make them out, but could see nothing clearly. She didn't want to move Bucky closer and alert her two companions. Uneasily, she studied the woods. She had been watching for some time when, behind her, Ryan put the sorrel mare to a gallop and moved up beside her.

"What are you watching?" the dark-haired young woman said. "What's in there, what are the horses looking at?" Both horses were looking toward the woods, their ears flicking nervously as they stared into the tangled shadows.

"Maybe rabbits," Charlie said. "I really can't see what it is. This time of year, maybe baby rabbits." Though none of their horses was in the habit of shying at rabbits.

Ryan frowned. With her dark Latin beauty and startling green eyes, Ryan Flannery looked, in Charlie's opinion, more like a model than a building contractor. Even this morning with her short dark hair tucked beneath a battered slouch hat and wearing faded jeans and faded sweatshirt, Ryan Flannery was striking, her mix of Irish and Latino blood creating a stunning and singular beauty. Riding Charlie's sorrel mare, turned in the saddle, Ryan peered into the shadows of the woods with curiosity but warily. She looked ready to act if action was needed.

Ryan's sister, moving up beside them so not to miss anything, watched the woods intently. Mounted on a dappled gray gelding whose coat exactly matched her short, well-styled silver hair, Hanni Coon was the glamorous one of the three. Hanni's designer jeans, this morning, were of a skillfully faded shade that dramatically set off her hand-knit coral-and-blue sweater. Her Western boots were too new to look natural; they sported rattlesnake insets and had been handmade by Tony Lama. Hanni's roping saddle was plain but expensive, elegantly understated, with a soft, elk-suede seat. The saddle blanket was hand-woven llama wool from Peru. Even the temperament of Hanni's gray gelding matched her own. He was as flamboyant as Hanni, a flashy, meddlesome Arab who would rather prance and side-step than take the trail at a sensible walk. As the three women watched the woods, Ryan and Hanni perhaps envisioning baby rabbits, Charlie knew that what she had seen wasn't rabbits. As they crested the next hill, she deliberately turned away.

"I guess it's gone," she said, hiding her nervousness. Ryan and Hanni didn't need to see what was there. The three women rode quietly for some time, caught in the beauty of the rolling green land and the muffled thunder of the waves crashing against the cliffs far below. The piping of a meadowlark shattered the air, as bright as tinkling glass. A hawk dropped from the clouds screaming, circling close above them; but the meadowlark was gone. In all the world, at this moment, there seemed no other presence but the birds and the innocent beasts of the forest. Of the creatures that followed them, only Charlie guessed their true nature. She told herself she was wrong, that probably those small, swift shadows *were* only rabbits.

Ryan and Hanni soon strung out behind Charlie again into a comfortable riding distance. She looked down at the fog far below her, the fog she had loved since she was a child, imagining hidden worlds among the mist's pale curtains. Even when she was grown, in art school in San Francisco, she had indulged herself in fantasies as she walked the city's steep streets where fog lay thick. Peering into mist-curtained courtyards and gardens, she had imagined all manner of wonders; as if, if she looked hard enough, she would glimpse unknown and enchanted realms.

Now below her hidden beneath the fog lay her own village, her home of two years — her home forevermore, Charlie thought, smiling. Molena Point was her own enchanted village — enchanted if one didn't look too closely, at the dark side that any idyllic setting could reveal.

Stroking Bucky's neck, she thought how lucky she was to have moved to Molena Point. She was certain that fate had led her to Max. To have married Max Harper was more than a dream come true. She wished he were here, riding beside her instead of home at the station slugging it out with the bad guys, with the dregs of the world.

So strange that she, eternal dreamer and optimist, had married a hard-headed cop. A man who, by the very nature of his work, was forced to be a cynic — at least in most matters.

But not a cynic when it came to her, or to his horses and dogs. There was not, in Max Harper's view, any reason to be a cynic regarding the nature of animals, for they were the innocent of the world.

Max had promised that they'd take this trip together, soon. A belated honeymoon, to make up for their original honeymoon plans a year ago, when their wonderful cruise to Alaska was aborted by the bomb at their wedding. A bomb that was meant to kill them.

That didn't matter now; though the bitter aftertaste was there. They were together, that was what mattered. And despite the perfection of this weeklong journey, she could hardly wait to get home.

She and Ryan and Hanni had ridden for three days down the coast, with a day's layover at the Hellman ranch to get the sorrel mare shod when she threw a shoe. It had been an easy trip, no roughing it, no camping out in the rain, no pack animal to lead, though they had carried survival gear, just in case. They had stayed each night at a welcoming ranch, dining before a hearth fire, sleeping between clean sheets and stabling their horses in comfort; had experienced nothing like what the first explorers and settlers had known traveling these hills, sleeping beneath drenching rain, eating what they could shoot or gather, fighting off marauding grizzly bears with muzzle loaders. It was hard to imagine grizzlies on these gentle hills; but this had been grizzly country then. The early accounts told of bear and bullfights, too, staged by the Spanish vaqueros and American cowboys in makeshift arenas; and Charlie shivered at the cruelty.

Now that they were nearing home again a bittersweet sadness touched her, but a completeness, too. Her soul was filled with a hugeness she could not describe; she felt washed clean. No religious retreat could ever, for Charlie, be as healing and inspiring as this open freedom, on the back of a good mount, wandering through God's country away from the evils of the world. As the sun began to burn through the fog, she could see the rooftops of Molena Point far ahead, a montage of red and brown peaks, hints of white walls softened by the deep green oaks and pines that rose between the cottages and shops. Soon she would be able to see their ranch, too, the white fences and oak trees of their own few acres. All three women were silent, drinking in the first sight of home, all with the same mix of sadness.

Hanni said, "I feel like an eighteenth-century traveler rounding the hills in a strange land, amazed to suddenly see my own rooftops." That made Charlie smile; but then she pulled Bucky up, again looking at increased movement in the woods. Had she heard a plaintive sound? A soft cry mixed with the wind and the crashing of the surf against the cliffs? Or maybe she'd heard only the faraway cry of the hawk? Dropping the reins across Bucky's neck, she sat listening.

The wind struck more sharply, hiding any sound. Above the pine woods a sliver of sun grew brighter as the clouds parted again. Pushing back her kinky red hair, Charlie brushed loose strands off her forehead and buttoned the throat of her jacket. Very likely she had heard nothing; she was as foolish as Hanni's gray gelding.

But no. Bucky had heard; he was watching the woods and he began to fuss, flicking his ears and rolling his eyes. Bucky, unlike the gray gelding, wasn't given to fantasies. Steady as a rock, the buckskin did not shy without good reason. Apprehensively Charlie studied the dark tangles among the pine trunks and deadfalls. She had not imagined that stealthy running, low to the ground among the dry branches and scrub bushes; had not imagined something intently following them. And she did not want — must not — let Ryan and Hanni know its true nature.

3

The lemon tree outside Chichi Barbi's window was useless for cover, and Joe had another thorn in his paw. He didn't like blood on his paws — not his own blood. Mouse blood or rabbit blood was fine. Now he had no choice if he wanted to learn anything, unless he clawed at Chichi's door and joined the party. Easing his position in the little tree he stayed on its far side, trying to conceal his white markings as he peered between the leafy twigs and in through Chichi's dirty window.

Her room was not as glitzy as Joe would have expected. But she was only house-sitting. The bedroom had pale blue walls and scarred, cream-colored Victorian furniture arranged on a worn, brown carpet. Chichi and the two men sat bent over the small night table, engrossed in the map. He couldn't see much; wherever he moved, one of the men was in his way. Both had their backs to him, so he had only to feel nervous at Chichi's possible glances.

Both men were fairly young. Smooth necks, smooth arms, smooth, strong hands. Both looked strong, hard-muscled. The gringo had styled his red hair in a harsh, spiky crew cut. He had masses of freckles on his neck and arms, more freckles even than Charlie Harper. On Charlie, the little confetti spots were bright and charming. On this guy, combined with the spiked hair and macho body language, they were blemishes. He wore a powder-blue T-shirt, and jeans. The back of his shirt proclaimed, "One Sweet Irish Lad." The Latino guy had straight black hair over his collar, and was the heftier of the two — a Peterbilt truck with legs. His red T-shirt advertised a brand of Mexican beer and had a picture of a cactus. The window glass must be single pane, because now that they had settled back to talk more normally, Joe could catch most of the conversation, which was centered on the map of Molena Point.

The redheaded man pointed to the intersection of Dolores Street and Seventh. "Little restaurant there," he said. "And a good view from inside the drugstore."

Good view of what? Joe tried to remember what else was on that corner. A country furniture store, one of those with faux country antiques. A bakery. And an expensive leather and silver shop. When Chichi leaned over to make a little mark at the intersection, she exhibited alarming cleavage. "That's seven," she said, sitting up. She glanced toward the window, making Joe wince, making him wish for the thousandth time that he was gray all over. Even among the tangle of twiggy branches he had to perch all hunched over to hide his white parts.

Well, but he was only a cat. So she saw him. So who would suspect a cat? And suspect him of what?

When Chichi kept looking, Joe began to fidget. Casually he turned away to wash, watching her obliquely. Only when she seemed to lose interest did he relax.

"You have it all laid out?" she was saying. "You're all set — sure you can handle this?"

The dark man's shoulders stiffened, and he raised his head in defiance. Chichi gave him a fetching smile. "Well of course you can handle it, Luis. You're a pro. A professional."

Luis's shoulders relaxed. "It's all worked out. Nothing *you* need to worry over."

Joe saw her temper flare, but it was immediately hidden as she glanced down. The redhead said, "The test run won't hurt nothing."

36

Luis glared at him, glancing in the direction of Clyde's house. "Keep your voice down."

"He won't hear you," Chichi said. "I don't hear a thing from over there, even when he has company — that woman carpenter. What kind of guy dates a carpenter? She doesn't have any clothes but jeans and muddy boots. So, what do I do for the test run?"

"The usual," Luis said. "You and Tommie." He nodded at the redhead. "Watch, listen. Keep count — numbers, direction. You know the drill."

Tommie punched at the map, picking out another intersection. "There's an alley here, north side of the street. One of them fancy alleys, a bench halfway down it, out of the way."

Chichi nodded. "I can't wait for the big one."

Luis laughed. "Just like old times."

"Better," she said softly. Joe saw a flicker of impatience cross her face, but it was gone at once. She gave Luis another dazzling smile and touched his hand. "What a blast." When Chichi looked up at the window again, Joe pretended interest in a branch above him, stealthily moving higher as if stalking a bird. What was the woman staring at? But then she looked away, and leaned for a moment on Tommie's shoulder. "Just like old times." That made both men smile.

Joe watched Luis fold the map and stuff it in his pocket. The men rose. He didn't want to leave the tree until they were gone. When at last they swung out the door, he leaped to the roof above them, peering over. Chichi stood in the doorway then moved to the drive, watching them approach their car. Joe followed above them, trotting along beside the metal roof gutter. When they turned to get into the car, he got a better look at their faces.

The redhead, Tommie, might be thirty, his face sharply sculpted, sharp nose, sharply pointed chin, angled cheekbones, his features as harsh as his stiff crew cut. The Latino guy was about the same age, but his broad, tanned face was more pleasant. He seemed to have a built-in smile, the kind of smile that would encourage anyone to like him, the kind of smile Joe seldom trusted. They swung into the brown Plymouth and backed out. As they pulled away, Joe headed back across the roof to the lemon tree, ignoring the voice in his head that said, "Watch your step, tomcat. Keep your eye on Chichi." Dropping down among the brittle twigs and sparse leaves, he glanced into Chichi's bedroom.

She had moved the night table back into place beside the bed. She was sitting on the bed with two pillows behind her, her feet tucked up, her eyes closed, her face so sad that Joe stared, amazed. What was she thinking? What sad memory filled her?

Likely some scam that went wrong, some crime left uncommitted. But for a long moment, as Joe watched her, his critical judgment almost softened. For one instant, he almost began to like the woman — until common sense kicked in once more, until the tomcat was himself again, suspicious and judgmental. Well, he *was* a cat, he could be as judgmental as he chose. That was his God-given feline prerogative.

Chichi was quiet for a long time, sitting with her eyes closed, lost in some scenario he'd give a brace of mice to understand. When at last she rose and left the room, moving away through an inner door toward the front of the house, he remained in the tree, thinking.

What was this plan involving the village? What he'd heard could mean anything. Some con game, maybe during a sports event? An onslaught of pickpockets? Nothing he had heard clearly indicated a crime in the planning, but what else could it be? He heard the TV come on from the living room. The daytime soaps? Oh, spare us, he thought irritably.

But the sound of those inane and tasteless melodramas would serve him well enough; and he studied Chichi's window, below him.

It was old, of the double-hung kind. Most such windows had old, round locks, frail or long ago broken.

Clyde would say he was overreacting, that Chichi had committed no crime nor had the trio actually talked about a crime. And maybe he would be right.

Or not, Joe thought. Whatever the truth, in the tomcat's view it was best to have a look, see what he could see.

He had leaped to the sill, his face pressed to the glass when the distant TV went silent. As he sailed back into the tree, she returned to the bedroom carrying a cup of coffee. Setting down the cup, Chichi looked right at him, right smack into his eyes. Panicked, Joe dropped into the scruffy grass and fled, his macho dignity forgotten.

Slipping around the corner of the house, he sailed to the top of his own wall and dropped to his own safe patio. That woman scared him, gave him the creeps. Crouched on the barbecue, he looked down at Clyde who was kneeling beside Rube, feeding him bits of the special diet the doctor had prescribed. The old Lab was not fond of what was best for him. Joe had to agree; most often, anything really good for you tasted like shredded bank statements. Clyde looked up, scowling.

"I take it you were eavesdropping, given your usual nosiness."

Joe fixed Clyde with a cool yellow gaze.

"Can't she have company without you spying on her? What did you do, watch them through the window?" Clyde would never admit that he, too, might be curious.

Joe shrugged and twitched his whiskers. "Probably tourists, friends visiting, deciding where they want to go, what sights they want to see." He didn't say any more. He wished the conversation had been more explicit. Why were humans so vague? Whatever was going on, he would prefer not to drag Clyde in. Clyde could be so opinionated.

At Joe's silence, Clyde raised an eyebrow and returned to feeding Rube, giving the sick old dog his full attention, making it clear that he thought Joe was imagining misdeeds where none existed.

It made no difference that Joe, his tabby lady Dulcie, and their young pal Kit had solved innumerable crimes in the village. With Clyde there was always that preliminary unwillingness to accept their skill and expertise, an inborn reluctance to face facts. Giving Clyde a cool glance, Joe considered Rube. At the moment, the old Labrador was far more in need of true understanding than was Joe himself.

"He's hurting, Clyde. I don't like the way he's breathing, don't like the way he smells."

"I just gave him his medication. You know it takes a while to kick in. I called Dr. Firetti again. He's increased the dose by a fourth. Said to watch him, see if I can get him to drink more. I made him some broth, he drank half a cup. Firetti said if he seems no better in an hour, bring him in."

Joe nodded and curled up next to Rube, pressing against the Lab's warm, black shoulder. Even the feel of Rube's body was different, more rigid and ungiving. The prognosis was not good, he knew that. Death would come; the old dog was dying, and there was only so much any human could do, no matter how skilled and attentive.

He thought about death, about their animal friends and human friends who had died. At one time he'd found the concept one of total emptiness, found it easy to fall into a deep malaise over a loved one's death. Dulcie had taught him differently, Dulcie and her housemate, Wilma. Plus a lot of thinking on his own, a lot of observation — and a few very strange experiences. Yet now when he thought about Rube's impending death, trying to come to terms with it, it was a very long time before he turned his attention again to Chichi Barbi.

4

When, within the pine woods, the fleeting shadows grew bolder, Bucky snorted and bowed his neck, nervously staring. Another sprint of shadows flashed among the trees to vanish behind a tumble of deadfalls; then across the leafy carpet, a stealthy creeping so subtle it might be only light shifting among the foliage as the sun rose. If there was something there, it was small and quick. But what kind of small animals would follow them? If they were in Ireland, Charlie thought, she'd imagine being tracked by some impossible mythical creature. Beside her, Ryan and Hanni watched intently. She was glad Ryan hadn't brought her big Weimaraner. Rock was becoming well trained, considering his uncontrolled first-year running wild and unwanted. But he still had moments when his highly bred hunting instincts and keen sense of smell — and his macho nature — tore him away from all commands and sent him, defiant and disobedient, racing maybe fifteen miles or more before Ryan could find him and bring him home again, the big silver dog worn out, deliciously happy, and not at all contrite. If Rock were here, he'd be running now, chasing those mysterious cats — and cats they were, she felt certain.

Though Rock would not normally hurt a cat, if they ran from him he would chase them. Any dog would. And who knew how far? This wilderness land went on for many miles.

Another shadow flashed through the mottled light, small and swift. If these *were* cats, they were not the three cats Charlie knew. Those three would not follow them secretly, they'd be right out in the open running beside the horses, begging a ride home across their saddles. Charlie had taken the young tortoiseshell up on the saddle with her several times, and the kit quite liked that excitement. Anyway, those three wouldn't be clear out here, miles south of Molena Point. Even on horseback, the riders were still a good hour from home. They were well south of Hellhag Hill, which was as far south, she thought, as Joe Grey or Dulcie ever ventured. Though the kit had come from much farther south when she first found the village, escaping from just such a band of feral cats. Small and hungry and troubled, Kit had taken refuge on Hellhag Hill and there, frightened and nearly starved, she had found the first two humans she'd ever been willing to trust.

Edging Bucky off the trail, Charlie looked back at Ryan and Hanni. "Go on. Whatever is there is small, I don't want to frighten it. I'm just curious. I'll catch up." And she headed alone into the woods, the buckskin stepping with exaggerated care and snorting. Behind her, the two women moved away, their horses' sorrel and gray rumps bright in the morning. Ryan glanced back at her once, frowning, then moved her mare up to match the gray's hurrying walk.

Charlie was glad Max wasn't there. If this was the feral band, Molena Point's police chief didn't need any more close encounters with speaking cats. He got plenty of that at home, though all unknowing. It was hard enough to keep the three cats' secret from him, without other sentient cats appearing. Approaching the dense woods, Bucky continued to stare and fuss, but he moved ahead sensibly. Bucky was Max's gelding, he was well trained and reliable. Though he would not so willingly have approached a band of coyotes or an unusually bold cougar. Cougars had attacked several hikers this year and, in one instance, a lone rider, raking and tearing the horse badly before the wounded rider shot him.

The three women were armed against that kind of danger. Three females traveling alone did not, to Max Harper's way of thinking, go into the California wilderness unprotected from some strange quirk of nature or a marauding human. These days, there could be a nutcase anywhere, the wild hills no exception. Particularly with marijuana growers squatting on state land, angry men who would kill to protect their lucrative illegal crops.

Charlie was police-trained in the use of a weapon and not, in any way, hasty or hotheaded. And Ryan and Hanni, having grown up in a law-enforcement family, had been well schooled from an early age. All three carried cell phones, but it would take a while for outside help to reach them. A Jeep could manage these hills, but they were riding the old original highway that had deteriorated over sixty years into a rough dirt track with patches of broken, washed-out blacktop — an impossible road for any car with only two-wheel drive. She entered the wood where the trees grew thick, the gelding picking his way among deadfalls, dry, rotting invitations to forest fire. Around them, nothing moved.

Where the trees parted sufficiently, thin shafts of light grew brighter as the sun rose. Away at the far side of the hill, the woods dropped into a ravine. Bucky's ears flicked and twisted, and his skin rippled with shivers. She could hear behind her the faint hush of the sea, then a distant click as one of the retreating horses stepped on a pebble. The pine forest was cold; she drew her jacket close. And suddenly for no reason she wanted to turn back. At the same moment, Bucky froze.

Something shone ahead, unnaturally bright between the trees, something glinting like metal. She frowned at the long silver streaks half hidden within the dark bushes.

No rock would glint like that, with those long, straight flashes where the sun shot down. Pushing Bucky closer, booting him deeper in among the crowding pines, she approached the bright gleams where a shaft of slanting sun picked out metal bars.

An animal cage. A trap. A humane trap, made of thin steel bars, not wire mesh as were most such cages. Its top, sides, and back had been covered with a heavy towel so that a trapped beast would settle down in the darkness and not harm itself lunging and fighting. A friend who worked for a cat-rescue group had told her that a trapped cat would fight its cage until it tore off hanks of its own skin, injuring itself sometimes so severely that it must be destroyed. The towel did not cover the front of the cage. She could see a cat inside, a big cat, crouching and silently hissing, its eyes dark with fear and hate.

Sliding off Bucky, she knelt to look. The cat fixed her with an enraged glare, a furious stare from keenly intelligent eyes. This was no ordinary cat. He watched her with intent human comprehension, and everything about him was demanding. Much as Joe Grey would have stared if he were caught in a trap. Though she could not imagine such a thing happening. Joe was far too wary.

How had this obviously intelligent creature let himself be caught? The huge, broad-shouldered tom exhibited such a deep and violent rage. This was a wild, rebellious intellect trapped not only in the cage but in a feline body with physical limitations that had betrayed him. With no hands to manipulate that complicated lock, he had no hope of escape. He glared at Charlie as if he would tear her leg off.

His rough coat was a mix of gray and tan and dirty white; his broad, boxy head scarred as if from fighting, his ears torn, his yellow eyes fierce. She had no desire to touch her fingers to the cage to see if this might be a domestic cat, an angry lost soul who might be longing to trust her. There was nothing lost about this soul. Enflamed, bedeviled, not to trust or be trusted.

His eyes never left her. His teeth remained bared in a snarl as lethal as that of any cougar, eyes like an imprisoned convict. She could see him debating how he could best use her, how he could force her to free him. Stepping away from the cage, she put her hand on Bucky's shoulder, steadying herself against the solid buckskin gelding. She stood silently for a long time watching the cat as he continued his careful assessment of her.

At last she knelt again, and spoke softly, though the other riders were on down the trail. "You run with the wild band. With the band that, almost two years ago, came to Hellhag Hill." Even as she said it, she thought, alarmed, that if he was one of that band, they might have come back searching for the kit.

But why would they? To take the little tattercoat back into their clowder? Why would they want her back? She had been nothing but an outcast.

Would they want to remove any cat of their kind from human company? Would they hurt Kit to keep their secret?

But that didn't make sense. If that was the case, why had they ever let her stay in the village? Why hadn't they taken her away at once?

Or was this a new and stricter leader? Charlie knew from Kit that the band had been ruled by a tyrant. Was there now a worse dictator, a beast even more predatory and controlling? Kit had said the leaders changed whenever a stronger male killed the old one. Was this tom even more anxious to keep his kind from being discovered? The cat continued to glare.

"If you will talk to me," she said, "if you will tell me why they trapped you — tell me how they managed to trap you — and if you'll tell me why you are here, I'll set you free."

His snarl rumbled.

"I promise I'll free you," she whispered.

In order to free him, she would have to handle the cage. If he chose, he could slash her fingers to ribbons through the bars before she could ever release the door and push it in.

Rising, she slipped her hoof pick from its little case on the saddle and fished her knife from her pocket. Because Bucky was tense and snorting, she was afraid he wouldn't stay ground-tied. She undid her rope from the saddle and tied him to a deadfall.

Opening her saddle bags, she found her leather gloves and slipped them on. Crouched again before the cage, studying how best to spring the latch, she heard Ryan call her from far up the trail. Oh, they mustn't come back.

"I'm fine," she shouted. "I'm coming. Give me a minute."

She had thought at first the cage belonged to one of the animal-rescue groups that trapped feral cats, that gave the cats shots and "the operation," then turned them loose again. But this cage wasn't like theirs. Though of the same humane design, it had stainless steel bars instead of wire mesh, and a different kind of tripping mechanism, too. A different way to release the door, and a far more complicated latch. But what gave her chills was the bungee cord.

The strong elastic cord was used to keep a trap open for many days so the victim would grow used to going inside for food. Normally, the cord was then removed, and the trap set. An ordinary cat would not realize the difference, but would go on in and trip the trigger, slamming the door shut before it could escape.

But this bungee cord hung in three pieces, frayed apart. It did not look chewed, but tampered with. The door had been sprung while the weakened cord was still in place, and it had pulled apart.

She looked into the tom's blazing eyes. "Was the cord on when you went in? So you thought it still held the door?"

The cat blinked, as if to say yes. It glared, and would not speak.

"You didn't chew it in two? It doesn't look chewed."

He lashed his tail, reluctantly letting her know he understood, but still unwilling to speak. This was too bizarre, kneeling in the wilderness talking to a trapped cat from whom she fully expected answers. This was a scene out of *Alice*, crazy and impossible.

But it indeed was quite possible.

"Tell me," she said impatiently. "Just tell me, and I'll free you! There are two more riders, they'll be over here in a minute. We can't talk in front of them."

The big cat studied her, ears back, teeth glinting.

She said, "This trap was not set by the rescue people. Whoever set it knew you, knew that he was setting it for an animal as smart as himself." She was studying the heavy, complicated latch when Ryan began calling again.

"Tell me now! Quickly! Speak to me now, and I'll free you. Otherwise I'll leave you. I swear I will."

The cat smiled with teeth like ivory daggers. His look said, Isn't this proof enough? My smile, my cognizance? That is all the proof you need, so get on with it.

Rising, she turned and swung onto Bucky and headed out, meaning to stop Ryan. She could feel, behind her, the cat's alarm.

Ryan had left the trail. Behind her, Hanni waited. "Go back," Charlie said. "It's all right. A feral cat in a cage, I don't want to frighten it. Looks like it's been there a long time. I'm going to free it; I think I can spring it all right."

"Let me help, I'll be gentle." Ryan booted her horse, moving beside Charlie before Charlie could stop her, and sliding from the mare. The cat, now crouched at the back of the cage, snarled and spit. Now its eyes were shuttered, giving away nothing. Charlie, opening her folding hoof pick and knife, began to work on the lock.

No cat could have opened this, it was hard even for her, with the simple tools she had.

As she wedged the pick into place, Ryan forced her own knife into the moving part of the mechanism; Ryan's knife was heavier and sturdier than Charlie's. By wedging in both knives, they were able at last to spring it. The moment they did, the cat surged forward against the closed door. But then, realizing he must get out of the way for it to be pushed open, he moved back. Ryan stared at him, puzzled. Immediately, he began hissing and growling as if frightened, trying to hide his too-intelligent behavior.

"I must have scared him," Charlie said, "when I stood up." Retrieving a fallen branch, she lifted the cage door.

As Ryan, using a second stick, pressed the door back into its open position, the cat moved a step toward the opening. He paused, looking fiercely up at them. Neither woman moved. He took another step. Another, toward freedom. His eyes never left them. He watched them secure the door open, wedging the branches in. Watched them back away from the cage. And he streaked out and through the woods — a flash and he was gone, they were looking at empty woods.

But then, from the shadows where he had vanished, the whole woods seemed to shake and shift, a violent stirring that came from every direction like silent small explosions. And then gone, the woods utterly still.

"What was that?" Ryan said, swallowing.

"I don't know," Charlie whispered, seeing in her mind's eye the swift, cat-shaped shadows vanishing among the trees. She watched the woods as Hanni joined them, her gray gelding prancing and fussing. Hanni took in the scene, the empty trap, and the woods beyond. The widening shafts of sunlight showed nothing alive, not even a bird flitting.

"I didn't know there were trappers up here," Hanni said. "But why a humane trap? If they're trapping for fur . . . ?"

"Cat trap," Charlie said. "Surely a 'trap and neuter' group."

"Why would they work way up here? How often do they check their cages? To leave a cat like that . . . No food, no water . . ." Hanni knew as well as Charlie that no animal-rescue group would have left a trap there unattended. "How long was it in that cage?"

Leaving Bucky tied, Charlie walked deeper into the woods, searching until she found a large stone. Returning, she knelt and began to hammer the cage, bending the bars as best she could; the metal was thick, hellishly strong. When her arm grew tired,

Ryan took the stone. Stronger, from years of carpentry work, Ryan struck with a force that soon collapsed the sides and sprung the door. When the cage lay bent beyond use, its lock and hinges broken, its door twisted into folds, Charlie carried it through the brush to where the land fell sharply, and heaved it down the ravine into steep, jagged rocks among a tangle of bushes.

By the time it rusted and the bushes grew over, it might never be noticed. Who knew what was hidden down in these draws? A rancher could lose a wily steer down there, or an old cow hiding her calf — a smart cow who would bring her calf out again only when the riders were long gone. Charlie wasn't sure why she had thrown the trap down there. It made more sense to leave it for whomever had set it, let them see it crushed. Yet she felt, for some reason she couldn't name, that she didn't want the cage found.

Behind them when they left the woods, there was no trace of the trap, only the trampled grass that would soon right itself; and their hoofprints, which Charlie wished she could brush away. She would not do that in front of Ryan and Hanni, drawing questions to which she had no answers.

Back on the trail, Charlie rode nearest the

woods, but saw no further movement. Maybe the cats, having regained their own, had headed away into the wild interior. She hoped they stayed away, prayed they wouldn't come down into Molena Point. Now, beneath the horses' hooves, where pieces of the macadam had washed away leaving only dirt, they found themselves following fresh tire marks. A single track, like that of a motorcycle.

Ryan frowned. "Do ranchers use motorcycles these days?" As they descended a steep slope, down into the blanket of fog, the horses began to shy and wanted to turn back. It was not the mist that made them spooky. Urging Bucky on into the thick mist, Charlie smelled the stench that had Bucky snorting and rearing.

Holding their breath, the riders forced their horses to the lip of the narrow ravine, and sat studying a swath of broken bushes and torn-out grass that led from the edge down to the bottom.

A motorcycle lay down there, flung onto its back, its bent front wheel pointing toward the sky, its rear tire stripped away in shreds leaving bare, twisted metal. The sweet stink of rotting flesh made Charlie want to throw up. A man lay beneath the bike, his black leathers dulled with dirt, his body swollen with the gases that form after death, his long black hair tangled in the ruined tire. The three riders reached for their cell phones.

"I'll call," Charlie said, leaning over Bucky, letting him spin away from the ravine as she dialed, giving him his head. She felt ice-cold. She prayed they had moved back into the coastal calling area. Listening to the first ring, she pulled Bucky up, and turned to scan the ravine and the land above it. She felt as if they were being watched. She was so unsettled that when Mabel Farthy picked up the call, Charlie had trouble finding her voice. Glancing at Ryan, tasting the sick, sweet smell, she told Mabel their location and what they had found.

Max came on the line almost at once. Her tears welled at the sound of his voice. All she could say was, "I need you up here, we need you." She could hardly talk. She felt so stupid, so weak and inadequate. You're a cop's wife, Charlie! Straighten up! "Can you get the cars up here?" she said. "On this old road? We could bring the horses down for you . . ."

"That's the sheriff's jurisdiction," Max said. "He has four-wheel, we'll be with them or in my pickup. You okay?"

Charlie nodded. "Fine."

"Hang on, we're on our way," he said. Was he laughing at her? Then, in a softer voice, "I love you, Charlie."

But Charlie, clicking off the phone, sliding off Bucky to hurry away and throw up in the bushes, felt like a failure, like she'd been no use at all to Max.

5

Twilight lasted longer on the rooftops than among the cottages below. Down along the narrow village streets dusk settled quickly beneath the wide oaks and around the crowded shops; as night settled in, the gleam of the shop windows seemed to brighten, casting darker the concealing shadows.

But up on the roofs, the evening's silken brilliance clung to the precipitous, shingled peaks and across little leaded dormers and copper-clad domes. Twilight washing across small balconies echoed the silver sea that lapped the village shore; and in the last glow, the gray tomcat racing across the rooftops seemed to fly from peak to peak.

Leaping shadowed clefts, dodging heat vents and chimneys, Joe Grey was not running simply for pure joy tonight, nor was he chasing criminals or the little brown bats that darted among the chimneys. He was heading across the village to supper, drinking in the heady scents of roasted chili peppers, of cilantro and garlic and onions and roasting meats — food that would put down most cats. Whiskers twitching with greedy anticipation, he sailed across the open chasm of a narrow alley and headed fast for the dining patio of Lupe's Playa. It was green corn tamale night at Lupe's.

He was approaching Lupe's rooftop, licking his whiskers, when suddenly from behind a chimney something leaped on him hissing and swatting him — and the tortoiseshell kit dodged away from him again, sparring. Behind her, tabby Dulcie appeared from around a chimney, her green eyes sly with amusement.

The kit rolled over, laughing.

Dulcie rubbed her face against his; and the three cats headed eagerly for Lupe's. Green corn tamales were a delicacy available only when the corn was young.

This early in the spring, they supposed the fresh corn must be coming up from Mexico, or maybe the hotter fields of southern California. It was still far too cold to expect fresh corn from California's nearby central valley. Racing past second-floor offices, it was all the three cats could do not to yowl with greed. Set apart so singularly from their feline cousins, these three had, along with human perceptions and human speech, stomachs as versatile as those of their human friends. Cast-iron stomachs, Joe's housemate said. Clyde told Joe often enough that their veterinarian would be shocked at what Joe ate. But there was a whole world about Joe Grey, and Dulcie, and Kit that Dr. Firetti didn't know.

Flying across the last narrow oak branch to the jumbled roofs of Lupe's Playa, they peered down among the overhanging oaks into the walled and lantern-lit patio. Lupe's was constructed of three old houses joined to surround a central patio, and closed on the fourth side by a high brick wall that offered diners privacy and warmth against the chill ocean wind. Within the patio, the pierced tin lanterns swinging from the twisted oak branches cast a soft, flickering light. The brightly painted tables with their red and green and blue chairs were already full of happy diners lifting beer mugs white with frost, and merrily chatting. Guitars played a Mexican melody sweet enough to bring tears. The dishes carried by hurrying waiters steamed and bubbled. The cats, dropping down to the wall, crouched just above their friends' regular table that stood like King Arthur's round table in the patio's sheltered northeast corner. Hidden within the wall's bougainvillea vine, the cats had a wide view of both patio and street.

Beneath them at the curb, having apparently taken the last nearby parking place, stood Captain Harper's king cab pickup, smelling strongly of the sweet scent of horses. Within the patio, at the round table, Max and redheaded Charlie sipped Mexican beer with Detective Garza and his niece, Hanni. Clyde and Ryan's chairs were still empty. Harper and Garza sat with their backs to the wall, with a clear view of the patio and the dining room to their left. Max Harper was not in uniform but dressed in the clothes that suited him best — soft jeans, a frontier shirt, and well-used Western boots — which set off his tall, lean, weathered frame.

The Latino detective wore jeans and his favorite old, soft corduroy sport coat, which, on anyone less handsome than Dallas Garza, might look like it just came off the rack at the Goodwill.

Beside Max, Charlie glanced up, sensing the cats on the wall above her or hearing them stir in the vine. With a little smile, she pushed back her mop of kinky red hair and began to prepare an appetizer plate for them, tearing up a soft tortilla and dribbling it with mild, melted cheese. Max didn't miss

her busy preoccupation, nor did Dallas and Hanni. Rising, Charlie set the plate atop the wall, chucking Kit under the chin and gently stroking Dulcie. The lady cats smiled and purred and rubbed their faces against her hand. Joe Grey gave her a twitch of the whiskers by way of thanks, and tucked into the rich appetizer.

Dulcie thought Charlie looked stunning tonight; the little cat did love beautiful clothes. Charlie was wearing a simple cotton print dress splashed with all the colors of summer, a combination of shades that made her hair look even redder. She'd tied her hair back tonight, with a tangle of multicolored ribbons. Even gorgeous Hanni Coon with her premature and startling white hair and dark Latin eyes, in her flamboyant and glittering silver stole over a low-cut black T-shirt, couldn't outshine Charlie.

"Up until this morning," Dallas was saying, "sounds like you had a good trip."

The cats stopped eating, they were all pricked ears. What happened this morning? They stared, listening, until Dallas glanced up at them. Immediately they lowered their faces again over their plates — though their ears remained cocked, their tails still, every fiber rigid with interest.

"A wonderful trip," Hanni said. "Nothing

as restful as a few days away from people, just the horses and the open land." Hanni's interior design studio and large clientele allowed her little time when she wasn't "on stage," when she could relax with her family or close friends. Even when she was at home with her husband, their two boys created demands that kept her on her toes, that didn't give her much downtime.

"Beautiful country," Charlie said. "Not a house, just the few ranches. So green, after the rains." The land would turn brown in the summer when the rains stopped, when it lay burned by the California sun. "Next time," Charlie said, "maybe we'll take Lori and Dillon; Lori is doing well at her riding lessons, and the two girls get along fine. Cora Lee's right, Lori needs a challenge and some real freedom."

Twelve-year-old Lori Reed had gone to live with their good friend, Cora Lee French, after Lori's father went to prison on two counts of murder, both killings of such pain and passion that no one really blamed him. It had been a hard year for Lori. Now, with the child settled in, Cora Lee was deeply aware that a twelve-year-old girl without her father needed to experience different kind of discipline and stre than she would enjoy in a household

older women, that she needed to be outdoors doing something bold and new and demanding. She had asked Max if he'd teach Lori to ride, as he had taught Dillon Thurwell two years ago, when she was twelve. Dillon, too, had seemed at loose ends and needed some positive challenge in her life.

Of course Max had agreed to Lori's lessons, and the Harpers had borrowed a wise, gentle pony for her. Oh, Dulcie thought, Lori did love that pony. She had seen Lori and the pony together up at the Harper ranch, and even Joe said that child and pony were a perfect match.

"I'm glad Lori wasn't with us this morning," Charlie said, "when we found the body. She doesn't need that, after all the death last year."

The cats were rigid as stones. *What body?* The tortoiseshell kit was so curious she began to fidget from paw to paw, and couldn't be still. And Dulcie could see in Joe's eyes exactly what he was thinking: If the riders had found a body this morning before they arrived home, Max and his whole department knew about it, had known all day. So Joe's human housemate had to know. Clyde and Max Harper were like brothers. Why the big secret? Why

67

didn't Clyde tell *me?* Joe would be thinking. And when Dulcie glanced at Joe, he looked mad enough to fight a pack of Rottweilers — almost mad enough to slash the hand that fed him — the moment Clyde walked into the restaurant.

Dulcie knew why *she* hadn't heard: her own housemate was in the hospital. Two days ago, Wilma had some routine surgery. Wilma had had to fight like a maddened cat herself to get Charlie to go on with her trip. "You have cell phones," Wilma had pointed out. "If I need you, you'll know it. It's a simple, routine operation. With Clyde here fussing over me, to say nothing of Max and Dallas and the senior ladies, I'll be smothered in attention. Go, Charlie! A few gallstones, for heaven's sake."

Even if Wilma called it minor surgery, Dulcie hadn't slept well, worrying. If she'd had her way, she'd have sneaked into the hospital and stayed there. Instead, she'd followed Wilma's stubborn instructions and gone to stay with Kit in the second-floor apartment above Ocean Avenue, which Kit's own two humans had rented.

When the cats heard Clyde's voice from down the street, Joe's eyes narrowed. In a moment, Clyde and Ryan appeared from around the corner, their footfalls quick on the sidewalk. Ryan would have left her truck at Clyde and Joe's house, where she would have shut her big silver Weimaraner in the patio. Likely, Clyde had put old Rube in the house where the ailing dog would have some peace, away from the energetic young hunting dog. The couple passed just a few feet below the cats. If they'd not had an audience, Dulcie was sure Joe would have leaped on Clyde, all teeth and claws and a lot of swearing. Kit reached out a paw as if to snatch at Ryan's hair, but Dulcie gave her a look that made her back off. Kit sat down again, looking innocent. If Clyde glimpsed the cats above him, he gave no sign. The couple disappeared around the corner, then appeared again, coming in through the front entry. They spoke with the hostess, then crossed the crowded patio, studying their friends' serious faces.

"What?" Clyde said as they sat down. "This is supposed to be a celebration that the girls are home — no one bucked off or kicked or itching with poison oak." He fixed on Charlie and Hanni. "Ryan told me about the body. Was it that bad? You've seen bodies before."

Ryan looked at her uncle Dallas. "Do you have anything yet on the prints?"

Dallas laughed. "You expect miracles?

Eight hours, and you think NCI's going to snap to with an ID?"

"But if you told them . . ."

"You know them better than that. We put on as much pressure as we could; you know the lab's always jammed up. Everyone wants everything ASAP. It isn't like this guy just died, he'd been down there a while."

"*We* know he was dead for a while," Ryan said, making a face. Ryan Flannery's fine Latino features mirrored her uncle's, though his face was more square; same expression, same faint dimples, same stern, serious look that hid a smile. Ryan's stare could be just as intimidating as detective Garza's. She had the same dark hair, but where Dallas's eyes were nearly black, often seeming unreadable, Ryan had her father's eyes, Irish eyes as green and changeable as the sea.

"Maybe by tonight," Dallas said, "we'll have something." The detective scowled comfortably at his niece. "The ID we found on the body, driver's license, social security card, belonged to a Mario Salgado. Denver resident, died some ten years back.

"Good job of forgery," Dallas added. "He even paid into social security, a couple of quarters, to make it seem legit." The detective looked around the table. "Coroner wouldn't commit as to the wounds on the face and throat. Said they *might* be scratches from blackberry vines, but he doesn't think so. There *were* heavy brambles in the ditch, but the scratches were too deep. They seemed more like wounds from some kind of weapon — but they sure looked like claw marks."

Clyde was very still. The cats could see Charlie's hands clench beneath the table. What had Charlie seen that maybe Ryan and Hanni hadn't? The cats watched her intently. Careful, Joe thought. She had gone way too tense. Careful, Charlie. Be careful. No human in the world noticed as much about a person's reactions as a cop did, no one was as perceptive to another's emotions. A good cop was nearly as keen as a cat at picking up the smallest hint of unease, the faintest change of expression.

In Joe's opinion, there was not a psychiatrist in the world who had half a cop's ability to correctly read a disturbed subject, who had the knowledge and skill to see through deception. You wouldn't catch a cat wasting his time on a psychiatrist's couch when all one really needed, for most emotional problems, was hard-headed logic, a dose of cop-style straight thinking.

Clyde would say he was inexcusably opinionated, that he didn't have a trace of compassion. Well, he was a *cat!* Cats weren't supposed to be socially correct. Cats could be as biased as they chose — or as right as they chose. A *cat* should be able to hold an unbiased opinion without fear of social censure.

But what was Charlie hiding? What had happened, up in the hills?

And what was making the kit so nervous? Beside Joe, Kit's eyes had grown huge. She looked so stricken and uneasy that Dulcie had to nudge her and lick her ears, trying to settle her down.

"No labels on the clothes," Dallas said. "No license on the bike. And those scratches . . ." The detective frowned. "Almost as if something leaped at him from the trail. Strange as it seems, I keep thinking he was attacked, that his bike was moving fast, something jumped on him, he swerved, lost control and went over the edge."

The detective looked at his friends. "But what? Not likely a bobcat would leap at a cyclist. Though a fast-moving bike would be a pretty tempting target, fast like a deer, and even the noise of a bike might not deter a hungry cougar if it was already used to such sounds.

"But those marks weren't made by a

cougar; this was something smaller. Anyway, a cougar would have gone down into the ravine after him, would have finished him."

"Guy apparently died of a broken neck," Max said. "Forensics should have their report in a few days." He looked around the table. "Sheriff's been up there all day, going over the area."

Dallas said, "Scratches of a domestic cat? No small cat would attack a man, no small animal would be so bold."

Up on the wall, the cats glanced discreetly at each other. There was one kind of cat that might attack a grown man, if it cared enough about who the cyclist was, or what he had done. If it wanted him dead.

But what had the guy done to enrage his attacker? And where had such a cat come from? There should be no other cat like themselves anywhere near the village.

Joe wondered if the attacker could possibly be Azrael. That evil Panamanian feline had first shown up in the village nearly two years ago, with his thieving human companion, and had returned a couple of times later without the disreputable safe-cracker. When Azrael disappeared the last time, into a seemingly bottomless cavern, carrying an emerald bracelet in his mouth, Joe had hoped they had seen the last of him, that he had ended up too far away ever to return.

Joe was washing his whiskers, listening intently but keeping his eyes half closed as if sleepy, when he saw Chichi Barbi crossing the patio, making her way between the tables following the Latino host, the curvy young blond bimbo swiveling her hips provocatively. She was alone, accompanied by neither of the men who had visited her that morning. Swishing between the tables she played the room, giving the eye to every male within view. Max and Dallas and Clyde exchanged a glance that the cats couldn't read. Ryan and Charlie and Hanni watched her with quiet amusement. Heading for a small table beneath the farthest oak, Chichi sat down with her back to the wall and immediately raised her menu, pretending not to see Clyde, pretending not to stare across to their table.

Dallas gave her a dismissive look, and turned to his niece. "We haven't talked since you got back from the city, you ladies were out of here the next morning. How did the legal stuff go?"

"Fine," Ryan said. "It went fine. Beautiful weather in the city, the tide was in, and the coast . . ."

Dallas scowled impatiently, making Ryan

74

grin. She had gone up to San Francisco to complete the sale of their house and the construction business she'd inherited from her philandering husband when he was murdered. "I wrapped up all the loose ends," she told Dallas, growing serious. "Sold the last of the furniture, cleared out the safe deposit box. Yes, deposited the checks," she said, giving him an unreadable look. Joe read her glance as a bit frightened.

Frightened of what? Of having all that money? Well, Joe had to admit, with the completed sale of the San Francisco firm, she would be rolling in cash. Maybe he'd be scared, too.

But it was money she could put into her new Molena Point construction business, and plenty left over to invest. Ryan could handle that. She should be as pleased as a kitten in the cream bowl. Yet he was sharply aware of her unease — as was everyone at the table.

"What?" Dallas said.

"Do you remember a Roman Slayter? A tall, handsome, dark-haired . . ."

"I remember him," Dallas said sharply. "I remember you sent him packing more than once while you and Rupert were married."

"He called me while I was in the city. Got

the name of my hotel from a new secretary at the firm, who didn't know any better."

"Came on to you."

She nodded. "Wanted me to go out to dinner, then demanded to see me." Her green eyes blazed. "I blew him off, but . . . I don't know. He left me uneasy."

"The smell of money," Dallas said. "He knows everyone in the company, sure he knew how much you got for the business. Knew when the sale closed escrow. I thought he'd moved to L.A."

"Guess he's back. Nothing fazes him. I told him I was busy with job contracts, that I was working long hours with a new business, that I was involved with someone," she said, glancing shyly at Clyde. Clyde grinned.

"Told him I was just leaving the city, that I didn't have *time* for him. He knew I'd moved down here to the village. Finally told him my live-in was a weight lifter and a hot-tempered gun enthusiast."

That got a laugh. "And that shut him up?" Dallas said.

"Nothing shuts him up. Doesn't matter what you say. Showed up in the office anyway, tried to kiss me right there in the reception room. I nearly punched him. When he grew really stubborn and refused to leave, I called security.

"As they dragged him out," Ryan said, laughing, "he said he'd see me in Molena Point, that he'd just run down to the village for a few days, get reacquainted. I told him, he showed his face here I'd file charges of harassment." She was half angry, half amused. She had balled up her napkin and was stabbing it with her fork. Her uncle leaned back in his chair, grinning, but he put his arm around her.

All the while they talked, Chichi watched them from across the patio, glancing over the top of her menu; she never looked straight their way, but her full attention was on them. Surely she couldn't hear them at that distance, with so many diners in between, talking and laughing; but her rapt concentration was unsettling. Then, just after the waiter arrived with their orders, Chichi left her table and came across to theirs, all smiles and swivels. She paused beside Clyde's chair, resting her hand possessively on his shoulder.

"Dear me, I couldn't help it, I had to see what you're having, it smelled so good when your waiter passed my table." She gave Clyde a four-star smile and beamed around the table. "Hi, I'm Chichi Barbi! I just ran over for a little supper, it gets boring, eating alone. I'm living in the house next to

Clyde's. You're Captain Harper! Well, I've heard great things about you! And you must be Detective Garza! It's so nice to meet you — you ladies, too." She looked down at Clyde's plate. "My goodness, is that on the menu? Green corn tamales?" She looked winsomely around the table. Clyde was still scowling.

"Well, I'll surely order the same," she gushed, waiting for an invitation to join them. When none was forthcoming, she stepped back, her hand lingering on Clyde's shoulder. "It's such an honor to meet you all. It does get lonely in that little back room, I just thought a nice dinner out, for a change . . ." Still she stood waiting, trying to look uncertain as she glanced from one to the other, managing the little girl act so well that even Joe began to feel sorry for her — or almost sorry.

The round table was, after all, plenty big enough if everyone slid their chairs around to make room. No one did, no one said a word. Cops in particular don't like pushy. At last Clyde rose, took Chichi by the arm, and headed her back to her table. The curvy blonde moved along close to him, brushing against him.

At her little table she sat down heavily, under what was clearly a forceful pressure.

Picking up Chichi's menu, Clyde spent some moments pointing to the page as if picking out the green corn tamales and the other specials.

Beside Clyde's empty chair, Ryan sat with her fist pressed to her mouth, trying not to laugh at his predicament. Above, on the wall, the cats pushed their faces into the vine, swallowing back their own yowls of glee. When Clyde returned to their table, still scowling, Ryan nearly choked with laughter. Clyde glanced up and saw the cats' amusement, gave them a cautionary frown and began hastily to break up a tamale for them, to distract them — and everyone grew silent, giving full attention to their fine dinner.

At her own table, Chichi fidgeted, waiting for her order; when it arrived, she finished her tamales quickly, not looking again in their direction. She left the restaurant long before they did.

The cats watched her from atop the wall, heading home, Joe swallowing back a growl. That woman was more than brash. Chichi Barbi made the tomcat as jumpy as a mouse on a hot stove.

"So, what did she want?" Dulcie said, when their own party had left the restaurant, Clyde and Ryan heading down the block hand in hand, and Max, Charlie, and Dallas squeezing into Max's king cab. "This Chichi Barbi," Dulcie hissed, "what is she all about?"

Joe wished he knew what Chichi was all about, what she wanted with Clyde; though half his thoughts were on the dead man and the suspicious scratches. "More important," he said softly, "what did Charlie see that she couldn't talk about?"

But the kit knew. She looked at them intently. "Cats like us," she said, her yellow eyes huge. "They're out there, the feral band is out there again, I know they are." She shivered and pressed close against Dulcie. "Those cats I ran with when I was little, they're out there again." She looked in the direction of the wild coastal hills where Hellhag Hill rose. "But why? And why did they kill that man?

"Those few, like me," Kit said, "the gentler cats, they could never stop the mean ones. Some of us only traveled with them for safety. Cruel as they were, they were better than bobcats and coyotes."

Dulcie licked the kit's ear and glanced up at the sky, where the moon had not yet risen; and soon she and Kit headed off to the kit's own rooftop terrace. Joe watched the two cats' dark, mottled tails disappearing into the moonlit night; and not one of the three had a clue to the excitement that would soon explode across the small village. Not one of the three cats glimpsed the shadowy figures many blocks away, slipping among the shops and dark streets. Nothing seemed to disrupt the peace of the evening. Nor did Max Harper's officers in their patrol cars glimpse the perps — until it was too late.

6

Approaching home across the rooftops, Joe slipped into his private tower, into the elegant construction that rose atop the new upstairs. Hexagonal in design and glass-sided, the tower afforded him a wide view of the village roofs and the shore beyond. Yawning, his belly full of Mexican dinner, he considered the soft cushions and the joys of a short nap. Glancing down at the drive, he saw that Ryan's truck still stood beside Clyde's car.

Though Ryan had designed and built his tower, it was Clyde who had put the idea to her; and Joe himself was responsible for the overall concept. One could say that the tower was a collaboration between the three of them, though of course Ryan didn't know that. She gave the credit to Clyde, actually believing in Clyde's perceptive understanding of feline psychology and desires.

"I want to see in all directions," Joe had told Clyde. "Not just the ocean. I want to look down on the entire village. I want windows I can open and close by myself without spraining a paw. I want a fresh bowl of water every day, a soft blanket, and plenty of soft pillows."

"You want the pillows hand-embroidered? How about a refrigerator? A TV? A telephone, maybe?"

"A telephone would be nice."

"And tell me how I explain to Ryan that a tomcat needs a phone line into his private retreat."

"You're so cheap," Joe had said, rolling over. "You don't want to pay for a second line." He had looked upside down at Clyde. "I would be perfectly happy to share the existing house line with you. But I guess you don't want to share. Did you know," he said, flipping to his feet and fixing Clyde with a steady gaze, "that there is already a manufacturer making cell phones for dogs, to be attached to their collars? So why not cats? I don't see why . . ."

"Joe, it's lies like that that really set me off."

"Not a lie at all. The honest truth, I swear. It's a company called PetsCell. I don't know any more about it than that; Dulcie found a mention on the Web, an old newspaper article. If you would just . . . I'll get you a copy, you can read it for yourself. If you would just stretch your mind a little, Clyde, not let yourself become so hidebound. That really isn't . . ."

Clyde had only glared at him. And no phone had been forthcoming, house phone *or* cellular. But even so, his tower was an elegant retreat, rising as it did atop the slanted shake roof of the new second floor. His private aerie that could be entered from the rooftops or from Clyde's office below. Ryan, in her innocence, had designed the layout so that Clyde could easily step up on the moveable library ladder in his study, reach through the ceiling cat door, and open or close the tower windows. She had no notion that Joe could do that himself. Now, as he pawed at his cushions, preparing to nap, the faint sound of a TV sent him back over the roof, to peer down at the house next door.

Chichi must have hurried right home after her pushy performance at Lupe's Playa. The light of the TV danced across the living room shades, picking out her shadow sharp as a lounging cameo. Maybe she'd felt logy from her big supper, headed home to curl up before the tube. He couldn't say much for her taste, he thought, listening to the canned laughter of a sleazy sitcom, a series that he particularly hated.

It all came down to taste. Some humans

had it, some didn't. Deciding against a nap, and wondering if Clyde had checked on Rube, he slipped down through his cat door onto the ceiling beam, and dropped to Clyde's desk.

Around him, the house sounded empty; and it felt empty. Maybe Clyde and Ryan were walking the beach, giving Rock a run. Galloping down the stairs, suddenly worried about the aging retriever, he found Rube in bed, lying quietly among his blankets in the laundry, on the bottom mattress of the two-tiered bunk. He could smell Clyde's scent, and Ryan's, on Rube's ears and face, as if they'd given the old dog a good petting before going out again. When Joe spoke, Rube opened a tired eye, sighed, licked Joe's nose, then went back to sleep. Above Rube, on the top bunk, the two older cats were curled together, softly snoring. But the young white cat lay curled against Rube, with her paws around his foreleg. She, in particular, loved Rube, and Joe knew she was hurting for him.

Easing onto the bunk beside the two animals, and speaking softly to the old retriever, Joe tried to reassure him. He was thus occupied, snuggled against Rube, listening to the Lab's rough breathing, when he heard Rock bark, and heard Ryan open the patio gate. Clyde and Ryan came in the back door joking and laughing; they grew quiet as they turned into the laundry, the way a person would enter the hospital room of a very sick patient. Outside the kitchen door, Rock whined and sniffed, but the big dog didn't bark now, he knew better.

Clyde started to speak, then caught himself. Joe could see on his face the clear question: How is he? Clyde blinked at his near blunder, looked embarrassed, and knelt beside Ryan, to stroke Rube. As the two talked to the old dog, the white cat looked up at them, purring. Ryan laid her ear to Rube's chest, her dark hair blending with the Lab's black coat; then she smelled Rube's breath in a very personal manner. Ryan had grown up with Dallas's gun dogs, she had helped to train the pointers, had hunted with them and had tended to more than a few ailing canines. She looked up at Clyde with the same look, Joe was sure, that Dr. Firetti would have given him. The time was coming when Clyde must make the big decision, when he could no longer let Rube suffer but must give him ease and a deserved rest.

No one that Joe knew would keep an animal suffering for their own selfish human reasons. He'd heard of people who did, but neither Ryan nor Clyde, nor any of their friends, thought that death was the end for the animals they loved, any more than it was for humans. They were sensible enough to give an animal ease when there was no other solution to its distress. Joe nosed at Rube, wishing very much that he could make the old dog better, and knowing he could do nothing. And soon he left the laundry and headed upstairs feeling incredibly sad. He wished he had as powerful a faith in the wonders that came in the next life as did Dulcie.

Leaping to Clyde's desk, disturbing a stack of auto parts orders, he sailed up into the rafters and slipped out through his cat door into the tower, where he curled forlornly among the pillows and closed his eyes.

After a long time of feeling miserable, he slept. At some point he woke smelling coffee brewing and heard the faint clink of cups from down in the kitchen; and when he slept again, his dreams were uneasy. The next time he woke, the house was silent and Ryan's truck was gone — workday tomorrow. He imagined Clyde would be giving Rube his medicine and sitting quietly with the old dog.

Rube seemed to have aged quickly after his golden retriever pal, Barney, died. Joe thought the household cats missed Barney, too. Certainly the cats felt a true tenderness for Rube, they spent a lot of time washing his rough black coat and sleeping close to him or on top of him. Two of the cats were getting old, up in the high teens. Someday there would be only the young white female, the shy, frightened little one, Joe thought sadly.

Such thoughts made him feel pretty low; he didn't like to dwell on that stuff. But, it *happens,* he told himself sternly. That's how life is, life doesn't last forever.

He wondered how much ordinary cats thought about death, or if they thought about it at all. He didn't remember any such thoughts before he discovered his extended talents — but he'd been pretty young. The thoughts of a young tom in his prime were not on death and the hereafter, he was too busy living life with irresponsible abandon.

Joe did not like to think about his own age. He and Dulcie hoped that, along with their humanlike digestive systems capable of handling food that would put down an ordinary cat, and with their more complicated thought processes, maybe their aging would follow a pattern closer to that of humans. This life was such a blast that neither cat wanted to toss in the towel, they were too busy fighting crime, putting down the no-goods. Who knew what came next time around, who knew if they'd like it half as much.

Scowling at this infrequent turn of mind, he dropped into sleep again, and this time he slept deeply and without dreams, floating in a restorative slumber — until sirens brought him straight up, rigid. Their screams jerked him from sleep so suddenly he thought he'd been snatched out of his own skin.

Half awake, he backed away from the ear-bursting commotion, from the ululating harbingers of disaster. The walls of his tower fairly shook with vibrations. He could feel through his paws, through his whole body, the banging ramble of the fire trucks. Then the shriller scream of a rescue unit joined in, then the whoop-whoop of Harper's police units. Sounded to Joe like every emergency vehicle in the village was streaking through the night, rumbling up the narrow streets heading toward the hills. Rearing up in his tower, all he could see was the racing red glow of their lights running along the undersides of the trees.

Slipping out of the tower and leaping up onto its hexagonal roof, he reared up like a weather vane, watching the wild race of red-lit vehicles hurtling between the cottages, heading up the hills — and he could hear, from up the hills, faint shouting, men shouting. Rearing taller, he could see an eerie red glow flickering. Fire. Fire, up around the high school. A tongue of flame licked at the sky, and another, and a twisting cloud of red burst into the night. He was poised to leap away across the roofs to follow when, below him on the dark street, three unlighted police cars slipped past him as silent as hunting sharks.

But these cars were not headed for the high school, they made straight for the center of the village, moving fast and quietly. He glimpsed them once, crossing Ocean, then lost them among the roofs and night shadows. He stood studying the silent village looking for some disturbance, but saw nothing, no one running, no swift escaping movement. He heard no shouts, no sound at all. Saw no sudden cops' spotlights reflecting against the sky. What the hell was happening? He was crouched to race across the roofs for a look when, from below in the study, Clyde began shouting. Joe stared down toward the study and bedroom, and dropped down to the shingles again and through the tower and cat door, peering down from the rafter.

Clyde's shouts came from the bottom of the stairs. "He's worse, Joe. His breathing's bad — we're off to the vet. Call him, Joe. Punch code two. Call him now, tell him you're a houseguest, that I'm on my way." And Clyde was gone, Joe heard the front door slam, then the car doors, and the roadster roared to a start and skidded out of the drive, took off burning rubber.

Leaping down to the desk, Joe hit the speaker button and the digit for Dr. Firetti; he felt dizzy and sick inside.

"Firetti." The doctor answered sleepily, on the first ring. Joe imagined him jerking awake in his little stucco cottage next to the clinic, pulling himself from sleep. "Yes? What?" Firetti said.

"This . . . I'm a friend of Clyde Damen, Clyde's on his way. Rube's worse, really sick. He should be . . ."

"Just pulled in," Firetti shouted from a distance as if he'd laid down the phone to pull on his pants. Joe heard a door click open, heard faintly Firetti shouting to Clyde; then the silence of an open line.

Seeing in his mind the familiar clinic with its cold metal tables, but with friendly pictures of cats and dogs on the walls, seeing old Rube lying prone on a metal table gasping for breath, Joe clicked off the phone. And he sat among the papers he'd scattered, thinking about Rube. Seeing Dr. Firetti's caring face peering down the way he did, leaning over you while you shivered on the table. Seeing Clyde's worried face, beside Firetti. And Joe prayed hard for Rube.

Then there was nothing else he could do. He hated idle waiting. He was crouched to leap back to the roof, when the white cat came up the stairs announcing her distress with tiny, forlorn mewls. She padded into the study and stood shakily below the desk staring up at him, crying.

Dropping to the floor, Joe licked Snowball's face, trying to ease her. She knew Rube was in trouble, this little cat knew very well what was happening. Snowball was, of all three household cats, by far the most intelligent and sensitive.

"It's all right, Snowball. He has good care. He'll be . . . he'll be the best he can be," Joe said gently.

Snowball looked up at him trustingly, the way she always trusted him, this innocent, delicate little cat. "It's all right," he said. "You have to trust Clyde, you have to trust the doctor."

Joe nudged her up into the big leather chair, where she obediently curled down into a little ball. He was tucking the woolen throw around her with careful paws when a muffled report, sharp as gunfire, exploded from the center of the village: a shot echoing between the shops. Distant tires chirped and squealed, racing away, then silence. But Joe, as hungry for action as any cop, couldn't bring himself to leave Snowball.

Licking her ears, he snuggled close, purring to her until at last she dropped off into sleep. The poor little cat was worn out, done in from stress and worry, from her pain over Rube. I guess, Joe thought, that ordinary cats — the kind of cat I was long ago — I guess there's a lot more understanding there than I remember having. I guess that even a regular cat is far more than he appears to be.

And that was the end of the night's philosophizing. He licked Snowball's ear again, though she was deep under, relaxed at last. "Stay here," Joe told her uselessly. "Stay right here, Clyde'll be back soon. And Rube will be . . . Rube will be the best he can be." As a second shot rang out, he leaped to the desk and was out of there, desk to rafter to tower and to the shingles, where he stood listening.

But all was silence now. He could see no lights moving beneath the trees. Only up at the high school was there increasing commotion as the fire licked higher across the night sky, heralded by the faint echoes of shouting men and by car lights appearing and disappearing as if moving back and forth behind the buildings.

Had kids set the fire? Students? That would be a first for this village. But he guessed every town had its troublemakers. Watching the red stain in the sky, he couldn't decide whether to take off up the hills to see what was happening, or seek out the mysterious events occurring somewhere on the dim village streets.

The decision took care of itself, quite suddenly.

The tomcat was crouched to leap away, when a figure appeared from the shadows in the neighbors' dark yard, a black-clad figure slipping swiftly through the bushes and around the far side of the house.

Sailing across to the neighbors' roof, Joe stood with his paws in the gutter peering down as the figure moved silently along the drive toward the back, heading for Chichi's door.

As much as he disliked Chichi Barbi, he didn't want to see something ugly happen to her. There she was, watching TV at the front of the house, and had likely heard nothing.

Above the raucous canned laughter, what could she hear? The woman was a sitting duck in there.

Slipping along the edge of the roof to follow the intruder, the tomcat had to laugh. Black leggings, black sweatshirt, black hood pulled up, and even black gloves, a character straight out of a cheap movie.

But that didn't make him any less dangerous. Joe watched him slip up the steps into the shadows beside the door. In a moment the door opened, the figure slipped inside, the door closed softly, then all was still.

Trotting across the roof again to the front of the house, he hung out over the gutter looking down through the front window.

Chichi's sharp silhouette hadn't moved; she appeared totally entranced by the insipid sitcom. Backing up and kneading his claws on the shingles, he trotted away to the pine tree between the houses. Leaping onto its trunk, clinging, he backed down to where he could jump into the little lemon tree — slashing his paws again on its wicked thorns. Why the hell did lemon trees have thorns! No cat could avoid them.

Looking into the dark room, trying to spot the intruder, he saw nothing at first but shadows. Nothing moved until . . . Yes. There. Black within black, slipping stealthily along beside the dresser. For a brief moment, Joe Grey was uncertain what to do. Shout at Chichi through the window to warn her? And jeopardize his own neck? Or wait, bide his time, try to see what the burglar would take, or what he was up to?

If this was only theft, and not the precursor of an attack on Chichi herself, his instinct was to stay put, to watch, and let this come down as it would. Tonight every cop was busy, the intruder had to know that. Joe thought he'd better play it by ear, maybe go for the evidence. With every cop in the department either up at the fire or chasing unseen miscreants through the dark streets, it was, indeed, a hard call.

7

Crouched among the thin, brittle branches, his nose tickling with the sharp smell of lemons, Joe stared in through the dark window watching the housebreaker's stealthy movements. In the inky-black room, he could make out very little even with his superior night vision. But suddenly he was blinded. Light blazed on, right in his eyes. Backing away, nearly falling, his every nerve jumping with shock, he was caught in the brilliance like a deer in a speeder's headlights.

Hunching down, trying to hide his white parts, he had no real cover. Light pooled in through the skinny branches and scruffy leaves. In its glare he couldn't see the intruder's face, the hood was pulled nearly together. Black might be melodramatic, but it was effective. There was a bulge in the intruder's right pocket. A weapon? Skinny guy, even in the oversized black sweatshirt. Opening the dresser drawers, real bold now. What was he looking for? Something in par-

ticular, or just any valuables he could find, money, credit cards, jewelry? Or was he putting something in the drawers? He seemed very casual and unhurried.

Either the lock on this back door had been easy to breach, a credit card lock, or the guy was mighty fast with the lock picks. Or Chichi had left it unlocked? Had she forgotten to lock it? Or did this person have a key?

Maybe the new owners hadn't changed the locks, some people just didn't think of those things. Or had Chichi given someone a key? From the front of the house, Joe could still hear dialogue and canned laughter. The way the burglar was bundled in the dark sweatshirt, it was hard to tell whether this was a man or a woman — until suddenly his quarry flipped back the hood, unzipped the sweatshirt, and tossed it on a chair — and Joe gulped back a yowl of surprise.

Chichi. It was Chichi. She smiled lazily, fluffed her frazzled blond hair, and ran her hand down her slim waist, pulling down her tight black T-shirt, showing plenty of cleavage. What was she doing sneaking into her own house under cover of darkness, sliding silently into the darkened room?

And who was out there in the living room

watching the tube? Did she have company? Why hadn't he seen someone before? Those two guys who came to see her, neither acted like he was living here. Suspicions formed in Joe's mind faster than he could process them; but they added up to nothing. Zilch.

As Chichi pulled off the tight black jeans and slipped into a red satin robe, he wanted to race around to the front window and have a closer look at that one-person audience. Maybe he could peer under the blind. But he wanted, more, to stay where he was clinging to the skinny branch. He watched her slip a black cloth bag from the pocket of the sweatshirt where it lay on the chair; and she stood looking around the room. It seemed like the kind of waterproof silk bag that expensive raincoats come folded into, for easy travel.

Kneeling, she opened the bottom dresser drawer and reached up underneath, making Joe want to laugh out loud. If she was hiding something, that was the first place a cop — or a burglar — would look.

But then Chichi seemed to realize this, too. She rose, clutching the bag, and stood considering the mattress — another laughable choice. Go ahead, Joe thought, twitching a whisker. The moment you leave, lady, or go to take a shower, I'll be in there slashing through the mattress, and out again with the loot . . .

But what loot? What did she have in the bag? And could he even get into the place?

Well, hell, he'd never seen a house he couldn't break into.

Kneeling, Chichi slipped the bag between the two mattresses. She didn't shove it very deep, she didn't slit the mattress ticking. Good show, Joe thought, itching to get his paws under there, get his claws into that black silk. For a long moment, she just knelt there. Then, almost as if she'd read his mind, she pulled the bag out again and set it on the bed, as if she meant to hide it somewhere more secure, harder to discover.

But maybe, Joe thought, he wouldn't have to retrieve it. Maybe he'd *know* what she'd hidden, as soon as he found out what had happened in the village. Chichi's stealthy arrival home while the sirens were still shrieking, plus the unanswered puzzle of who was watching TV, had to add up to trouble.

The thin branch was cutting into his belly, and its thorns had stuck his hind paw so deeply he could smell his own blood. Hurt like hell to back away when, within the bright room, Chichi turned suddenly and approached the window.

100

She stood looking out, her eyes on a level with his own, which were slitted closed, his white parts hidden in an uncomfortable crouch. Did the bedroom light pick him out like a possum on a leafless branch?

But so what? What difference? So there was a cat in the tree, a neighborhood cat. Clyde Damen's cat, harassing the sleeping birds, maybe snatching baby birds from their nests.

She didn't remain long at the window, but bent down to root around in a suitcase that lay open on a chair beside the dresser. Hadn't she unpacked? She'd been there two weeks. That spoke of a transient, fly-by-night attitude that made Joe smile with satisfaction at his own astute character assessment.

But when she drew from the suitcase a long, sharp-looking bread knife, and looked up directly through the glass, he swallowed back a yelp of surprise and nearly fell out of the tree. Backing away into the tiniest twiggy branches, he lacerated two more paws and bent the limbs so far that he swung and wobbled wildly before he righted himself, nonchalantly licked a paw as if he hadn't seen anything frightening but had just lost his balance, and crept back to a safer perch. Maybe, with the inside light reflecting against the glass, she had only seen her own reflection.

But why the knife? What made her pick it up and peer out so intently?

And what, in the next instant, made her draw the shade?

Maybe she'd heard something, the soft hush of his scrabbling among the brittle branches; maybe that was all. There was no reason for her, even if she'd seen him, to feel threatened. By a cat? Why would she?

Annoyed at his own cowardice, Joe dropped from the lemon tree and sped for the front of the house. Rearing up with his paws on the sill, he peered through beneath the shade, stretching and tilting his head, his nose pressed against the cold glass.

Studying the dim room in the TV's flickering light, Joe laughed softly. Little Chichi had some artistic flair, some talent as a sculptor.

Maybe she had worked in department store window display, or maybe on stage sets. Or maybe she was simply talented. She had created a very lifelike silhouette using a mop and several other common household items.

The mop formed the body; it was one of those old-fashioned mops with twisted rags on a stick; these were the woman's tresses, tangled like Chichi's blond coiffure. The figure wore a blue sweat suit, artfully padded out in just the right places. The head itself was made of wadded and pasted newspapers. A small table lamp behind the figure gave off the weak glow that helped, with the flicker of the TV, to silhouette her against the shade. The creative dummy was, at the moment, being treated to an old rerun of *Lassie*, a series Joe found particularly disgusting.

It was one thing to see animal stories that were obviously imaginary takeoffs, like *Alice in Wonderland*, or the Narnia series, or *The Lion King*. Children knew this was make-believe, and they loved it. It was quite another matter to subject children to animal tales that purported to present impossible animal behavior as real life. The things Lassie understood and did were not at all how dogs really acted or thought, and yet the series wasn't presented as fantasy. The result, in Joe's opinion, was generations of children who hadn't a clue how to train and deal with their new Christmas puppies or kittens, and generations of parents who were just as ignorant.

When Joe compared those tawdry stories to the very real and wonderful feats of well-trained police and drug dogs, and of herding and search-and-rescue dogs, Lassie's idiocy came off as dangerously and foolishly misleading. No wonder children grew up knowing nothing about the animals with whom they shared the earth.

Clyde would once have said he was grossly opinionated. But Clyde's views on the subject had undergone some serious changes, and were now pretty much the same as Joe's own. As for Joe and Dulcie and Kit's situation, the cats themselves understood that *they* were far beyond the pale. That no sensible adult could easily believe that a cat could talk, and for this they were eternally grateful.

Continuing to admire Chichi's display-window handiwork, he wondered if this figure had been here before Clyde went off to dinner. Clyde and Ryan must have walked right by it, passing this window as they headed for Lupe's Playa. Clyde, seeing what he thought was Chichi in there, should have wondered at seeing her so shortly afterward walking into Lupe's.

But maybe not. It was only a few blocks. Or maybe she'd had this figure all set up within the darkened room, had watched through the front window until Clyde and Ryan left the house walking up toward the village, and then had turned on the lamp and TV, and had slipped out of the house to follow them.

But why? To establish an alibi to her whereabouts, tonight? But dinner was a long time before whatever came down in the village. How could her appearance at Lupe's afford her a tight alibi?

Maybe she'd wanted to get friendly with the Molena Point cops, make nice to Harper and Garza. She'd tried hard enough to get herself invited to join them. To gain their goodwill, while at the same time establishing an alibi. Fat chance, with cops. Anyway, that really didn't wash. How would she know Clyde was having dinner with Max and Dallas?

Unless Clyde had told her? Quite possible. She often came knocking; maybe earlier this evening he'd used dinner as an excuse to get rid of her. Or maybe, seeing Ryan arrive and the two of them go off, Chichi took a chance and followed?

Whatever, they'd all left the restaurant long before the sirens started. She'd had plenty of time to take care of whatever business involved the little black bag.

Filled with questions, he considered waiting until her lights went out and she was in bed asleep, then find a way inside;

try to wriggle under the mattress without waking her.

Right. And end up backed into a corner by that businesslike bread knife.

But again, he was only a cat. She shouldn't be overly alarmed by his presence; when she saw him in the yard or on his own porch, she looked at him with distaste, but not with fear; she didn't go pale and back away as a real ailurophobe would be likely to do, exhibiting shortness of breath and possible heart palpitations. A person like that, you really couldn't con them with purrs, with face rubs against a stockinged ankle. And long ago, in San Francisco, she'd played up to him big time.

Now, probably the worst Chichi would do if she found him in her room would be fling open the back door and chase him out into the night.

Right. With the bread knife.

Dulcie would say his plan was more than stupid, she'd call him totally insane, say he'd abandoned the last shred of his previously astute feline mind. Maybe he'd wait until tomorrow, take the sensible route, lay low until Chichi walked into the village early, as she often did, carrying her big canvas tote.

Leaving Chichi's front window, scorching up the pine tree to his own roof, he shouldered into his tower and through his cat door, dropped down to Clyde's desk, and went straight to Snowball in the big leather chair.

She was awake, looking small and lonely, just a frightened wisp of white fluff. Charlie had said once that cats, when they were sick or hurt or afraid or grieving, seemed to shrink to half their size, to collapse right in on themselves. Slipping up into the chair beside Snowball, he began to lick her ear and to talk gently to her.

Of the three household cats, Snowball had been the first to get used to his human speech. Her initial shock hadn't lasted long, and then she'd been more fascinated than appalled.

"It's all right, Snowball," he told her now. "Rube will be all right, he's in good hands now, he's not in pain now." But even as he said it, Joe shuddered. What did he mean, he'll be fine? What did that mean, in good hands now? What did that mean, not in pain now?

He didn't want to think what those expressions might really mean.

Giving the grieving little cat a gentle wash, he sat with her snuggled close, waiting until she dozed again, tired out with missing Rube. Only then did Joe leave her. Leaping from desk to rafter and through to the roofs, he headed fast for the center of the village, his gaze focused on the reflection of slow-moving car lights and handheld spotlights that now glanced skyward, bouncing against the edges of the roof gutters and flickering along the undersides of the oaks. Cops with spotlights, moving fast and silent.

He approached the scene expecting any second to hear sirens blast; but none did. Just the silent racing lights and the whisper of voices that, from a distance, only a cat could hear; and then, soon, the muted static of police radios turned low. As he neared the scene he could make out more clearly the soft resonance of the cops' voices, the voices of men he knew. There were no sirens, no staccato sounds of men running, no cars taking off with squealing tires; no more shots fired.

But suddenly just below him four patrol cars took off fast in four directions, racing silent and swift along the narrow streets. Joe knew the sound of the big Chevys that Molena Point PD drove, knew their purr as well as he knew his own. Approaching the scene over the shingles, he paused, waiting and watching, half his mind even now on old Rube, on Clyde and on Snowball.

Clyde would be alarmed when he got

home and Snowball wasn't in her bed, when she wasn't anywhere downstairs or in the patio. Eventually he'd look upstairs, where she sometimes went when she was very upset, when the other two household cats took her toys or took all the food. Clyde would find her in the leather chair and would likely take her into bed with him, to comfort her — to comfort each other. Clyde would be feeling low himself, maybe very low, Joe thought forlornly.

Long before the first alarm sounded on the police switchboard, before any call came in to the dispatcher, Max and Charlie Harper had settled in for the evening, replete with their good Mexican dinner. They had made a pot of coffee and brought the two dogs in for a relaxed evening before the fire. Charlie, tired and happy after her pack trip, lay on the rug before the blazing logs, lulled by the fire's crackle, by the faint crashing of the distant surf, and the music from an Ella Fitzgerald CD. The two big dogs lay near her, eyeing her coffee, though they didn't like that bitter brew. Max sat sprawled in one of the two red leather chairs, enjoying the beauty and peace of their home and admiring Charlie's neat butt in her snug jeans.

Above them the ceiling of the great room rose to a high peak that towered over the rest of the house, its cedar rafters perfuming the room. In the daytime the long glass wall offered a wide sweep down across the pastures to the open hills and to the sea beyond and, off to the right, the rooftops and dark oaks of the village. The thin, pleated blinds pulled high and the lamps unlit they enjoyed the night sky. As yet there was no hint of trouble, no faint finger of red touching the sky, no faint, distant sounds of unrest in the small village.

The furnishings of the room were simple, the red leather chairs, the bright primitive colors of the Turkish Konya rug that Charlie had found at an estate sale, the long wicker couch with its fluffy pillows. Opposite the windows, the fireplace wall was faced, floor to ceiling, with round river stones and flanked by tall bookcases. The other two walls of the room were stark white, setting off Charlie's framed drawings of horses, dogs, wild animals, and of the three cats. One wall was broken by a sliding glass door that led to the wide stone terrace; the terrace, in turn, joined the kitchen. Charlie was telling Max about the quarter horse ranch where she and Ryan and Hanni had spent two nights, when

Max's cell phone buzzed. "Damn!" she said violently.

"Maybe it's nothing," Max said, flipping the phone open.

The next moment, she could tell by his face that it was the end of their quiet evening. He listened, asked several questions, then rose. Neither said anything. Charlie got up from the floor and kissed him. He hugged her hard, grabbed his jacket and was out the door — gone while she stood there wondering, for the thousandth time, why she had married a cop.

But she knew why.

Pouring another cup of coffee from the pot by the fireplace, she lay down again among the cushions, thinking that she should pull the shades now that she was alone. Thinking she really ought to turn the police scanner on, find out what was happening. But she was far too comfortable to do either. She'd know what was happening soon enough. Rolling over on the rug, snuggling between the two dogs, she said a prayer for Max, as she always did. He would not like knowing that she prayed for him; this was his job. But she prayed anyway. What could it hurt; she couldn't help how she felt, no matter how she tried — and then she began to worry about the three cats.

They'd be right in the middle, you could bet on it, drawn to the crime scene like kids to a fire. Three little cats, so small, three rare little souls, so strangely blessed with human talents, out in the night peering down from the trees or rooftops, keen with predatory enthusiasm for whatever crime was coming down.

Though her prayers might not make anyone safe, and though she would not change the cats any more than she would change Max, Charlie prayed for them all.

8

As Max headed down the hills to the village, their friends listened to the sirens that he hadn't heard from his distant position, and saw the reflections of flames up around the high school, and they paid attention. Max and Dallas would be heading up there, as would their other friends on the force. In the hospital, Wilma Getz woke from dozing before her TV, turned off the set, and listened. The tall, thin, wrinkled woman wished she had the little police scanner she had bought recently for just such occasions, for times when she knew Dulcie would race off into the middle of danger.

Dressed in her own red flannel nightgown instead of the hospital gown that had left her chilled and irritable, Wilma was comfortable enough despite the fact that she didn't like hospitals. Her long, silver-white hair had, until tonight, been bound into a bun in an effort to keep it confined under the cap they put on you before surgery. Now that she had been allowed to wash and blow-dry it, she felt better. Her clean hair lay smooth and comfortable, pulled neatly back in a ponytail.

Reaching for the little mouse that would allow her to raise the back of her bed, she tried to track more precisely the scream of the sirens as they hurried up the hills. Swinging her feet to the floor, wincing at the pulling pains, she made her way to the window, supporting herself on the night table, then along the back of the visitors' chair.

It hurt to raise the venetian blind. Lifting her arm high and pulling hard sent a sharper pain cutting along her incision. Time to start exercising, get herself back in working order. Her young, enthusiastic surgeon, Jim Hallorhan, had only this morning pronounced her ready to start some serious rehabilitation.

It hurt less to slide the window open. The chill night air felt fresh and good on her flushed face. Her room faced east, away from the village, toward the hills. High up, cutting the blackness, she could see a thin smear of red dancing against the sky, very near the high school. She made out the whirling red lights of the patrol cars and fire rig and what was probably a rescue unit. She prayed that the three cats, if they insisted on racing up there, would keep to the residential rooftops and out of the way. She thought it wasn't a big fire, maybe trash cans or an outbuilding. Very likely the units would quickly get it under control. She had been watching for some time when something else alerted her. She stood still, listening in the other direction, from the village beyond the hall and the opposite line of rooms. Had she heard a shot, faint and muffled?

Crossing the hall, she slipped into an empty room where the blinds were open to the village below, to the dim, narrow streets and little shops that lay snug beneath the leafy canopies. She watched the moving beams of police torches flashing along the faces of the buildings, and shadowy uniforms searching among the shops; farther away along the darkest streets she sensed, as much as saw, occasional swift movement. This was a strange, phantom kind of search. She stood for a long time, making little sense of it. What had gone down? Burglary? Robbery? Murder? There would be nothing on TV until it was over. She stood worrying about the cats, knowing that if they weren't already down there, they soon would be. She wished she had her binoculars. She tried to spot Joe Grey's stark white markings stalking the roofs; he was so much easier to see than her own Dulcie or the kit.

Perhaps it had been a break-in that the officer in charge had decided to handle with a quick canvassing search, while the perps had successfully fled or were hiding nearby. She could only pray the cats kept clear. After a lifetime of considerable control over the criminals she handled, she felt helpless as a civilian. Helpless, indeed, when the action involved the three cats.

Worrying but knowing there was nothing she could do, she returned at last to her room, chilled, and slipped into bed. She wished they gave you more than two thin blankets. Well, Dulcie was with Lucinda and Kit; maybe, somehow, the Greenlaws would manage to keep the two in.

Fat chance, Wilma thought.

But the Greenlaw terrace was so close to the action that maybe the two cats would be content to watch from that vantage. Maybe. She turned over, wincing at the pain, reminding herself that the surgery was over, that her gall bladder was gone and that was no big deal. A few minor changes in her diet, a small price to pay for a cessation of sudden pain. Tomorrow she'd be up at Charlie and Max's, able to start exercising again — while Charlie waited on her, she thought, amused.

She ought to be home in her own house, making her own meals, but Charlie wouldn't hear it. Charlie said it was the only excuse she had to enjoy her aunt as a houseguest.

As if Charlie needed a houseguest right now, with the new addition barely finished and a hundred chores and details to tend to, trying to get settled into her new studio so she could get on with her several commissions for animal portraits, and with the children's book she was writing.

That, for Wilma, would be the biggest treat, to tuck up with Dulcie before Charlie's fire on these chill days, after Max went off to work, when Kit could speak freely, telling the fascinating tales of her kittenhood when she traveled with the wild band of ferals.

Charlie's book would include no speaking, sentient cats. Just the story of a band of feral cats trying to survive. Even so, it was turning into a magical tale, as the best realistic story should be. Magical, too, when illustrated with Charlie's drawings. Not long ago, Charlie had cursed her art education, calling it a total waste of time and money, a squandering of four years of her young life. Now, look at her, Wilma thought, grinning.

It was earlier, ten minutes before the first siren shrieked heading up the hills to the high school, the village streets still quiet and nearly deserted when Dulcie and Kit arrived on the terrace of the Greenlaws' second-floor apartment. Full of Mexican supper, they had taken their time meandering home over the rooftops, detouring to lazily chase a little bat, then to sit by a warm chimney and have a nice wash and enjoy the evening.

Their dawdling, circuitous route brought them, yawning, to the tall pine tree beside the Greenlaw terrace. As they dropped to the terrace, they could smell coffee; Lucinda stood in the shadows, her cup balanced on the terrace wall, as she, too, enjoyed the evening.

But as the two cats landed on the terrace, a siren screamed only blocks away, heading away from the fire station up toward the hills. And another siren, another. Fire trucks and then an ambulance, then patrol cars racing by nearly bursting their eardrums. Dulcie and Kit leaped to the low terrace wall, ready to follow.

"Wait," Lucinda said.

"But . . ." Dulcie began, looking up the far hills where a red glow was beginning to lick at the sky. The cats, not seeing Pedric, thought he'd likely gone to bed early, aching with arthritis.

"Wait, you two!" Lucinda said with urgency.

"What?" Kit said. "You never want us to go. We'll stay to the rooftops, we're safe there." Both cats crouched to run, staring up to the hills at the brightening flames, both ready to bolt and follow the fire trucks. Below them the village was still, the streets quiet. Imperatively, Lucinda put her hand on Kit's back.

Kit stared up at her. "You never want . . ."

The old woman spoke softly but with harsh command. "You've missed something. Look down! Something else is happening! Help me look, quick, you two can see in the dark better than I!" She pointed down across the street to the corner shop opposite their building; looking, the cats went tense.

Molena Point had no streetlights; only the soft glow from the shop windows. Between these, the sidewalk was shadowed and dim. They all three watched the dark windows of Marineau's Jewelry store; Lucinda could see little within, but the cats' eyes grew round, and they crouched, their tails lashing.

"Two shadows," Dulcie said softly. "Moving inside. How . . . ?" Then a thin, shielded light flicked on, as if from a miniature flashlight. The next instant a sharp tinkling, almost like music, and tiny jagged glints of light flickered and fell.

"Before the sirens headed up the hills," Lucinda said softly, "I heard the faintest sound. The little light flashed once, and went out. I thought I heard glass break then, too, but muffled. As if by a towel." She held up her cell phone. "I called the station. What else can you see?" Even as she spoke, the tiny light flickered again, and they heard a sharper crack as of heavier glass breaking, more bright shards fell.

"Why doesn't the city put in some decent lighting?" Lucinda snapped irritably. "Ambiance is all very well, until something ugly happens."

Max Harper had tried to get the city to install decorative, soft-glowing streetlamps. The city council said that would spoil the quaint sense of Old World mystery that the tourists liked. Max had pointed out that there was plenty of crime on the dark medieval streets, that robbery and murder were common during those times. He said modern tourists didn't need *that* much ambiance. Several members of the city council had laughed at him. But the shopkeepers hadn't laughed, particularly the jewelry store owners.

The lighting Max wanted would not have spoiled the atmosphere, but it sure would have hindered such stealthy break-ins as was occurring below. Lucinda and Dulcie and Kit watched as a dark figure slipped out the broken glass door and fled, vanishing among the street's shadows.

"Two are still in the store," Dulcie said, watching the pair of black-clad figures barely visible in the blackness, even to a cat's eyes; watching them moving about at their work. Then, "Oh!" Dulcie hissed. The thieves came bolting out and took off up the street, disappearing — and before Lucinda could grab Kit, the cats were after them, racing away unheeding of the old lady's cries.

Sailing from the rooftop terrace into an oak, they crossed the street on bending branches into another tree, leaped four feet to the shingled roof of the jewelry store and raced across it following the thieves. Running, the cats heard the purr of an engine; a car swerved around the corner and skidded to a stop, and the two figures piled in and were gone.

★ ★ ★

Lucinda stood looking after the cats, half annoyed, half filled with fear for them. But she couldn't stop them, couldn't change them; they were doing what, according to their rules, they *must* do. As the little cats were swallowed by the night, two squad cars slipped around the corner without lights. Four darkly uniformed officers emerged, moving to cover the door and the broken display window. She cursed herself for calling the cats' attention to the burglary, for putting them in danger. If she'd kept her mouth shut . . .

But it would have made no difference. If they hadn't seen the burglars, they'd be off to the fire, and that could be worse. Or, if they had paused before they raced away to the hills, they would have heard the jewelry store break-in for themselves, the tinkle of shattered glass.

For a long moment Lucinda stood envying the cats, wishing she, too, could race across the rooftops leaping from peak to peak as free and sure of herself as they. She caught a glimpse of movement down the alley where other officers were approaching, friendly shadows slipping silently through the dark streets. How many men could Harper spare, with something happening up in the hills, too, where the red glow bloomed brighter and another siren screamed?

9

It was some time later that two more patrol cars pulled to the curb facing the jewelry store and switched on their lights to blaze in through the broken window. Now, in the harsh glare, Lucinda could see every detail, the glitter of scattered glass as bright as spilled diamonds, the smashed display cases gaping empty, stripped of a fortune in jewels — surely a large portion of James Marineau's livelihood. She could see, now, that the front-window glass had been secured, before breaking, with wide strips of silver duct tape. Maybe that was the thunk she'd heard, the sound of a hard object striking a dull blow into the taped glass. Several blocks away, two more squad cars raced by while three others cruised more slowly, shining their spotlights into doorways and alleys.

She heard, farther up Ocean, the screech of tires as a car braked, then another car skidded behind it. Both sets of lights came racing down Ocean and onto the side street, to stop before Marineau's: Max Harper's truck followed by Dallas Garza's green sedan. Had the burglars escaped? Had there been silent arrests? She wished she'd been able to see more clearly, to offer up some description of the men. How many had there been? Maybe even the two cats hadn't seen the robbers clearly. Thank goodness they were on the roofs now, and not down there! Safety, with those three, never seemed a prime concern.

As Lucinda watched the captain and detective enter the jewelry store, up the hills north of the village two of the thieves, free of danger now, slipped into a darkened house. They carried no loot from the job, no little bags filled with diamonds, no pockets bulging with Cartier watches, though Marineau's was the most prestigious jewelry store in Molena Point, the kind of shop where every entering patron was treated with courteous respect but even the most elegantly dressed among them, if they were not regulars, were carefully observed.

The house they entered was dark, tall, built against the hillside, the drive climbing steeply up beside it. The thieves had not emerged from a car — there was no car in the drive or on the street. They appeared out of the shadows, moved halfway up the drive and onto the little porch, and slid noiselessly in through the front door. They did not speak until the door had closed softly behind them, then the two resumed arguing, but quietly; dark-haired Luis angry and cursing in whispers, his redheaded partner snickering until Luis turned on him with cold rage, grabbing him by the collar.

"Shut up, Tommie! He's not your brother!"

"You said you'd as soon be rid of him! You've said it a hundred times, he's a damn screwup! Now he's out of your way. What trouble can he get into, in jail? Safest place for him!"

"We don't need a screwup in the hands of the cops, you dummy!" Luis pulled off his dark windbreaker, dropped it on a chair, and headed down the hall through the dim house toward the kitchen. "Cops hassle Dufio enough, he'll spill everything."

"Nah. He knows better. Even Dufio ain't that stupid."

"Keep your voice down."

"Knows damn well," Tommie muttered, "stoolies die in jail." He followed Luis into the kitchen, shutting the door behind them as Luis turned on the light. Luis didn't call his sister to the kitchen as he usually did, to fix their meal. They stood at the counter,

eating what Maria had left out for them —
cold beans, cold tortillas, a dozen small cold
tamales, a twelve-pack of beer. Around
them in the silent house the other residents
slept, or pretended to sleep.

Only in the back of the house, in the
smaller bedroom, did anyone make a sound.
There, from within a cage, came the faintest
mewl as one of the captive cats woke. The
men didn't hear her, nor would they have
paid any attention as long as the beast didn't
yowl loud enough to wake the neighbors. In
the shadowed bedroom, the cat looked
around her. She listened to the two women's
breathing. She listened to the men's harsh
arguing from the kitchen, her ears catching
small sounds that the women, even awake,
would not have heard.

She stared at the crusting food dish in the
corner of the cage, but she didn't approach
it. She drank a little water, listened shivering
to the voices, then curled up tightly again on
the wadded cotton towel and stuck her nose
under her tail, trying to get warm.

She was a pale calico color, her white coat
marked with bleached gray like pussy willow
buds, and with pale orange, a subtly colored
cat with a rather long, distinctive face, and a
look of distrust in her green eyes. The three
cats had been in the cage for two weeks.

They kept careful count of the days, not that it did them much good. In all that time, they had not been able to breach the lock. They had tried every way they could think of, but no cat, not even one with their talents, could open a padlock. Even if they'd had the key that Luis kept in his pocket, even though they understood the functions of lock and key, they could not have manipulated such a tool. It would take fingers to do that, and opposable thumbs; these were among the few blessings they wished they possessed along with their ability to speak and understand human language.

The hinges and joints of the cage were welded, too, so there was no way they could force them apart. Their only chance of escape was when, once a day, Luis's sister, Maria, removed and changed the litter box — except that Luis was always there, watching her. Luis would unlock the cage, then slam the door shut the instant Maria pulled out the litter box. He would slam and lock the door again when she'd put the box back inside. She seldom changed the sand, just scooped out the wet and dirty part, so the box stunk bad. That made the food and water taste bad. Even the air tasted like poop. Willow felt sick all the time, confined so. All she wanted to do was growl and hiss and hunch to herself and not eat. She thought they'd die there. She longed for the green hills and fresh winds, for cold fresh water.

She even longed for the clowder of cats they had run with, even as mean as those cats were, even as much as she feared the leaders. She was not a brave cat; she felt safer in the clowder than trying to survive alone.

From the kitchen came the clatter of dishes, then the men's voices rose, and they went stumping down the hall to the front bedroom. She could smell their stink of beer beneath the closed door like a sour wind, she could taste the beer smell.

She heard Maria come awake in one of the two beds, her breathing suddenly quicker and shallower. But, wary of the men's approach just as Willow herself was, Maria lay still and made no sound. Only when both men had used the bathroom and gone back into the bedroom and shut the door, only when at last they could be heard snoring, did Maria settle down once more, pull the covers over her face, and go back to sleep.

Willow didn't sleep. She paced the cage, stepping around the sleeping forms of white Cotton, and dark tabby Coyote of the long, canine-like ears. Ever since they'd been trapped, she didn't sleep until she was so exhausted she could no longer hold her eyes open. Pacing, she thought about where this house must be in relation to the hills south of the village where they were captured. How foolish they had been to get caught, to trust those spliced bungee cords that had come apart and let the three traps spring closed. Their only excuse was that those traps had been rigged like no other they'd ever seen.

Usually, the door to a cage-trap was held open for a week or more with a brightly colored, elastic bungee cord, and new food would be added every day. This was meant to lure a cat inside again and again, they all knew that. They all knew it was safe to snatch out the food when a bungee cord was in place — but that when the bungee was gone, no matter how delicious the bait smelled, no sensible cat would go near.

How unfair, that these three traps had been rigged differently. Once the doors had sprung closed behind them, they'd been as helpless as mice skewered in their own claws.

Someone had known what kind of cats they were. But why did these humans want them? Willow's fears combined with the stink and the sour food and the crowding, were becoming nearly intolerable. She had never known, until she was caged, how very dear was her freedom. How precious was their ability to run free across the grassy hills, to curl down at night in the leaves or bushes in the cool wind, looking up at the vast sky and endless stars.

All that was gone now, and Willow was afraid.

She thought about that horrible noisy ride down the hills in a tiny cage tied on the back of the motorcycle, its roar so loud that their ears nearly burst. They had been shaken, thrown against each other, and miserably cold in the sharp wind. That terrible fear and noise and cold had left her shivering for hours after they were brought into this room and locked in here.

But coming down the hills, flung about in the bouncing cage, they had seen clearly where they were going. They had recorded every scent, every change in the wind, had looked down on the village rooftops and the crowded hills on the north, and looked back at the hills from which they had come. They had learned about the house as they were carried through.

The house had two bedrooms and a lower floor of some kind. At night she could hear

Hernando and Dufio descending the stairs; she thought they slept down there. She hadn't heard Hernando in a day or two, though. Alone down there, Dufio had been quiet, except for a TV. Dufio didn't like cats, none of the men did, and that made their capture all the more frightening; they didn't like to think what Hernando and Luis intended for them.

Maria was kind to them, though, when her brother wasn't around. She brought them nicer food and even milk sometimes. But she was afraid of Luis. Maria was, Willow thought, almost as much a prisoner as were they.

Of course, they did not speak in front of Maria; they whispered among themselves only late at night, when they were certain that Maria and the old lady slept. Maria called her Abuela. Willow watched Maria sleeping now, and the calico cat was filled with questions about the young woman who seemed more Luis's servant than his sister; questions she supposed would never be answered.

Maria woke when she heard the men come in. As usual, they were arguing. They always made a mess in the kitchen for her to clean up in the morning. She prayed their job had gone okay, so that Luis would be in a decent mood. Her arm and back were still black and blue from the last beating. To Luis she was property, not good for much.

One of the cats was fussing around in its cage. She hated seeing those cats there, pacing like wild animals. She fed them through the bars. And when Luis unlocked the cage door so she could clean the sandbox, they always looked like they'd bolt. She didn't know what would happen if they tried and Luis grabbed them. She had no idea why Luis and Hernando had trapped cats or what they meant to do with them. She'd heard them talking and whispering, but what they said didn't make sense. Maybe Hernando had been drunk, or smoking a joint. She hated when he did that. But no cat could talk, that was what she'd thought Hernando said. And something about the cats knowing something, having seen something. Crazy talk, as crazy as Dufio, but in a mean way, not just dumb like Dufio.

Maybe Luis was just doing what Hernando wanted; Luis treated his older brother with more respect than he treated poor Dufio. She wondered where Hernando was, gone so long. It angered Maria that Luis and Tommie had taken the big front room, Abuela's room. That Luis made

Abuela sleep back here with her and the stinking cage. She was, after all, his grandmother, and he should show respect.

Until Maria came, Abuela had lived here alone. But after she fell twice, once tripping on the worn carpet, once on the stairs, she asked Maria to come live with her. She was afraid of breaking a hip, of lying there unable to call for help. Maria was her only granddaughter.

Maria had been eager to get away from Luis. Estrella Nava was ninety-three; God knew she needed someone to take care of her. Maria had been so happy to be off by herself, to take the bus up from Irvine. But then, months later, Luis and their two brothers and Tommie McCord had decided to come here. Maria thought they were ditching the L.A. cops. They didn't ask Abuela if they could come, they just moved in, greedy for the free rent and a new territory to make trouble.

Well, at least Hernando had gone off somewhere with his noisy motorcycle. Luis didn't look for him, so probably he was with a woman. And Dufio . . . Sometimes she thought Luis felt sorry for Dufio, because Dufio was so different.

Luis had nailed the bedroom windows so she could only open them a few inches.

What did he think? That she'd run away and leave Abuela, leave her grandmother? Or that she'd haul the frail old woman out through the window? And take her where?

But as crude as they were, they were her brothers, they were family. She would not have considered trying to call the police to report that she and Abuela were prisoners or nearly so. Maria had no clear notion of alternate choices, she trusted fate and God. Her decision to get on the bus and come to Abuela had been a singular and frightening moment, she might never again do such a brave thing.

Though she had gone to American schools, though she had been in Los Estados Unidos since she was ten, she was nothing but a poor Mexican girl in a strange country. Luis told her that over and over. In a country she could not understand and that would never understand her, Luis said, no authority would care what happened to her.

When she heard the three-colored cat's tiny little mewl, she got out of bed and poured some kibble through the bars into the bowl, on top of the stinking canned food. There was nowhere else to put it, they were crowded in there with the two bowls and the sandbox. The cat mewed again; it always sounded like a kitten; it looked at her for a long time, a look that made her feel strange — as if it was asking why she didn't free it.

"I can't!" she whispered, shivering. Then she hurriedly crossed herself and moved away. She was getting as crazy as Hernando.

Returning to her bed, she listened to the cat picking kibble off the top of the little heap, and crunching it. In the other bed, Abuela snored with the harsh breathing of old age. When the calico cat finished eating it stared out at her again. She could see the shine of its eyes from the window where the night clouds reflected pale light. The cat looked and looked at her, then closed its eyes. As if, like Maria, it had no hope left. As if it could never expect anything different from this imprisonment.

But Willow had not lost hope. She was determined they would get out of there, she did not mean to die there. Despite her kittenish voice and her terrible fears, she was a stubborn cat, and in her own way, she was bold.

She only suspected what these men wanted: they talked about selling them for money, or putting them on television or in the movies. Then, they said, they would drive fancy cars. But they wanted, as well, to make sure that she and Cotton and Coyote did not tell other humans about the money they stole. And about the men they had killed.

But who would she and Coyote and Cotton tell? And why? All they wanted was their freedom.

They had discussed a dozen plans for getting out of the cage, had talked late at night, in whispers. But no plan seemed to be the right one. Cotton wanted to attack Luis the minute he opened the cage, leap on him, rake and bite him and streak past him to freedom. Coyote wanted to pretend to be sick, but she thought if they did that, Luis would indeed kill them.

Thinking fearful thoughts, for a long time she didn't sleep. She huddled into herself thinking of possible new ways to escape that would be less violent. She was not a brash warrior like the two males; she was the kind of hunter who liked to run her prey down and trip them, then make a quick and humane kill. She hunted because she had to eat, not because she enjoyed killing. Praying for sleep, she worried and planned until at last she dropped into exhausted dreams, into the only escape she knew.

10

The roof was so steep it was all Dulcie and Kit could do to keep from sliding down the shingles into the face of the cop below. Claws were no good at this angle. Bracing their paws as best they could, they watched Officer Brennan fasten a belly chain on a handcuffed Latino guy dressed in dark jeans, black T-shirt and black sneakers. He was maybe thirty, with a scruffy little beard and one earring, his expression a strange mix of anger, puzzlement and guilt. Brennan and his partner had chased him for blocks, as Dulcie and Kit raced along above them over the rooftops. The arrestee was small and light, and was a fast runner, zigzagging through back streets and alleys. Three times the cats had nearly lost him, as had Brennan. But then at the corner of Fifth and Dolores, where a low roof dropped nearer the sidewalk, Kit had skidded on a loose shingle, knocking it off right in the guy's face. Scared him so bad he spun back swearing in Spanish — into Brennan's hands.

Brennan was just as surprised as the perp. Nearly as surprised as the kit who, Dulcie told her later, had made her first arrest, or nearly so. "This," Dulcie said, licking the kit's ear, "should make you an honorary officer."

Kit, watching Brennan cuff the guy, had shivered with mirth and with smug triumph, though she was glad Brennan hadn't seen her. On the roof, they followed Brennan and his captive back to Brennan's squad car where he forced the belly-chained prisoner into the back seat, pushing his head down so he wouldn't crack his skull. No one wanted an inmate suing the department. Seemed like cuffs and belly chain were a lot, Dulcie thought, when the distance to the station was only a few blocks. But Brennan, with the extra weight he packed, sure wouldn't want to chase this one again. As Brennan headed for the station, Dulcie and Kit were still laughing; and as they dropped down from the roof to a little bench that stood in the shadows, they could see into the jewelry store where officers' lights flashed.

The exploding brilliance of strobes made them shutter their eyes as Detective Garza photographed the broken, empty display cases. Max Harper stood talking with two officers and with Garza, but soon he left the scene again, swinging into his pickup, driving off in the direction of the high school. Dulcie thought about the lovely chokers and bracelets the cases had held, and how often she had reared up to peer in through Marineau's windows, admiring those treasures — wondering how she would look in platinum or emeralds. Except that the idea of a confining collar gave her the shivers; even such a multimillion-dollar confection as a sapphire choker from Tiffany's would scare her if she couldn't claw it off and free herself.

Both cats felt sad looking in at the ruined shop, at the shattered glass cases, at the silk-covered walls now scarred with ugly gouges. An inner door had been torn off its hinges. The thick, creamy carpet had been ripped back as if the thieves were searching for a floor safe. Such destruction by humans sickened them.

If Dulcie had her way, the people who did this would be cooling their heels for a lifetime. And not in a cushy cell with free TV, three hot meals, laundry service, ample medical care, and unlimited phone privileges. In her view, the universal need for freedom ended when it was used to destroy the lives and livelihood of others.

"How much do you suppose they got?" Kit said.

"In value?" Dulcie said, surprised by Kit's uncharacteristically practical turn of mind. "Whatever they got, they didn't get what they deserved. Come on," she whispered, dropping down into deeper shadows beneath the bench as Detective Garza turned in their direction.

The Latino detective had finished photographing and was putting away his camera equipment. They waited, very still, until he turned away again and, with his back to them, began to dust showcase and door surfaces with black powder. As Garza lifted prints, two officers approached along the sidewalk, stopping before the window.

Wearing thin surgical gloves, the uniforms began collecting broken glass from the sidewalk and the little garden that ran along the front of the shop, sealing each piece in an individual evidence bag. And as the officers drew close, the cats backed away around the edge of the building, into a bed of begonias.

When Dulcie glanced up, Joe Grey stood on a rooftop across the street watching the scene, his white parts clearly visible, white chest, the long white triangle down his nose. His white paws were hidden in the roof gutter. He studied the scene, then leaped into an awning, dropped down onto a bench, and trotted across the street toward them, between half a dozen police units that were parked to block approaching traffic. Pushing in among the begonias, he gave Dulcie a whisker kiss. "What did I miss?"

"Tell us what happened at the high school," Dulcie said.

"I haven't the faintest, I wasn't up there. I was . . . watching someone."

"Watching who?"

Joe ignored her, teasing; so it had to be important. He glanced casually away in the direction of the PD. "Maybe Mabel Farthy's on duty. We'll hear something there, or maybe we can cadge a look at the report."

Dulcie held her tongue; she wasn't begging for answers; he'd tell her quicker if she didn't prod him; and she followed him across the roofs to the courthouse and down the oak tree to the door of Molena Point PD. Joe's expression was so smug it was all she could do not to belt him.

While the cats were waiting for the dispatcher to open the heavy glass door, Clyde arrived home from the vet's. He arrived alone, without old Rube. He was feeling very low. He wanted to talk with Joe, he wanted Joe's company, wanted to stroke Joe and hold him — though he would never tell the tomcat how much he needed him at that moment.

Coming in the house alone, he turned on some lights and called to Joe. Called the tomcat again and again, until he was certain Joe wasn't home. Hurrying into the laundry, he looked for Snowball. She wasn't in the bunk bed. With an unaccustomed feeling of dread for her, too, he hurried upstairs.

There she was, the little white creature curled up in his study, in the big leather chair. Someone had tucked the woolen throw warm around her.

Ryan wasn't there, there was no note as she would have left on the kitchen table if she'd come in. Only Joe had been here in the house, to fold the throw gently around Snowball like that, and that touched Clyde deeply. Kneeling before the chair, he stroked Snowball and put his face down against her. She looked up at him pitifully. As if she knew very well what had happened. Just ordinary cats, Clyde thought, know a lot more than we suspect of them.

Snowball sniffed his hands for a long time, smelling each finger, then she dropped her head into Clyde's hand. He remained very still, holding her.

It was a long time later that he rose,

picking Snowball up, cuddling her in his arms. Carrying her to the desk, he sat down, making the little cat comfortable in the crook of his arm; and he called Ryan.

He told her about Rube. They talked for a long time. Her gentle voice, and her own tears, eased him. When at last he hung up, he felt better.

But he was still lonely, so lonely that he did something he'd never done before. He dialed the dispatcher on the nonemergency number, asking innocently if his cat was there. He told Mabel he'd heard a terrible cat fight, off in that direction, and he just wondered . . .

Mabel Farthy had cats, she was a sucker for cats. She wouldn't think his call was odd. Everyone knew that Joe often hung out at the station. Harper complained bitterly about cats wandering so casually in and out, but Clyde thought Max was secretly growing fond of Joe. He tried not to think how mad Joe was going to be. The tomcat would give him hell for making this call. Right now he didn't care, he just wanted Joe to come home.

Mabel's raspy voice was amused. "All three cats are here, Clyde. Sitting on the counter eating pastrami on rye."

"With *mustard?*"

"Of course not. I know cats don't like mustard."

Clyde repeated how much the catfight had alarmed him, and said he hoped Mabel got some of her dinner and didn't go hungry. "You could throw the little beggars out. You don't have to feed them."

Mabel laughed. "You know I'd go hungry to see the satisfied smirks on their furry faces and hear the little freeloaders purr."

On Mabel's counter, lolling between two stacks of reports, Joe heard Clyde's voice on the phone, and went rigid. They were talking about cats, about *him,* and he was wild with anger. Clyde had called about *him*. But the next minute his anger vanished, and he knew.

Rube. This was about Rube.

Clyde wouldn't have called if this were good news. Joe's stomach felt like it had dropped to the cellar, he was cold all over and lost, felt sick all the way to his paws.

He was about to take off for home when Officer Blake came in. The tall, thin officer tossed a handful of Polaroids on the desk, color shots of the fire at the high school. Slipping closer again, between Dulcie and Kit, Joe stared at candid studies of smoke and flame licking up a building, and of the burned interior of a classroom. It was the kind of mess you'd see in some L.A. street riot, not in Molena Point. What was coming down here?

There had been no trouble at the school, no student unrest or complaints building up to this, and no hot issue that might draw outside agitators. Keen with predatory curiosity, longing to paw the photos out across the desk to see every detail, Joe turned away instead. He was too torn by Clyde's need, too conscious of Clyde's pain to attend even to this perplexing crime.

Glancing at Dulcie with a look he hoped she would understand, he leaped from Mabel's counter to the front door and reared up against the glass, pawing impatiently until Mabel came around the counter and let him out. And he headed fast for home, a wild gray streak racing over the rooftops and across the highest oak branches above the narrow streets, heading home. Going home, where Clyde needed him.

11

Dulcie seldom hung around Molena Point PD, spying and picking up intelligence, without Joe Grey by her side. Sitting with Kit on the dispatcher's counter, with cops milling all around them, she tried her best not to look interested in the pictures of the fire. The four officers who had just returned from the high school smelled nose-itchingly of smoke. Their faces and hands were smeared black, their uniforms torn and wet.

Dulcie did not want to appear to be reading their reports; but she could hardly look away. A schoolroom had been deliberately set afire, as well as some trash cans under the wooden grandstand. Kit kept crowding her, staring so intently at the pictures that Dulcie could not distract her. This kit did not know the meaning of finesse. As much as Kit hung around the station, as many cases as she'd helped to solve, some spectacularly, the little tortoiseshell still was impetuous to the point of alarm. Terrified that any minute Kit would forget herself and blurt out some burning question, Dulcie hissed softly at her and pressed a paw on her paw.

But only when, glancing up through the glass door, they saw Dallas Garza approaching across the parking lot, did Kit back off and curl up as if for a nap, tucking her nose under her tail. Dulcie washed her own hind paw, then feigned great interest when a rookie dropped a wadded-up gum wrapper on the floor; she made a show of creeping along the counter peering down, lashing her tail.

Dallas Garza swung in through the heavy glass door looking sour and angry. He said very little but double-timed on down the hall, followed silently by the officers around the desk and half a dozen who came in behind him. They turned into the coffee room-cum-squad room. The cats waited a moment, then leaped down, wandered along behind them, and crouched outside the door. The room smelled of overcooked coffee.

"Store window was already broken when the call came in," Garza said. "Security alarm disabled. They were in and out before the first car arrived. Cameron's in the hospital, shot in the leg. Lucky as hell it missed the bone. She should be out in a few days."

Jane Cameron had been on the force only a few months. She had come down from San Jose PD where she'd graduated from the police academy. "She didn't want to fire her weapon in that neighborhood. Guy doubled back on her. His first shot took her down, hit her twice before she fired and killed him," Garza said. "She's feeling more mental pain than pain from the leg wound." It was doubly hard for a rookie to live with having killed someone. There would be a routine investigation, which would surely amount to nothing.

Dulcie was just glad that Cameron was alive. The tall, soft-spoken blonde always had a smile and a pet for a visiting cat. The cats listened with switching tails as Garza described the action.

"Besides the man Cameron killed, we have one arrest and the make on two cars." He glanced at Officer McFarland.

"McFarland pursued a black Ford Neon, no lights, forced it into an alley against the brick wall of The Patio restaurant. Car took out three feet of wall. McFarland might never have spotted it — but the license plate flat fell off."

McFarland grinned. "Bounced and rattled like a barrelful of tin cans." McFarland was a young, fresh-faced cop with soft brown hair that, when freed from his cap, immediately fell over his forehead. "Puny little guy. Fought me like a nut case, bit me twice. Flailed around until I shoved my gun in his ribs. Little twerp, Latino. Dark eyes, dark complexion. Long bleached hair and a nose ring. Made me want to lead him along like a ringed bull. We're towing the car in.

"We ran the plates," McFarland said. "Stolen off a '99 Cadillac DeVille, West L.A. address. There was ID on him, driver's license, couple of credit cards. Likely turn up fake."

Detective Garza read off the jewelry store inventory of stolen items, which the store's efficient assistant had prepared for him. "She'll have pictures of some of the pieces by morning."

Dulcie was wondering why the elderly owner of the jewelry store hadn't shown up after the break-in, when Garza said, "Sam Marineau's visiting his daughter in Tacoma, be gone a week. Left Nancy Huffman in charge, she's over there now, with Davis." Juana Davis was the department's other detective, a solid, no-nonsense Latina with a quiet, reassuring way that could quickly calm an upset victim. She and Nancy Huffman must both have arrived just after Dulcie and Kit and Joe raced away from the demolished store. Garza unfolded Nancy's inventory and began to read, listing the items. Their value added up to a sum large enough to keep every village cat in caviar through the next century. Garza said, "We've contacted all departments in the Western states." The wonders of electronics, of the department's ability to contact all those offices within seconds, still impressed Dulcie, as did so many of the accomplishments of human civilization.

She expected that if the insurance company offered a sizeable reward, the fence might cooperate, too. Maybe give them a line on the crooks. When the cats heard Captain Harper come in the front door, they vanished from the hall, slipping into the first darkened office.

Harper stopped to speak to the dispatcher, then passed their shadowed door, heading for the squad room. His shoes and pant legs reeked of smoke and wet ashes. They crept out behind him to crouch, again, outside the door.

Harper stopped just inside to pour himself a cup of coffee, then moved to the front to face his men. His thin, tanned face was drawn into long, angry lines. "It was arson," he said. "Payson and Brown picked up oily rags, two empty gas cans.

"One classroom trashed and set afire. The amount of smoke and flame, I thought at first the whole school was burning. Books pulled from the shelves, desks overturned, stuff pulled out of cupboards. The other fires were on the grounds. Two in trash barrels near bushes and trees — we got them before they spread. Fire on the football field under the stands, in trash bins. Another few minutes, those wooden stands would have gone up, as well as the pine trees in the greenbelt, and then the buildings.

"Williams Construction is boarding up the burned classroom." He looked around the room. "We have no arrests. Fire alarms were deactivated. They were in and out before the neighbors heard anything or anyone saw flames. Crowley? That's your patrol."

Officer Crowley's square, jowled face reddened. One big bony hand came up, then rested again on his lap; his broad shoulders seemed to hunch lower. "We were south of the village on a drunk and disorderly when the call came. We'd just left the high school. Ten minutes. Didn't see or hear a thing. Maybe they were waiting, hiding in there? And when we pulled out, they cut loose? There were no trash cans turned over, trash cans were standing in a row outside the maintenance room, the lids on. Maintenance door was padlocked, I got out and checked. Nothing under the grandstand, we swept our lights in like always.

"We always circle the classrooms. That room they set afire, it backs on the parking lot. We look in those windows, shine a light in. Looked in there tonight, room was tidy as an old maid's bedroom. Nothing, no one. They had it all worked out, had to. Went to work the minute we pulled out." Crowley looked at Harper. "You think the high school was a diversion?"

"It's possible," Harper said. "But that makes a good number of players, a big coordinated group. Whatever the story, we've got egg on our faces." He gave the men a sour smile. "One dead perp. Make on two cars that got away. Two arrests." But in the chief's long, thin face, there was a spark of satisfaction, too. "Lab is lifting prints, collecting clothing particles. Let's see what we get."

Dulcie wanted badly to hear Harper and Garza interrogate the prisoner. But she thought maybe they wouldn't do that until they had a make on the prints, a little ammunition to nail him in his lies, to turn his untruths back on him. *If* they got a make on the prints, if the guy had a driver's license or a prison record. He might just have come into the country; if he were illegal, he might have no identification at all.

The thought of arson made the tabby shiver. Fire, to a small animal, was a horrifying thing, more terrible even than to a human. An animal had no way to fight a fire. An ordinary beast had no concept of the sophisticated technology to control and subdue killing flames. All an animal could do was run, driven by panic. When Dulcie thought about the millions of animals and people killed and injured in deliberately set fires, it seemed to her that arson — as well as rape and murder and child molestation — deserved the most severe and ultimate punishment.

But Dulcie was a cat. Her concepts of right and wrong were clear and precise. A cat's code of justice had no use for the subtle and nuanced, not when it came to deliberately destroyed and crippled lives. To a cat, hunting and killing to be able to eat, or to teach one's kittens what they must learn, those matters were necessary to survival. But maiming and killing to see others suffer, that hunger stemmed from a pure dark evil for which Dulcie had no smallest shred of sympathy.

As the officers rose, Dulcie and Kit galloped up the hall to mew stridently at

Mabel, dragging her out from behind her electronic domain again.

"You cats are mighty demanding tonight! Bad as lawyers, snapping your fingers and expecting me to jump!" But the hefty blonde was grinning as she opened the front door and obligingly set them free, into the night.

Trotting away waving their tails, Dulcie and Kit heard Mabel rattle the door behind them making sure it was locked. Glancing back, Dulcie felt a warm spot for Mabel. For some minutes, the stocky blond dispatcher stood inside the glass, watching them with as tender a look as that of a mother sending her children out to play.

But then, hurrying away in the chill wind, Dulcie let her thoughts return to Joe.

She'd put the thought aside, but she knew something was very wrong at home. Why else would Clyde call the station looking for his cat? He'd never before done such a thing. What had Clyde said to Mabel that had jerked Joe away so fast, his ears down and his stub tail tucked under? A deep chill filled Dulcie. Was it Rube? The old dog hadn't been well, not for a long time. She shivered suddenly, and a heavy sadness filled her. But on she went, following Kit. Slipping past the jewelry store that was now being boarded

up, they watched two carpenters nail plywood over the broken window and broken
glass door. Dulcie watched Kit sniffing
along the sidewalk and around the carpenters' feet, her ears sharply forward, her body
suddenly tense.

"What?" Dulcie whispered.

Kit turned to Dulcie, phleming and
hissing. "Cats. Other cats," she said quietly.

"So? There are cats all over the village.
What cats? What *is* the matter?" Of course
there were cats — housecats, shop cats, even
an occasional tourist's cat on a leash like a
confused stand-in for a toy poodle. "What is
it, Kit?"

Kit looked at her strangely.

"What?" Dulcie repeated.

"I . . . I don't know," Kit said uncertainly.
She nudged against Dulcie, quiet and still.
"It's gone now," she said. "Now all I can
smell is raw plywood." Lashing her fluffy
tail, she leaped away across the empty street,
and into the jasmine vine that led up to her
own terrace.

Suddenly Kit wanted her warm bed, she
wanted her own human family and safety.

Dulcie heard her race across the terrace
above and into the apartment. What had Kit
smelled back there? What kind of cat would

so upset her? She didn't know whether she should follow Kit or go to Joe.

But if something bad had happened to Rube, Joe and Clyde would be comforting each other. Maybe this was a time just for family.

Slowly and sadly, certain in her little cat soul about what had happened, she made her way up the jasmine vine, to the Greenlaws' terrace. She wished Wilma were home, out of the hospital.

Lucinda had left a light on for them. Dulcie heard, from the bedroom, the old lady's slow, even breathing and Pedric's faint snores. The Greenlaws were, after all, in their eighties; and it had been a busy night.

She found Kit in the kitchen, lapping up a lovely custard. Kit had, in a rare fit of generosity, left Dulcie's custard untouched. Kit looked up with custard smeared on her whiskers, and yawned; both cats yawned.

Dulcie ate her custard slowly, thinking about Joe and about Rube; then she curled up on the couch, watching Kit trot away to the bedroom. Tomorrow, she thought. Tomorrow morning early I'll find out what happened to Rube. Though I really don't want to know.

Tomorrow! Oh, tomorrow Wilma will be

home. And at once, her spirits lifted. No matter that Wilma had said the operation was routine and simple, she had been very worried. No operation was without pain and without risk. Dulcie wanted Wilma home again, home and safe.

She guessed she wanted, too, to be spoiled a little; to snuggle close at night as they shared the pages of a favorite book. The two of them would be up at Charlie's tomorrow night, and Charlie would spoil them both just as she would spoil Kit. At Charlie's house, Kit would tell more of her tales for Charlie to write down, and Wilma could be cosseted and cared for even if she said she didn't need that. In Dulcie's opinion, a little spoiling never hurt anyone. Ask a cat, spoiling was what made the rest of life worthwhile.

And maybe tomorrow Charlie would tell them what had happened on the pack trip. Tell them what she had left out of her story, over dinner at Lupe's Playa — what she had *not* told everyone else, about the dead cyclist. Tell them what had caused the nervous twitch of her hands under the table, and her evasive glance. Maybe tomorrow, after Captain Harper had gone off to work, they would learn Charlie's secret.

12

Joe had dreaded going home. He felt in every bone that old Rube was gone. Leaving Dulcie and Kit stealthily gathering information within the offices of Molena Point PD, he scrambled up to the rooftops, worried by Clyde's call, heading home fast and feeling heavy as lead; he was already mourning for his old pal, was sure that Rube was gone or close to it. There was no other reason Clyde would have called the station asking for him. He needed to be with Clyde, needed to comfort him and to be comforted.

He'd known Rube since he himself was a kitten, when Rube was a young, strong dog. When Joe was half grown and feisty, it was Rube who had mothered him. Already mourning Rube, Joe felt like half of him had dropped away into an empty abyss; life would be very strange, with Rube gone.

Dulcie had read something to him once, in the library late at night as he lounged on a table among the books she had dragged off the shelves, something about part of your life suddenly breaking away, sliding away, forever gone. Even then, the words had stirred a huge emptiness in him. He was filled with that same dropping feeling now as he raced over the rooftops toward home.

The thin moon and stars were hidden, the sky gone dark and dense with clouds, and the sea wind blew harsher, too, and more cruel. Jumping wearily across the last chasm from an overhanging cypress branch to the rooftops of his own block, Joe glanced down automatically at Chichi Barbi's small front yard.

There were lights reflected there, no light from the living room window and no flickering from the TV. The house beneath him was silent, and when he looked around the side, down the drive, no light reflected from her bedroom. Making one last mournful jump from Chichi's roof to his own, landing heavily on the fresh cedar shingles, Joe padded into his cat tower dreading what lay ahead.

"Joe?" Clyde spoke from the study just below him. Joe studied the flicker of firelight that reflected through his plastic cat door, sniffed the nose-twitching scent of burning oak logs, and pushed through under the plastic flap flinching as it slid down his spine. Padding out along the rafter, he

dropped down to the desk, trying hard not to scatter Clyde's papers.

Clyde sat in the leather chair holding Snowball, stroking and cuddling her. They were alone. He had not carried the invalid dog upstairs. Joe thought Clyde would not have left Rube downstairs alone.

Clyde looked up at him, and there was no need to explain.

"I brought his body home," Clyde said sadly. "So the cats could see him, so maybe they'd know and understand. He's downstairs, tucked up on the loveseat on the back porch, as if . . . so they can see him there."

Joe nodded. If animal companions were not allowed to see the dead one when he passed, their grieving was far worse; they never understood where their friend had gone. The finality of death was, for an animal, far kinder than thinking a loved one had simply gone away, far less stressful than waiting for the rest of their own lives for that pet or human to return.

"I wrapped him in his blanket. I'll take him in the morning, to be cremated."

Again, Joe nodded. They would bury Rube's ashes beside old Barney's ashes, at the foot of the high patio wall beneath the yellow rosebush. There was room there for all the animals. Room for me someday, Joe

thought, and felt his paws go cold. Leaping from the desk to the arm of Clyde's chair, Joe rubbed his whiskers against Clyde's cheek, then crawled into Clyde's lap and curled down beside Snowball. And for a while he was only a cat, safe in Clyde's arms, at one with Snowball and with Clyde in the pain of their grieving.

Only after a very long time, when the fire had burned to ashes and the moon had come out again gleaming down through the skylight, did Clyde get up and warm some milk for all four cats, and break up bits of cornbread into the bowls, a special treat they all enjoyed. He waited at the kitchen table while the cats ate, then settled the two older cats cozily among the blankets in their bunk. He made himself a rum toddy. Carrying Snowball and his toddy, he headed upstairs behind Joe, and the three of them tucked up in bed.

But as Snowball slept in Clyde's arms huffing softly, all worn out, and Joe's eyes drooped and jerked open, Clyde insisted on hashing over Rube and Barney's puppyhood in a maudlin display of memories that Joe found more than painful. Clyde reminisced about how he would take the young dogs to the beach to chase sticks in the ocean, how

he judged his girlfriends by how they related to the two dogs. On and on, trying to get rid of the pain. The red numbers on the bedside clock flipped ahead steadily toward morning. It was after four when Clyde finally drifted off. Exhausted, Joe curled down deeper in the blankets, but he couldn't sleep. All the joyful and irritating and funny memories of Rube crowded in to nearly smother him. Long after Clyde was snoring, Joe lay atop the pillow wide awake, his teeming thoughts too busy to settle.

He tried to pull his mind from Rube, to examine again the jewelry store scenario, to see Chichi all dressed in black slipping into her dark house carrying that small black bag, hiding something important, while a dressed-up kitchen broom sat in her easy chair watching sitcoms. Thinking about anything was better than lying there wide awake, thinking about Rube.

Right now, was Chichi asleep over there? How deeply did the woman sleep? Frantic for distraction, Joe rose and leaped off the bed.

What was the best way inside?

He considered the tried-and-true methods: check all the windows; if he couldn't claw one open, then try a roof vent and go in through the attic.

Except that moving those plywood doors that opened from an attic could get noisy, and they were heavy as hell. Most weren't even hinged, and you had to lift them away. Usually, Dulcie was there to lend some muscle.

But who knew, maybe Chichi had left a window unlocked and he could claw right on through the screen. Worth a try. He wasn't doing himself any good lying there fretting, listening to Clyde and Snowball snore.

Trotting across the little Persian rug into Clyde's study, he leaped to the desk, so preoccupied he sent the stapler clattering to the floor. Cursing his clumsiness, he sprang to the rafter and pushed out through his cat door.

Scorching across the shingles to Chichi's roof, he backed down the jasmine vine and dropped to the scruffy yard. First thing, he tried the front door just to make sure, swinging like a monkey with his paws locked around the knob. When the knob turned, he kicked hard with both hind paws.

But it was bolted, all right. The door didn't budge. Well, what did he expect? Trotting around the side of the house he peered up at the evenly spaced roof vents.

They all looked pretty solid, as if they

were not only nailed but sealed with several generations of paint. Circling the house, he pawed at the eight under-house vents, shaking them as hard as he could. All were screwed down tight. His nose was filled with the damp smell of earth and moldy wood, and of the dusty old bushes that pressed around him.

Making his way around to the door of Chichi's bedroom, he swung on that knob, kicking vigorously while trying to make no noise. Of course it was locked. But hey! From the power of her sleeping scent, and the tiny sounds of her slow, even breathing that came from the far window beyond the door, he knew that window had to be open.

Leaping up onto the narrow sill, Joe smiled. She had locked the window open six inches, a space no human burglar could breach. Pressing his nose to the screen, he looked in sideways at the bolt that locked the sliding glass in place. Lifting a paw, claws rigidly extended, he ripped down the old, rusty screen wincing at the dry scraping sensation as it gave way under his pad. The long, jagged tear jerked and caught at his paw, then at his fur as he slipped through.

The room smelled of dust and of Chichi, that distinctive sleeping-woman smell, as rich as baking bread. In the dim room,

Chichi lay curled up around her pillow. She slept naked, with the covers thrown back, even on this chill night. She was tan all over, no strap or bikini marks. Maybe a salon tan. Or maybe sunbathing on her San Francisco rooftop? When he and Clyde lived in the city, Clyde always hurried home on sunny days, to enjoy the view from their apartment window.

Stepping down onto the dresser among a mass of bristly hair curlers, loose change, and wadded tissues, he reached down a paw, to pry gently at the top dresser drawer. Not likely she'd hide anything of value in the first place a burglar would look, but you never knew. Silently he slid the drawer open.

A jumble of panties and panty hose, a box of tampons, an open box of Hershey bars with almonds. He pawed underneath the clutter but found nothing of interest. Dropping down to the carpet he reared up to close the drawer, then clawed open the next two. His search netted him a pile of folded T-shirts, more panty hose, a lacy slip, balled-up socks. No little black bag, no package, mysterious or otherwise. No precious jewels tucked beneath her lingerie. No faintest scent of metal, no hint that such items had been there and had been moved. The drawers smelled only of old, sour wood, of Chichi's sweet perfume, and of Hershey's chocolate.

Making quick work of the lowest drawer, rummaging between and under half a dozen folded sweatshirts, he checked the undersides of all the drawers, then squirmed inside the dresser itself, to paw around behind the drawers. Maybe the jewelry was taped inside the back.

He found nothing but dust. He was growing edgy. He crawled beneath the dresser to look up under the bottom.

Again, nothing. He tackled the rest of the room, the cushions, the underside of the upholstered chair, the undersides of two straight chairs, the small drawers in the little dressing table, and, carefully, the night table, working not a foot from Chichi's face. She slept on. The deep sleep of innocence? Or of someone without conscience? Stopping to scratch his shoulder with a hind paw, he had turned toward the closet when suddenly she came awake. He had his back to her when he heard a movement of the sheet, a tiny hushing that jerked him around, wanting to run.

She was sitting up in bed, the sheet pulled tight around her. She stared down at him, frowning. She looked at the torn screen, then looked again at Joe. In her eyes he saw fear and rising anger. He was starting to pant, he had to get out of there. He was crouched to leap to the dresser, but then thought better of that. Instead, he smiled up at her.

"Meow?" he said weakly, trying to look cute. "Meow?" He tried hard not to glance toward the window. It took all his willpower to roll over on the rug giving her the round-eyed innocent-kitty look. He purred as loud as he could manage, given the way his heart was thundering. Something about Chichi scared him, scared him bad. He had the feeling that this woman would grab him, that she didn't like nor trust cats — that Chichi Barbi could hurt a little cat.

Her hands looked strong. Long, capable fingers. Lean, well-muscled arms. Chichi Barbi was, Joe thought, not all curves and bleached hair and girlie giggles.

He wondered if he *could* make it to the top of the dresser and out before she swung out of bed. Somehow, he was afraid to try, that might really set her off. Instead, he continued his rolling-over, inane-purring routine.

"Hi, kitty, kitty. Nice kitty." Chichi threw back the covers and approached him, half crouching, her hand out as if to stroke him. Or to grab him. He didn't relish being attacked by a naked woman. She looked far too predatory, too intent. Staring into her eyes, Joe lost it. Filled with terror, he bolted to the dresser, sliding on the jumble of loose change, and flew through the screen snagging his fur, its metal fingers snatching him.

But he was out of there. Out. Free. Leaping to the grass and scorching away through the graying early shadows, his heart banging like kettledrums. Beating it for his own front porch; he crouched before his cat door, shivering and looking back, he half expected her to come racing around the corner chasing him. Above the rooftops dawn had turned the sky the color of faded asphalt. What was wrong with the woman? Why was he so afraid of her? Why was she so intent on grabbing him? Particularly when, during past encounters as she passed him in the yard or came to Clyde's door, she had avoided him as if she did not want to be near a cat — not at all like she'd been in San Francisco.

But that didn't necessarily make her a cat abuser, that didn't mean she would hurt a little cat. Did it?

Watching her house, he could see no bright reflection on the grass or in the branches of the pine tree as if a light had come on inside. He heard no stealthy sounds, no creaking floors, no stirring at the windows.

Maybe he should have stayed, kept on playing friendly kitty. Maybe he'd only imagined her cruel intent. Maybe she would have knelt on the carpet petting him and baby-talking him, even offering him a midnight snack. If he'd made friends with her, gotten cozy, he could have tossed her place at his leisure. Could have pretended he was bored living at Clyde's house, started hanging out at Chichi's. He would soon have the run of the place, have her leaving the window open so he could come and go at his pleasure.

And why not? Dulcie had once played lost, starving kitty for over a week. Moved right in with a murder suspect and come away with information that nailed the killer.

But Joe shivered, remembering the look in Chichi Barbi's eyes, and he knew he couldn't have done that. That woman put a cat off, big time. Even Dulcie would hesitate to play easy with Chichi Barbi.

Yet no matter his fear, no matter how he distrusted her, Joe fully intended to find out what she had stashed in that black silk bag.

13

The big family kitchen of the Harper ranch smelled of freshly baked shortbread and fresh coffee, and of homemade custard for Wilma. She sat at the round kitchen table in her best tartan robe and new slippers, having come straight from the hospital where Lucinda and Pedric had picked her up. They had brought Dulcie to be with her, and brought Kit so she could continue telling Charlie her story. On the window seat Dulcie lay curled among the quilted pillows. But Kit sat straight and alert, her fluffy tail twitching. She was very much onstage and she had a most attentive audience as she told about her early life running with the wild band. At the table, Charlie was writing it all down.

Writing a book about *me,* Kit thought with excitement. And she's making the pictures, too. Pictures of *me!* Charlie had already collaborated — that was a new word for Kit — on a big, thick novel, so Kit guessed she knew how to write a book by herself, and she even had an agent who said it wasn't wise to make pictures for your own story except if you were a real artist, which Charlie was, so that was all right.

This story wouldn't have anything about how Kit could speak or was in any way different from other cats. Nothing about how the wild band was different, just a wonderful story about the adventures of a band of feral cats and an orphan kitten that they didn't want, that no one wanted but who tagged along with them because she had nowhere else to go.

"I was always hungry," Kit said, "and we were always moving on and on. I ate the scraps from the garbage cans, if they left any. They stole other cats' food from yards and porches but they never left any for me. The best place we ever came to was all among the green hills where there were rabbits under the bushes and in the little hollows and the big cats could catch them. I tried but I couldn't, they were too big and fast and the big cats didn't want to teach me to hunt, no one wanted to teach me like a mother cat would. My mother was dead. On the hills sometimes the coyotes came hunting us but there were oak trees to go up, and once I found a bird nest in the branches and I ate the baby birds but the big birds flapped their wings at me and swooped and pushed me out of the tree and I fell." The kit sighed. "I wanted to stay on the green hills but the others moved on, no one cared what I wanted, I was only a dumb kitten and I was scared to go off on my own."

Sometimes Kit felt shy telling her own story out loud, but she was excited, too. The same kind of excitement she'd felt when she'd sneaked onstage that time when Cora Lee was playing the lead in little theater and the whole audience watched *her*, Kit, the whole theater was still and she and Cora Lee did the whole scene together with Cora Lee singing, and they were stars that night, stars together for the whole play. *Thorns of Gold* ran for weeks and weeks and *her* picture was in the paper right there with Cora Lee, and Wilma and Clyde wanted to take her away and hide her and hide Joe and Dulcie too before anyone figured out that they were more than ordinary cats, but then Wilma thought of a way to make it all right, to make her, Kit, seem like just a trained cat that didn't talk but just had learned to do tricks.

Now telling her story she felt like she had felt on that stage in the bright lights; and her human friends listened and sipped their coffee and Dulcie purred. "When summer got real hot," Kit told them, "there was no more water in the hills and the grass turned all brown and more coyotes came real hungry all hunting us. We moved on then and I got so tired and so hot and hungry and thirsty. When I thought I couldn't go another step we came to a city with garbage in the alleys falling out of big metal cans and thrown away wrappers with bits of pizza and hot dogs still in them and the leaders ate and ate but they would never share. There were some empty houses with boarded-up basements, too, that we could get in when boys chased us or it rained, but once two boys shot at us with a gun and we ran and ran into a canyon and never went back there except to sneak food and run again. Arroyo Secco the canyon was called and it had bamboo jungles and broken concrete water pipes to hide in and we lived *there* a long time and came up among the houses at night to get food and to drink from the puddles where people watered their lawns. I was getting bigger and I learned to fight for something to eat but once I got bit and clawed real bad and that hurt for a long time so I could hardly walk."

Kit stopped for breath and for Charlie to catch up. Charlie was writing as fast as she could. When Kit looked out through the wide window, Ryan Flannery's big

Weimaraner, Rock, looked in at her wagging his short tail. Beyond him across the grassy side yard, Ryan knelt on the roof of the stable tearing off the shingles, getting ready to raise up the roof the way she did on Clyde's house. Ryan would jack the roof's two sides right up to make new walls for a second floor. Kit thought that was amazing, what humans could do — what they would think of to do.

Ryan's uncle Scotty and her other carpenters would help her lift the two halves of the roof and nail them in place and then, like magic, they would put on a new roof, way high up, and there would be a whole new room up there, a big guest room right over the stable.

But right now there was just a lot of *screeing* and *scritching* as Ryan pulled out nails, and *chunking* sounds as she tossed the shingles down on the bed of her big red pickup.

Kit turned back when Charlie set two bowls of warm milk and a plate of shortbread down on the window seat for her and Dulcie. Everyone kept watching the side yard in case Ryan came down the ladder and headed for the house because Ryan didn't know that she and Dulcie could talk. They would be silent then like ordinary cats having a nap on the window seat. And they all watched the long drive, too, that came from the main road in case Captain Harper came home unexpectedly because he didn't know, either. How complicated life could be. Kit looked up at Charlie.

"What happened, Charlie, up on the hills? That you couldn't tell when we all had Mexican dinner?" Though she thought she already knew. She thought she knew very well what had made those scratches on the dead man's throat and sent him careening over the cliff to die crumpled under his heavy motorcycle.

Charlie looked at Kit a long time, and sipped her coffee. "I think your wild band has returned, Kit."

Kit shivered again and licked milk from her whiskers. When her wild clowder came there before to Hellhag Hill when she was little, that was when she saw Lucinda and Pedric there having a picnic and the Greenlaws knew right away that she was not an ordinary cat. They had shared their picnic with her and told her stories of her ancestors and she loved them right away, they belonged to one another right away and she left the wild band for this new life with the most wonderful people in the world. Now she looked at Lucinda and Pedric and purred and purred and they looked back at her all warm and happy. But even though she was safe with them, when she thought of the wild band so near, she trembled. Why would they come back? Why had they come here?

Oh, they couldn't want *her?* Why would they want *her?* They'd been happy to be rid of her.

But Charlie was telling how she'd freed the big tomcat from the trap, and when Charlie described him, Kit felt cold and scared. "That was Stone Eye," Kit whispered. "That big gray-and-brown tom with eyes the color of rust. He runs everything. He bosses everyone. He always slashed and bit me. He did worse to the older female kittens." Thinking about Stone Eye, Kit wanted to crawl under the pillows into the dark where nothing would find her, but of course that was silly. That was how she felt, though. She wished Charlie had left him in that cage.

But Charlie would never do that. And when Charlie said she thought maybe other cats had been trapped and taken away prisoner, Kit remembered something scary, and she hunched down deeper next to Dulcie.

"What, Kit?" Dulcie and Lucinda said together. Lucinda rose and came to sit on the window seat beside her and to stroke her. "What is it?" the thin old lady said. "What did you remember?" Lucinda always knew how she felt.

"There was a man," Kit said. "In one town, when I was little, watching us when we were eating garbage in an alley. He watched us from the back door of a shoe shop and he had canned baked beans maybe for his lunches and every day he put out some beans for us and the hungriest of us sneaked up after dark and ate but always the man was there behind the screen watching and watching us. Stone Eye told us not to go there, and drove us away. He said we had to go away from that city but we went back anyway one more time the next day and there were other men there too and they put out those big traps for us with food in, humane traps they're called but we knew what they were and we left those streets. We stayed in the ravine and didn't ever go back there again."

Kit sighed. "There were three ordinary cats that traveled with us that couldn't talk but felt safe in the big clowder and they went back, they went in the traps every day and ate the food. Stone Eye didn't drive *them* away. When they got caught, he said what did it matter? When those men took the bungies off and the ordinary cats got caught, Stone Eye laughed and said they were just stupid beasts, but some of us . . ."

She paused to peer through the window toward the main road, where a car had turned into the drive, moving way too fast toward the house. Charlie rose angrily and hurried to the door, and ran out to tell the driver to slow down. Pedric got up and stood at the kitchen window, looking out.

"A black Alpha Romeo," he said crossly. "Damn fool." They watched the car skid to a stop right in Charlie's face, and the driver's door opened.

Kit could hear Charlie through the closed window, but Pedric slid the glass open so he could hear. "You don't drive like that on my property!" Charlie snapped. "What do you want?"

The driver was dark-haired and handsome. He stepped boldly out of the car. "Your property? I thought this was Chief Harper's property."

"I am Mrs. Harper. What do you want?"

He looked past her to the stable roof, where Ryan had paused in her work, kneeling on the roof. "It's really none of your business. I came to see Ryan."

"Everything on my property is my business." Charlie looked at his license plate.

"Go on over there if you have business with Ms. Flannery. When you leave you will drive slowly." Kit and Dulcie smiled. Everyone said redheads had a temper. The man looked amused. Charlie's eyes flashed as he turned away. In the kitchen, Pedric glared as if he wanted to barge out and protect Charlie. Kit thought that wasn't smart at his eighty-plus frail years. Dulcie's ears were back and her tail lashed. Kit was fascinated, her nose pressed to the glass, watching.

The man was tall and indeed very handsome, with a smooth, angled face and short, well-styled black hair that, Lucinda would say, had been artfully blow-dried. He wore a pale tan shirt, powder blue tie, and a beautiful cream-colored suit. His sleek loafers looked like the handmade Italian shoes that Pedric liked to admire in the most elegant village shops. Beautiful shoes that were dulled now with dust from the yard. He approached the stables, smiling up at Ryan, but stopped abruptly when Rock burst out of the shadows growling, moving toward him stiff-legged.

Beyond the Weimaraner at the pasture fence the Harpers' two big dogs stood with ears flattened and lips drawn back in twin snarls. Ryan shouted at Rock from the roof, and swung on to the ladder; the silver hound backed off a step, his head lowered, teeth still bared.

Charlie had returned to the kitchen; she came to the window seat where she could watch, and she had her cell phone open. Kit thought, from the bulge in her pocket, that she might have additional protection, too.

Ryan came down the ladder, scowling. "What do you want, Roman?" Rock approached the man stiff-legged, snarling — but then the dog paused, sniffing. He glanced up at his mistress uncertainly, sniffed again at the man, and his short, docked tail began to wag.

The stranger smiled wryly, and knelt in the dust, knelt right down, facing Rock, and began talking to him, making little lovey sounds, kissy-baby sounds to the big Weimaraner. Kit and Dulcie watched Rock, amazed. The big dog had gone totally mushy, smiling and wagging and pushing right up to the man. Dulcie was so irritated she was shifting from paw to paw, growling — as if she'd like to race out there and tackle the man herself — and give Rock a whack on the nose. Pedric and the three women watched the scene, unbelieving.

Ryan took in the scene without expression and commanded Rock to heel. The cats knew she would deal with Rock later, in a

181

little training session. Her voice was cold and clipped.

"What do you *want,* Roman?"

"It's Sunday, Ryan. I'm amazed to see you working on Sunday."

"Why would you come here? I didn't ask you here."

"I came by to see if you'd have dinner with me. For old times' sake?"

"There are no old times. I told you in the city I don't have the time or patience for you. Nor the inclination. I am involved, Roman. Do you understand that? Do I need to spell that out?"

In the kitchen, the little party glanced at each other. Too bad Ryan's lovely big bodyguard had suckered up to the man. No one could understand what was wrong with Rock; this was not his way, Rock was fierce as tigers when it came to Ryan. Dulcie and Kit looked at each other wishing, not for the first time, that the big, beautiful, intelligent hound could speak, that Rock could tell them what was going through that incomprehensible doggy mind.

14

Clyde liked to fix a big Sunday breakfast for himself and Joe and the household animals, preparing special, vet-approved treats for Rube and the three cats, who could not eat the exotic foods on which Joe Grey thrived. This morning he cooked, but his heart wasn't in it. Rube was not in his usual place on the throw rug before the kitchen sink, drooling as he waited; he would never be there again.

Sitting on the breakfast table in the middle of the Sunday paper, Joe looked sadly at Rube's empty place on the rug, which the cats had left between them. Despite Clyde's presence at the stove and the good smell of scrambled eggs and bacon and sautéed chicken livers, everything in the kitchen seemed flat and off-key. Joe felt so low that he hadn't even clawed the funnies and front page to enliven Clyde's morning.

He looked at Clyde hopefully. "Will Ryan be coming for breakfast?" Ryan could always cheer them up.

"You can see I only set two plates," Clyde snapped. "She's working up at Harper's, getting the barn roof ready to lift." Joe looked at Clyde and shrugged. He looked at the nicely prepared breakfast plate that Clyde set before him, the bacon artfully arranged between the scrambled eggs and the golden chicken livers. Clyde had even grated cheese on his eggs, a nice morning start with plenty of comforting cholesterol.

But he didn't feel like eating.

Setting his own plate on the table, Clyde put the cats' dishes aside to cool, then set them down on the rug. The cats looked up at him, then the two older cats turned away, headed back into the laundry, and crawled up into Rube's lower bunk. Snowball just sat, hunched and miserable.

"He's out of pain," Clyde said. "You wouldn't have kept him here when he was so tired out. When he looked at you, he was all but saying he was ready."

Joe nodded. "I know. I know he's better off. But they don't understand. We all miss him."

Clyde looked hard at Joe. "You're down about more than Rube, too." He looked into Joe's eyes. "When you went out early, I thought . . . What happened? You're ready to claw the world apart."

Joe didn't usually share with Clyde the early stages of an investigation. Clyde could be so judgmental. And talk about worry, talk about overprotective. But this morning . . .

"That woman . . ." Joe began.

"What woman? What woman would you see before daylight, before . . . Chichi? What?" Clyde set down his coffee cup. "What did she do to you?

"Or what did you do to her? What have you done, now?"

That was the reason he didn't share crime investigations with his housemate. "Eat your breakfast," Joe said. "Then we'll talk."

Clyde reached into his shirt pocket and produced a slip of paper. "Message," he said. "Almost forgot. You had a message." He said this with that bemused expression that drove Joe up the wall. Joe waited, trying to be patient.

"Lucinda called. Early, before they picked up Wilma at the hospital and headed for Charlie's." Clyde glanced at the scrap of paper. "These are Lucinda's exact words, exactly as Dulcie told her. 'The prints haven't come in yet, on either man. Harper and Garza both think the high school was a diversion.'"

Clyde sat looking at Joe. "You want to fill

me in? I heard the sirens last night, I saw the fire, but I . . . my mind was on Rube."

"It's part of what I have to tell you," Joe said. "Eat your breakfast." He knew he'd have to give Clyde the whole story. The minute Clyde picked up the paper he'd see it — the high school fire and the jewelry store burglary were smeared all over the front page. Pawing at the front section, Joe turned it around and shoved it over in front of Clyde: color pictures of the broken store window and showcases; and spectacular, bright flames licking up from the high school.

"Read it," Joe said. "Then I'll tell you about Chichi."

Clyde glanced at the headlines then quickly skimmed the articles, giving Joe an incredulous look. "You're telling me Chichi was part of this? Come on, Joe. The woman might be . . ."

Joe licked cheese from his whiskers. "She might be what? Only a small-time thief because she only stole five hundred bucks from you? She wouldn't do anything worse?" He sat looking at Clyde, one paw lifted. "Some people will just steal a little, but not a lot? Is that what you're saying?"

"Well she didn't exactly steal the money from me, she . . ."

Joe stared, silent and unblinking.

"Well," Clyde said. "Well . . . maybe she stole it." He returned his attention to the front page. Joe returned to his breakfast. Clyde could be annoyingly argumentative and opinionated, but if properly directed he usually managed, after a little time, to face facts and be reasonable.

"So," Dulcie said when Ryan's visitor had gone, spinning out of the yard in his black Alpha Romeo, leaving a cyclone of dust clouding the kitchen windows. "What did he want? Who is he? Why did he come here and force himself on Ryan?"

Charlie shrugged. "Roman Slayter. Ryan and her husband knew him in San Francisco before their marriage broke up; their construction firm did some work for him. Remember what she said at Lupe's that night? She thinks he'd like to get his hands on her money from the sale of the firm."

Dulcie rolled over among the cushions, her peach-tinted paws waving idly in the air, her dark, ringed tail lashing. "Or maybe he wants something even more than money?"

"Like what?" Charlie said, coming to sit on the window seat beside the two cats.

"I don't know," Dulcie said uneasily. Beyond them, out the window, all that was left of the Alpha Romeo was a long snake of dust hanging over the yard like a murky jet trail. "That man's up to no good," the tabby said. "He gives me the twitches. I can't believe Rock would make up to him like that! Rock's only a simple dog, but . . ."

Charlie wanted to tell Dulcie that sometimes she imagined too much, let her imagination run wild; but Dulcie's speculations, and those of Joe and Kit, were too often on target, their perceptions about humans as keen as the instincts of a seasoned detective.

"She told me this morning," Charlie said, "that he called her last night, she'd hardly gotten in the door after dinner. Insisted she go out for a drink, was really pushy." Charlie grinned. "She hung up on him.

"When Ryan was in the city, when Slayter showed up at the construction office . . . Well, she says Slayter can smell money like a bloodhound." She glanced at the phone pad where she'd written his license number; and they watched Ryan storm back up the ladder, scowling.

"Ryan says he worked in real estate for a while, but she thinks he was into a lot of things, most of them shady, including some questionable stints as a private investigator of sorts, probably unlicensed.

"I guess, though, the men he represented

in the real estate ventures paid their bills, if the firm kept building for them." Charlie shrugged. "If I know Ryan, he'd play hell getting any of her money." She looked at Wilma. "Are you getting tired, ready to tuck up in bed for a while?"

Wilma laughed. "I don't need to be in bed, I won't heal lying in bed, I need to walk." Refusing more coffee, she rose, her long silver hair bright beneath the glow of the soft overhead lights. Charlie and her aunt looked a lot alike, with their lean, angled faces and tall, lean figures. Only their coloring was different: Charlie's red hair vivid against Wilma's pale silver mane. Wilma had wrinkles instead of freckles, and her eyes were dark where Charlie's were green; but their comfortable, reassuring smiles were the same.

Though Wilma's career had been in federal probation, her master's was in library science. She had, just out of college and before she went with the federal courts, worked two years in state probation. During that time she'd gotten her master's degree, taking courses at night. Her plan, which she had made early in her life, had been to fall back on her library degree when she was forced to retire from probation work, a retirement that then had been mandatory at fifty-five. "Way too young," Wilma had told Clyde, "too young to stop working."

Ever since Dulcie came to live with Wilma as a kitten, Wilma had worked in the library, and Dulcie was glad of that; the little cat had had wonderful adventures among that wealth of books, to which she would otherwise never have had such easy access.

Wilma and Clyde had been friends since he was eight, when she was his neighbor; she had been his first love, Dulcie knew. A beautiful blond graduate student. Now, Wilma was the only family Clyde had left, Dulcie thought sadly.

Wilma had her niece, Charlie. But of course Wilma and Charlie and Max, Clyde, and Dallas and Ryan and Hanni, had one another, so close that they were like family.

Dulcie glanced out to the back patio where Wilma, walking briskly in her robe, knew she would not be seen from the front drive. At the moment Dulcie was more interested in the yard by the stable, where Roman Slayter had stood harassing Ryan.

Slipping out, the two cats wandered the yard where Slayter had walked, picking up a distinctive medley of shoe polish and musky aftershave that masked subtler scents. But then both cats caught a whiff that made them laugh.

Somewhere, on his shoes, Roman Slayter had picked up the scent of female dog, female in heat.

That was what Rock had been making up to! Dulcie looked at Kit and smirked. What a timely accident . . .

Or was it an accident?

Dulcie sat down, staring at the dirt beneath her paws.

Had Slayter acquired that scent on his shoes on purpose? Though the aroma was partially destroyed by shoe polish, it had certainly been strong enough to charm the young Weimaraner.

But now Rock, having found no lady dog to go with the distinctive message, lay in the sun, watching Ryan tear off shingles. Approaching him, Dulcie sniffed noses with him in a friendly way and lay down beside him. She so wished he could tell them what had gone through his thoughts when he'd snarled at Roman Slayter. As Kit uselessly chased a bird, Dulcie lay considering the accumulated puzzles of the last twenty-four hours: The jewelry store robbery, the high school fires, the dead cyclist, the return of the feral cats and their capture.

She thought how deeply afraid Kit was of that wild band, and how cruel they had been to her. Kit still had scars under her fur from their teeth and claws. In the car this morning, while Lucinda and Pedric went into the hospital to get Wilma, Kit had sat silent and worrying. "They haven't come back looking for me," she had said. "They wouldn't want me, Dulcie! Why would they?"

"They wouldn't want you, Kit. They didn't want you before, when you ran with them!" But Dulcie wondered.

Would the leader want to prevent any speaking cat from being out in the world, a cat that might give them away, might let someone know their secret?

She didn't want to consider such matters. Why would they wait until now? Kit had been in Molena Point for nearly two years. Dulcie tried to force her thoughts back to the fire at the high school, and the broken store windows. But it was hard not to worry and not to be frightened for the kit.

She made herself think about what they had learned at the PD, trying to tie the scattered facts together. Except that nothing wanted to go together. Too many pieces were still missing, so nothing made much sense. And it was not until that evening when the chief got home that they learned any more about the investigation — or, for that matter, about the feral cats.

15

The wind off the sea had calmed. Beneath the dropping sun, the water gleamed with an iridescent sheen; the Harpers' stone terrace and the green pastures beyond were stained with golden light. The cool air smelled of burning hickory chips and spicy sauce. Charlie stood at the barbecue, turning racks of ribs on the grill, their sweet-vinegar aroma prompting the two cats' noses to twitch and their pink tongues to tip out.

On the chaise Wilma sat tucked under a blanket, sipping a weak bourbon and water, possibly against doctor's orders. She could see Ryan through the kitchen window, tossing a salad and gathering silverware and plates onto a tray, and assembling Wilma's own supper. She'd be glad when she could eat more solid food. Well, it wouldn't be long. In Wilma's lap, Dulcie reared up as Max's truck turned onto the drive. Behind it Clyde's yellow roadster appeared, coming over the crest, its top down. Joe was standing up on the passenger seat of the Model A, his white paws on the dash, the white strip down his nose bright in the evening glow.

As Clyde parked by the house, Dallas's car turned in behind them. The scent of exhaust from the vehicles battled with the good barbecue aroma. As the cars killed their engines, the kit woke blearily, tangled in the blanket at Wilma's feet. She looked around her, fighting her way out of the folds, and her first thought was of disappointment that Lucinda and Pedric had not stayed for supper.

The older couple meant to look at four houses the next day. Lucinda said, at eighty-some, one tired more easily. Kit did not like to think about them tiring, could not bear to think about them growing older. She wanted to be with them all the time, but she just couldn't stand the house hunting. All those strange unfamiliar spaces with unfamiliar smells, where other people and animals lived. House after house after house, with the Realtor going on about the new roof and the hot-water heater. Who cared? Realtors had no notion of the important things — a nice tangled garden with sprawling oak trees to climb, plenty of deep windows with wide sills to lie on, a clean thick carpet to roll on and maybe a few hardwood floors for sliding. A nice warm fireplace and tall bookcases to sleep on, and a comfortable rooftop with a wide view down onto the village. Was that too much for a little cat to ask?

Lucinda and Pedric knew what kind of house she liked. And of course it should not be too far from Joe's and Dulcie's houses. Lucky they wanted much the same — except for the climbing part. Kit longed for them to find the perfect home and for the three of them to be settled in. Though Kit's true home *was* Lucinda and Pedric themselves; life with the old couple was the only real home she'd ever known.

Kit watched Max Harper and Clyde come across the patio, talking about hunting dogs. They both bent down and hugged Wilma, and drew chairs close to her chaise. Max said, "About time you got out of the hospital."

"Two days." Wilma laughed. "I'm a tough old bird. Is Jane Cameron out yet? I went to see her twice while I was there, she wasn't far down the hall. She wasn't sure when they'd release her."

"She should be out tomorrow," Max said. "She'll be tied to a desk for a couple of months, before she can go back on the street. Right now, I could use every officer. She'll be able to drive, though. And she can fire a weapon just fine."

Wilma looked a question at him, but said nothing. Across the patio, Dallas turned away into the kitchen to join Ryan and Charlie. Through the glass doors, the cats could see him hugging his niece, then petting and talking to Rock. He said something that made the two women laugh, and in a few moments he came out onto the terrace with Rock trotting beside him, the big Weimaraner pressing close to the squarely built detective. At sight of Joe Grey, Rock barked and bowed and gave the tomcat a lick on the face. Joe grimaced and hissed, but Dulcie knew he liked it. The tomcat, stubbornly extricating himself from the big silver dog, leaped to the arm of Wilma's chaise and settled near Dulcie, giving them both an inquiring look.

Dulcie looked back at him wide-eyed. So frustrating, that they couldn't talk in front of Max and Dallas and with Ryan there in the kitchen.

But really, she had nothing to tell him. She and Kit had learned nothing new at the station after Joe left. Now, all three cats waited impatiently for some news. The subject of hunting dogs could get old fast.

But it was not until everyone was seated for dinner around the big patio table that Max and Dallas returned to the burglary and the school fires — sharing information unknowingly with their snitches. It was Wilma, glancing at the fidgeting cats, who nudged the conversation.

Setting down her drink, she straightened her robe, looking a bit embarrassed that she had not dressed properly. "Do you have anything yet on the prints from the jewelry store? Or an ID on the men you arrested?"

Max's leathery face creased into lines of amusement. "One is Dufio Rivas. Does that ring a bell? We have nothing on the other."

Wilma frowned, pushed back a pale strand of hair. "Does he have brothers? A Luis Rivas? Short, square, heavyset?"

Max nodded.

She said, "There were three brothers. Luis, Dufio, and I didn't know the third one."

"Hernando," Harper said. "Information came in about an hour ago. All three have long rap sheets, mostly around L.A. Petty burglary — small stores, home break-ins. Hernando is our John Doe, the body from up the hills."

"Well," Wilma said softly. "The murder and the burglary are connected."

"Dufio, our arrestee, he's a strange little man. Apparently a total screwup. The bad penny. Amazing, his brothers let him run with them. Apparently, every now and then, they try to dump him. Never seems to last, I guess they feel sorry for him."

Charlie brought more ribs to the table and sat down again.

"In Indio," Max said, "Dufio robs a 7-Eleven at gunpoint, red bandana over his face, knit hat and gloves, the whole rig. Gets the cash, runs into the backyard of a nearby house and hides the money in the bushes. So he won't get caught with it on him, means to come back for it. He hides every-thing incriminating — bandana, gloves, hat, .357 Magnum, and his jacket, and takes off.

"Cops arrive with a dog, find the stash. Find, in the jacket pocket, Dufio's property identification card from county jail. Name, photograph, fingerprints, date of birth, jail booking number."

Everyone smiled. Max took a sip of beer, ate a few bites of his dinner. "Dufio does his time, gets out. Two weeks later he's waiting in the car with his cell phone while Hernando, a block away, is robbing a small bank. Dufio is supposed to swing around at Hernando's call, pick him up and take off. He sees this guy come out of a luggage shop, out the back door with one of those canvas cash bags, heading away toward the bank. Dufio decides while Hernando's grabbing the bank money, he'll make a second hit."

Harper took another slice of garlic bread. "This is noon, rainy midweek day. There's not much foot traffic. In the process of knocking out the luggage-store guy, Dufio drops his phone, messes it up so it doesn't ring, and misses Hernando's call.

"Hernando comes careening around the corner with the bank money, mad as hell. The alarm is going in the bank — and Dufio, when he got out of the car . . . He'd locked their only set of keys inside."

Chuckles exploded all around; and on the chaise the cats turned their faces away, hiding their own amusement. There was something deeply satisfying about the bad guys screwing up, even the clumsy ones.

Dallas said, "Dufio might be inept, but he has survived. You have to give him that."

Max nodded. "Just as Luis has. Luis seems always the first to slip away, leave the others on the hot seat. The other two dozen hoods who have run with them at various times are either serving time, or dead."

Charlie rose to pour the coffee. Wilma said, "I remember two jobs with maybe eight or nine guys, some kind of car insurance scam."

"They ran that for over a year," Max said. "Again, around L.A. Did pretty well until they hit on an unmarked car carrying four drug agents. When they tried to maneuver the car in between them, to rear-end it, all hell broke loose. The agents were armed and knew what was coming down and were mad as hornets.

"Now," Max said, "Luis has likely added new blood. Last job they pulled, in Thousand Oaks, they had five new recruits, and they got away clean. Next job, four of them pose as DEA agents. Two o'clock in the morning, burst into a private residence carrying handguns, a shotgun and a rifle. Said they were searching for drugs, on a tip. Tied up six people, hit one in the face with the shotgun, and broke a woman's arm. Swept the house, got off with eight thousand dollars in jewelry, couple thousand cash. Used handheld radios to communicate with those outside the house. That's the most sophisticated job they pulled, that we know of."

"What do they look like?" Clyde said, glancing only for a split second toward the chaise where Joe lay washing his paws, apparently half asleep after his big supper.

"Luis Rivas is thirty-five," Max said.

"Maybe five-foot-five, hundred and eighty pounds. Broad and heavy-boned. Coarse features, broad nose, fairly dark skin. Hernando was taller, thinner. Dufio is slight, lighter complexion, pale brown eyes. Long hair, bleached blond at the moment.

"Tommie McCord runs with them. Five-ten, hundred and sixty. Red hair — even brighter red than Charlie's hair," Max said, grinning. "Wall-to-wall freckles, blue eyes. No idea yet who else might be with them. They have a sister, sometimes travels with them. Maria Rivas. About seventeen. Apparently does their cooking and laundry. She's never been in trouble, never been arrested even as an accessory. Couple of the reports imply that she thinks she has nowhere else to go, no choice but to run with them, as their maid."

Immediately after supper, the three cats broke into a wild chase out across the pasture, where they could talk, heading for the tallest spring grass, where only the grazing horses could hear them. Rock didn't follow them, he'd been scolded too many times for chasing the cats, both by Ryan and by the cats themselves. Rock meant only to play, but a big dog's playful enthusiasm could get out of hand.

Crouched in a forest of grass, Dulcie and

Kit told Joe about the caged cat up in the hills that Charlie had freed. "Charlie thinks Hernando was trapping cats. The cat wouldn't speak, but clearly he understood her."

Kit said, "He is the leader of the clowder that I ran with. Stone Eye. He's mean as snakes. Charlie should have left him to rot."

Joe looked at her, surprised. Dulcie said, "Question is, did Hernando know what *kind* of cats? Charlie thinks he did, and that he's trapped others."

"And he died for it," Kit said darkly.

"If he did trap others," Joe said, "where are they?" His yellow eyes narrowed. "And does his brother Luis know? Could Luis have them, hidden somewhere?" The tomcat sat considering. "I think I've seen Luis and that Tommie McCord, next door in Chichi's room."

"Chichi?" Dulcie said.

Joe smiled. "Little Chichi Barbi, sitting in her room with those two hoods, going over a map of the village."

Dulcie's and Kit's eyes widened; they were considering the ramifications of this when Clyde started calling them.

"He's getting ready to leave," Dulcie said, rearing up to look over the tops of the tall grass. "Hurry up, Joe. You know how impatient he gets." Joe was reluctant to head home, but the cats took off for the house. Dulcie and Kit would stay with the Harpers, settling in with Wilma in Charlie's studio. The minute they hit the patio, Clyde scooped Joe up and headed for his car.

Ryan walked beside them for a moment. "I'll be by, then, first thing in the morning."

Clyde nodded, and tossed Joe onto the leather seat. He was silent starting the car, silent heading away up the drive. Then, "The water faucets were delivered. Ryan's going to install one, to see how it works."

"To see if *I* can work it."

Clyde glanced at him, and shrugged. When Ryan was working on Clyde's extensive remodel, adding the second-story study and master bedroom, Clyde had asked if she could get faucets that a cat could turn on, but that would turn off by themselves. He'd spent a lot of time explaining how he planned to train Joe and the other three cats to turn the faucets on for a drink of fresh water. "I can train them to turn the water on," Clyde had explained. "But you can't expect a cat to turn the water off. A cat doesn't pay the water bill. He would see no reason to do that."

"I think you're crazy," Ryan said. But she'd searched until she found the proper faucet, in the catalog of a North Carolina specialty shop. She had ordered five.

Joe said, "She coming for breakfast? She does like your ham and cheese scramble."

Clyde shook his head. "She said she'd have a quick bite somewhere before she picks up Dillon and Lori so they can ride. Lori's taken really well to that pony." He glanced at Joe. "It's a teacher's day or something, kids'll be out of school. No wonder kids don't get an education."

Joe had his own thoughts about childhood education. But at the moment, his mind was on the Rivas brothers and Tommie Mc-Cord, and on that band of feral cats. Had some of those cats been captured? Were there speaking cats somewhere, shut miserably in a cage? And that night, he lay awake worrying about the feral cats. About cats like himself and Dulcie and Kit locked up in cages. Why? What did Luis mean to do with them? Sell them? Force them into some kind of animal act? He didn't want to consider clearly what those crooks might attempt. The thought of animal prisoners and how they might be treated made him shaky.

But one thing sure. If Luis knew those cats could speak, he wouldn't hurt them; they were too valuable to be harmed.

And if there *were* captive cats, and if

Chichi knew about them . . . He sat straight up on the bed. If Chichi knew what those cats were, knew they could speak, had she guessed that he was the same?

Was that why she had looked at him so strangely, the night he "happened to wander" into her bedroom? He sat shivering and terrified, and he did not sleep anymore that night.

16

Ryan Flannery loved the dawn. The world seemed cleanest then, before people cluttered it up with roaring engines, exhaust fumes and shouting voices. Waking in her high-ceilinged studio apartment, as the first pale glow touched the white walls and rafters, she gave Rock a good-morning hug and let him out into the fenced backyard. Plugging in the coffeepot, which she had set up the night before, she showered quickly, pulled on jeans and a T-shirt, let Rock in again.

Outside, a gull landed on the railing, peered in through the wide windows, then flew off again. Since Rock had come to live with her, she hadn't bothered to draw the draperies at night. Rock would let her know if anyone came up the stairs onto the deck, in the small hours. The duplex studio belonged to Charlie Harper. Ryan paid her rent, in part, with carpentry and maintenance work, a nice arrangement all around — except perhaps in the eyes of the IRS, a governmental leviathan which, in Ryan's opinion, was badly in need of a severe overhaul.

While Rock was crunching his kibble, she took her coffee out on the front deck to enjoy the brightening sky and sea. High, creamy clouds floated above the village rooftops, catching reflections of the sun's first gleam from the hills behind her. The world, at dawn, seemed to belong only to her and Rock, and to the screaming gulls and the seals that were barking happily out on the rocks.

But while Ryan sat relaxed enjoying the fresh beginning of a new day, Rock pushed the door open and paced the deck looking up at her, wanting to start the day, hungering for action. He was so insistent that soon she gave it up, grabbed her gloves and battered briefcase that was jammed with house plans and receipts and work orders, snatched up her car keys, and they hit the road for a quick breakfast.

As she and Rock entered the patio of the Swiss Café, the big dog wagged his tail madly and surged ahead toward the back wall. Bringing him quickly to heel with a sharp command, she looked across the brick terrace to a small table where Lucinda and Pedric Greenlaw waved at her. Grinning, she moved to join them, keeping Rock close. Making her way between the tables, she took the one empty chair. "You don't mind company? This isn't a private tête-à-tête?"

Lucinda laughed. "We're celebrating — or almost celebrating. We think . . . we may have found the right house. We haven't seen it yet, but from the brochure . . . We're meeting the Realtor first thing this morning." The old couple was just finishing their pancakes and bacon and coffee. "It's just a stone's throw from Wilma's," Lucinda said. "You can see her roof from the deck."

"That'll be handy. You can walk right over."

Lucinda nodded. She had an almost secretive smile, and Pedric's blue eyes twinkled — both looked as if this house included something very special. "Tell me what it's like," Ryan said, intrigued. The Greenlaws were such a lively couple; their venerable age had not dimmed the intellectual sharpness and enthusiasm that made their friends treasure them.

"Everything we'll want is on the main level," Lucinda said. "Huge living room with a freestanding fireplace you can see from the dining room. High rafters, much like your studio. All one side is tall windows looking down on the village. One nice big bedroom on the main floor, with a big dressing room and bath, and two closets. It even has a double garage!" Garages, in the heart of the village among the crowded cottages, were at a premium, a big selling point for any house. As they talked, the waitress appeared and Ryan gave her order.

"Downstairs," Pedric said, "is a big family room, two bedrooms and a bath and laundry."

"Will you want all that?"

"We thought," Lucinda said, "to remove the inner stairs. Turn the downstairs into a separate apartment for a live-in housekeeper. If this is the house, we hope you'll take a look at the job." She glanced across the patio, watching someone.

"That blond young woman," Lucinda said, "in the pale blue sweat suit. She was finishing breakfast as we came in." She glanced at her watch. "Over forty-five minutes ago. She's been sitting there ever since, sipping coffee and watching something out the window, and making some kind of notes."

Ryan reached down to adjust Rock's leash where he lay under the table. Bent over, she managed a quick look. She straightened up, shrugging. "That's Clyde's new neighbor, Chichi something. She was in Lupe's the

209

other night. Nervy. She came over to our table, tried to join us. Clyde hustled her away, back to her own table. She was alone and maybe she was lonesome, I get that she doesn't know anyone in the village. But she was pushy."

Lucinda said, "You can see that the waitress would like to clear her table. What can she be watching, of such interest?"

Ryan turned her chair then, fussing with Rock's collar. Across the street from the restaurant were two galleries, a leather boutique, an antique clock and watch repair, and a small bookstore specializing in local history. The waitress came quickly with her order, setting down a stack of thin Swedish pancakes, a side order of ham, and a paper plate. She leaned down to give Rock a pat. The young brunette kept two lovely boxers, and Ryan asked her about them.

"They're fine, but they're wild in this cold weather. They'd run the beach all day if I had time." She refilled Ryan's coffee cup. "At least they have each other to play with, and a big backyard." As she turned away, Pedric looked at his watch, laid some bills on the table with their check, and he and Lucinda rose.

Lucinda's eyes were bright with excitement, looking forward to yet another house to consider. Maybe this would be the one, Ryan thought. They had been house hunting for weeks. Having spent the first year of their late-life marriage traveling up and down the coast in their RV, they were anxious now to get settled, as impatient as a young pair of first-time home buyers. As Ryan watched the tall, thin couple make their way across the patio, Chichi watched them, too.

The young woman avoided looking in Ryan's direction, though they had met Saturday night at Lupe's. She probably doesn't remember me, Ryan thought. Except . . . I *was* with Clyde. And with Dallas and Max, and she was pretty interested in them, in getting to know them. She was all over Clyde. And Ryan's sudden shock of jealousy dismayed her.

She didn't like jealousy, it was a constricting and enervating emotion. If Chichi was after Clyde, if she had moved next door to get close to Clyde, that was Clyde's problem.

None of the three men at their table that night had seemed particularly drawn to the young woman. She might be good for a one-night stand, but she didn't seem to be a person who would wear well. Sipping her coffee, Ryan studied Chichi then turned away. Taking her notebook from her purse, she began making a list of hardware for the Harper loft. She loved this kind of project, turning unused space into something of value. Creating a spacious and cozy guest room where there had been nothing but stored feedbags and breeding mice.

As she completed her list, Danielle brought her the check. She just had time to pick up Lori and Dillon then swing by Clyde's and install one faucet — see if that one worked as he hoped. By the time she got up to the ranch, Scotty should have the rest of the shingles off the roof, and have the big metal jacks in place. She was fishing out small bills for the check when Rock stirred restlessly.

"I'm about ready," she told him, reaching down to scratch his ear. He settled, looking up at her expectantly for another treat, though he'd had a third of her order. "That's all," she told him. "No more." Less than a year ago, when she first adopted him, Rock had been running wild in the hills, a beautiful, unwanted stray. It had taken her some time to manner him. He'd been so unruly that she'd been on guard every moment in a public place, never sure how he'd behave. She was digging for change when Rock came out from under the table, growling. Startled, she looked up.

Roman Slayter was approaching her table. She was pleased that Rock's reaction today was totally different.

"What a nice surprise," Slayter said, raising an eyebrow at Rock's growls, but giving her that charming, boyish, brown-eyed smile. Without asking, he pulled out a chair. When Rock's growl deepened, Slayter paused. "May I join you? Are you alone?"

"Sorry, I'm just leaving. I have an appointment."

Roman sat down anyway, stretching his legs out under the table. Rock sniffed at his shoes, and at once he began to wag his tail.

What was wrong with the dog?

Roman smiled, looking up when the waitress arrived. "I'll have whatever Ryan had."

Ryan rose, shrugging on her jacket. Slayter gave her a pleading, lost look designed to gentle the meanest female. "Just for once, Ryan, indulge me. I have something of interest to tell you."

"I don't have time to talk." Slipping her cell phone from her belt, she flipped it open. "You show up in San Francisco asking questions about the money from the sale. You were all over me with questions that were none of your business. How much did I get, where did I bank it? You weren't even subtle. And you barged into the Harper place, pushy and uninvited. Why would I want to be friendly?"

Roman's smile was innocent and charming. "I'm sorry, Ryan. I only wanted to help — about the money. You know I've done financial advising, that I worked for Thompson and Marrick for a while. I never meant to pry, I just thought . . . Well, with so much sudden money dumped in your lap, that you might . . ."

"That I might not know what to do with it? That I might not know how to handle my own money? That I'm too dumb to protect it?" She was so angry she thought her face must be flaming red. She stood staring down at him, wanting to hit him. But then she smiled.

"If it's of any interest to you," she lied, "I've put all the money in annuities and trusts. Where no one, no one on earth can touch it, Roman." Speaking to Rock, she turned on her heel. But Roman's next words stopped her.

"Before you go, Ryan, I have information about the recent jewel robbery."

She spun around to face him. "Tell it to the cops, Roman. Why would you tell me? Go down to the station." She heard, beneath the table, the soft crunching and smacking that told her Roman had slipped Rock some treat. Leaning down, she snatched a Milk-Bone from his mouth. "And don't ever, ever feed my dog!"

Calling Rock to heel, she held up the slobbery Milk-Bone and gently dropped it in Roman's coffee.

With Rock at heel, she stalked out. Her heart was pounding. What the hell did he want? Let him pick on someone else! Driving over to get Dillon and Lori, she fumed. Rock was quiet, watching her. She felt only a little ashamed that she had snatched his treat. She began to think seriously about giving him poison training, where he would not accept food from anyone but herself, or would accept it only with a particular command.

At Dillon's place, she had to honk for the girls. They came hurrying out, Lori carrying her little overnight bag and a piece of toast, the brown-haired, big-eyed child wiping egg from the corner of her mouth. Redheaded Dillon Thurwell, two years older, took one look at Ryan's angry face and climbed silently into the back seat of the king cab.

Taking off, Ryan resisted the urge to burn rubber. In the back seat, Dillon gave Lori an amused glance. All the way to Clyde's, neither girl spoke. She must look mad enough to chew nails. Beside her, Rock looked back at the girls with a hangdog expression that made her want to laugh, and that shamed her.

But she was still puzzled by the change in Rock's reaction. Why growl at Roman, and the next minute cozy up to him? And the fact that he would so eagerly take food from a stranger frightened her badly. Looking into the rearview mirror, she tried to make small talk. "What did you have for breakfast?"

"Pancakes," Lori said hesitantly. "With a gallon of syrup," she said, rubbing her tummy. "Bacon, two eggs. A piece of chocolate cake."

"That should keep you until midmorning." These two would burn it off riding, cleaning stalls and doing chores for Charlie, burn it off just with the energy of their wild young spirits. Lori had so blossomed since she came out of hiding in her cave in the library basement, since going to live with Cora Lee French and the senior ladies. She was such a bright, eager child, and so resourceful and ready for adventure, now that she was among caring friends. Ryan hoped her adventures would remain positive.

"I'll only be a minute," she said, parking in front of Clyde's house. She grabbed the bag of faucets, took Rock with her, and left the girls in the truck. This project did make her laugh. Just thinking about it soothed her anger. The idea that Clyde's cats liked to drink from the bathroom sink and he was tired of waiting on them — and that he could teach four cats to turn on the water faucet by themselves. How many men would even have the patience to try? How many men would *care* where their cats drank?

She really didn't think this would work, but Clyde did. They had a dinner bet on the success of the project, steak and champagne at any upscale restaurant of the winner's choice. The whole project was a belly laugh.

But who knew? Maybe he *could* teach them; what did she know about cats? Swinging out of the truck, she stopped still.

The scene on Clyde's front porch amazed her. Made her angry all over again. Apparently, Chichi had left the café right after she did. The blond bimbo stood on Clyde's porch snuggling up to him, or trying to. She was all over him, petting his face and laughing with a high giggle that set Ryan right on edge; all that pulchritude and sex thrown at

Clyde was just too much, made her feel like a jealous schoolgirl.

But then Ryan's common sense took hold. Looking Chichi over, her sense of humor returned with an explosion that made her want to double over laughing. This was pitiful! The woman was more than a joke, this was a scene straight out of the daytime soaps or out of the cheapest comedy. Clyde's face was red with embarrassment or with anger, or both. Glancing past Chichi to Ryan, he looked so uncomfortable she thought he might expire right there on the porch. Even Clyde's cat seemed amused, staring out at them through the front window with, Ryan could swear, a malicious grin on his gray and white face.

17

Much earlier that morning, before Ryan left her apartment and before the Greenlaws entered the Swiss Café, Joe Grey was jerked from sleep. He'd been dozing in his tower after a little hunt. He woke to the sound of water pounding in the pipes, from the house next door — a sound for which he'd been listening, even as he slept. Chichi was up early again.

Slipping out from among the warm pillows and out of the tower, he sat down on the roof. Night was just drawing back, in the wake of a clear, silvered dawn. He gave himself a quick wash, working fastidiously on his front paws until he heard the rumbling in the pipes stop, then the faintest rustling from within the house next door, a sound no human would hear. Then, louder, an inner door closing, maybe the closet door. He waited until he heard Chichi's outer door open and close, and heard the lock turn. He listened to her walking through the grass below him, her footsteps softly swishing.

Heard her hit the sidewalk in her soft shoes, walking quickly. Only then did he follow across the shingles, peering over.

Wearing a pale blue sweat suit and what looked like good running shoes, she was headed toward the heart of the village. Joe didn't picture Chichi as a runner, certainly not a serious one. As, above him, the silvered sky brightened, he watched her cross Ocean beneath its shelter of eucalyptus trees. He hungered to follow her. But he wished, far more, that he knew how long she'd be gone.

He'd heard her leave early like this on several mornings, but until the night of the robbery he hadn't paid much attention. He thought that those times she'd been gone for at least an hour. Dropping into the pine tree on the far side of her house, he backed down, sprang into the little lemon tree, cursing the sting of its thorns, and leaped to the sill, hoping she hadn't repaired the screen.

When he examined his recent handiwork, he almost laughed out loud.

Tape? She'd put duct tape on the torn screen? Smiling, Joe took a corner of the tape in his teeth and gently pulled, peeling it back neater than skinning a gopher.

But then, pressing his paw sideways

against the glass and exerting all the force he could muster, he was unable to slide it.

Where before she'd had the slider locked open a few inches with a little peg, now she had secured the window completely closed. Had shut it tight so he wouldn't come back? He felt a chill course down through his fur.

But how likely was it that Chichi knew his special talents? He was just a cat; and she didn't like cats. He pressed his face against the glass, mashing his whiskers, to peer in.

He could just see the lock protruding. It was one of those that slid up or down along the metal frame when one closed the window, the kind that usually locked but not always. That sometimes, in these old windows, didn't work at all.

This one had caught, though. Hadn't it?

Pressing against the window, he shook and rattled the moveable section as hard as he could.

And at last, slowly, the little lock slid down the metal frame and dropped to the bottom. Now, with sufficient body pressure, he was able to slide the window back as far as the little peg, which was still in place. And in a nanosecond he was in, searching her room, his ears cocked for her approach through the overgrown yard.

Carefully, he went through every dresser

drawer again, searching for the little black bag, flinching at every faintest sound. He didn't want to be caught in the closed room with her again. He told himself he was magnifying the danger, but there was something totally focused about Chichi Barbi, a singular determination that unnerved him.

He searched the closet among her few clothes and shoes, searched the top closet shelf, leaping up stubbornly forcing open three suitcases and badly bruising his paws. All were empty. The latches weren't as bad, though, as zippers, which were hell on the claws. He searched under the bed and in between the mattresses as far as his paw would reach, then as far as he could crawl without smothering. He'd hate like hell for her to catch him in that position. He searched the under-sink bathroom cabinet, the night-table drawer, peered into the two empty wastebaskets, checked the carpet for a loose corner under which she might have loosened a board.

He found nothing, nada. He was nosing with curiosity at the back of the little television set when he heard her coming, brushing past the overgrown bushes.

Leaping to the dresser he crouched, ready to bolt. He watched her pass the window, heading for the door. As the door handle turned, he slid out through the window and shouldered the glass closed behind him.

He hardly had time to paw the tape back over the torn screen when the inside light went on. Praying she wouldn't notice that the tape was wrinkled, not smooth the way she'd left it, he dropped down to the scruffy grass.

He was crouched in the dark bushes beside the foundation of the house, poised to scorch for home, when he thought about those two empty wastebaskets. And a sure feline instinct, or maybe acquired cop sense, stopped him in his tracks.

Waiting in the bushes until he heard her cross the room to the bathroom, he beat it past her door and past the kitchen door, to the tall plastic garbage can that stood at the rear of the house.

The lid was on tight. He tried leaping atop Clyde's plastered wall and reaching down with one paw to dislodge it, but the distance was too far, he could get no purchase without falling on his head. Stretching farther, he lost his balance and dropped to the top of the lid — embarrassing himself, though there was no one to see him.

Dropping to the ground, he hung one paw in the can's plastic handle and pressed up on the lid with the other. He should have done that in the first place. The lid popped right off and felt silently to the grass.

Leaping up to perch across the mouth of the can, his hind paws on one side, his left front paw bracing him on the other, he hung down into the dim stinking world of Chichi's rotting garbage: sour grass cuttings, moldy food cans, and a sour milk carton, and he sorted through Chichi Barbi's trash like a common alley cat.

Well, hell, FBI agents did this stuff. So did DEA. If those guys could stomach the stink and indignity, so could he.

Surprisingly, the moldering grass was the worst. It stuck to him all over, clung to his sleek fur, got into his ears and in his nose and eyes. Part of Chichi's job as house sitter was to mow the tiny scrap of weedy lawn. She used a hand mower that was kept in the narrow one-car garage, which occupied the south side, between her living room and Joe's house. As he balanced, pawing and searching, he was painfully aware that he was in plain sight of Clyde's guest room window, not six feet away.

If Clyde saw his gray posterior protruding from Chichi Barbi's garbage can, he'd never hear the last of it. He sorted through food cans and wrappers, wadded tissues, run panty hose, used emery boards, empty spray bottles of various smelly cosmetics, and a dozen other items too gross to think about. Pawing through a layer of discarded papers, he retrieved a dozen store bills and cash register receipts, stuffing them into an empty peanut can. They'd absorb some oily stains but they should still be legible. He did not find the black bag itself, and could catch no scent of metal jewelry. But in this mélange of garbage, who could smell anything? The most talented bloodhound would be challenged.

At least there wasn't too much sticky stuff, thanks to garbage disposals; not like San Francisco garbage when he was a homeless kitten. Rooting in those overflowing bins for something to eat, that had been a real mess.

Taking the peanut can in his teeth, he backed out, pausing for an instant balanced on the edge of the garbage can. He was tensed to drop down when a faint noise made him glance up, at the window of his own house.

Clyde stood at the glass, his expression a mix of amazed amusement and harsh disapproval. The next minute he burst into a belly laugh that made Joe leap away nearly dropping the can.

He heard Clyde come out the back door

heading for the patio wall, as if to look over at him. Racing away around Chichi's house, gripping the metal can in his teeth, he headed for his cat door. He would never hear the end of this one.

But then as he was approaching his cat door, his nose twitched with the smell of burning bacon wafting out from the kitchen, and he smiled. Clyde's unwelcome curiosity had created a small and satisfying disaster.

Spinning in under the plastic flap, he dodged behind his clawed and be-furred easy chair, set the can down, and crouched, silent and still. While Clyde dealt with the bacon, he would just dump the receipts out on the rug and have a look.

But even as he reached a paw in, Clyde rushed into the room, flinging open the windows, turning the house into a wind tunnel that would scatter those papers clear to hell.

Taking the can in his mouth again, he raced away behind Clyde's back through the living room and up the stairs to the master suite. The smell of burned bacon followed him up along the steps. Bolting into Clyde's study and behind the leather love seat, he dumped the papers on the carpet and began to paw through them — until Clyde went racing into the master bedroom, opening those windows, too, then headed for the study.

"Don't open the windows in here!" Joe shouted, leaping to the back of the love seat. "Stop! Don't do that!"

Clyde stared at him. He took two steps toward the love seat. Joe dropped down again behind it. Clyde knelt on the love seat, peering over the back. "What have you got? What did you take out of her garbage? What the hell did you steal this time?"

"You don't steal trash. Things that have already been thrown away are . . ."

"What do you have, Joe?" Clyde frowned at the wadded papers. "Bills? Cash register receipts?" Despite his attempt at anger, Clyde eyed the little collection with interest.

Resignedly, Joe spread out the little bits of paper. Together, they studied a drugstore receipt that included two disposable cameras and a spiral notebook. He pulled out a Kinko's receipt for twenty machine copies. He put aside the wrinkled phone bills. It was the receipt from Kinko's that held him. "What did she make copies of?"

"Well I don't know, Joe. Business papers? How would I know? Just because you saw her slip into her house the night of the jewel burglary, just because . . ." A knock downstairs at the front door stopped Clyde.

"That'll be Ryan with the faucets." And he headed for the stairs.

Pawing the papers back into the peanut can, Joe pushed it safely into the corner between the love seat and chair. And he followed Clyde. Twenty copies of what? It wasn't as if Chichi ran a business. And this was February, no one wrote Christmas letters in February. He could hear Clyde's voice, but not Ryan's. Hurrying down the stairs, hitting the last step, he froze.

That wasn't Ryan. It was Chichi.

Had she seen him in her room or in her garbage can, and come over to complain? Swerving into the kitchen, out of sight, he stood listening.

Sounded like Clyde had moved out onto the porch. Well, at least he hadn't let her in. Hurry up, Clyde. Blow her off, send her packing. Joe could hear her cooing sweet enough to make a cat throw up, and softly laughing in an insinuating way. Disgusted, but as fascinated as any eavesdropper, Joe trotted into the living room and peered out through the partly open front door.

18

Joe could see little more than Clyde's back, and their two pairs of feet on the porch — Clyde's old, dirty jogging shoes, and Chichi's little high-heeled sandals. She had taken time to change? He wondered what else she had put on, to vamp Clyde. Those shoes had to be cold and uncomfortable, had to hurt like hell if she walked a block in them. Her feet were very close to Clyde's — until, suddenly, Clyde backed away and turned as if to slip inside. Chichi laughed softly and moved against him again. Joe stared up indignantly as she tenderly stroked Clyde's cheek, petting him in a way that sickened the tomcat.

"Just to use your phone, Clyde? What's the matter? Just to report my phone out of order . . . What do you have in there that your neighbor can't see? I'll just be a minute, and I . . ."

"Don't you have a cell phone? Go on down to the corner and use the pay phone." Clyde went silent as Ryan's truck pulled up.

Slipping up to the windowsill where he could see better, Joe was glad he had a front seat for this one. Chichi glanced at the big red king cab, scowling. Ryan's lumber rack was stacked with big beams and two-by-fours, ready to build the end walls and place the rafters for the Harpers' new guest room. As Ryan swung out of the truck, Chichi snuggled. Clyde backed off like he'd been burned. Joe could see Dillon and Lori in the back seat staring out, wide-eyed. He watched Ryan hold the door for Rock to leap out. The big dog always rode in the cab, never in the truck bed. Ryan said it was barbaric to subject a dog to the dangers of riding in an open truck where he could easily be thrown out in case of a wreck, and cruel to leave him in a truck for hours tied up in the beating hot sun.

Ryan came up the walk, barely hiding a grin at Clyde's predicament and at Chichi's low-cut pink sweater, her big boobs half out, and her tight black pants riding up her crotch. Under Ryan's amused glance, Chichi looked uncertain and unsure of herself. Ryan was swinging a heavy paper bag bearing the hardware store logo, and her toolbox. She pushed past Chichi, giving her a cool, green-eyed look-over, and headed through the house as if she lived there, making for the upstairs bath. Joe rumbled with purrs. He was not only getting his own personal, cat-friendly water faucet, he was witnessing an entertaining moment of defeat for Chichi Barbi that made his day. The woman looked mad enough to chew off the old faucet for Ryan — or chew Ryan's hand off. As Ryan disappeared upstairs, Clyde fended off Chichi with frustrated finality, and closed the door in her face.

Watching her stalk away, Joe could hear Ryan upstairs unscrewing the faucet. From the bottom of the stairs, Clyde shouted, "Need to turn off the water?"

"Turned it off under the basin. I'll be just a few minutes." Ryan had installed the two upstairs basins, so Joe guessed she knew how to cut off the water. He had dropped off the sill and was heading for the kitchen when there was another knock on the door. Clyde stared at the closed door in disbelief.

Joe gave him a look that said, Don't open it. Clyde looked at him and shrugged. And the minute he foolishly cracked the door open. Chichi pushed inside.

"I never heard of a woman plumber," she said. "She's been around here before — you must have a lot of plumbing problems."

"If you want to report your phone out of order, go in the kitchen. Make it quick, I have to get to work."

"You're leaving a plumber in the house alone? Aren't you . . ."

Clyde just looked at her. "Where is your cell phone?"

"The battery . . ." she said, helplessly gesturing with upturned hands. Scowling, Clyde led her into the kitchen. Following them, Joe watched Chichi slip a scrap of paper from her pocket and punch in a number, then enter a series of numbers as a tape gave her instructions. Joe hated those taped replies. Though he seldom had reason to call a number that employed that particular form of dehumanization. Your highly skilled, undercover snitch didn't waste time on taped messages. Most of Joe's calls were directly to Molena Point PD, clandestine, short, and conducted directly between himself and the law, usually the chief.

When Chichi had reported her out-of-order number she moved to the kitchen sink, draping her hand on Clyde's shoulder, and at the same time taking in every detail of the kitchen. Joe swallowed back a growl. She'd love to be left alone to snoop. The tomcat said a prayer of thanks that he'd carried the little can of her purloined bills upstairs, out of sight. "Could I have a drink of water?"

Patiently, Clyde poured Chichi a glass of tap water, pushed it at her, and stared pointedly in the direction of the front door. Joe listened to a series of small metallic clicks from above, then a short rumble as water surged back through the pipes. He was eager to try the new faucet. As Clyde took Chichi's arm and headed her out toward the front door, Ryan came down the stairs.

At the foot of the stairs, the two women looked at each other like lady cats sparring for territory. Joe waited for the fur to fly, but Clyde shoved Chichi on through the living room and out the door, and locked it behind her. He leaned with his back against the door, trying to collect his temper. Ryan looked at him for a long moment, the corner of her mouth twitching.

"Come on," Clyde said stiffly. "It's not funny. Come have a cup of coffee, help me calm my temper."

Ryan chucked him under the chin. "Your temper? Or your libido? I can't stay for coffee, the girls are in the truck and I'm late, Scotty's waiting." And she was gone before Clyde could point out, with sarcasm, that *Ryan* was the boss, that she made her own hours.

Clyde didn't see Ryan again for three days, during which time he grew increasingly irritable. "You think she's mad? Because of Chichi, because Chichi was here?"

Joe just looked at him. They were in the kitchen having breakfast, waffles and fried ham, with kippers on the side for Joe.

"She didn't give me a chance to explain." Clyde looked across at Joe. "If she's jealous, you think she's seeing that guy who came up to the ranch? This Roman something?" That was two days after Ryan installed the faucet. That night, Clyde paced the house for an hour, before Joe got him to settle down. "If she's not jealous, why hasn't she called?"

Joe had licked a smear of Brie off his paw, a late-night snack, as Clyde waited, fidgeting, for the phone to ring. "So call her," the tomcat had said impatiently. "What's the big deal?" But maybe he shouldn't have laid it on so thick, shouldn't have repeated everything that Dulcie had told him about how handsome this Roman Slayter was and how stubbornly Slayter had pressed Ryan to go out with him. And maybe he shouldn't have ribbed Clyde so much about Chichi.

"Doesn't Ryan know I can't stand the woman?"

"*Call* her!"

Instead of calling, Clyde poured himself a double whiskey, and kept pacing. "What's with you," Joe said. "Call her! There was a time when men did all the calling!" Clyde was so damn stubborn. And then two nights later as Clyde was passing Binnie's Italian on his way home from work, he saw Ryan going into the cozy restaurant with a tall, handsome fashion plate who had to be Roman Slayter.

Clyde got home mad as hornets — and found Rock in the back patio, complete with his bed, a rubber bone and a bowl of kibble. And a cryptic message on the phone from Ryan, saying she was leaving the dog there for a little while, that she wouldn't be late, that it was all very strange and she would explain when she came to get Rock.

"I'll just bet she'll explain! She goes out with this guy like it's a big secret, can't tell me where she's going or who with, just brings Rock over here like I'm some kind of paid babysitting service!"

Joe *tried* to talk to him. "Maybe she had a reason for not telling you, maybe she was in a hurry and didn't want to take time to explain. Why don't you . . ."

"Why don't I *what?*" Clyde didn't pet Rock, didn't let him in the house. He shut the door in Rock's face, and fastened the cover over the big dog door, leaving Rock alone in the patio, looking hurt indeed. When Joe peered down at him through the kitchen window, Rock looked up at him, devastated. Never before had Clyde shut him out. His yellow eyes were incredibly sad, his ears down, his short tail tucked under in misery.

That wasn't like Clyde, to be mean to a dog. Clyde loved Rock. Incensed at Clyde's unfair attitude, Joe waited until Clyde had settled down in the living room with a book, then slipped out to the kitchen, slid the cover of the dog door open a few inches, and went out to snuggle down with Rock on his big, cedar-stuffed bed. Sighing, Rock laid his head over Joe, badly needing sympathy. It wasn't Rock's fault that Ryan had gone out with someone else when Clyde didn't call her, Joe thought indignantly. Nor was it Rock's fault that Clyde had let Chichi make an ass of him in front of Ryan.

19

Maria was bringing the newspaper in for Luis, before she put his eggs on, when she stopped in the doorway to sound out the English headlines. The words made her feel weak. She leaned against the door, her heart starting to pound. Dufio was in jail. Again. Oh, poor Dufio. That was why Luis was so angry last night.

Dufio was always getting arrested. And every time, it made her feel worse.

Closing the front door she headed down the hall for the kitchen, slowly reading the front page, frowning over the words. She wished she hadn't had to go to a bilingual school, that they'd made her learn English better. Luis said she didn't need English, except kitchen words. He'd never wanted her to learn anything.

She could make out, in the paper, enough about last night's burglary to know they had stolen jewels worth more than a hundred thousand dollars American. That would be a huge fortune to a family in Mexico, enough to keep cousins and uncles and all the children for the rest of their lives. The police had spotted two of the cars, but Luis didn't have any identification on them, just the stolen plates. Luis had been real mad when they came in last night, maybe because Dufio let the cops get him. She hadn't been able to hear much from her bedroom, they'd had the kitchen door closed. Whatever happened now, there would be trouble. She wished she had the nerve to run, before the police came. Take Abuela away now. Run away now.

But where would they go? Abuela was an old woman, she was slow and she wore out easily, even when she was in the wheelchair. And wherever they went, Luis would find them.

She wouldn't have the heart to leave those poor cats behind, in that cage. She would have to free them, too. And she didn't have the key. Maybe they *were* only dumb beasts. In Mexico, people would laugh at her. But she didn't think she could leave those helpless cats to Luis. She wished she had the nerve to take the key from Luis's pocket while he slept.

But even if she could, he'd know she did it, and his beatings hurt bad. It didn't matter that she was his sister. To Luis, women were for cooking and beating and for the bed. Though even Luis wouldn't do that with his sister.

Well, he did keep the others off her. Even if he didn't go to mass anymore, Luis knew that if he let them touch her, or touched her himself, he'd surely burn in hell.

Returning down the hall to the kitchen, she gave Luis the paper, cooked his and Tommie's eggs with the chorizo, then stood at the sink scrubbing the skillet. Behind her at the table Luis and Tommie ate silently as they read the paper. She thought about when she and her three brothers were children, in Mexico. When Mamacita made breakfast for them and dressed them nice and took them to mass. Thought of them all crowded into the pew, her and Dufio and Hernando and Luis lined up on the bench, and her feet didn't touch the floor. She was the smallest. They all wore shoes on Sunday. Her brothers had feared the word of God, then. And feared the anger of the priest, too.

But when the boys were bigger they got smart-mouthed and started stealing and didn't care what the priest said. That was after Mamacita died, and they lived with their aunt and her drunk husband. The boys stopped going to confession. Then they all three went away to make money in Los

Estados Unidos and she was left there alone with her aunt and uncle.

She was eleven when Luis came back for her and they crowded into the back of a vegetable truck and crossed the border into California and lived with a third cousin's family in San Diego, ten to a room. Luis was stealing big and fancy then, and she worried all the time. Then the three boys moved into a room of their own and she cleaned and cooked for them and kept her little suitcase packed like Luis said. She was only twelve, and she did what Luis told her.

But then they were arrested, were all three in jail. She ran, then. Went to work for a Mexican woman who cleaned houses; slept on a pallet in the woman's kitchen — until Luis got out of jail and found her. After that it was one town after another, living out of his rattley old car, all their life was robberies and leaving town in a hurry, late at night. Not like in Mexico, when the boys had no car and couldn't get away fast. They weren't in so much trouble then.

When Luis and Tommie finished breakfast and went to bed because they'd been up all night, she picked up their plates, folded the newspaper, and wiped egg and crumbs from the table. She didn't want to read any more of that paper.

She made Abuela's breakfast and went to bring her into the kitchen. While Abuela was eating, Maria returned to her and Abuela's bedroom and fed the cats, scooping the dry food through the bars into the dirty bowl. She couldn't clean the sandbox until Luis got up again, with the key, until he stood right over her, making a face and telling her to hurry up.

As she spooned the dry food through the bars, the three cats looked up at her, then at the cage door. They looked like they were asking her to open it; quickly she crossed herself.

"Luis has the key," she told them; but it scared her even more that she was speaking to them. As if some voodoo spell was on her. The biggest cat's eyes burned into hers like he understood her, too. As if he wanted to say, "Can't you *take* the key? *Can't* you let us out?" She grew frightened, indeed, watching him. It did no good to remind herself that they were only cats, only stray cats.

There were stray cats all over Mexico, they hunted rats and mice, and they died. In Mexico, there were always more cats.

It was Hernando who trapped the cats, away in the green hills beyond the village, which she could see from the window. Some of the cats had gotten away, slipped out of the traps. Then Hernando bought different ones. He said those cats knew how to open traps, but no cat could do that. Someone had let them loose.

Hernando believed it, though; he said they weren't regular cats. He talked real crazy, said they were worth money. But now that Hernando had gone away somewhere, why didn't Luis turn the cats loose, get rid of them?

She wished, with Hernando gone and Dufio in jail, that Luis would go away, too. She wanted to pray to the Virgin that Luis and his men would all go to jail for the jewel robbery and she and Abuela would be free. But she guessed she would go to hell if she prayed for such a thing. When she looked at the biggest cat, his eyes were so like a person's that she backed away from him, whispering her Hail Marys.

Binnie's Italian was a small, family-operated café that had been a fixture in Molena Point for three generations. The Gianinni family had been a part of the village since the dirt streets of Molena Point were traversed by horse and buggy. In the early days, many Italian families had emigrated from the old country to California's central coast, to farm and work and open businesses, to become doctors and lawyers and bankers, to settle in and help create the lively economy that now existed.

Other, fancier restaurants than Binnie's came and went, but Binnie's was part of the community, a constant favorite with its roasted-vegetable pizzas and seafood pastas and locally made wines and beers. A few years ago, Binnie's had redecorated, shocking the old-timers with bright abstract murals that covered the walls and ceiling and even the tabletops. Every surface became a feast of color, every chair a work of art painted differently. The effect was cozy and welcoming, a warm and cheerful retreat.

On this chill spring evening, Ryan Flannery entered Binnie's as Roman Slayter held the door for her in his most courteous manner. Having erased a dozen of Slayter's messages from her machine over the last four days, Ryan had at last given in, driven by curiosity at Slayter's latest message. She knew the taped message was a ruse, but she couldn't resist: "I think I know something about this burglary, Ryan. The jewelry store? Some facts . . . Well, I don't want to go to the police myself. I can't explain exactly why. You'd have to trust me on that. I thought if you passed on the information, it might be helpful . . ."

Oh, right, she thought. What kind of scam is this? But still, she had to know what he would say.

He'd reserved a table at the back, complete with a little bowl of flowers and a candle. Pulling out her chair for her, then folding his slim six-foot-four frame onto a red-and-blue ladder-back bench, Roman grinned at her, his brown eyes more familiar than she liked. He was wearing a tan cashmere sport coat over a black shirt and cream slacks. A flashy gold Rolex watch gleamed on his tanned wrist, and he wore some kind of gold signet ring with an onyx stone.

Up at the ranch, she hadn't noticed his jewelry, she'd been too angry and then too shocked at Rock's chameleon behavior. She still didn't understand what had gotten into Rock. She'd seen him, too many times, threaten to attack strange men who approached her. Tonight, she'd dropped the big dog off at Clyde's before Clyde got home from work. Had left a message on Clyde's machine. She hoped he didn't mind keeping Rock. It had been days since she'd seen him, and he hadn't once called her. She probably could have left Rock at home, he was much more dependable than when she'd first taken him in. But even now, when left alone, he was still inclined to panic and tear up the yard or the furniture.

Slayter had ordered wine as they were seated. Now she glanced briefly at her menu, then sat watching him. "What did you have to tell me? What was so urgent?"

Slayter had begun to speak when the waiter approached, uncorking a nice merlot. He remained silent, nodding and tasting at the right moments. Ryan watched the little ritual impatiently. The dark-haired young waiter was nervous, was probably new at this — one of Binnie's many nephews, young men who had, over the years, worked in the restaurant while they were in high school or college. She kept a cool gaze on Roman.

When the waiter left, Slayter lifted a little toast to her, which she ignored. "The night of the burglary," he said, "I saw a woman running . . . Not from the store itself, but from that direction, that block." His brown eyes never left her, a soft, disingenuous look, concerned and innocent. He'd apparently just had a haircut, she could see the tiny white line below his neat, dark hair — and he smelled of some expensive, musky after-shave. "Just as the sirens started, I saw her running down the street from the direction of the jewelry store, keeping to the shadows.

She was carrying a small black bag, a shapeless cloth pouch that bulged at the bottom. She was darkly dressed, with a hood pulled around her face. Running south, away from Ocean.

"Two blocks south of Ocean she ducked into a driveway, old shingled cottage next to a two-story house on Doris, that Spanish-style place with a new shake roof."

Ryan startled. That was Clyde's house, Slayter had to know that. It was the only two-story house for several blocks south of Ocean, the only house with a new shake roof. She looked at Slayter, frowning.

Could the woman he saw, if he had seen anyone, could that be Clyde's blond neighbor? She didn't know what Slayter was up to, but she didn't think she wanted to hear this.

No matter how much she disliked that woman, she liked even less what she was hearing.

"I was just headed back to the motel after dinner," Roman said. "Heard the sirens and turned up there instead." He gave her a boyish smile. "Idle curiosity. Rubbernecking, I guess. She ran into the driveway of the brown house, disappeared at the back, I heard a door close somewhere at the back. There was a woman in the front of the house, watching TV, I could see her silhouette through the shade."

Ryan frowned. She'd thought Chichi was staying there alone, that the owners were up in the city. "If you thought she was running from the burglary, why didn't you call the police? Why are you telling me?"

"I . . . I was in some trouble not long ago," Roman said diffidently. "Not of my doing, but the police thought it was. I . . . didn't want to get involved. The police . . ."

"You could have called them anonymously. They might have caught her. Might even have recovered the jewels." She watched him intently. "What is this, Roman? What kind of scam is this?"

"It isn't a scam, Ryan. What would I get out of tipping you off? I saw her and thought I'd pass it on. Well . . ." Roman leaned closer over the table. "I think she's a friend of your friend, I think she lives next door to him. I didn't want to make trouble for someone you're fond of."

The hell you wouldn't, she thought. "Why would that make trouble for him? Are you implying that Clyde's involved?" Ryan did her best not to laugh in his face. "You're going to have to spell it out." What scared her was that he'd taken great pains to learn about Clyde, to learn who she was seeing.

She watched the waiter set down their anti-pasto and salad and refill their wineglasses.

"I thought maybe your friend . . . That this might touch you in some way, that you wouldn't want to . . ."

She rose, shoving back her chair so hard it fell clattering to the floor. "Call the police, Roman! Tell *them*. This has nothing to do with Clyde, or with me! If you have information, call the department!

"Unless you want to be charged with withholding information," she added hotly. And she stormed out of the restaurant, her stomach churning with anger — and with disappointment at abandoning Binnie's shrimp-and-ham linguini.

Heading for Clyde's to pick up Rock, she did her best to simmer down; but she was still steaming when she knocked softly on Clyde's door. One light was on in the living room; looked like the reading light by Clyde's chair. She could hear a Dixieland CD playing. At her knock, she expected Rock to bark and then to catch her scent and whine, but she heard neither. "Clyde? It's me, it's Ryan."

He opened the door, scowling. He didn't move back out of her way, but stood blocking her entry.

"Where's Rock? I . . ."

"Have a nice evening?"

"What's wrong? Is there . . . Clyde, where's Rock? I brought him . . . Is he all right? Did you get my message?"

"He's in the backyard where you left him."

She stared at him. "What's he done? What are you mad about?"

There was a long silence. Clyde stood frowning. She stared at him, and began to laugh. "You're mad! Mad because I . . ." She pushed past him into the room, and turned to look at him. She took his hand and, against his mild resistance, led him to the couch, pulled him down to sit beside her. She was still holding his hand.

"Listen to me, Clyde. I met Roman Slayter for dinner because he said he had some kind of evidence about the jewel burglary. He called and called."

"Right."

"Just listen . . ."

From the kitchen, Joe Grey listened, too. Having slipped back inside through the dog door, he'd slid it shut in Rock's face, had left Rock outside pawing and scratching at the plywood. Joe stood in the kitchen, engrossed in Clyde's anger and Ryan's amusement, and in her explanation of why she'd agreed to have dinner with Slayter. He was heartened that she'd left the restaurant in a rage before dinner was served. Surely Clyde would be pleased at that.

When Ryan repeated Slayter's "information" about Chichi, Clyde played dumb, as if Chichi's stealthy behavior was news to him — as it should be. They made up with a lot of mushy talk that embarrassed Joe, then Clyde opened a bottle of Chablis and made Ryan a grilled shrimp sandwich that was, she said, far superior to Binnie's linguini. They let Rock in before he tore up the door; and Joe went up to his tower and curled down among the cushions, leaving the lovebirds alone. Below him the house was quiet, except for the romantic forties music that Clyde had loaded onto the CD player. Joe must have been asleep when Ryan and Rock left, he didn't hear her truck pull away.

About the same time that Ryan left Binnie's so abruptly, abandoning her dinner, Lucinda Greenlaw called Charlie. Charlie and Wilma were tucked up by the fire in the Harpers' new living room, with Dulcie and the kit, having had an early dinner before Max went back to the station.

"We've found a house," Lucinda said, her voice bright with excitement. "We waited to call until our offer was accepted. Tell Kit . . . Is Max there . . . ? Could I . . ."

"Max is at work," Charlie said, laughing. "You can talk to Kit. She's all over me, pawing at the phone." Kit had sprung to her lap and was rearing up, paws on Charlie's shoulder, pressing her ear to the phone, her long, fluffy tail lashing. She was so excited that when Charlie turned the speaker on, she yowled twice like a little wild cat before she could get a word out. "A house, Lucinda? A house! What kind of house! Does it have a tower like Joe Grey's? Is it near Dulcie's? With a big garden and trees and a window seat with pillows and a nice fireplace and . . . ?"

"Stop, Kit! Stop and listen! Window seats, yes. Trees and a tangle of garden just the way you like. There's no tower but it does have a surprise . . ."

"What surprise, Lucinda? What?"

"Would it be a surprise if I told you? You'll have to wait and see. Of course there's a fireplace. You'll love this house. We'll pick you up first thing in the morning, seven-thirty, have breakfast in the village, then meet the Realtor at nine. Oh, Kit, we can hardly wait for you to see it."

Kit was purring so loud that it was hard for Charlie to get a word in. "Shhh, Kit."

She stroked the excited tortoiseshell. "Lucinda, have breakfast here! A mushroom omelet and fresh mangoes?"

"That sounds wonderful, Charlie, but that's way too early to be entertaining company."

"No it isn't. You're not company, you're family. Ryan's bringing the girls, to ride. They can help me before they saddle their horses."

When Lucinda said they'd come, Charlie clicked the phone off, and looked into Kit's wide, yellow eyes. The little cat was seething with anticipation, so wired that Charlie thought she'd fly apart. It took a long time for Kit to settle down again and to resume telling the story she had begun.

Charlie felt certain that Kit's early life, with a judicious retelling to remove the little cat's unusual talents, could be a wonderful book — if she could do the story justice. Wilma had read the first five chapters, which were in rough draft, and she thought the story was as compelling and as real as *Watership Down*. Charlie knew it was foolhardy to ask the opinion of one's friends when it came to creative matters, whether to the written word or to a painting. But Wilma was, after all, a well-read librarian with a keen perception of what her own readers loved. The fact that both Wilma, and Charlie's agent, were excited about the beginning chapters had left Charlie amazed and even more eager to write the finest book she could. Life was, indeed, full of wonders.

Now, long after Max got home and they were tucked up in bed, and both cats were settled in with Wilma in Charlie's studio, Charlie lay awake, filled with too many thoughts to find sleep. The fire in the master bedroom had burned to coals, and still she lay thinking about the book and about the pictures she was doing for it; seeing the newest drawing clearly, as she liked to do before she began it. Beside her, Max tossed restlessly. Even in sleep, his mind would be busy with police matters.

She thought about the jewel theft and the increasing complexity of the suspects; profiles that Max and Dallas had put together. About their growing suspicion of a larger scenario, perhaps a dozen burglaries to hit the village at one time. Though she tried never to succumb to fear, the more she learned about this little nondescript Luis Rivas and his men, the more uneasy she felt. She turned over, shivering, pressing close to Max, clinging to the comforting sense of his goodness and strong capability. He and Dallas and Davis had the situation well under control, she told herself, or they soon would have.

But still the worries were there, silly, disjointed fears about matters that probably meant nothing, like Ryan's dinner with Roman Slayter and his accusation of Clyde's neighbor.

Ryan had called her when she left the restaurant, so mad she could hardly talk. Charlie lay puzzling over what Slayter had told Ryan, puzzling over Slayter's arrival in the village at just this time, as well as Chichi's sudden appearance right next door to Clyde. And she began to wonder why Max had received no anonymous phone tips on this case.

Still, though, Max and Dallas were gathering information and biding their time, waiting for more police files to come in from L.A. So maybe Joe and Dulcie were doing that, too.

She was smiling to herself in the dark, thinking about two little cats wandering the station, pawing through reports, tucking away sensitive facts, when she heard, in the still night, one of the cats in the kitchen crunching kibble.

That would be the kit, she thought, grinning. In a little while, she saw the little cat's shadow prowling the patio, restlessly stalking, her long, fluffy tail twitching. Was Kit, too, thinking about the jewel robbery? More likely, about the new house. Charlie thought about the amazing accident that had brought Kit here, to the Greenlaws. That wild band had never before, in Kit's lifetime, traveled this far north. What had drawn the clowder to Hellhag Hill, and drawn the Greenlaws to picnic there? Surely that had been a wonderfully happy accident. Or had it been more than an accident?

That meeting between Kit and the Greenlaws, then Charlie herself moving to Molena Point, had resulted in Charlie's book in progress. Serendipity? A happy accident? Or a gift of grace? A gift she would do her best to honor.

Snuggled close to Max, Charlie promised herself that she would produce, in this book, the best work she could create, an adventure to touch the heart of every reader. She lay smiling, lost again in the story — and the next thing she knew the alarm was buzzing and she was out of bed before she came fully awake. Pulling on her jeans and sweatshirt and boots, she went to feed the horses and dogs and then to start breakfast.

20

Picking up the two girls again the next morning, Ryan headed straight for the ranch, no stopping this morning for breakfast; she and Rock had shared a bowl of cereal; though he'd had his dog food to himself. She wanted to get the upstairs dried in before any chance of rain. Early spring on the central coast could be temperamental, California wasn't all sunshine and warm beaches. The roughing in was finished, the roof raised and the new studs in place. Today they would get the exterior sheeting and roof sheeting on. The flooring was being delivered this morning, too, and the drywall, all of which needed to be stacked under cover before bad weather hit. When she stopped for the girls, they climbed in the back seat sleepy and quiet; they were silent until, in the center of the village, Dillon came alert, suddenly glued to the window.

"There she is again!" They were passing a small café patio that was half filled with early breakfast customers. "What does she do, at the crack of dawn? For hours, like that? Looking up and down the street and writing things down. She's spying on someone. How long's she been sitting there?"

Ryan glanced in her rearview mirror. "What?"

"That same blonde," Dillon said, "that lives next door to Clyde, that bimbo who was all over him yesterday when we pulled up at his house. Who is she?"

"That cheap blonde with the tight sweaters and big boobs," Lori specified.

Ryan glanced at Lori, amused, and turned off Ocean up the highway, heading for the Harper place.

"We've seen her four times," Lori said, "sitting in different restaurants early in the morning. For hours, alone, watching the street. Writing something in a notebook. She's never eating, just coffee. How much coffee can a person drink?"

"Hours, Lori? How would you know that?"

"We've been taking the dogs to the beach," Lori said. "Susan Brittain's dogs." Susan was one of the four senior ladies Lori had lived with since her father went to prison. Lori loved the standard poodle and the Dalmatian, and got along well with them. "I don't like that woman, she's a tramp."

Ryan gave her a stern look in the mirror, trying not to laugh.

"Well she is. She's there when we go down, real early before school, and she's there when we come back. Once was later, Saturday. We were in the library." She glanced at Dillon, who grinned sheepishly.

Dillon's current English teacher was assigning long, detailed papers, and would not let the kids go online to do their research. It had to be from books, with the sources properly noted, all footnotes in correct form — and no adult help.

Dillon had never worked this way, she said all the kids complained. Two dozen parents were so angry they were trying to get the teacher fired. But a dozen more applauded her. Dillon found the new method very hard and demanding. She didn't care, at the moment, that the training would put her in the top ranks when applying for college. She didn't care that she was learning to do far more thorough and accurate research than anyone could ever do online, or that you couldn't do adequate college work without those basics. But while Dillon wasn't happy with the assignments, Lori was having a ball.

Two years younger, Lori tried not to be smug that she knew her way among the reference books. Before Lori's mother died, she'd often taken Lori to work with her in the library, and had often let her help with reference projects.

No one had said Dillon couldn't have help from a younger child. Surely her teacher had never imagined that a twelve-year-old would have those skills. And while Lori was hugely enjoying the challenge, and Dillon was learning, the situation deeply embarrassed the older girl.

Below the highway, the sea gleamed in the brightening morning, the little waves flashing silver up at them. The tide was in, the surf pounding high against the black rocks, the smell of the sea sharp with salt and iodine and little dead sea-creatures. Ryan glanced at the girls. "So what do you think she was watching?"

Dillon shrugged. "Hard to tell. I didn't see anything very interesting. A man from the shop across the street watering his garden. Cars creeping by. Couple of tourists walking their dogs."

"Which shop, Dillon?"

"That posh leather one," Lori said. "With the Gucci bags."

"And the other times?"

"Dormeyer's Jewelry once," Lori said. "When we took the dogs down before supper, and were coming home. Sunday night, gray-haired man closing up, locking the door."

"That was Mr. Dormeyer," Dillon said. "He owns the shop."

"Was anyone with him?" Ryan asked. "His wife?"

"A woman left about an hour before," Lori said. "Gray hair, a long skirt and sandals. He left last, locked the door."

Ryan nodded. Gray-haired Mena Dormeyer usually wore long, flowered skirts, and sandals, even on cold winter days, varying her wardrobe only with a heavy, hand-knit sweater. And maybe with wool tights under the skirt, she thought. She slowed for a car to pass in the opposite direction, then turned left onto the Harpers' lane. Moving slowly between the white pasture fences, approaching the barn, she studied the new end walls of the second story, their skeletons pale in the early light. The side walls had been stripped of the old roofing shingles but were still covered with age-darkened plywood. Scotty's truck was parked in the yard. She caught a flash of his red hair and beard as he disappeared around the back of the barn, where they had stashed their ladders and equipment out of the way of the horses. Parking the truck, she watched the girls head into the house to get permission before they saddled the horses.

Ordinarily, Dillon would have been welcome to work on the construction, doing odd jobs, but Ryan didn't want her on the second floor, balancing on open joists. Dillon's work permit spelled out clearly the safety precautions Ryan would take. Ryan had not only signed the agreement but had of course promised Dillon's parents that she would be closely supervised. This was not medieval England, where a fourteen-year-old was expected to do adult work and was paid a bit of stale bread and a lump of coal.

Swinging out of the truck, she gave Rock his command to jump out behind her; and as the girls hurried out, she headed for the barn.

She was up on the beams when the Greenlaws' car pulled in. They were gone again when, at midmorning, she went in to have coffee with Charlie and Wilma. Sitting at the kitchen table, she mentioned the two girls watching Chichi and commenting on Chichi's early-morning vigils. On the window seat, Wilma's tabby cat lay stretched among the pillows, next to Wilma's overnight bag. Like a patient traveler waiting to depart, Ryan thought, amused. Wilma was going home this morning, after several days' pampering, but how could the cat know? The familiarity of the overnight bag? Knowing that where it went, Wilma went? That had to be the explanation.

Though this cat often gave Ryan a sense of the unreal. All three cats did. Well, but cats were strange little creatures, she didn't understand cats.

Yet even Rock seemed to view these particular cats in a strange way. With unusual respect? Yes, that was it. And often with a puzzled look that seemed almost to be amazement.

Maybe the cats had clawed Rock at some time, had put him in his place, and he was unusually wary of them. Rock was, after all, a very big dog. He was daunting to most cats, so maybe it surprised him that these three would stand up to him — as they surely had, in the beginning. Now they were the best of friends.

"But what do you think she was doing, what was she watching?" Wilma said.

"Chichi?" Ryan shook her head. "I haven't a clue." She grinned. "The girls decided she was spying on the shopkeepers. Leave it to kids to find the most dramatic spin."

Charlie said, "Maybe what Slayter told you wasn't so far off, what he said when you had dinner with him last night — or started to have dinner."

When Wilma looked inquisitive, Ryan told her what Slayter had said about Chichi running from the scene of the burglary. "That could be a figment of his imagination," she said carefully. "Or could be a lie — Slayter's the kind who would lie for no good reason, just to entertain himself." She glanced out the window, saw that Scotty was back at work carrying two-by-fours up the ladder, and she rose, hurrying out.

She was on the roof again when Charlie and Wilma came out, Charlie carrying Wilma's overnight bag. She watched Wilma's cat gallop by them, heading straight for Charlie's SUV. The minute Charlie opened the door, the cat leaped up onto the seat in what, Ryan was certain, was surely not normal feline behavior.

But then, what did she know? Maybe cats *were* as smart as dogs.

The kit, full of Charlie's lovely mushroom omelet and warm milk, prowled the empty house ahead of Lucinda and Pedric, far too impatient to give the old couple a chance to show her around. Leaping to every sill to look out, nosing into every corner lashing her tail with interest, leaping atop every bookshelf catching cobwebs in her whiskers, she decided she liked this house. Liked it quite a lot.

The two-story dwelling was on such a steep hill that, even after the Greenlaws had made their offer and given the agent a check, the conscientious agent was uncertain about the old couple living on such a slope. But to Lucinda and Pedric, the house was perfect.

The high rafters of the great room filled Kit with delight as she leaped from one to the next. But where was the surprise? She could not ask in front of the real estate agent. Even if Mrs. Thurwell was a friend, she didn't know Kit's secret. The old couple had chosen her because she was Dillon's mother, and had decided to work with her exclusively because she was a quiet, sensible agent who didn't push. Who had, during all their weeks of searching, left them alone to prowl each house as they pleased, without comment. Unless of course, they asked a question. Neither one of the Greenlaws could abide a pushy Realtor, and neither could Kit.

Now, even though she must remain mute, she raced about eagerly looking, her tail lashing, drawing Lucinda's frown because she was not behaving like a normal cat, making Mrs. Thurwell glance at her, puzzled.

"She's always been like that," Lucinda said. "As hyper as a terrier. The vet says she has a thyroid problem. Makes her wild. We worry about her, we keep hoping she'll settle down. She's such a dear, when she's quiet. But anything new sets her off — new people, new places . . ."

Lucinda laughed, as guileless as a cat herself. "I guess everyone thinks their pet is special. Do you have figures on the utility costs?"

Managing to divert Mrs. Thurwell, going over the utility figures and then leading the slim brunette into the kitchen to discuss the dishwasher, Lucinda freed the kit — and freed Pedric to lead Kit to a dining room window and open the latched shutters.

Leaping up to the sill of the open window, Kit looked and looked, then she turned to look at Pedric. The thin old man held his finger to his lips. Kit stared at him, then sailed out the window into the oak tree — into a realm that took her breath. Into a little house right among the tall branches. This was the surprise! A little house, hugged within the branches of the oak.

Scorching from the branch in through a small, open door, Kit was beyond speech. Lucinda and Pedric had never hinted that there was a tree house! She looked back to the window, to Pedric. Her tall, wrinkled friend grinned, his eyes sparkling. "It's yours," he whispered, mouthing the words. "Yours, Kit."

Oh, the wonder!

Joe Grey had a tower on his roof but *she* had a tree house! A tree house sturdily made of thick cedar boards, a beautiful tree house with its own little deck and door and windows. She imagined beautiful India cushions inside, a tumble of pillows in which to snuggle; it was a retreat far cozier and more elegant even than Joe Grey's wonderful tower.

At the moment, there was a lovely pile of dry oak leaves that had blown into the corner. Flopping among them she rolled and wriggled, lay upside down purring, looking up at her own raftered ceiling. She prowled her own deck, sniffing the salty sea wind and looking away to the hills where scattered cottages rose, half hidden among pines and oaks. She looked down to the south, to Wilma's house, and could see Wilma's roof! When she looked to the center of the village, she could pick out Joe

Grey's tower. She looked through the branches down into the window of the dining room where Pedric stood looking up at her, his eyes bright, his wrinkles curved with pleasure. "Yours," he mouthed again. He turned away as Mrs. Thurwell joined him.

21

In her cozy living room, Wilma paused from serving drinks, set her tray on the desk, and placed three saucers of milk on the blotter. Beyond the open shutters sunset stained the sky, as bright red as the rooftops in the painting hanging above the fireplace behind her. A reflection of sunset played faintly across her long, silver hair. As she passed drinks to Lucinda and Pedric, the three cats set to lapping warm milk, their own version of before-dinner cocktails.

Charlie had brought Wilma home at midmorning and ordered her to rest. Wilma, after a half-hour nap, had grown so restless she began to call her friends to tell them she was home and on the mend, ready to go back to work. Now, this evening, an impromptu dinner to celebrate her homecoming, as if she'd been gone for months. The Greenlaws had brought a salad, and Clyde was picking up takeout on his way to get Ryan. Charlie had promised a dessert.

Joe Grey had left the station before

Harper did, galloping across the rooftops burning with information on the Rivas brothers, with statistics from arrest sheets and reports that had just come in by fax. He was tense with news to share; but with Kit so excited, he hadn't been able to get in a word.

"It's a real tree house, it was a child's tree house and it's so beautiful all hidden in the tree and it's mine! Wait until you see!" She was lapping milk and talking so fast that she spluttered most of the milk across the blotter and on Dulcie's ears. Joe waited patiently. With Kit's nonstop narration, Dulcie and Joe and Wilma soon knew more about the Greenlaws' new house than the real estate agent who had sold it.

"There will be cushions," Lucinda said. "And a water bowl on the windowsill that Kit can easily reach. We thought maybe Lori or Dillon would take the pillows up, with a sturdy ladder. That is," she said, "if they understand that the tree house belongs to Kit."

Kit purred with contentment. Life was indeed wonderful. But beside her Joe Grey fidgeted and laid his ears back until at last she paid attention and shut up and let him talk before he exploded like a wildcat.

"Faxes are coming in, on the Rivas brothers," Joe said, twitching an ear.

"Twenty-seven burglaries and street robberies in two years, and those are just the arrests. Who knows how many when they weren't caught? Luis has a rap sheet long enough to paper this room, and so did Hernando.

"Most of the time, Luis and Hernando worked together, apparently kept Dufio out of the way." Joe licked his paw. "Poor Dufio. By the time Dallas finished reading off the details of his arrests, half the department was standing around the fax machine, grinning. I had to crawl under Mabel's counter to keep from breaking up laughing.

"Dufio's full name's Delfino. I guess he's been clumsy like this all his life. Last year he robbed an Arby's in Arcadia, two o'clock in the afternoon, got out with the money okay. But for the second time, he locked his keys in the car. Can't the poor guy learn? When he couldn't get in, he dropped the paper bag full of money and took off running.

"Two blocks from Arby's, three patrol cars were on him, bundled him off to jail. But, as they recovered the money, the judge went easy on him. He did seven months, got out, his brothers wouldn't have anything to do with him. On his own again, he broke the padlock on a storage locker in Anaheim, backed his truck up to it, and somehow in the process he set off the alarm. Chain-link gate swung closed, and he was trapped."

Lucinda and Pedric looked a bit sorry for Dufio, but Wilma was laughing. Whatever embarrassment Dufio Rivas had suffered at his own mistakes, the entertainment he afforded those in law enforcement was deeply satisfying.

"When he got out of L.A. County jail," Joe said, "he pulled a holdup on a 7-Eleven. He had his keys in his pocket this time. But he flashed a holdup note at the guy. He got away all right, for six blocks, then a customer ID'd his car. A patrol car stopped him, asked for identification and registration." Joe purred, twitching a whisker. "I love when humans do this stuff. He opened the glove compartment, handed them all the papers in it, including the holdup note."

This made Lucinda and Pedric chuckle, too. They were still smiling when Clyde and Ryan pulled to the curb out front, Clyde's yellow Model A roadster gleaming in the falling evening. Charlie's new, red SUV parked behind them, then Max's truck. They all crowded in through the back door, setting their bags of takeout on the kitchen table.

Now, with Ryan and Max present, the cats must remain mute; they turned their attention to supper, committing themselves fully to a dozen Oriental delicacies that Clyde and Charlie served for them on paper plates. The highlight was the golden shrimp tempura. Clyde had brought three extra servings. Kit ate so much shrimp that everyone, human and cat alike, thought she'd be sick. She slept so soundly after supper that when Pedric lifted her up into a soft blanket and carried her out to the car to head home, she didn't wiggle a whisker.

And it was not until Joe and Dulcie had wandered away to the rooftops, alone in the chill evening, that they discussed the Rivas brothers again. Then they laid out a businesslike schedule for shadowing Chichi Barbi, to discover what she found of such interest during her long, solitary vigils.

Joe could see her leave the house in the mornings, so he would follow her until noon. Dulcie would prowl the rooftops in the evenings when most of the shops were closing. Kit would be going back to Charlie's in the morning for a few more days of storytelling; she had no desire to accompany Lucinda and Pedric on a spree of furniture shopping, any more than she'd wanted to look at houses. She might revel in a velvet love seat or a silk chaise, but she didn't care for the shopping.

The Greenlaws had no furniture, they'd sold everything before they moved into their RV to travel the California coast. After the RV was wrecked and burned, the old couple, though safe, had owned little more than the sweatshirts and jeans they were dressed in; plus their ample bank accounts. The task of furnishing a whole house seemed monstrous to Kit; the only shopping that interested her was a nice trip to the deli. Besides, she was so looking forward to sharing more of her adventures with Charlie. Charlie's book about *her* was far more exciting than furniture stores and pushy salesmen.

"She's getting big-headed," Joe told Dulcie as they wandered the rooftops. He rolled over on a patch of tarpaper that still held the heat of the day. "You think it's a good thing, for Charlie to be writing about her?"

"Charlie's not putting in anything she shouldn't. No talking cats." Dulcie twitched her whiskers. "Kit'll calm down. How many cats have their life story written in a book for all kinds of people to read, and with such beautiful portraits of her? You wouldn't spoil that for the kit."

"I guess I wouldn't." Joe nuzzled Dulcie's cheek. "But you have to admit, she does get full of herself."

Dulcie shrugged. "That's her nature." And the two cats trotted on across the rooftops, thinking about Kit's mercurial temperament as they headed for the courthouse tower — until Joe came suddenly alert, stopping to watch below them.

Some of the restaurants and shops were still open, the drugstore, the little grocery that catered to late-shopping tourists. From the edge of a steep, shingled roof, they looked across the street to the grocery's side door. "That's . . ." Joe hissed, and the next instant he was gone, scrambling backward down a thorny bougainvillea vine and racing across the empty street. Dulcie fled close behind him.

Slipping into the shadowed store, they followed the short, stocky Hispanic man along the aisles, their noses immediately confused by a hundred scents: onions-coffee-oranges-sweet rolls-raw meat-spices, a tangle of smells they had to sort through to pick out the man's personal scent — which, at last, was recorded in their scent-memories: a melange of Mexican food, sweat, and too much cheap after-shave. They flinched as an occasional tourist glanced down and reached to pet them; though the locals paid no attention. This family grocery store had cats, it was not unusual to see a cat in the aisles. Quickly down past cereal and bread they followed Luis, then down between shelves of canned vegetables and canned soup and then soft drinks. At pet food, Luis stopped. Pet food?

He began to fill his cart with the cheapest tins of cat food. He tossed in a fifty-pound bag of cat litter as if it were a little bag of peanuts. They watched him add a large bag of cheap kibble. He didn't seem to give a damn for favorite brands or flavors, for what his cats might like or what might be good for them.

His cats? Luis Rivas did not seem to them to be a cat person. Dulcie's green eyes were wide, her voice no more than a breath. "Are you sure this is Luis Rivas?"

Joe wouldn't forget the scowling, burly Latino who had visited Chichi the morning before the burglary. And as Luis filled his rolling cart and joined the checkout line, it became more than clear that this man was, indeed, no cat lover.

The checker was a pretty, young brunette, probably still in high school. She looked at Luis's purchases, and gave him a sunny smile. "You must surely love your cats. How many do you have?"

"Not my cats!" Luis snapped. "Far as I'm concerned, every cat in the world should be drowned or strangled."

In the shadowed aisle, Dulcie's eyes narrowed with rage, and Joe flexed his claws; but patiently they waited, filled with escalating excitement.

They followed as he slipped out the side door. He stood with his grocery cart, looking around, then headed up the sidewalk.

Following, they kept away from the shop lights, clinging within the black shadows of steps and curbside plantings. Two blocks away, on a narrow side street, Luis tossed the bags into the back seat of an old, white Toyota. Swinging in, he took off in a cloud of black exhaust. Phew. The car was one of the last square models, a rusted vehicle with a loose front bumper and a dent in the right front fender.

Committing the license number to memory was a no-brainer, and made them smile. Luis's plate, in the standard succession of letters and numbers issued by California DMV, read 7CAT277.

Scrambling up the nearest tree to the rooftops, they took off after him, watching his lights for as long as they were visible. Before they lost him among the hills and trees, they heard his radio come on. They followed the loud Mexican music for several blocks more, up into the residential hills. As the brass and guitar grew fainter, they could catch an occasional glimpse of headlights high up the hill, flashing between the branches of oaks and pines. Far up the hills they caught one last flash as the car turned abruptly, and then the light was gone; the blast of trumpet stopped in midsquall.

"Ridgeview Road," Joe said, studying the narrow ribbon that snaked along the far crest. "He turned off Ridgeview, maybe a quarter mile up, that's the only road that goes along the side of that hill."

"Come on!" Dulcie flew from the last roof into a willow tree and dropped down to a little hiking trail. Racing along the greenbelt above the sea, the cats dodged into the bushes whenever they met a nighttime jogger or biker; and prayed they wouldn't meet anything wilder; there were coyotes up here, and bobcats.

Dallas Garza's cottage lay to the east of them, the senior ladies' house to the northeast. The houses far ahead crowded ever closer as they rose higher, half hidden among overgrown oaks and shrubs. And suddenly, Dulcie didn't like it up here.

She pushed on stubbornly, but this was not their regular hunting territory. Even in daylight the meanly crowded houses on this part of the hills seemed to her somber and forbidding; not friendly like the good-natured crowding of the village cottages, with their exuberant gardens. She slowed to catch her breath, shivering with an inexplicable fear. "We'll never find it at night, with no scent trail. If he put the car in a garage . . ."

"You're tired," Joe said softly. "You feel okay?"

"I'm fine. I just . . ."

"Let's go home," he said, untypically. "We'll come up in the morning. If they're cooking breakfast maybe it'll be chorizo, smell up the whole length of Ridgeview with Mexican spices."

She leaned against him, yawning, imagining the kit at home snug and safe in her bed, and wanting to be in her own bed. Joe studied her, concerned. "We'll find the car in the morning," he repeated, and together they headed toward home, down the long, lonely path through the chill night, then up to the roofs again, Joe's thoughts seething half with concern for Dulcie, and half with tangled questions surrounding Luis Rivas.

22

But while Joe and Dulcie hurried home, each thinking of a midnight nap, Kit was not in her bed at all, but out in the night on her own mission. Having left the rooftop apartment after Lucinda and Pedric slept, much too wide-awake to stay in, Kit lay on a copper awning above a little cigar shop, watching Chichi Barbi across the street in the Patio Café.

Chichi sat at an outdoor table, observing the shops that flanked the cigar store just below Kit. I'm a spy spying on a spy, Kit thought. That's what Dulcie would say. The curvy blonde, pretending to read the newspaper by the soft patio lights, glanced up every few seconds then wrote something down in the small spiral notebook half hidden beneath the sports section. Kit stretched out to see, but felt too impatient to remain still.

Dropping from the awning to the low-hanging cigar sign then to a raised planter, she landed among a tangle of bright cyclamens. Choosing a pair of late shoppers, she padded across the street behind them: a bare-legged woman in flat sandals and a man who smelled of the leather jacket he wore. Once across, she sprang atop the two-foot brick wall that defined the patio and approached Chichi from the rear.

She could not see the pages of the notebook until she was up on the next table, behind Chichi. Most of the other diners had left, their tables stacked with dirty plates waiting to be cleared. She had time only to glimpse Chichi's odd notations when a dark-haired waiter double-timed across the patio, his black, hard-soled shoes ringing on the bricks, and waved to shoo her away.

"Scat! Get down! Cats on the bricks, that's allowed! Cat on the table, bad, bad! You village cats know better!" Swiping at her with a dish towel, he picked up a plate that contained several scraps of leftover shrimp, set it under a chair, picked her up and set her down beside it, then began to gather up dishes. Laughing to herself, Kit scoffed up the shrimp.

Chichi glanced down, frowning at her, but then returned to her notebook. When the waiter left, Kit returned to the cleared table, to peer around Chichi's shoulder.

She got a good look at the page before

Chichi turned and saw her. But Kit was gone, racing away up a trellis to the roofs, where she disappeared from view.

Hidden among the chimneys she closed her eyes, concentrating until she saw Chichi's scribbles again, clearly in the blackness; and she held them there, committing them to a strange kind of memory that even Joe Grey and Dulcie couldn't match.

As a kitten, her one joy and wonder in life was to hide in the cold shadows where the wild band had gathered for the night, and listen to the old Celtic tales they told, the stories of their beginnings. To listen, and to remember so she could tell the stories later to herself when she was alone and frightened.

Now she saw sharply in memory Chichi's mysterious notes, as strange as the hieroglyphs from some ancient Celtic tomb. She needed Lucinda, Lucinda could write them down. Whatever this was, it was important. Holding that clear picture in her head, Kit bolted desperately for home.

Racing across her own terrace and into the bedroom, leaping onto the bed, she mewled at Lucinda and lashed her tail and patted at Lucinda's face. "Wake up! Wake up, Lucinda. Now! Wake up now!" Dropping down again, she raced to the living room and onto the desk to snatch a pad of paper and a pen in her mouth. Carrying them clumsily, she flew back to the bedroom.

Lucinda had flipped on the bedside lamp. She sat muzzily against the tumbled pillows. Beside her, Pedric still snored; he had heard nothing. "What, Kit!" Lucinda demanded. "What happened?"

Dropping the pad and pen in Lucinda's lap, Kit said, "Write. Write what I tell you . . . try to tell you . . . Oh, please."

Obediently, Lucinda wrote as Kit spelled out the senseless words.

"Dn lv, dot."

"Period?"

Kit nodded. "Then eight double dot forty, period. Next line, 2 cust. Then Bev dn shds lts off, period." Kit had to spell it all, it was very difficult. Had to talk with her eyes closed to see it all clearly.

"Next line, nine oh four period out lock, period, then, wlk wst period. Then, Dn period. Eight double dot forty, period.

"2 cust. Bev dwn shds lts off, one sec in.

"Nine double dot oh four out lock wlk wst.

"That's all," Kit said at last, collapsing among the covers.

"What kind of code *is* this? Where were you, Kit? Where did you get this?"

Kit told her where she'd been and how she'd watched Chichi making notes.

Lucinda frowned, then slowly began to translate. "Don. That would be Don Blake — Blake's Watch Shop? Don leaves the shop at eight-forty? Then . . ." Lucinda scanned the page, "then two more customers. Then fifteen minutes later, Beverly Blake pulls the shades and turns off the lights?"

Kit licked her whiskers, thinking. "Yes, that happened. I saw from the awning, I saw the lights go off, I saw the woman leave. I didn't see the man. I guess he'd already gone?"

"Bev leaves one security light on inside?" Lucinda said, frowning. "She leaves the shop at four after nine, locks the door, and walks west?"

"Yes, she did that!" the kit whispered, pleased that Lucinda was quick at these matters. To her, the little squiggles were maddening. She hoped she'd gotten them right.

But Lucinda looked at Kit and stroked her. "You are quite amazing. Do you know that you are amazing?"

Kit rubbed her head against Lucinda's hand and purred and purred. She looked up at Lucinda. "Why is all that so important that she has to write it down?"

"I'm not sure. But, Kit, maybe we're both thinking the same." Lucinda frowned. "When Beverly leaves a little later like that, she often meets Don at the grocery. They like pastrami hoagies for supper. He sometimes leaves earlier to order and pick them up. My goodness, Kit." Lucinda touched Kit's shoulder. "Chichi? Is this from Chichi Barbi?"

Kit nodded.

Lucinda's eyes widened. "Blake's Watch Shop is known for its Rolex watches and valuable antique clocks." She reached for her robe. "Maybe it isn't urgent enough to call, at night, but I . . ."

But Kit was already streaking for the living room. Leaping to the desk, she hit the phone's speaker button and punched in the station. In seconds she had Dallas Garza on the line and was describing what she had seen and what Chichi Barbi had written in her little notebook. She did not want Lucinda to call, Lucinda could never explain how she knew Chichi's secret.

The old stucco house stood jammed into the steep hillside as if it had been pressed into the earth by giant hands. It was two-storied in front, on the downhill side, one story at the rear where it pushed into the earth. This early in the spring the rising sun still hung in the south, casting a rich amber glow across the front of the worn stucco box, bringing to life patches of faded tan paint that had worn away to reveal the ancient gray plaster. The asphalt roof shingles were curled and mossy; the low picket fence beside the steep drive had perhaps never seen paint. But the rosebushes along the fence were lovingly tended, heavy with huge pink and red blooms.

The basement appeared to be a bedroom, the blinds drawn down halfway to reveal the crooked hems of limp lace curtains. The windows of the upper-floor living room were dressed with lace, too, giving the house an appearance of having not changed in decades, as if its residents had been settled within its dated rooms for a lifetime. The kind of house occupied by aging folks trying to exist on an ever-shrinking income that was eaten away by inflation and rising medical costs. The kind of house where an elderly widow might be too settled in emotionally to sell for a nice profit and move on. Such a widow might have few options, when all California real estate was out of reach for a person on a fixed income.

Joe and Dulcie had already circled the dwelling, leaping from tree to tree, peering in past lace tiebacks above the shorter lace curtains that covered the lower panes. They could see an oversized velour couch and chairs, their backs draped with Mexican weavings. And a dining table of the old-fashioned waterfall style, same as the end tables, the bedroom dressers and a round-topped radio. They saw no TV. They saw no human occupant until they reached the back bedroom.

There by the window sat a lean, wrinkled old woman with graying black hair tied back severely. Her gnarled hands were folded together in her lap. A Bible lay closed on the table beside her, next to another round-topped old-fashioned radio. This room did have a TV, an ancient box set on a little table in the far corner, facing two narrow beds. Dulcie imagined the old woman holding a rosary; though at the moment her wrinkled hands clutched only a fold of her faded apron. She sat facing the dulled glass and the backyard rose garden, but apparently was asleep in her chair. At least, she had her eyes shut. If she had spied the cats in the pepper tree, she gave no indication. Facing the bedroom door stood a cage set up on a table.

All along Dulcie had hoped it wasn't true, that there were no trapped cats. They peered in past the frilly pepper leaves and lace tiebacks at the three captives, feeling scared and sick.

The cage was made not of wire but of thin, strong bars, impenetrable as a jail cell, and was closed with a heavy padlock. The three cats slept inside huddled together, filling the small space. The white cat's tail lay across the dirty sandbox. The dark tabby with the long ears had his hind feet pressed against a dish of stale food. The bleached calico huddled miserably between them, her eyes squeezed shut.

Swallowing back a growl, Joe studied the window.

It was an old, double-hung casement. Joe's eyes widened when he saw it wasn't locked, that the round metal lock, in plain sight, was disengaged. He tried to determine if the old woman was indeed asleep. If they dropped to the sill and slipped through, would she wake and shout for Luis? She seemed, dozing in her rocker, totally unaware of them.

23

Estrella Nava sat admiring her rose garden, waiting for Maria to make breakfast, when two cats appeared in the pepper tree outside her window. Wanting to watch them but not scare them away, she pretended to be asleep. No animal liked to be stared at. They crouched among the pepper tree's delicate leaves, peering in at her through the glass. Nosy little creatures. Dark gray cat with white markings, and a dark-brown striped tabby. Not neighborhood cats, she knew every cat for blocks, they all came into her yard to pee. Hundreds of cats over the years. What were they staring at? She remained still and kept her eyes shuttered. They were looking at the cats in the cage, the cats Hernando had caught before he went away. Likely off again with some woman.

Grandson or no, Hernando wasn't her concern. She hadn't asked him and his brothers to come here. They might be family, but she didn't like them much and didn't want them here. She had asked only

Maria. Had meant for only Maria to come. She needed Maria. She didn't need those three.

This house had been her home since she came as a bride. She'd buried Manuel from this house twenty years ago, he had lain right there in his own parlor, for the viewing. She had lost their five children, but only one from this house, laid out properly with mass said over him. The others had died far away. She had only herself now, hanging onto life like a cockroach clinging to the wall, and she had Maria. Maria's brothers didn't count. Maria was the only grandchild she could trust. She didn't know how to get rid of those boys. She didn't know enough about their comings and goings to call the police, but she suspected plenty.

That would be very hard indeed, to report her dead daughter's boys, no matter what they had done. That would deeply shame her.

At least Hernando was gone, for a while. And now Delfino gone, too. From the way Luis and that Tommie McCord talked, she guessed Delfino was in jail again. Though he never seemed to stay there long. She wished they were all three in jail. Then she would let those cats free and not have to smell that cage anymore. And Maria would not have to take care of them. Crazy. Hernando and Luis trapping cats. *Muy loco*.

And now, more cats, looking in the window. What could they be looking at? If they had any sense, they'd get away before Luis saw them and caught them, too. Glancing under her lashes at her old, frail Bible that was written comfortably in her own language and that had been her own grandmother's, she wondered what life had come to. She was eighty-two years old, was losing control of her own life, and was still wondering what life was really about. Wondering what God had in store for her. She'd borne and raised and buried five children, and that was God's will, but she kept wondering if there wasn't something more. Father Mahoney would be shocked that she did not always cling to the thoughts the Church expected of her.

She did not like sharing her bedroom, even with Maria, though she loved Maria. Nor did she like that those cats in the cage watched her — as if they thought she could let them out of there. Estrella Nava crossed herself. She could only go to sleep at night with her back to them, and even then she could feel them watching.

Luis slept with the key in his pocket.

Maria had already slipped into his room at night to try to get it, but Luis kept his pants under his pillow. If Maria got caught, he'd beat her, maybe beat them both. It was shameful for a man to beat his own sister. He would surely burn in hell for that — not that Luis cared.

He never went to confession. Wouldn't drive her to mass, either. If Maria took one of the cars, he checked the mileage before they left and again when they returned. They'd rather walk, but it was fifteen blocks to the mission.

She startled when, outside the window, those cats leaped suddenly onto the sill, peering in at her. But when she struggled up out of her chair to chase them away, they spun around before she could reach the window and leaped to the pepper tree, shaking its branches, and again to the roof, and were gone. She was dozing when Maria called her to breakfast.

Maria had made fresh coffee and had baked empanadas for the two of them. It was nice when Luis and Tommie didn't eat with them. Maria didn't like to cook properly for Tommie and her brothers, she bought things in cans and packages. How would they know the difference when they washed everything down with beer?

Estrella said grace with Maria, and she said to herself a little prayer of her own, regarding Maria's fate. But her prayer for Maria's brothers was a different matter, a different kind of fate. Maria didn't need to hear that.

When the old woman had left the room, Joe and Dulcie returned to the windowsill to press against the glass, studying the cage and the three cats. The cats had waked when the old woman came to the window; they looked steadily back at them through the bars, with an intelligence and pleading that left no doubt of their true nature.

With swift claws Joe ripped a hole in the screen. Reaching through, catching his fur along the torn wire, he flipped the screen's latch free of its little ring. Pulling the screen out a few inches and slipping underneath, he and Dulcie clawed and pushed at the double-hung window. It stuck so hard they thought it must be nailed.

"More!" Joe hissed. "Push harder!" She pushed, they fought the double-hung panel until at last they were able to slide it up a few inches — but no farther. Something was stopping it; when they examined the molding, they could see where nails had been driven in to prevent it from rising higher. No human could get through, but fresh air could blow in.

Slipping under, they hit the floor as softly as they could, and leaped to the table that held the cage. They stood nose to nose with the three captives.

None of the three cringed away in fear or charged the bars with territorial rage as an ordinary cat might do, on first meeting. No one made a sound; no hiss, no threatening yowl. No claws or teeth bared in confrontation. But no one spoke. The three captives glanced toward the partially open door where at any moment the old woman or Luis might appear.

The one male was as white as snow, his long fur surprisingly fluffed and clean despite the crowded conditions. His blue eyes stared back at Joe with challenge, but it was only a good-natured tomcat challenge. The tabby male was darker than Dulcie, and long-furred, with a huge, fluffy tail. His ears were as tall and erect as those of a coyote. A strange cat, with eyes that were black-rimmed and then circled with palest cream. The female did not approach Joe and Dulcie, but pressed away against the bars as if she was afraid. She was a lovely, faded calico with a long face and a questioning look in her green eyes, the look of a cat who trusts no one.

For a long time, the three feral cats stood silently assessing Joe and Dulcie, taking their measure. The look in their eyes was a hunger for freedom, as powerful as that of three convicts on death row. It was Joe who spoke.

"Where is the key?" he said softly. "Tell me quickly." They could hear the two women talking out in the kitchen, could hear their cups clink on their saucers.

"He keeps the key in his pocket," the white tom said. "I am Cotton. I would kill him, if I could get my claws on him. The key is always there in his pocket. Maria says he puts his pants under his pillow when he goes to bed." The cat sneezed with disgust. "Can *you* get the key? Or get the lock open?" Intently, he studied Joe. "Would you dare to free us?"

The tabby tom said, "I hear them talking late at night, Maria and the old woman. *They* would free us, if Maria wasn't so afraid of her brother."

Joe and Dulcie circled the cage, examining the lock and hinges, and how the bars were set in place. Every joint was securely soldered, and there was no way those strong, thin bars could be bent or broken.

Not without human hands and the right tools. There was no way to separate the barred walls at the corners; the hinges were soldered or welded, just as was the hasp. No way out of that prison, except with the key.

"Bolt cutters?" Dulcie said.

"If we had a pair of bolt cutters, how do you propose to lift them?" Joe snapped. "Let alone put enough pressure on them!" He stared in frustration at his paws. It wasn't fair, this human ability to use tools, while a clever and intelligent cat was so cruelly hampered.

"Maybe there's a second key," Dulcie said. She had that determined, stubborn look. "If there isn't, then we have to toss Luis's bedroom, slip his pants out from under the pillow."

Joe looked at her. "Is Luis someone you'd want to catch you while you're stealing his pants?"

Dulcie flicked a nonchalant whisker. "Bring him on, I'll shred him." But her green eyes reflected fear. The truth was, this Luis Rivas, with his interest in speaking cats, left her chilled and cringing.

24

Hanni Coon's Interiors occupied a handsome, used brick storefront two blocks off Ocean, the shop's softly tinted windows displaying unique and intriguing fabrics and accessories. This week Hanni had arranged a lush tangle of hand-woven cottons and carved furniture from the coast of Africa. Some weeks, it was all silks and damasks and period pieces; other times, an esoteric collection from Italy or Latin America. As flamboyant and self-assured as Hanni herself, the shop could exhibit any number of elegant personas.

It was barely seven in the morning when Charlie and Ryan parked Ryan's truck in front of the design studio. Approaching the elegant entry with its potted trees and theatrical displays, the two women looked out of place indeed dressed in their old, worn jeans and wrinkled boots; but neither cared, nor did Hanni. Peering in through the leaded-glass door, Ryan grinned at her sister. Hanni unlocked the door and opened it to the wonderful smells of freshly brewed coffee, something with onions and cheese, and the warm French rolls for which the corner bakery was famous. She was dressed in persimmon silk pants and flowing tunic, and sandals, with dangling gold circle earrings setting off her vivid complexion and short white hair. Ryan and Charlie moved quickly to the blazing fire and stood rubbing their cold hands.

Locking the door behind them, Hanni sat down at the end of the couch to pour coffee from a silver carafe into flowered porcelain mugs.

"You are a gem!" Ryan said. "I'm starved."

"You're always starved. Come sit." Hanni flipped back a lock of white hair, and passed them plates of miniature quiches, of fresh mango and papaya with lime wedges, and the basket of warm French rolls cosseted in a linen napkin. "You can't pick out rugs on an empty stomach."

"You sure you want to do this?" Charlie said. "Sell me rugs with no markup? Your rugs . . ."

"It's a fair trade. I take no markup. You let me ride Redwing whenever you don't have the time. Now, while you two fill your tummies, I'll just flip through the rack, find a few pieces you can study while you're eating." Rising, she began to slowly swing the metal arms of the ceiling-high rack that occupied the far wall, bringing the hand-made rugs into view one at a time. Charlie could hardly eat for admiring the bright, primitive patterns. She wanted them all; she was asking Hanni the prices of several when she glanced out through the shop window and grew still.

"What?" Ryan and Hanni said together, craning to look.

"Don't turn around, Ryan. She's looking right in here. I can't believe this."

"Who?" they chorused. Ryan paused with her cup raised, glancing up sideways. Hanni stood unmoving beside the hanging rugs.

"Chichi Barbi," Charlie said. "Across the street in front of the drugstore, sitting on that bench. Staring right across at us, bold as brass. Staring right in! How much can she see, in here?"

"Can't see much, with no lights," Hanni said. "That blonde? Oh, of course — that woman who barged up to our table . . ."

Charlie nodded. "I . . . We think . . . Wilma and I think she's casing the shops for burglaries. We . . . My God, Hanni. With this new line of imported rugs, you have one of the most expensive inventories in the village."

Hanni looked alarmed for only a moment, then she grinned and shook her head.

"What?" Charlie said.

Hanni laughed. "I'm not a cop's kid for nothing. I won't show you, in case she *can* see in. I just had this baby installed, when I ordered the rugs and new rack. I can slide metal doors out from behind the walls, across the rack, and lock them. That, and the sophisticated alarm system . . . Someone could break a window, but they won't get the rugs." Leaving one of the most beautiful weavings facing Charlie, Hanni returned to the table, helped herself to breakfast, and sat down where she had a clear view of Chichi. "Does she always dress like a street-walker?"

Ryan said, "She's making notes." She looked up at her sister. "Dallas and Max have gotten a call, one of those anonymous calls, that she's casing the more expensive shops. They think she might be part of the jewelry store bunch, that they could be planning one big hit, multiple stores all at one time."

"Chichi Barbi is part of that?" Hanni said. "I've been gone so much, I haven't talked with Dallas."

"They're working on backup," Ryan said. "Contacting other districts, to borrow officers. You know Uncle Dallas and Max! They'll have more men than they need, never doubt it."

Hanni took another quiche and wolfed it. "That's the kind of thing that makes me think about sleeping in the shop for a few nights, even with my new security."

"Dallas would have your hide," Ryan said. "Putting yourself in that kind of danger."

"We're not Dallas and Scotty's little girls anymore." Hanni reached for a second helping of mangoes.

"I wouldn't be too sure about that," Ryan told her. "Can you imagine their rage, or Dad's, if they caught you hiding out in your own shop waiting for armed robbers — or if you got shot?" But as the two talked, Charlie's attention was no longer on Chichi but on the dark little shadow crouched on the roof above her as Chichi made her mysterious notes.

Kit had been sitting on the roof for some time, intent on Chichi, who, in turn, was intent on the shops across the street, particularly on Hanni Coon's Interiors. Kit had seen Charlie and Ryan go in, and guessed they were shopping for Charlie's rugs. Next door to Hanni's, the owner of the antique shop had the front door open, and the round, elderly woman was sweeping the entry and sidewalk. Next to her at the Tweed Shop, the driver of a brown UPS truck was unloading several large brown boxes. On down the street at the Gucci shop with its diamond-paned windows and small, elegant garden, the tall, slim, bald owner was watering his miniature roses and ferns. Chichi, making notes behind a newspaper that she pretended to be reading, was watching them all. And she was making the same kind of cryptic notes in her spiral-bound notebook as she had before. Kit wished she'd spell it all out; that stuff was hard to remember. Occasionally Chichi glanced at her watch as if recording the time of each occurrence. Kit did her best to commit the entries to memory — that seemed easier since Lucinda had written out the first batch for her last night, when she'd spied on Chichi in the Patio Café. Now Chichi's scribbles made sense; now all she had to do was call the station.

In Hanni's firelit shop, the three women polished off breakfast while they watched Chichi.

"I wonder if that's her real name," Hanni said. She glanced at Ryan. "Have you seen her around the village with anyone, any strangers? Has Clyde? She's living right next door to Clyde."

Ryan shrugged, and said nothing.

"Well, she has your back up," Hanni said, grinning. She glanced at Charlie. "Could she be a writer? Doing some kind of research? Why *did* she move in next to Clyde? She was so friendly, that night at Lupe's." But then Hanni frowned. "Wanting to get friendly with Dallas and Max? To get on their good side? Or to draw their attention away from someone or something?" Her eyes widened. "Distract them from the burglary that night?"

Charlie said, "It was more than an hour between dinner and the burglary. But . . . she makes me uneasy, too." She studied Ryan, her dark-lashed green eyes, her clear tan and bouncy dark hair. "You needn't be jealous over Clyde, certainly not jealous of the likes of her."

Charlie left the shop with Ryan, having selected three beautiful primitive rugs that would set her back a bundle, even at wholesale prices. Picking up her own car, she headed up the hills to inspect a new job and a new cleaning crew. Pulling out into light village traffic and turning up into the north hills, she was glad she'd have little, wizened

Mavity Flowers to oversee the two new crew members.

This was the fourth year for Charlie's Fix It, Clean It, and the business she'd built had grown to be nearly more than she could handle. But she was proud of what she had created, and it was too successful to let go; she didn't want to sell. For one thing, her customers had come to depend on her. Hers was the only service in the village where the same crew would clean the house, make all the minor household repairs, even fix fences and roofs, run errands and feed the dog.

She would feel ashamed at discontinuing the service, at letting down her regulars — to say nothing of the very nice income. She was helping to pay for the new construction on their house, and would, in turn, take a tax write-off on her new office-studio. What she badly needed was a manager for the cleaning business; so far she'd found no one she trusted who wanted to take on the extra work and responsibility.

Winding up into the hills, checking her map to make sure of the address, she was a block from the new job when she hit the brakes. Stopping dead in the empty residential street, she stared up a long, steep driveway.

But then hastily she pulled on past; she

didn't stop again until she'd parked a block away, pulling in behind her old blue van with CHARLIE'S FIX IT, CLEAN IT lettered on the side. She sat a moment behind the wheel, smiling, then flipped open her cell phone.

How often did this happen? She could hardly believe what she'd seen.

The house she had passed was a tall, old stucco badly in need of paint, two stories in front, one story behind, old-fashioned lace curtains at the windows, unpainted picket fence along the steep drive. Halfway up the drive, pulled to the side into some concealing bushes, or perhaps so another car could go past into the closed garage, stood a brown Toyota pickup.

It was maybe ten years old, dull and battered and with a dented tailgate and a missing back bumper. It was without doubt one of the two getaway cars the department had ID'd. Glancing in her rearview mirror, she hit the button for the station.

25

Max Harper was headed downstairs to the department's indoor firing range when the dispatcher came out from behind her counter and called down the hall to him. "You might want to take this, Captain. Caller won't give her name." Mabel smiled; she knew that voice. She didn't know who it belonged to, no one did, but this was a caller the chief always found of interest. "I tried to take the message," she said, amused. "She wasn't about to do that."

Harper turned into his office and pushed the door closed, shutting out the joking and laughing of several officers heading downstairs. As he sat down at his cluttered desk, he could hear through the floor the faint, random popping of the first group as they fired at the moving targets. With his usual wariness at talking with this particular snitch, he picked up the phone.

"Captain Harper, I watched that woman again. She was making notes about the shopkeepers again early this morning before opening time. Just after seven. The Gucci shop, and Hanni Coon's studio. Maybe it isn't important, but . . ."

"I'm always interested," Harper said softly. She sounded hesitant this morning, as if she thought he might not like her calling. "I always welcome your calls." He sure didn't want to lose her; this snitch and her partner had been responsible for a considerable number of arrests and prosecutions. Hitting the RECORD button, he snatched up a pen and pad. Harper liked to hedge his bets, not rely totally on electronic equipment.

"That same blond woman, writing down when people get to their shops or when they close up, if they open the door early to sweep or take deliveries. This morning she wrote down that Mrs. Harkins swept the front walk and watered the flowers then locked the front door again and went down the street for a cup of coffee at Ronnie's Bakery. She wrote down the time that she left, and how long she was gone."

Where had the snitch been, to see all that *and* to see what Chichi had written? He burned to ask her how she'd done that, ask her some details of her own movements, but she'd hung up on him.

She told him she had seen Charlie and

Ryan inside Hanni's studio, looking at rugs, and that made him smile. Charlie would be high just looking at those rugs — the soul of an artist, he thought. Same kind of kick *he* got from locking up some skuzzy felon.

When the snitch had hung up, he sat at his desk trying to put down the uneasy feeling her calls gave him.

Yet every one of these calls, though they made him squirm, had supplied the department with valuable leads. Facts and evidence they might otherwise never have uncovered; or would have done so only after a long and expensive, drawn-out series of searches. Dallas called it uncanny. Max didn't like the word "uncanny."

Pouring the last of his cold, overcooked coffee into a mug, he sipped the bitter brew, studying the notes he had made, taking advantage of a moment of seclusion that his private space and closed door offered.

This kind of solitude had been unavailable when the department was one big open squad room with its clatter and bantering officers and constantly ringing phones. He didn't miss the busy friction and din. His new, well-organized space added up to a welcome sense of ease. The tall oak bookcases, Charlie's drawings of Bucky on the paneled walls, the leather couch and chair and the handsome Oriental rug — Charlie had combined the furnishings to create a comfortable retreat where he could enjoy a few moments of peace — except for, as at the moment, whatever edgy feeling he brought in with him.

Chewing over his notes, he at last gave up wondering how she'd gotten the information, and rose to head downstairs. He stopped when Mabel put through another call. "It's your wife, Captain. It's Charlie."

He returned to his office, picking up the phone to Charlie's excited voice.

"I think I found the second car, the brown truck. Toyota pickup, maybe 1980 or so. No back bumper, and a dented tailgate." She gave him the address up in the north hills, described the house and how the car was parked.

"How close are you? Get away from it, Charlie. Did you see the plate?"

"I couldn't see the plate for bushes. I didn't want to get out and be seen from the house. I drove on past."

"Good. We'll take a look. Don't go back there, for any reason."

When they'd hung up, he called for two cars to meet him several blocks away from where the truck was parked. As he headed out, Dallas met him by the front desk.

Joe and Dulcie crouched beside the metal cage describing for the three captives how Charlie had freed the brindled tom from the humane trap. "That's Stone Eye," Coyote said, narrowing his ringed eyes and flattening his long, tufted ears. "Stone Eye, our self-appointed leader. Your friend should have let him rot. How did *he* get himself caught?"

"Hitler with claws," Cotton said, hissing. Both the white tom, and the dark, striped tom lashed their tails and kneaded their claws, crouched as if for battle.

But the bleached calico female clung in the corner of the cage looking as fearful as if she faced Stone Eye himself. "Brute," Willow hissed. "His henchmen are just as bad. I'm not going back there. If . . . if we get out," she said, with a frightened mewl.

"We'll get you out," Dulcie whispered, pressing against the bars to nuzzle Willow. "But if Hernando's dead, why are they keeping you?" Dulcie's green eyes widened. "Do they *know* he's dead? Or do they think he's coming back?"

"They know," Cotton said. "They saw it in the paper. They haven't told Maria and the old lady — not that there's any love lost."

"Then why are they keeping you here?" Dulcie repeated, frowning.

"Hernando talked wild," Coyote said. "His brothers believed him. Foolish talk about performing cats on TV and in the movies, about Hollywood and big houses and expensive cars. Tons of money, like in the newspapers and on TV we hear through people's windows. He could never make us do those things; no cat I know would want to live like that." Coyote licked his striped shoulder, his circled eyes narrowed with rage.

"He might *make* you do those things," Joe said.

"What, torture us?" Cotton hissed. "What kind of performers would he have, if we were half dead?"

Dulcie said, "Maybe he thought that soft beds and servants and gourmet food . . ."

"He wouldn't ply me with such things," Willow mewed. She had a small little voice that didn't seem to match her elegant stature and markings. "I would not be slave to some hoodlum!"

"Luis has to know that's a foolish dream," Joe said.

"There's more to it," Cotton said, licking his silky white paw. "Hernando thought we knew something about them stealing cars and about two old murders, in L.A., wherever that is."

"We don't know anything," Willow said, growing bolder and coming to press against the bars. "We couldn't make much of what we heard. And what would we do about it? Go to the police?"

Dulcie and Joe exchanged a glance; they said nothing.

Cotton's blue eyes were filled with disgust. "They have wild ideas about us. But the truth is, we *are* different. Given their greed, and their superstitious fears that we could tell what they've done, they have no intention of letting us go."

Coyote flicked his tall, canine-like ears at a sound from the front of the house. They all listened. A car was pulling up the drive. Dulcie glanced toward the window, but Joe headed for the shadowed hall. Dulcie pressed close to him as he made for the front bedroom.

The unoccupied room stunk of male human and stale cigarette smoke. With its little damask chair and delicately carved dresser and vanity, clearly this room belonged to the old lady. Looked as if the men had evicted her, taken it for their own. Smelling fresh cigarette smoke from outside the open window, they slipped up onto the sill.

A blue Camry stood in the drive behind an old brown Toyota truck that was pulled off into the bushes. The windows of the Camry were open; cigarette smoke drifted out, and in through the bedroom window. Luis and Tommie sat in the front seat, their voices sharp and angry.

"Those dummies," Tommie said almost in a whisper. "Bringing the truck back here, parking it in plain sight! If the cops made that truck . . ."

"They didn't make the truck. No one saw the truck!" Luis snapped. "Dumb bastards. What was Anselmo thinking. Get over here and drive!"

"But if we can get it in the garage . . ."

"No damn room in the garage, old woman has junk in there up the wazoo."

"If I shove everything over, I can squeeze it in. Ought to set a match to that stuff."

"Shut up, Tommie. Go on, back the car out! Meet me over there!" Luis swung out of the car and into the truck, leaning down, apparently to fish the keys from under the seat. Tommie backed down the drive, hit the brakes, and squealed off down the street. Luis started the truck, swung a sharp U-turn in the drive, plowing down three rosebushes, and took off after him.

From the windowsill, the cats glanced

down the hall in case Maria stopped clattering dishes and came out of the kitchen. "They *were* the ones," Dulcie said with satisfaction. "How many more men are there? Harper needs to know where they are."

"Let's see how much more we can pick up," Joe said, "before we call the station." And he dropped to the floor, to search the room.

The men were gone maybe ten minutes. When the blue car came scorching back and Luis and Tommie headed in the house, the cats were under the Victorian dresser, crouching at the back among the cobwebby shadows.

Luis hated that drive down from San Francisco. Too many damn trucks. They'd been up all night and he needed sleep. This stupidity with Anselmo and the truck didn't help his mood. Stepping out of the car, he hustled on into the house, Tommie behind him. He'd *told* Anselmo to keep the damn truck out of sight. Just because Anselmo's landlady came snooping was no excuse. Well, he'd knocked Anselmo around before, it was good for morale, let them know who was boss.

"Four men crammed in one room," Tommie said, "they were bound to get edgy."

"Edgy's not all they'll get." Luis wanted his breakfast. Shouldering down the hall, he yelled for Maria, then saw the light on in the kitchen, saw the dirty plates in the sink. He picked up the coffeepot and shook it. Still hot but nearly empty. Damn woman, lounging around in the kitchen when he was out, but never there when he wanted her. Shouting again for her, he sat down at the table and pulled a roll of bills from his pocket. Tommie had gone to wash, always had to wash when he got home, said staying up all night made him feel skuzzy. Said his hair itched. Well, red hair wasn't healthy, he ought to know that. Tommy'd said he didn't want a spicy Mexican breakfast. But he had no say in the matter. It was his choice to run with them, not theirs. If he didn't like it, he could cut out.

"Maria! Get your tail out here! Get us some breakfast." Man was up all night, driving half the night, he needed to eat. Why didn't she think of that!

Maria came into the kitchen sullenly, scowling at him. She jerked open the refrigerator, pulled out a box of eggs, a package of chorizo, pepper sauce, tortillas. As the frying pan heated and the kitchen filled with the spicy smell of frying chorizo, Luis counted the money.

On the floor beside the dresser under which the cats crouched was an overflowing wastebasket. Stuffed inside, among the crumpled candy and cigarette packs, was a wad of crocheted doilies that must have covered the dresser and vanity and chair arms. The cats pawed through these and through the trash but found no gas receipts, no receipts or bills of any kind. In the closet, jeans and shirts were tossed on the floor with a tangle of men's shoes. The twin beds were unmade, the blankets half on the floor. Dulcie imagined the room as it must once have been, with the care that Maria's abuela would have given it.

She had seen in Maria's room photographs of several generations, from Abuela down to babies and small children. She imagined this house full of children and grandchildren. Maybe little Luis and his two brothers before they grew big and mean, and the child Maria still innocent. She imagined them growing up and drifting away. It seemed strange for a good Latino family to wander apart. Dulcie preferred the loud, quarreling, close and happy Latino families who lived around Molena Point. From beneath the dresser, the cats could see straight down the hall, the kitchen table in their direct line of sight.

Dulcie's eyes widened as Luis removed a large bundle of greenbacks from his jacket pocket. "That's some bundle," she whispered to Joe. "How much has he got? There was no cash taken during the burglary."

"You want a closer look? Ask him a few questions?" Joe whispered back dryly.

Maria stood at the stove cooking breakfast; the house was redolent of frying chorizo. She glanced at Luis several times, her eyes wide at the stash of money. As if she, too, was wondering.

"Fence," Joe said softly. "I'll bet he fenced the jewels. Maybe he just got home."

Tommie emerged from the bathroom and went on down the hall to the kitchen. He looked unhappily at his plate of eggs and chorizo, ignored the tortillas, and took a slice of white bread from the package Maria handed him. Luis and Maria began to argue in Spanish. The cats knew only a few words, not enough to make sense of it. Tommie replied to Luis in Spanish; but he spoke the language without grace, with a flat American accent.

Dulcie didn't like being in the house with these men. She didn't see how they were going to get the key when it was in Luis's pocket and then under his pillow. But they had to try, they had to free the caged cats. Luis was complaining about being up all night, so maybe they *had* been to a fence, maybe in the city. Maybe, tired and full of breakfast, they'd sleep.

And, yes! The next minute, when Maria asked Luis if he wanted more eggs, he snapped at her and rose, shoving back his chair. "I'm going to bed! Keep the damned house quiet." Dulcie glanced at Joe, excited because they could get on with searching. But scared out of her paws to try for the key. When Luis went to bed, would he take his pants off? In the daytime?

No cat would be fool enough to slip a paw into Luis's pocket when Luis was still in the pants.

Or would he? She looked at Joe, and wasn't so sure.

They drew deeper under the dresser as Luis headed down the hall — and as another car pulled up the drive. They heard its door open, and then the click of high heels. The front door opened. A woman called out: "Luis? Maria? You home?" Chichi's voice. The cats listened to her strident, whisker-wilting giggle as her high heels clicked across the entry. Luis, coming down the hall, quickly stuffed the roll of bills in his

317

26

"The list is shaping up," Chichi sang out, waving a notebook at Luis and taking his arm to turn him back toward the kitchen. They sat down at the table across from Tommie; she dropped her purse on an empty chair. Silently Maria set a cup of coffee before her, then returned to shoving dishes into the ancient dishwasher. Their voices lowered, as if not wanting Abuela to hear, Luis and Tommie studied the notebook.

Listening, Joe slipped out from under the dresser, heading for the hall. Dulcie grabbed the skin of his rump in her teeth. "Let me," she said through jaws clenched firmly onto his hide. "I don't have white markings, I can fade into the carpet. And Chichi's seen you. I could be any stray that wandered in."

Joe looked at her doubtfully, but he drew back. His look said clearly that if anyone laid a hand on her, he'd skin them with his bare claws.

319

Creeping down the hall, Dulcie hugged the baseboard, her belly sliding along the faded runner. Just outside the kitchen she melted into the shadow cast by the partially closed door. The room smelled of chorizo and sour dishes. Luis sat with his elbows on the table where he had spread out a large sheet of paper that must be the map. As Chichi read off her notes, he repeated the names of several village streets and shops, which she helped him find. Dulcie peered up at the tall refrigerator, longing for a higher perch from which she could see.

Was this woman the brains of their burglaries, or only the messenger gathering information? Listening to Chichi's detailed rundown of the times that the jewelry stores and other shops opened, of how many employees were there to both start and end the day, whether male or female and approximate age, Dulcie was soon so wired she could hardly be still. They were taking great care with their plans.

Chichi had run her surveillance both morning and evening, as if the thieves had not yet decided the best times for the burglaries. *Were* they planning multiple burglaries all at one time? They were smug indeed to think they'd get away with that. With the information Dallas and Harper now had, and would soon have, these hoods would be in jail before they broke the first window.

"People will be coming in all week," Chichi said. "Cluttering up the streets. And a jazz parade on Saturday. I don't think . . ."

"Cops'll be up to their ears," Luis said, smiling with satisfaction. "Snarled traffic, a real mess. Their minds'll be on tourists and crowd control."

"You want traffic and crowds, why not wait until the big antique car show instead of this local yokel jazz festival. I don't see . . ."

"That's months away. I've got twenty idle guys about to go nuts. You think they're going to wait all summer?"

"Give them something else to do. Take them up the coast, hit a few beach resorts."

"You want to pay their gas and rent and food bills? Twenty guys? And that antique car show, they'll bring in every cop on the coast *and* the whole damn CHP. Those cars are worth a mint. Cops cluttering the streets everywhere. That's the trouble, working with a woman!"

"I got the information, didn't I? And I'll tell you this, Luis," she said sullenly. "You're going to use the jazz festival, you better look at the early evening closings, when the town's jammed. Some of those stores'll stay open, but the jewelry stores won't. And your cover's no good, first thing in the morning. No one'll be on the *streets* in the morning. All the mornings I've wasted getting up early . . ."

"This stuff's none of your business anyway. You do what you're told, you don't tell *me* what to do. It was different in L.A." He looked her up and down, taking in her tight pink sweater that offered plenty of cleavage, her skintight black jeans. "Half of these, you got no closing time. I said to . . ."

"I got closing times on the jewelry stores. I'm not finished." She flipped the notebook page. "Here's the frigging closings." But, confronted with Luis's rising rage, she seemed to draw back, turning suddenly as docile as Maria.

When Luis finished marking his map, Chichi tore out the pages, handed them to him, and put the empty notebook in her purse. Where had her spunk gone, all of a sudden? The woman's brassy nerve seemed just to have vanished.

Did Luis beat her? Dulcie could see no marks on her, but that didn't prove anything. The puzzled tabby cat remained crouched on the faded hall runner until the men began yawning again and started to rise; then she streaked for the bedroom.

Their shoes scuffed down the hall as she fled under the dresser, ramming into Joe. She was barely hidden when they came in. Luis sat down on the unmade bed nearest the door and pulled off his shoes, dropping them on the floor on a tangle of blanket. His feet smelled awful. How often did he wash those socks? Was he going to take off his pants and shove them under his pillow, or keep them on? The cats grew so nervous, waiting, that they could hardly breathe. From the kitchen they could hear Chichi and Maria talking softly among the clicking sounds of cutlery and plates and running water.

What would they be talking about, dumpy little Maria who looked so browbeaten, and brazen Chichi Barbi with her carefully collected hit list — brazen until a few minutes ago? Yet the two women seemed close; there was a gentle sympathy in their voices, which intrigued Dulcie.

Joe laid his ears back in annoyance when Luis lay down on the bed fully clothed, tucking his feet under a lump of the blanket. Well, Dulcie thought, so much for that. How comfortable could it be to sleep with one's pants on? That was another plus to being a cat: no confining pants and shoes. Tommie pulled down the yellowed blinds under the lace curtains, stripped down to his shorts, and dropped his clothes on the floor, grumbling as he pulled up the tangle of covers and crawled underneath. The cats waited some time before both men were snoring. Then they slipped out from under the dresser and, despite any fear Dulcie might harbor, Joe reared up against Luis's bed, looking.

He was just reaching out a paw when Chichi came down the hall.

Quick as a pair of terrified mice the cats were under the dresser again, crouching in the dusty dark peering out at her. She stood in the doorway observing the sleeping men.

When she was satisfied that their snores were indeed real, she came on in and began to toss the room. The cats looked at each other, fascinated and amazed. What was coming down, here?

Chichi was as methodical as a cat herself as she searched in and under every piece of furniture. When she approached the dresser, they nearly smothered each other, pressing back into the darkest corner. She slid open the drawers above them almost soundlessly, and rifled through. Then, in the closet, she investigated every garment, felt into every pocket. She didn't approach Luis, but she went hastily through Tommie's pockets, lifting his heaped clothes with distaste.

Only then, dropping Tommie's wrinkled shirt back atop his pants, she approached Luis's sleeping form.

When she was two feet from him, Luis snorted. She jerked her hand back. She waited, then stepped near again. She wouldn't be looking for the key. Did she mean to take the money? He muttered and turned over, throwing out his arm, and she was gone, backing out of the room, apparently losing her nerve. She was halfway down the hall when Luis opened his eyes blearily. But then he only grunted and turned over, and was soon snoring once more.

Chichi did not return.

Dulcie had thought Chichi Barbi was a nervy, brazen young woman who wasn't afraid of much. Who maybe hadn't the sensibilities to be afraid. Now, she wasn't sure. She didn't know what to make of Chichi — brassy and confrontational one minute, cowed and uncertain the next.

But whatever the truth, Chichi *was* conspiring with these crooks, was diligently helping them. Dulcie watched warily as Joe approached Luis again, his paw reaching; and she moved close behind him. If Luis woke and snatched Joe, the more teeth and claws the better.

Luis lay on his back, his snores loud and rhythmic. The cats were so close that their noses stung not only with the smell of his feet but with his garlic breath. Rearing up with his left paw against the edge of the mattress, Joe eased his right paw toward Luis's pants pocket. And Dulcie slipped silently up onto the nightstand, ready to spring into Luis's face if he grabbed for Joe. Ready to defend her tomcat, she looked as lethal as a coiled snake.

Faster than she could blink, Joe's paw slipped into Luis's pocket.

Reaching delicately to the bottom of the pocket, Joe felt two car keys on their chain. Then, among a tangle of loose change, he could feel another key fob. Round, with some kind of raised emblem, attached by its short chain to a lone, fat, stubby key. That sure felt like a padlock key.

Soft as butterfly wings, his paw caressed the hard metal. Gently he hooked his claws into the chain. Luis grunted, stopped snoring and scratched his leg. He turned over, reaching automatically to his pocket, in his sleep. He nearly touched Joe. The tomcat panicked, reared away from him and dropped off the bed — without the key.

Angry at his own clumsiness, Joe wondered if he had tickled Luis. He crouched beside the bed, scowling, until Luis began snoring again with little uneven huffs, then he slipped up for another try.

Luis's snores continued unbroken until Joe's paw was again in his pocket; but suddenly Luis jerked upright, thrashing his arm, flailing out, then rubbing his eyes. Joe was gone, vanished beneath the bed, Dulcie beside him.

Directly above them, Luis sat up, bouncing the springs so close to their heads they ducked. Swinging his legs to the floor, he sat on the edge of the bed yawning, then, in his socks and his pants but no shirt, he headed down the hall to the bathroom. Not until they heard the shower running did the cats come out from under the bed, to crouch before the closed bathroom door.

Dulcie didn't want to go into that small closed space with Luis. Joe leaped, grabbing at the knob until he had a secure grip between his clutching paws. Swinging with all his weight, he turned the knob. Beside him, Dulcie pushed the door open.

The shower water pounded, its thunder

hiding whatever noise they might make, its steam and the mottled shower door hiding them from Luis's view — they hoped. The room was like a sauna, steam blurring the porcelain fixtures. Behind the obscure glass door, the ghost of Luis's squat, broad figure genuflected and scrubbed.

On the closed toilet seat lay Luis's wadded-up pants. Faster than the speed of the pounding water, Joe's paw was into the pocket among the tangle of keys and loose change. This time he knew what he was looking for. Beyond the shower door Luis bent one knee as if washing his feet — an indication to Joe that he was about to finish up and step out, that any minute he would slide the door open and snatch a towel from the rod. Glancing at Dulcie, he saw a sharp mix of fear and predatory determination in her wide green eyes.

Pawing deeper into the pocket, he tried to separate the little fob with its single fat key from the other keys, and to catch its chain in his claws. At last, with it securely hooked, he drew it out.

The fob at the other end of the chain held the carved picture of a long-tailed quetzal bird, its image half worn away from use. Gripping the bird in his teeth, he pushed quickly out the door, Dulcie by his side.

When, behind them, the shower door slid open, Dulcie swallowed a mewl. They shouldered the bathroom door closed and were gone, twin shadows streaking down the hall into the empty living room and behind the couch, the first piece of furniture they encountered.

Crouched in the shadows, they listened to the two women in the kitchen. ". . . Must be tired, Maria," Chichi was saying. "Abuela to take care of, Luis and Tommie to cook for, and those cats to tend, cleaning their cages . . . Would you like to get out for a while?" There was a jingle of keys. "Go on, take some time for yourself. Bring home some groceries, you can say you were doing the shopping. Go have a sundae, a look in the store windows. I'll take care of Abuela, see that she's comfortable, make her a nice cup of tea."

Slipping through the living room and into the dining room, the cats peered through a second door into the kitchen. Maria stood by the table, pulling on a red jacket over her blue sweat suit. "You sure you don't mind?"

"Go while you have the chance." Chichi hugged Maria. "Before Luis comes out of the shower. I'll tell them you had to go to the store."

"That we were out of beans and milk,"

Maria said quickly. "Chorizo. Onions. And sand, that cat sand."

"Why does he keep them? What's he mean to do with them, now that Hernando's . . ." Pausing, Chichi glanced toward Abuela's bedroom.

Maria's expression went solemn. "He . . . Hernando said they were worth money. Luis believed him. He's too stubborn to turn them loose, he's sure he can sell them, make a bundle. I guess that's all," she said uncertainly.

"Stray cats! Not worth shooting. And the poor things stuffed in that cage. I'll clean the cage before I go, so it won't smell so bad."

"You can't clean it, Luis has the key. Can't clean it properly. You can reach the scoop in between the bars, though."

Chichi sighed. "How can a grown man be so stupid?" She gave Maria a little shove. "Go on, before he comes out." The two women looked at each other with a bond of friendship, and Maria slipped away, out the front door. The cats heard her start the car and back down the drive.

In the kitchen, Chichi immediately resumed her search, going through the pockets of Luis's windbreaker that he'd left hanging over a chair. When she pulled out a small, empty, black silk bag, Joe swallowed back a hiss of surprise that almost gave them away.

"So," the tomcat said when they were behind the couch again, "she did give the bag to Luis. And Luis came in this morning counting money." Luis had gone back to bed, they could hear his snores chorusing off-key with Tommie's. "*Is* she looking for the money? Or something else, too? Go on, Dulcie. Follow her. I'll go in Abuela's room; if she's asleep I'll open the lock."

Dulcie looked at him uncertainly. She didn't like to split up. And she was afraid of Chichi.

But what was the woman going to do if she saw her? She was a cat, totally innocent; and she was faster and more agile than Chichi. Not liking to act the coward in front of Joe, she slipped quickly away following Chichi, padding down the shadowed hall toward the stairs with only a small shiver, only a few beads of sweat on her paws.

27

Dallas Garza was preparing to release Dufio Rivas. The detective had sent three men up the hills to watch the old house where Charlie had spotted the brown pickup. Two officers were wearing gray fatigues marked with Molena Point Gas Service logos, and were driving a gas company truck. The third officer, stationed just down the block, was dressed in greasy jeans and was changing the tire on an old car he had pulled to the curb. Dallas had a fourth man waiting near the jail to follow Dufio when he left.

He had checked the ownership of the hillside house, and knew it belonged to an Estrella Nava, an eighty-two-year-old village resident who had lived there alone since her husband died twenty years before. The detective had run the Washington state plates of the truck Charlie spotted, and had run the Nevada plates of the car they picked up the night of the burglary. That night, the truck's plate had not been visible. Both plates came up stolen. Neither belonged to the vehicle to which it was affixed. Dallas had some concern that when they released Dufio, he would spot the tails they had on him. Max didn't think so. "We could probably send him home with a chaperone, he wouldn't catch on."

"He's stayed out of jail better than his brothers," Dallas said. "Just hope he hightails it for the Nava house, gives us reason to get a search warrant. Charlie's pretty sure that was the truck?"

"I've never known Charlie to be wrong about what she's seen. She's an artist, she looks and she remembers."

"Let's get Dufio moving, maybe we'll see some action."

Harper rose, grinning at Garza's unrest, and they headed down the hall and out the back door. Crossing the officers' parking lot within its chain-link fence, they entered the small village jail.

Molena Point jail was a holding facility for short-term detainees and for prisoners awaiting trial or being tried. Once a sentence was imposed, those sentenced were moved to the county jail or to a state facility. There were four small cells, two on either side of the concrete hall. Four bunks to each cell. Down at the end were two large tanks, one on either side, each built to accommodate ten prisoners. The right-hand tank was empty except for Dufio. Its other three occupants had been released an hour earlier, when they had sobered up sufficiently and been bailed out by their wives. Dufio Rivas lay stretched out on his back on a top bunk under a rough prison blanket, his face turned slightly to the wall. Maybe the drunks had kept him awake all night, maybe now in the welcome silence he was trying to catch up on his sleep. Dallas unlocked the door.

"Come on, Dufio. You're free to go home."
Dufio didn't stir.

"Wake up Dufio," Garza said. "Get the hell out of here." When Dufio didn't move, Dallas drew his weapon and stepped over to shake the prisoner's shoulder. Before reaching him, he swung around.

"Call the medics!" He rolled Dufio over fast, generating a last few spurts of blood. The man's face and neck were torn, a mass of blood. Dallas reached uselessly for the carotid artery; he couldn't be breathing.

There was a bullet hole through Dufio's neck, and two in his head. Small holes, as if from a .22 — but big enough for the purpose. Max, having called for medical assistance, glanced up at the cell window studying the bars.

The bars were all in place. He looked at the branches of the oak tree outside, but nothing seemed different. Activating his radio again, he put out an arrest order for the three sobered-up drunks who had, an hour earlier, been released to their wives. In seconds, they heard the back door open, heard officers running out to their units and taking off. The same action would be occurring at the front of the building. The emergency van came screaming through the chain-link gate, and two medics ran in with their emergency packs.

Climbing up to stand on the lower bunk, they began to work on Dufio, stanching the last trickle of blood and checking for a heartbeat. But soon they turned away, shaking their heads. "You call the coroner, Captain?"

Max nodded, looking up as the coroner arrived, stepping into the long hall and heading for the back cell. John Bern was a slight, balding man with glasses. He glanced at Max and Dallas, stepped up on the bottom bunk as the medics had, and began to examine Dufio.

"Shot from the back," he said, turning to look down at Max. He glanced around the cell, then up at the window as the other officers had done. He asked about the position of the body before the officers moved it, then he readied his camera and began to take pictures.

He ended with several close-ups of the hole in the mattress and, once the body was removed, he employed forceps to carefully pick out the one bullet he could locate, from the thick cotton padding.

"Twenty-two," Bern said. "Guess the other slugs are still in him." The overhead light reflected off Bern's glasses, off his bald spot, and off the fragment of lead he held in his forceps. "Good shooting, to kill him with a twenty-two." He glanced up again at the barred window. "Like hunting deer from a tree stand, the way they do in the South. Only this was more like shooting fish in a barrel. Quarry can't run, can't get away. Was probably sound asleep, never knew what hit him."

They searched the cell but found no casing. They heard two more squad cars leave. Garza sent Brennan to search the yard, meaning to join him. He wanted to get up in that tree, maybe lift some fiber samples. Max turned and was gone, they heard him double-timing across the parking lot and into the building, heading for the control center.

Garza remained with Bern until Dufio, tucked into a body bag, was taken away to the morgue. Strange, Garza thought, watching the medics carry Dufio away. He had an almost tender feeling for the poor sucker with his long list of screwups. Strange, too, that it wasn't a screwup that finally got him. Not directly, anyway.

But who would want to kill the poor guy? He watched Bern collecting lint and hair samples, giving the cell and bunk a thorough but probably fruitless going-over. This cell housed a vast turnover of men, all of whom would have left traces of themselves. But John Bern was more than meticulous. At last Dallas turned away, his square, tanned face pulled into unhappy lines, his black-brown eyes dark with annoyance that someone had committed a murder in their jail.

With Maria gone in Chichi's car, Chichi herself downstairs, and Luis and Tommie asleep, Joe approached Abuela's room, the key clutched uncomfortably between his incisors, making him drool. Crouching beside the bedroom door, he looked across at Abuela. Sound asleep in her rocking chair, softly huffing. Her cane leaned against the chair arm. The window was closed now, and the shades pulled down to soften the harsh morning light.

The three cats looked down at him

through the bars so forlornly they made Joe's stomach flip. But then Coyote saw the key, and his yellow eyes blazed. At once the other two pushed against the bars, in their terrible hunger for freedom. He only hoped he could manage this. He had never yet been able to manipulate a key; not that he hadn't tried. This time, he had to pull it off.

Shouldering the bedroom door nearly closed, hoping no one would hear the tiny squeak of its hinges, he waited, listening. No sound from the hall. Abuela slept on. He leaped to the table beside the cage, the metal key and chain dangling from his teeth like the intestines of a metal mouse.

All three captives nosed against the bars sniffing at the key, their eyes wide and expectant. None of the three spoke.

Bending his head, Joe placed a paw on the dangling key fob and fumbled the key into position between his front teeth. He had the key in position — but when he guided the key into the hole in the dangling padlock, immediately the lock swung away.

He looked at his three silent observers. But how could they help? The bars of the cage door were too close together to allow even a paw through, to steady the lock. And the way the lock dangled, every tiny movement sent it shifting.

Rolling down onto his shoulder, on the four-inch strip of table, he peered up from that angle, hoping he didn't swallow the key. Reaching up with careful paws, humping up as close as he could get, he tried to line up the key.

Voilà! It was in position! Carefully he eased the key in, his heart pounding. He was starting to turn the key when it fell out, fell into his mouth and nearly into his throat, scaring him so badly he flipped over, coughing and hacking.

Spitting the key out, he sat trying to calm his shattered nerves. But he took the key up again, tried again. Again it fell, again he nearly choked. Again and again, a half dozen frightening failures before, on the seventh try, slowly, carefully twisting his head with the key in place in the lock, it turned!

The lock snapped open. He wanted to yowl with triumph. Employing his claws in a far more natural operation, he hooked the padlock, lifted it, and twisted it out. It fell with a thud, the key still in it. Six round eyes stared at it, and stared at him with wonder. Eagerly they pressed against the door, as Joe clawed to free the hasp.

A sound in the hall; a shuffle behind him. The bedroom door flew open, banging against the wall. Hands grabbed him, big, hard hands. He flipped over fast and sunk his teeth and twenty claws into Luis Rivas's arm, biting, raking, tearing him, tasting Luis's blood.

Dulcie padded soundlessly behind Chichi down the stairs to the lower floor. She watched the blonde in her tight sweater and tight jeans stretch up to the highest bookshelves and closet shelves, searching, then crouch to peer under chairs and dressers, to feel beneath cushions and to open drawers. What was she looking for? If Chichi's job was to help Luis and Tommie scope out their hits, to assess the number of staff and the best times to make those hits, then what was this stealthy search? Chichi seemed most interested in small niches, small drawers, cubbyholes. Not until Chichi had entered the small laundry room did Dulcie catch a whiff of what she might be seeking.

Dulcie did not want to go into the laundry and be trapped in that tiny space with only one way out. She crouched in the shadows beside the door. The concrete room stunk of dirty laundry from the overflowing hamper that stood beside the washer, and of laundry soap and a whiff of bleach. But Dulcie caught, as well, another scent. A pungent oil, a smell she knew. She sniffed deeply.

As sure as she had whiskers, that was gun oil. The same as Wilma used to clean her .38, the same smell that was always present around the PD, the smell of well-oiled handguns.

The smell came from beneath the washer. Chichi was crouched on the concrete floor looking under, pressing her face against the washer, squinting into the dark; she was bound to smell it.

But apparently not, with the other stinks in the room, and with Chichi's own sweet perfume, which carried considerable heft. Dulcie waited, tensed to race away. Chichi squinted and looked, but at last she rose and left the room, heading down the hall. Slipping into the laundry behind her, Dulcie peered under washer and dryer into the same shadows Chichi had scanned.

The gun lay far back beneath the washer, where maybe only a cat would be able to make out its dim shape. So far back that a human, even if he found it with a flashlight or knew it was there, could only fish it out with a stick.

Slipping behind the dryer, pressed in between it and the wall, she crept back behind the washer. Making sure the gun was pointed away from her, she lay down and reached a paw in, and gingerly fished it out by the grip, careful not to turn it toward her or touch the trigger.

There it lay, under her nose, in the dusty dark space between the wall and the washer. A blue-black revolver with a roughly textured wooden grip and, on the side of the grip, a round embossed metal seal that showed a rearing horse and read *Colt*. A revolver very like Wilma's Colt .38 special.

This had to be what Chichi was searching for. What crime had the revolver been used for? How did she know, or suspect, that it was here in this house? And what had she intended to do with it? Or, after all, was she searching for something else, and not the gun?

Carefully pushing it out of sight again, as far under as she could, she backed out of the tight space, shook off the dust, and hurried to catch up with Chichi.

Like two mimes, one silently mimicking the other, she followed the young woman in her futile search. Padding unseen through the dim rooms, Dulcie was Chichi's shadow.

Only when the blonde had exhausted every crevice, or thought she had, did she head back upstairs. She was halfway up when shouting erupted from above: Luis's enraged yells coming from Abuela's bedroom, accompanied by furious tomcat yowls as if Joe was being strangled.

28

Streaking past Chichi up the stairs, Dulcie fled for Abuela's bedroom, which rang with Joe's yowls and Luis's screams. She burst through the open door into a storm of swinging arms, flying fur, and Spanish swearing. Pausing for only an instant to sort out the action, she leaped straight into Luis's face, clawing, clamping her teeth on his ear, trying to make him drop Joe.

Luis tried to pull Joe off his arm, but the enraged tomcat clung and slashed and bit. As Luis fought to knock him loose, Dulcie glimpsed the cage door where the three cats pressed frantically. It was unlocked, the padlock was gone, but the hasp was still in place, held tight by the swivel eye where the lock had hung.

The three cats were so close to the swivel eye, just inches from it. But they could not reach through, no paw could fit between those tight bars. She was crouched to leap to the table when the old lady joined the fray. Estrella Nava, with a cry of dismay, rose from her rocker and flew into action, beating at Luis with her cane, shouting Spanish expletives that sounded as vile as those Luis was yelling. Luis turned on her, lunging against the cage so it rattled and slid, and Dulcie and Joe clung to him raking flesh, bloodying Luis with claws and teeth — until the bedroom door banged open, hitting the wall, and Tommie burst into the room.

He grabbed Dulcie, tore Joe off Luis, making Luis scream with pain. Jerking open the cage door, Tommie shoved Joe and Dulcie in, forcing the captives back against the bars.

Slamming the door, Tommie turned the swivel, effectively locking it. The five of them were jammed inside like kippers in a sealed can.

But Tommie couldn't find the lock. He searched the floor and under the table and in the corners, swearing; then he ripped off his belt and stuffed it through the swivel eye.

Standing back, he smiled. Not his carefree Irish grin, but a cold leer, his red hair on end, his freckles hardly visible in his red, excited face. Tommie stared at Luis, and turned to look at Abuela.

Estrella Nava had slipped back to her rocking chair; she sat glaring at the two men, her eyes, defiant and angry, reflecting passions Dulcie wished she could read. But as the old woman turned in her chair to look out the window — as if dismissing the two men — Dulcie glimpsed a flash of metal in her hand. She saw it for only a second, then it was gone.

"Where's the lock?" Luis was shouting, crawling beneath the table. "Where's the lock and key?" He was so covered with blood he could hardly see; he looked like butcher's meat. Backing out from under the table, he swung up to face Tommie. "Where's the damn lock? Where's the *key?* Who took my key?"

"I don't have it!" Tommie snapped. "Look under the bed, maybe it got kicked away . . . Wait!" He spied the padlock underneath Abuela's chair.

Following his gaze, Luis snatched it up. The key wasn't in it. He stood holding the lock, staring angrily at Abuela. "Where's the key! Give me the key!"

"I don't have your key, Luis. Leave me alone." Her voice was quiet, cold and disdainful. From within the cage, Dulcie watched her with interest. Abuela Nava was, despite her frail age, a woman of strength and dignity. Her eyes on Luis showed plainly her hatred of her grandson. "Why would I want your key? I don't want it, or you, in my house, Luis."

Luis was snapping the lock on the cage door when Chichi appeared behind him. Stepping into the bedroom, she took in the scene with disgust. "Get yourself cleaned up, Luis. You have bandages? Get some, and a towel and a wet washcloth." She saw Abuela then, and went across to the old woman. "What did they do to you? Did they hurt you?"

"They hurt only the cats," Abuela whispered. "They hurt the cats."

Chichi's eyes widened at the sight of more cats in the cage. She stared hard at Joe — at Clyde Damen's cat — but said nothing. She laid a hand on the old woman's arm. "Maria will be back soon. I . . ."

"Quit messing with her!" Luis screamed. "Where's the damn *key!*"

"*I* don't have your key! I just came in! How could I have it! Get some stuff to clean yourself up!"

Luis hit her a glancing blow across the face. She didn't flinch, didn't step back. Stood staring at him until he backed off, then she turned and stormed out of the room. They heard the front door open and slam. Dulcie wondered if Chichi would wait outside for Maria, for her car. Or if she was so mad she'd go off without it, and come for it later. She stared at the bars trapping them, and out at the two men. Joe looked sick, his ears down, his short tail tucked under, his whiskers limp. She couldn't bear the pain and defeat in his eyes, she wanted to nuzzle him, but she would make no such show of emotion in front of this human scum. The five cats were pressed so hard against one another that Coyote and Cotton were pushed into the dirty sandbox, and Willow stood with three paws in the water dish. It wouldn't be long, they'd be hissing and striking each other, frantic with their confinement. Closing her eyes, she tried to calm herself, to get centered, to not give herself to defeat. She was so miserable she hardly heard the sound of a car in the drive, or Chichi and Maria's voices, or the car pull away again. All she could think of was their frantic need to be out of there, to be free.

It was noon when Charlie finished looking over the new job, near where she'd seen the brown pickup. She had reset the hinges on the sagging gate, checked on the work of the two new cleaning girls, and told them she was pleased. One of the girls had horses and needed to work to take care of them. She was a lean, strong young woman, more than used to hard work. An employee Charlie would like to keep. The young man who was doing the yard was a musician, a bass player working to support his music, which was not yet supporting him. He did the gardening wearing heavy gloves to protect his hands. He'd last until he got a regular gig, then he'd leave her. That was the trouble with owning this kind of company — or maybe any small business, these days. That, and all the forms she had to fill out, all the details and red tape. To say nothing of the insurance rates! She thought again about selling the business.

Her best, most dependable employees were, like Mavity Flowers, past middle age. Up in their years and settled in; but the sort of folk who truly liked cleaning houses. There were not many of those anymore. All the young people wanted top-flight jobs the minute they were out of school; no climbing the ladder for them, they deserved to start at the top — or thought they did.

She hadn't grown up like that, she'd done all kinds of odd jobs to get through art school. Had come out of school glad to find any beginning art job. Her first year, she'd washed brushes in a small commercial-art studio, then done rough layouts for wastebasket designs and frozen-lemonade cans, work far more tedious than scrubbing floors. She'd had no chance to design anything. When she was "promoted" to painting finished art for a set of willow-ware canisters and metal kitchen items, that was the most tedious of all. All those tiny cross-hatch lines and little details nearly drove her mad. She still couldn't stand willow ware. But she'd paid the rent, that was what mattered. Today, a kid coming out of art school expected to step right in doing layouts for major magazine advertising, or to be offered a top position with some prestigious interior design studio in New York or San Francisco. Few got the chance. If those kids, when they were still in grammar school or high school, had had to work at menial jobs every summer, they'd take a different view. And that made her smile. Opinions like that, bemoaning the lack of work ethic in the young, sure as heck showed her age.

Well, maybe not being a kid anymore wasn't a bad thing, maybe what she knew now, about the world, served her better than the feel-good illogic of her youth. Turning into the courthouse parking lot, she swung into the red zone before the glass doors of the police station to wait for Max. Strange that he'd called her to have lunch, he seldom had time to do that. He'd said only that he and Dallas needed to get away from the shop.

She and Max had been married for not yet a year, but she'd learned a lot about being a cop's wife — how to hold back her questions, curb her curiosity, wait and bide her time until Max was ready to share with her. That was not always easy, it was not in her nature to be patient.

It hadn't been easy, either, to keep her fear for him at bay. Nor, she thought, amused, to learn to make dinners that would hold for hours.

Parked beneath the sprawling oak before the door of the PD, she sat enjoying the gardens that flanked the courthouse. Molena Point PD occupied a one-story wing at the south end of the two-story courthouse, a handsome Mediterranean complex with red tile roofs, deep windows, and flowering shrubs bright against the pale stucco walls. An island of garden filled the center of the parking area, which was shaded by live oaks. The huge tree under which she sat served not only for shade over the station door, but also as a quick route to the roof for the department's three feline snitches. To the roof and to the small, high window that looked down into the holding cell, into the temporary lockup where arrestees were confined until they were booked and taken back to the jail or were led off to the interrogation room for questioning.

Joe and Dulcie and Kit could easily spy through the holding cell window, or slide the window open and drop through the bars down into the cell — then slip out through the barred door to the dispatcher's desk. Though on most occasions it was easier for the cats to simply claw at the glass front doors until the dispatcher, usually Mabel Farthy, came out from her electronic world and let them in. Mabel hadn't a clue she was admitting the department's secret informants.

Charlie was idly watching the parking lot when a white Neon pulled in, not twenty feet away. Chichi Barbi got out, dressed in tight black jeans, a low-cut pink sweater, and high heels. She stood leaning against the car, watching the street. Charlie pulled her sun visor down, hoping not to be noticed; she watched as a black Alpha Romeo turned off the side street, pulling in to park beside Chichi. Well!

Ryan hadn't mentioned that Roman Slayter and Chichi were connected. Maybe she didn't know. Chichi was from San Francisco, and Roman was, she thought, from L.A. Chichi stood leaning against his car, leaning down talking with him. They knew each other well enough to argue. Charlie's windows were down, but with the breeze rattling the oak leaves it was hard to hear much.

Roman said something that sounded like, *Not in front of the station, for Christ's sake!* Chichi's answer was lost, but her reply made Roman laugh. She turned away to her own car, and in a moment they were both gone, the black Alpha Romeo following Chichi's Neon out between the bright gardens, surely headed somewhere together. When she turned back, Max and Dallas were coming out of the station.

"Been waiting long?" Max swung in beside her. Dallas got in the back. "Clyde and Ryan are meeting us," Max said. "Tony's okay?"

"More than okay. What's the occasion? What are we celebrating? You make a reservation?"

"Of course I made a reservation." He put his arm around her and blew in her ear, dangerously hindering her driving. "Have you forgotten this is our six-month anniversary?"

Charlie blushed. She loved it when he was this romantic. He was so down-to-earth, so much of the time a hard-nosed cop, that such moments were special.

"Well it almost is," he said. "Close enough to celebrate. There's a parking place, guy ready to pull out."

She waited for an SUV to leave, then slipped into the space. The meter maid was just leaving, she had just missed them.

Tony's was a popular lunch place for the locals, a high-ceilinged structure of heavy timbers and glass, decorated with ferns and other lush plants in huge ceramic pots. Medleys of ferns in baskets hung from the rafters. The dining room seemed as much a garden as did the patio beyond. They followed the waiter to a table in the back patio where Ryan and Clyde waited, Rock stretched out under the table at their feet. Several other dogs lay beneath the tables, all on their best behavior, seeming hardly to notice one another. Restaurant dogs, Charlie thought, would make a nice series of drawings. They had ordered and were talking about the Harpers' new addition, when Charlie glanced across the patio into the restaurant, and saw Chichi and Roman Slayter being seated.

"What?" Max said. Though his back was to the wall, his view in toward the dining room was partially blocked by the ferns.

"Chichi Barbi and Roman Slayter. They met in front of the courthouse while I was waiting for you. I didn't know they knew each other."

Ryan said, "I didn't either; but they're a perfect match."

"Maybe Slayter will keep her occupied," Clyde said hopefully. "I wonder if she's a pickup."

"I don't think so," Charlie said. "They know each other well enough to be arguing, she seemed really angry."

"How long were they there?" Dallas asked. "Could you hear any of it?"

"Only that he didn't like meeting in that particular location." Charlie studied Dallas. He nodded offhandedly, and said no more.

Max asked for the French bread and sipped his O'Doul's. He didn't seem interested in what Chichi Barbi did or who she met. He seemed, Charlie thought, strangely miffed at Dallas for his own interest.

But he could be annoyed over anything, could have had a bad morning. Some small problem in the department. Both men seemed edgy.

"They're still arguing," Ryan said with interest. "They do know each other well."

"I'd like to be a fly on the wall," Charlie said. She thought Chichi could be really attractive with less makeup and better taste in clothes. She longed to know what they were talking about.

But even as she wondered, she saw that a spy was already on the scene.

Crouched between two tall pots of ferns beside Roman and Chichi's table, the kit, with her dark fur, was nearly lost among the fern's lacy shadows. How intensely she was watching them, ears sharp, tail very still, her whole being fixed on the couple — as intent as if she were crouched over a mouse hole.

29

The tiles beneath Kit's paws felt smooth and cool. The potted ferns helped hide her; their shadows blended with her darkly mottled coat, providing a nice disguise. But the restaurant's delicious smells distracted her, made her want to leap onto the next table, into the middle of that broiled lobster or into that great brimming bowl of meaty spaghetti. It took all her strength to resist. But then the conversation directly above her became so fascinating that she forgot her hunger.

"That time in L.A. was hard on you," Roman Slayter was saying. He was very handsome, lean and tall, his dark short hair blow-dried just so, and those gorgeous brown eyes — like a movie star, Kit thought. Yet he scared her.

"I'm glad to be out of that friggin' town," Chichi said. "I'm never going back there, damn L.A. cops are a bunch of hoods."

Slayter's voice turned serious and gentle. "I know you miss him, Chichi. We all do."

"They murdered him! Damn cops murdered him — friggin' cops never pay for what they do. Cheap, lying Gestapo. 'Line of duty,' my ass. *He* wasn't in the damn bank, *no* way they could put him there!"

Slayter gave a sympathetic murmur, patting her hand and looking around them like he hoped no one was listening. Quietly he sipped his wine as the waiter appeared with a bowl of French-fried onion rings. Their scent made Kit's claws itch with a powerful need to snatch a pawful. Slayter took some onion rings onto his bread plate and sat munching one, watching Chichi; Kit could not read his expression. She wouldn't want to be trapped with this man. If she were a human lady, she'd stay away from Roman Slayter.

"Never even had a proper funeral," Chichi said. "Stuffed in that vault like a side of meat." She looked up accusingly at Slayter. "And everyone ran, saved your own skins. You vanished quick enough, Slayter."

"What could we do, Chichi? Get *ourselves* killed? You didn't hang around!"

"Luis dragged me! Luis . . ."

"Bank guards and cops all over. What the hell *could* we do but run?"

Kit's heart was pounding. Slayter *was* part of that gang with the two men Joe Grey saw in Chichi's room. A gang that had robbed an L.A. bank, and the village jewelry store.

Roman stroked Chichi's hand. "Why did you come up here with us? Frank was dead. You could have . . ."

"I guess I came because Frank would have. I guess," Chichi said softly, "I just did what Frank would do."

Kit itched to find a phone. Captain Harper and Detective Garza needed to know about this. Chichi had started to cry — the kind of crying when a person doesn't want to talk about something, when a woman hides her silence with tears and most men think they're real tears. "And . . . I didn't have any money. That's part of why I came. Nowhere else to go. That's why I found that house-sitting job, a free place to live. I didn't want to stay up there with Luis . . ." She looked at Roman. "I'm still pretty broke, Roman. Could you . . . ?"

"I have men in place, Chichi. Rent to pay, food. Those guys don't live on air!"

Chichi reached to stroke his cheek. "But *you're* living in a nice place, the Gardenview is really nice, I could stay with you. It wouldn't . . ."

"It's a tiny room, Chichi. The cheapest they had. And right now . . ." Roman shook his head. "Wouldn't work. You're better off where you are."

He had men in place? Rent to pay, and food? What men? A whole gang of men? And why was Chichi so interested in moving in with him?

To get in his bed? Was she feeling like a queen in heat? Kit thought, shocked. Or did she want to snoop, search his room? Kit's imagination soared, she could hardly be still. She had to tell Captain Harper, had to tell him now.

She looked across the dining room into the patio where Captain Harper and Detective Garza sat. They would have their cell phones, and if she could tell them now . . .

But she couldn't use a phone in this public place. The idea made her laugh. She had to go home, to call him. And this person named Frank who was killed by the cops, who was he? She was so excited she had to put a paw on her tail to keep it from lashing. She watched Slayter move his chair closer to Chichi's.

"It hurts me to see how you miss Frank, I wish there were *something* I could do." He took Chichi's hand again, in both of his. "There's nothing either of us can do about cops," he said angrily. He removed his hand only when the waiter appeared, bearing elegant plates of pasta. The smell of shrimp and scallops made Kit lick her whiskers.

There was only silence, then, as the couple occupied themselves with their lunch. She looked around the restaurant. All the tables were full, and people were waiting, too. Those who'd been served were happily enjoying lovely things to eat. And it was not until she looked again into the patio at the Harpers' table, that she saw Charlie staring at her. Staring right into her eyes, trying not to smile.

I'm not doing anything! Kit thought fiercely, giving Charlie a flick of her tail. Cats are born curious! But then she smiled, too, because Charlie only wanted to know what Chichi and Roman Slayter were saying; Charlie was just as curious as she was.

The caged cats were very hungry. Even Joe and Dulcie were growing hungry, and they'd been eating better than the prisoners. The kibble, which had been old and dry anyway, was all gone. To Joe and Dulcie, kitty kibble was meant for a dire emergency. The stale cat food at the bottom of the bowl stunk so bad it made them all flehmen, baring their teeth and pulling faces. Joe thought the three ferals must surely be longing for fresh game, for freshly killed squirrel or rabbit; Joe thought lovingly of the delicacies that Clyde regularly provided, and of the fresh selections that might be waiting in the alley behind Jolly's Deli, gourmet fare laid out for any village cat who cared to partake — who was free to enjoy George Jolly's largesse.

Maria had returned from shopping just after Chichi went flying out the door. They could hear her in the kitchen putting away groceries, and then soon they could smell searing meat. The three captives sniffed the good scent and looked hopelessly at each other. And Cotton pressed his white face to the bars, searching the floor. "Where did they drop the key? You think it's really lost?"

"It's lost," Coyote said. He smiled a wolfish smile. "That Luis was mad as a rabid raccoon."

"But didn't you see?" Willow said softly. She glanced across at Abuela, but the old woman slept. "Grandma took the key, I saw her."

"Abuela?" Cotton said. "Are you sure?"

Willow twitched her whiskers. "She slipped it out of the lock and into her pocket. She slid the lock under the cushion of her chair, but when she moved, it fell."

Even as they spoke, Abuela came awake. She looked around the room, looked at the closed door. She slipped her hand under the cushion of her rocker and drew out the key. They stared at each other, rigid. Had she heard them?

She rose, dragging her cane along with her. Was she going to let them out? They were frozen, watching, their five hearts pounding so hard Joe thought everyone in the house would hear them.

She moved to the double-hung window, which was open the few inches from the bottom. Finding the screen unlatched, she frowned. But she reached through. Bending down awkwardly, she managed to reach her arm through and swing. They saw the bright flash as she tossed the key in the direction of the far bushes.

She returned to her chair. The cats were silent until they were sure she slept again, her mouth a little open, a tiny glisten of drool appearing at the corner.

"Oh, my," Willow said softly. "No one will ever find it now." She looked at Joe and Dulcie, a tear running down her pale calico nose. "Now there's no way out."

"Not so," Joe said.

The three cats looked at him.

"We have friends," Joe said.

Dulcie licked her whiskers. "Do you remember a scrawny tortoiseshell kitten who once traveled with your clowder? Who came to Hellhag Hill with you, and stayed there?"

"That scraggy kitten?" Cotton said haughtily.

Willow said, "So that's what happened to her! She went away with you!"

"Sort of," Dulcie said. "She found two humans who . . . who knew what she was without her telling them. Without her ever speaking."

"Oh, my," Willow said. "How very strange." Her look said that she'd like to find such a human, but that she would be too shy and afraid to make friends.

"That scrap of tortoiseshell," Cotton said. "*I* thought she went down Hellhag Cave and the ghost got her."

"She's alive and well," Joe said. "If no one else finds us, she will."

Coyote sneezed. His eyes danced with amusement within their cream-and-black circles. "That tortoiseshell . . . always nosing into everything, asking a million questions." He shook his whiskers, flicked his tall ears. "You don't believe *that* skinny scrap will save us?"

Dulcie smiled. "When we've been gone long enough, she'll come looking."

"So?" Cotton said. "She'll find you, just like that? And then what?"

"Kit has her ways," Dulcie said. She hoped Kit would be as stubbornly curious as she usually was. Hoped she wasn't preoccupied with some other matter, too busy to notice how long it was since she'd seen them — that soon Kit would indeed decide they were in trouble, and come searching for them.

Charlie had the horses groomed and saddled when Max's truck turned in off the main road and headed down their long dirt drive. What a lovely day, she thought, tightening Bucky's cinch. Lunch with Max, and now a long evening ride together. This was how a happy, newly married couple was supposed to live. Shrugging into her heavy jacket, she led Bucky and Redwing out into the stable yard and slid the main barn door closed behind them. She'd fed them early and lightly, and would feed them again when they got home; they were used to evening rides when the weather was bright. Waiting for Max to take his papers in the house and get a jacket, she stood looking down over their pastures to the sea, filled with a deep contentment.

In the setting sun, the green hills were awash with golden light, and the evening air chill and clear. Calling to the dogs, she let them out the pasture gate. The two fawn-colored half-Danes bowed and danced around her, eager to be off, though they'd been running in the pasture most of the afternoon. She needed the exercise more than they did, after that huge lunch at Tony's. Waiting for Max, she stood thinking about Kit, there in Tony's, crouched among the ferns, spying. What had Kit heard? What had Chichi and Roman Slayter been talking about?

After lunch, when she'd dropped Max and Dallas at the station, she'd stopped by Lucinda's hoping Kit might have come home, but she hadn't. Lucinda hadn't seen her since breakfast. It was an exercise in futility to try to keep track of Kit, she was worse than Joe or Dulcie. Watching Max come out and lock the door behind him, she was filled with dismay that she couldn't share with him the cats' secret. It hurt her that she must lie to Max.

But she could never tell him. Not only would she breach the cats' trust, she had no idea how this particular truth would affect him. Max Harper was a realist, a down-to-earth man who believed in clear and objective thinking, in statements that could be proven. Yet if the cats' secret were proven to him, in the only way it could be, if he were to see and hear his three best snitches speak to him . . . She didn't like to consider his possible reaction. That truth, to a hardheaded realist, could be more than unsettling. Yet, though such a thought frightened her, there were times when she was so deeply amused at the situation that she had to turn away from him to hide a smile.

Watching Max cross the yard, she admired his long, easy stride, his lean body and leathery face. His brown eyes were fully on her.

As he swung onto Bucky, he gave her a grin that made her stomach twist with love for him — and because there must be this one secret between them. The only secret except, of course, for occasional police business. Winking at her, he moved Bucky out at a fast walk.

The chilly evening made the horses immediately want to run, fussing and rattling their bits. Ahead, the sea shone deep gold as the sun settled into it, the sea's swells reflecting fire. The hills seemed aflame, too; but their long shadows darkened then vanished as the sun dropped. Who needed to fly to Italy or France or the English downs? It was all right here, a perfect world. As long as Max was in it.

When the horses had warmed up, they

gave them a nice gallop across the south pasture, and moved on through their locked gate and out onto open land high above the Pacific. Both horses were fast walkers, eating up the miles. As dusk thickened, they trotted along beside fenced acreage, skirting their neighbors' pastures. Max was quiet tonight, as he was when his mind was on department business. He looked over at Charlie quite suddenly.

"What do you think of Clyde's blond bimbo?"

"Chichi?" she said, surprised.

"Give me your impression, a woman's impression."

"Well, she's . . . First off, I don't think she's Clyde's bimbo. Maybe she was once. Now he seems to want to avoid her at all costs. She's . . . she seems cheap, but I don't know her well." She laughed. "Even his cat doesn't like her. Don't animals always know?"

"Know what, Charlie?"

The question startled her. "If a person's to be trusted. Dogs seem to know, don't they? Know if a person is threatening, if they should keep away." She looked hard at him. "Surely dogs sense those things? Why wouldn't all animals?"

"Animal sense," he said, and shrugged. "They do sometimes."

She said, "You told me Chichi was watching the village shops, keeping a record of who opens up and what time, of who closes up, how many clerks. What's she up to?" He'd said the snitch had told him what Chichi was doing. "Well," she said, "I guess you can't arrest her for . . . as an accessory?"

"Accessory to what? Nothing more has happened."

"Arrest her on suspicion? Or on some kind of drummed-up charge, before there are any more break-ins?"

He laughed and shook his head. "We'd really have to stretch, to do that."

"But if there are more burglaries, and she has the list of those places . . . ?"

"When and if that happens, yes. You know that, she'd be an accessory, then." But he was brief, as if holding back. There was something he wasn't saying, that he didn't feel free to tell her. Of course that was sometimes necessary, but it always made her burn with curiosity. She guessed she was as nosy as the cats.

"Meanwhile," she said, "at least the list your informant gave you helps know what shops to watch, doesn't it? Helps you know what places they might rob?"

Max nodded. "Particularly if they're planning one grand snatch-and-grab, all the shops at once. Get out fast, head for some prearranged destination."

Charlie watched him. "Would you have enough men?"

"If they're planning this in conjunction with some kind of diversion, where we're busy with crowd control, for instance, we might not."

"But what kind of diversion? Oh . . . the jazz festival's next week."

"Or maybe this growing dispute over water control. If there's a full-blown protest, if someone were to bring in a hundred or so protesters to clutter up the streets, slow down traffic . . ."

She shook her head. She'd hardly paid attention to the battle over the area's water supply, it seemed a part of central coast life, seemed to go on and on.

"It's been done before," Max said. "Bringing in professional protesters for various causes — so far, never in Molena Point."

She eased in the saddle and flicked a hank of Redwing's mane straight. "A diversion? A protest? The jazz festival? Or why not the big classic car gala? Except that's months away. Oh," she said, "and you bring in extra police, then. And CHP."

"Exactly. I don't think this little group is

that high-powered. And now, with Luis Rivas's brothers dead, maybe Luis will change his plans. But still there's Tommie McCord and I'd guess a dozen others." He looked intently at her. "How much is Ryan seeing of this Roman Slayter?"

"*Slayter* is part of this?"

"I don't know, Charlie. Just a hunch."

"The snitch, again?"

Max grinned. "Maybe. How much is Ryan seeing of him?"

"She's not seeing him at all, if she can avoid it. She hates Slayter. She had dinner with him a night or two ago, because he told her he had information about the jewel burglary. She said she stormed out of the restaurant before their dinner was served."

"She told me about that," he said. "In L.A. the Rivas brothers ran with a dozen men. They could all be here, holed up in motels, rented rooms."

She looked bleakly at Max. "That's not a pleasant thought. That house where I saw that truck . . ."

"That house belongs to an elderly widow, Estrella Nava. She's the Rivas boys' grandmother. Dallas dug that out this afternoon after you found the truck."

"Can't you get a search warrant on that?"

"We'll search at the right time. Dallas and

Davis are talking with the jewelry store and shop owners, the ones Chichi's been watching." He shifted in the saddle, looked down at the sea, then back at her. "Store owners are pretty much in agreement." He let it lie and busied himself leaning forward over Bucky's neck to straighten Bucky's mane under his headstall.

"Agreement on what?" she pressed. "What can they do?"

He smoothed Bucky's mane all the way down the withers, exasperating her.

"You're such a tease! What are the store owners planning? What are you planning?"

"The owners like the idea of a sting," he said. "There are eighteen stores on Chichi's list. If it's the jazz festival, some of the streets will be closed off, curb-to-curb crowds. Hard to get a squad car through in a hurry. If the robbers come in on foot, and if they have enough men to hit all the stores at once, they'll grab and vanish in the crowd while we're cruising traffic and keeping order.

"Or they could plan to hit in early morning, just before or during opening time when there's maybe only one person in most shops. Or even the middle of the night, two or three a.m., if they can get a handle on the stores' security systems. We're not sure these guys are sophisticated enough to deactivate many of the alarm systems, but we don't know that."

"So what's the sting? What are you and the shop owners planning?"

He gave her a look that needed no words, that said this was totally off-the-record confidential, and that made her nervous. If she promised not to share what Max told her, she was promising not to tell Joe Grey and Dulcie and Kit — not to tell the three snitches who relayed to Max the very information he was relying on.

There were times, Charlie felt, when promises *must* be broken, no matter how shabby that made her feel. It could be far shabbier not to tell the cats, to leave them only half informed, and thus perhaps in twice as much danger.

30

At the same time that Charlie and Max set out on their evening ride across the hills, Kit began to miss Joe and Dulcie. She hadn't seen them since the night before, at Wilma's house, hadn't seen them all day while she was spying on Chichi Barbi and then racing home to Lucinda to call the station. Where were they, all that time? Where were they now? As evening settled onto the Greenlaws' terrace, throwing soft shadows across the rooftops, Kit fidgeted and paced, increasingly uneasy until at last, losing patience, she sped away, hit the roofs, and went to search.

Kit seldom worried about the two older cats; *they* were usually looking for *her*. She might wander away or she might get angry and go off in a snit, but that was different, *she* knew where she was. Now, in the falling dusk, muttering softly to herself, she prowled among the shadows of balconies and peered down into the streets and alleys. Had they gone off to the hills hunting without her? Oh, they wouldn't! She did not choose to remember that she herself had recently vanished for several days, that she had worried not only Joe and Dulcie but all their human friends, that they'd all gone searching for her. Well, *she* couldn't help *that,* she'd been locked in. Locked up in that old rental house and she couldn't get out and that wasn't *her* fault. Locked in, trapped in there and scared out of her kitty mind.

Locked in? Kit thought, and felt her fur ripple with unease. That idea gave her a very bad feeling . . .

But Joe and Dulcie wouldn't be locked in. Where could they be locked in? Who would lock them in, and why? That couldn't happen to them.

Yet why this terrible, sinking feeling? Now that she'd thought of such a thing, she got so nervous she had shivers in her belly and her paws began to sweat.

She searched every inch of the village rooftops, or tried to; she looked and searched until it was deep dark. There were clouds over the moon, low and heavy. Were they at home by now? Maybe Clyde was cooking something special or maybe Wilma was making chicken pie? The slightest scent of chicken pie on the breeze would always draw Dulcie home. Well, she'd just trot by Clyde's and then by Wilma's and sniff the air. She was all alone anyway; Lucinda and Pedric had gone off with Ryan's sister, Hanni, the gorgeous interior designer, to look at furniture — instructing her to go to Wilma's if they were very late, to stay there with Dulcie — leaving a poor little cat to fend for herself.

Well, Lucinda *had* left an elegant supper in the apartment for her, laid out on the kitchen table with creamed sardines and kippers set into a double bowl of ice. Kit licked her whiskers. She would look a little more for Joe and Dulcie and then return to the rest of the creamed sardines; and she headed first for Clyde and Joe's house.

Approaching across the roofs, she saw Clyde's car in the drive. The living room lights were on and she could smell something nice, a deep slow beefy smell, like maybe a roast in the oven. With that good aroma filling the evening, Joe would surely be home. She was headed for Joe's tower when she heard Clyde's voice yelling, blocks away behind her, calling, calling Joe Grey.

But at the same moment two other voices exploded, closer, ringing out from the house next door, from Chichi Barbi's bedroom: a man shouting and swearing and Chichi shouting back at him.

"The hell you don't have it! Give it over, Chichi! Why the hell would you take the key! What the hell would you *want* with the damn key! You said you didn't want nothing to do with them. Hand it over!"

"I don't *have* your key, Luis! Why would *I* take it!"

Shivering with the violence of the man's anger, but keening with curiosity, Kit sped across Clyde's roof for the back of Chichi's house and dropped down into the twiggy branches of the lemon tree. Clinging among its thorns and leaves, she peered in through Chichi Barbi's window.

Max and Charlie returned to the ranch well after dark; the cloud cover was breaking apart, and the full moon picked out new details across the pastures and fence lines, making the horses shy. Bucky was more teasing than startled, having fun with Max. Redwing was naturally more nervous, she bowed her neck and snorted but she didn't try to bolt.

"Just being a female," Charlie said. "Likes a little drama."

"And you?" Max said, riding close to her. "How do you like your drama?" In the moonlight he couldn't see her blush, but he knew she was; it didn't take much. He loved that about her, that she blushed so easily, that he could gently embarrass her.

"Don't try to distract me with your ways, Captain. I want to hear the rest of the plan — if you want to tell me."

"The jewelry store owners have been meeting, getting together two or three at a time, in someone's shop at odd hours. Making their plans as quietly as possible." He moved Bucky aside from some ground squirrel holes, though Bucky was perfectly aware of where he was stepping and cocked an ear back at Max in annoyance.

"But what *is* their plan?" Charlie said patiently.

Max eased Bucky against their own pasture gate so he could open the latch. "Fake jewels," he said, looking up at Charlie. "John Simmons and Leon Blake suggested it." He swung the gate wide. They rode through, and he closed it. "They're collecting every realistic piece of imitation jewelry they can lay hands on to replace the real stuff. They've already begun to switch the jewelry in the cases every night, using pieces as much like what they have in the daytime as they can manage. In the heat of the break-and-enter, they're counting on no one taking the time to examine the take closely."

He had lowered his voice as they approached their own stable yard, watching the lighted sweep of yard and barn, the shadows beneath the trees and around his truck and around her SUV, though the dogs sensed nothing amiss; they raced ahead sniffing and checking the territory in their untrained, rowdy way. When dismounting, Max slid open the stable door, the dogs raced in, circled the open alleyway between the stalls, then shoved their black-and-tan noses deep into their bowls of kibble.

As Charlie slid off Redwing and undid the girth, her thoughts were full of elegant jewelry cases lined with fakes. She was still smiling as she walked Redwing to cool her down, then led her into her stall, took her halter off, filled her water bucket and tossed her a couple of flakes of hay. But *would* those men notice the switch? Would one of them think to put a jeweler's glass on a diamond, or take a careful look at the rich settings?

She began to worry about what she would tell the cats — what she dare tell them. And to wonder what danger she might put them in if they weren't told, if they didn't fully understand the operation. And she knew she had no choice.

Besides, when she promised Max to tell no one, in Max's mind the meaning was that she would tell no human. Max had made no mention of cats.

The short, dark, square man was roaring drunk. The stink of secondhand alcohol through Chichi's open window made Kit want to retch. What was wrong with his face? He had adhesive bandages on it and on his hands, under his long-sleeved shirt.

Chichi stood facing him, very angry. "I don't *have* the key to your cage! What would I want with those stinking cats! I don't even know what *you* want with them!"

Cats? Kit's heart was pounding. *Cats in a cage? What cats?*

"There was no one else to take the friggin' key! Them cats couldn't!"

Kit's whole body was rigid. Only her tail moved, lashing wildly against the branches. She concentrated hard to make it still. Sometimes her tail was like a stranger, all out of control. *What cats? In what cage? And where?*

"And now them two others," Luis said with triumph. "They're the same, you can bet! Why else would they be in there?"

Kit began to shiver. She had to find out where, and fast! She pressed against the screen, drawing in a great breath, sniffing Luis as he rounded on Chichi, trying to smell past the whiskey for some other scent, for cat scent — for the scent of Joe Grey and Dulcie.

But she could smell only the booze.

"Did you search Abuela?" Chichi asked suspiciously.

"Of course I searched her. *She* don't have the damn key."

"You searched Abuela!" Chichi screamed. "You pig, you searched your own grandmother! You are scum, Luis. Pure scum!" Chichi lunged at him and slapped him. Luis grabbed her hands, twisted her arm behind her until she screamed. As he turned, forcing her against the dresser and raised his arm as if to hit her, his sleeve brushed the screen right across Kit's nose.

And there it was: Joe Grey's smell. Sharp on Luis's sleeve. The smell of the enraged tomcat, mixed with the smell of blood and medicine.

Kit was shaking so hard that for a moment she couldn't move. A cage . . . Trapped in a cage . . .

Where? She had to find out where.

She moved fast, springing out of the tree

and across the damp grass and weeds and around the house to the front and across Clyde's yard onto the porch. She was crouched to bolt through Joe's cat door, when she stopped.

He wasn't in there; she could still hear him far away, calling for Joe. *Oh, Clyde, he's in a cage, they're in a cage and no one knows where, no one but Luis and Chichi — if they're in a cage, how long before . . . before . . . ? But Chichi knows where, she knows this Abuela so she must know where* . . . Kit needed Clyde. She needed him bad, right now. Clyde could make Chichi take them to where Joe and Dulcie were in a cage. Chichi had been there, *she* knew where, Chichi would have to lead them . . .

But if the key was lost? Well, Kit thought, then Clyde would have to break the cage. Clyde was strong, he'd know how to do that . . .

Rearing up on the porch, she looked down the street where Clyde was shouting for Joe, and she streaked away through the night toward his impatient voice . . .

31

Clyde was headed home when something bounded at him out of the night, hitting him in the chest like a bullet; and Kit was clinging to his sweater, blathering in his face trying to tell him something about Joe and Dulcie. In a cage? What cage?

"Slow down, Kit. Take it slow." He undid her claws and pulled her off, and cradled her in his arms. "Shhhh, Kit! Don't talk out here, wait until we're inside." He double-timed home, and they were hardly through the door when she blurted it all out, talking nonstop, in a panic.

"In a cage, Joe and Dulcie, and no one knows where but Luis and Chichi. Chichi must know where, she saw them there! Hurry, Clyde! You have to make her take us there. Oh, hurry! Locked in a cage and Luis lost the key and maybe someone *took* the key so you'll have to take a saw or some kind of cutters. Oh hurry before Chichi leaves because she has to take us there she's the only one who knows except Luis. But

Luis . . ." She stared in the direction of Chichi's house praying that Luis would go away and Chichi wouldn't, so Clyde could make her help them. Rearing up in his arms she stared nose-to-nose at Clyde.

He was deathly white, as if she'd scared him bad, landing smack on him out of the night and then telling him about the cage. "Locked in a cage, Clyde, and Chichi can take us, you have to make her take us before she goes away again, oh, hurry!"

Clyde unhooked her claws again, held her close, and swung out the door, heading for Chichi's house. "You are not to talk, Kit! Not a word!"

"I won't talk but Luis is in there and he's mean, he's drunk and mean."

He set her down on the drive. "Go get in my car, Kit. Right now. In the back." He jogged around the corner of the house, heading for Chichi's door.

Of course Kit didn't go to his car, she followed him, scorching up into the lemon tree again, expecting to hear Luis shouting. But there was nothing. Not a sound at all, not of fighting, not anything. Dead silence. Were they gone?

But then a door slammed, and Luis came charging out along the side of the house and up the drive to the street, then up the street to a dark blue sedan. As he ground the car to a start and spun away with tires squealing, Clyde headed up the steps for Chichi's door.

Abuela's house was dark. The old woman's bedroom was dark except for the thin wavering light of the TV bouncing and receding as Maria and Abuela watched a movie. They were tucked up in their beds, laughing out loud.

"What are they watching?" Dulcie whispered. She was surprised she could think about anything else but being crammed into the stinking cage maybe never to get out again. But Maria and Abuela were having such a good time.

"*Secondhand Lions,*" Joe whispered. Both women seemed comforted, watching those two old men in their rocking chairs on their front porch laughing as they blasted away at traveling salesmen with their shotguns. Maybe, Joe thought, Maria and Abuela would like to do the same to Luis. A thin drift of pale light filtered in through the window, too, from the full moon. In the locked cage beside Joe and Dulcie, the three ferals slept or seemed to sleep, tangled miserably together, tabby head on white flank, calico nose under Coyote's front paw in the kibble dish.

Maria had done nothing to try to find the key. Joe had hoped that, once Luis left, she would go out to the backyard and look for it, where Abuela had thrown it. He guessed she was too afraid of Luis to do that.

He didn't know how long the five of them would last, crowded in there, before they'd all get sick or start to fight, seriously harm one another in their panic to be free. The crowding and stink, combined with the flashing light and noise from the TV, had Joe himself ready to claw anything within reach. He was trying to lie down without waking Cotton when a looming shadow darkened the moonlit window: a man's shadow, a broad-shouldered figure with a lump on his shoulder. Joe went rigid with disbelief and then with excitement.

A man looking in, a man with a cat on his shoulder, its fat, fluffy tail switching. And on the night breeze that filtered in through the four-inch crack at the bottom of the window Joe could smell Clyde. That familiar miasma of automotive shop gas-oil-grease-metal-paint-primer and the sweet smell of industrial hand-cleaner; all this mixed with Clyde's aftershave and with Kit's own scent. Rearing up against the bars, it was all he could do not to shout and cheer.

He waited for Clyde to open the window

wider, then remembered that it was fixed closed at four inches. As Clyde leaned into the glass, looking in, examining the molding, Kit's dark little face came clear beside his, her round yellow eyes taking in the scene.

But out of the dark behind them, Chichi appeared, and Joe knew that all was lost.

Pushing Clyde aside, Chichi bent down, looking through the open part of the window. "Maria? Maria! It's me." Beside her, Clyde produced a small electric screwdriver. The music from the movie was loud, and the women were laughing. No one heard her.

Clyde pushed a bigger hole in the screen where Joe had made a small one. He unlatched it and removed it and leaned it against the house. Reaching in, he found the screws that held the window in position, and began to remove them. In less than a minute he slid the glass up.

Joe was pretty sure Luis had gone out, but he didn't know where Tommie was. The men had left Abuela's bedroom door ajar, and a person could see down the hall. There was no light on from the living room or bedroom or kitchen. Either Tommie had gone out, too, or had gone to bed early. Kit leaped in and pressed against the cage, licking

Dulcie through the bars. Clyde climbed into the room, and then Chichi. What could Clyde have done, to make Chichi bring him here? How had he known where they were? Joe had no idea what had happened, but from Kit's smug look he could see she'd had a paw in the matter. Maria had seen them, she watched, wide eyed.

Kit licked and licked Dulcie's ear, and she stared at the three feral cats. The cats looked back at her, their eyes merry with recognition. Their looks seemed to say, See how she's grown. Look how beautiful she's become, that skinny little waif. Joe watched Chichi shake Maria gently by the shoulders.

"Where's the key, Maria? What did he do with the key?"

"You can't, Chichi. Luis will be . . . He'll kill me. He would beat Abuela. He thinks she took the key. If you . . ."

Chichi shook her harder. "You have rope? Cord? Your belts . . . the belt on your robe, on Abuela's robe. Take them off. Get belts, all you can find." She looked at Clyde. "Forget the key. Use that saw. Get busy . . ."

Clyde got to work with the hacksaw, jamming the padlock at an angle to hold it steady. The saw's rasping was incredibly loud even over the sounds from the TV. Joe pressed against Dulcie tight between the captive cats, watching Chichi tie up Maria and Abuela with a bright collection of belts, binding them to the curved bars of their antique iron beds like a scene in some Western melodrama. Abuela was grinning ear to ear, as if the cats' impending escape filled her with wicked delight, now that she and Maria would not be blamed for it. Chichi, tying knots, glanced nervously at the bedroom door watching for Luis or Tommie to come barging through. The minute she had the two women secure, she headed for the window and safety.

"I'll be in your car!" she hissed, and she was through the window and gone. Clyde calmly removed the lock and opened the cage door. Coyote and Cotton squeezed through both at once, their tails lashing. Coyote's ears were erect and eager as he sniffed the fresh outdoor air. Cotton pushed past him and they leaped to the sill. Both toms turned to look at Clyde, a silent moment of thanks, then they were gone, racing away through the moonlight. Willow followed more slowly, pausing on the sill for a long moment, looking back at Joe and Dulcie and Clyde, a deep and loving look. Then she exploded away behind the others.

When the captives were gone, Joe and

Dulcie came out from the cage, licked Kit to thank her, and rubbed against Clyde's hand. But as Clyde scooped them up in his arms and reached for the kit, prepared to climb back out the window, Kit drew away.

Racing ahead of them, she stopped in the bushes and lifted a paw, but backed away when Clyde stooped to reach for her. "I heard something, I have to tell . . ."

"Come on," Clyde said. "We're out of here, you can tell us later."

"Now!" Kit said with an imperative yowl that startled them all. "Right now! That man . . . Slayter, that handsome obnoxious man? He's part of this gang, with Luis, it's a big gang. *They* broke in the jewelry store. He's part of it and he's staying in the Gardenview Inn and Chichi wants to get in there and search for something, I don't know what. She . . ."

A sound from the house, a hush of muffled footsteps in the bedroom, made Clyde snatch at her again. He missed and she leaped away and Clyde could only follow, clutching Joe and Dulcie. When they heard the bedroom door bang open Clyde ran, Joe and Dulcie clinging to him with all forty claws. But Kit was gone, racing away through the night.

"Kit, come back!" Dulcie hissed. "Kit,

wait . . ." They heard her leaping away through the bushes, following the wild ones.

Shocked, Clyde clutched Joe and Dulcie closer as he rounded the house, heading fast for the car. No one said what they were all thinking — that Kit might stay with the feral band. Might race away with them into the hills to take up that old life once more. Swinging into the car, Clyde still watched the bushes, but Joe and Dulcie knew she was gone. Kit's wild streak had taken her, Kit's longings that could never be tamed.

They were all three strung with nerves as Clyde dropped the two cats in the back of the roadster and slid in beside Chichi and headed home. They were all three hearing Kit's words . . . *Slayter . . . staying in the Gardenview . . . Chichi wants to search . . .*

Chichi, all scowls and fidgets, watched warily for Luis's car, as if it would appear at any instant racing after them or waiting on some dark side street. Joe considered her with interest.

She did not look like a vamp now, but like a lost soul. She sat hunched and miserable, perhaps imagining what Luis would do to her when he found the cats gone, certain that she was responsible. All her lipstick had worn off, and her pale hair hung limp and lifeless. She seemed not to care. There wasn't, at this moment, much pizzazz left to Chichi, and Joe liked her better this way.

But then the next minute she whipped out a comb and lipstick and got to work fixing herself up in the dark. She seemed to be skilled in such matters. Fishing out a little vial of perfume, she had soon restored the old Chichi. She watched Clyde with speculation.

In the back seat, Dulcie peered out, longing for a glimpse of Kit and feeling cold inside and lost and frightened. She was far more upset than she wanted to let on. Oh, Kit, she thought, you *won't* go with them, not forever. Not back to the clowder. You won't go for good, you won't do that, you can't.

But when she looked at Joe, his whiskers drooped and his yellow eyes were filled with misery, and she could smell fear on him. Fear that Kit *had* gone for good with the ferals, that the little tattercoat had let her hunger for crazy new adventures magic her away — that the unfettered wildness of her kittenhood had filled her right up again so she could think of nothing else.

Clyde's yellow convertible, having no power steering or power brakes, took his full attention — or he let Chichi think it did as he negotiated the dark, narrow, hilly streets down into the village. Three times Chichi asked him how he knew Luis had his cat, when he hadn't known anything about Luis.

"Damn, that was lucky," Clyde said. "I was just coming home from walking the streets shouting for Joe — he'll usually come when I call him. I was getting mad *and* worried. I guess you think it's foolish, to be that fond of a cat, but I've had him a long time. I'd about given up, and was going in the house when I passed that guy leaving your place." Clyde looked across at her. "I heard him *muttering*. Talking to himself about cats. Something about a cage, a key. Muttering about cats in a damned cage."

Joe, crouched in the back seat with Dulcie, glanced at her with amusement. Clyde wasn't the greatest liar. Still, it wasn't bad. He watched Chichi sidle closer to Clyde, looking up at him engagingly.

Ignoring her advances, Clyde parked across the street from her place, didn't pull into his own drive. He glanced at her. "You know how cat lovers are. The guy looked . . . I just had this feeling he was talking about *my* cat! That he was some nutcase, had caught my cat here in the yard, and put him in a cage." He left the engine running, glancing at Chichi. "This time, my hunch was right. Thanks, Chichi. I really owe you."

He swung out to open her door. "You want me to walk you back? That driveway's dark."

Chichi looked at him with speculation. "You want a cup of coffee? Or a drink?"

Clyde shook his head. "I need to run Dulcie home, her owner's worried, too. She called me twice."

"Could you walk me in, though? It is dark back there. If Luis — if he's come back . . ." She shivered. "If he got home and saw the empty cage . . ." She did look frightened. Joe wished he knew what she was thinking, wished he could read her thoughts.

He'd been startled at how tender she was with Abuela, as if she really cared for the old woman. Strange, he thought as he watched Clyde walking Chichi down the drive. He hoped Clyde wouldn't go in, wouldn't succumb to this out-of-character side of Chichi Barbi, and to the charms that would likely follow.

32

As Clyde walked Chichi down the dark drive, Joe leaped to the front seat and reared up, looking out the window. He heard Chichi's key turn the lock, and her soft "I'll just check my room . . ." Heard her door squeak open. Dulcie hopped over the back of the seat and stretched out beside him, her dark tabby stripes tiger-rich in the gleam of the moon. "I'm bummed, after that cage."

"We were in there only a few hours." But Joe felt much the same, wrung out with the stress of being locked up. He couldn't half imagine how the others had felt. He'd never before been in a cage, except at the vet's, and he could open those cages if he wanted. Besides, Dr. Firetti treated him royally. Well, he guessed his cat carrier was a sort of cage, but of course he knew how to open that.

Dulcie's pink tongue tipped out, licking nervously at her front paws. "The padlock and those heavy bars, the awful crowding.

And the stink." Her emerald eyes were round with stress. "I was really scared. I never felt like that before."

Joe lay down and put his head against her. "I knew we'd get out. If not Clyde or Wilma or Charlie, if not Kit, then we'd find some way."

"I wasn't so sure. Thank God for Kit." But she looked at him mournfully. "Where is she? I couldn't stand it if she never came back."

Joe licked her ear. "She'll come back." He only wished he believed that. "Kit likes her luxuries too well. She won't get filet mignon and Alaskan salmon and imported cheeses up on those wild hills. Or silk pillows and cashmere blankets. Anyway, she loves Lucinda and Pedric far too much to leave them, or to hurt them."

"But she . . ." Dulcie sighed, and shivered, and was silent.

"She's just having a lark. She'll be home. I never dreamed Chichi would help us."

"You really think she'll come home, that she won't stay with that wild band?"

Joe listened to the hush of Clyde's step coming back up the drive and crossing the street. "She'd be crazy to do that. All the time she was a kitten, running with them, she longed for someone to love her." He nuzzled Dulcie's shoulder. "Kit might go off for a while. But it won't last."

Clyde slipped into the car and started the engine. "What won't last?"

"Kit wouldn't stay with them."

Clyde glanced at him. "Maybe she's already home with Lucinda and Pedric."

"Maybe," Dulcie said hopefully. "Tucked up warm, with a tummy full of goodies. Maybe she just showed the ferals the best way out of the village, where to cross, to avoid the traffic . . ." Trying to convince herself, she rolled over on her back, watching the treetops swing by upside down as Clyde headed across Ocean for Wilma's. She could smell home, smell the scents of her neighborhood, before ever Clyde slowed the car.

Wilma Getz's low, stone house stood so close to the hill that it had no backyard, just a narrow walkway before the hill rose steeply up. Wilma had made up for this lack by turning her deep front yard into a lush English garden with rock paths, great tangles of flowers and ferns beneath the sprawling oaks. A rich floral gallery that thrived under Wilma's care.

Both the front and back doors faced the street, the back door at the south end near the garage, the front door near the north end of the low Norman structure. Clyde killed the engine and sat staring at the dark house. "Where is she?" He turned to look at Dulcie. "Out searching for you? And she's just out of the hospital."

"She can go out if she wants," Dulcie said, standing with her paws on the window. "The light's on in the back, in the bedroom — the reflection against the hill. She's tucked up in bed, reading, that's all. She knows I'm all right."

"You damn near weren't all right!" Clyde snapped. He glared at the thin glow of light washing up the hill behind the house brightening the tall grass, and glanced at his watch. "It's only seven."

"She just got out of the hospital," Dulcie hissed. "At sixty-some years old, she can go to bed early and read if she wants."

Clyde opened the driver's door. As he stepped out, the cats leaped out over their own side of the open car and headed for Dulcie's cat door. The air smelled of woodsmoke: a fire would be dancing in the little red stove in Wilma's bedroom. *Home!* Dulcie thought. Wilma would be reading Bailey White's magical stories. Dulcie, able to think of nothing but snuggling down with her housemate beneath the flowered quilt, bolted away through her plastic door far ahead of Joe.

Before Clyde could ring the doorbell, Dulcie heard Wilma at the front door. She must have swung out of bed the minute she heard his car. Oh, Dulcie thought as she raced across the laundry, she *must* surely have been worrying. Looking through to the living room, she watched Wilma shut the door behind Clyde, and the two of them head for the kitchen. How lovely to be home, with Wilma all cozy in her red plaid robe, barefoot, her long gray-white hair hanging loose down her back.

In the kitchen, Wilma said not a word to Dulcie or to Joe. She and Clyde exchanged a long look, then stood watching as the cats fought the refrigerator door open. No one helped them.

Wilma had been worried all evening, and was feeling grumpy. She didn't know why she'd been so uneasy, since the cats were often gone for long periods. Somehow, today had been different. Dulcie could at least have called.

That thought made her want to giggle. Though it was perfectly true, the tabby cat could have called and saved her endless worry.

As to opening the refrigerator, already the cats were dragging out Dulcie's plastic dishes from the bottom shelf, which belonged exclusively to her. Hauling the covered bowls onto the kitchen rug, flipping off the lids with practiced claws, they devoted their full attention to the sliced roast chicken, the homemade custard, and cold beef Stroganoff that Wilma had left for them. They heard Wilma ask Clyde if he wanted coffee or a drink, glanced up to see Clyde open the lower cabinet where Wilma kept her meager supply of bourbon and brandy, retrieve the bourbon, and fetch two glasses. But everything tasted so good they could think of little else but their supper. They hardly paid attention until Wilma sat down at the table, saying to Clyde, "You look as angry as I feel. What have they done this time?"

Dulcie and Joe stopped eating and glared up at her.

"I swear you two have taken twenty years off my life," Wilma told them. "The idiot who said that living with a cat lowered your blood pressure didn't have a clue."

Dulcie's tail switched with annoyance. Clyde poured a double bourbon and water for himself and a light one for Wilma. "Tonight," he said, "I guess we shouldn't hassle them." He sat down opposite Wilma. Wilma's eyes filled with uneasy questions.

"So what happened?" she asked tensely. "And where's Kit? Is Kit all right?"

"It was Kit who saved the day," Clyde said. "But . . ."

"What happened? Lucinda's so worried. It's as if . . ." She looked down at the two cats. "Lucinda and I have been edgy all evening, for no real reason."

Joe and Dulcie looked at each other. Clyde waited for them to answer.

"Where's the kit?" Wilma demanded.

Dulcie looked up at her quietly, her green eyes round.

"What?" Wilma said.

"She's all right," Dulcie said around a mouthful of Stroganoff. She leaped into a chair, looking up at Wilma. Wilma put out a hand but didn't touch her; she sat tense and waiting.

Dulcie tried to begin at the beginning but had trouble deciding where the beginning was. She didn't want to tell Wilma all of it. Though Wilma had experienced plenty of danger, herself, before she retired from the federal probation system, when danger threatened Dulcie or any of the three cats, that was another matter. She told Wilma how they found the caged cats, but left out that they had tossed Abuela's house while the crooks slept. Immediately, Wilma saw there were omissions.

"What's the rest of it, Dulcie? You're leaving things out."

Dulcie sighed. It was no good living with an ex-parole officer; Wilma saw everything. She told her housemate about their search, but did not make much of it. Then told how Clyde and Chichi and Kit had gone in through Abuela's window and Clyde had cut the padlock and freed three captive cats. But Wilma sensed another lie of omission, and made her tell the rest, how she and Joe were locked in the cage, too. Then Clyde told how Kit had discovered where they were and brought him to rescue them. When they'd finished, Wilma poured herself another drink, stronger this time.

Sipping her bourbon, Wilma absently bound back her long hair into its usual ponytail and tied it with a piece of string from a kitchen drawer. "And they meant to *sell* those poor cats? They *knew* what they were, and meant to sell them! And to sell you!"

"We think it was more than that, too," Dulcie said. "The captives heard the men talking. Luis seemed to think they would tell someone about their robberies, and about some murder."

Wilma swirled the ice in her drink. "Could it be Dufio's murder? Oh, did Luis kill his own brother?"

Joe said, "Maybe Luis was afraid Dallas or Harper would trap Dufio into telling their plans, or into naming the gang members. Dufio wasn't famous for his quick wit." Joe licked up the last of the custard, and leaped into the fourth chair, rubbing his face against the edge of the table, smearing custard. Dulcie gave him a chiding look.

Joe licked his paw and cleaned his whiskers. "Luis and Tommie talked about 'the others.' Men apparently staying in half a dozen places around the village, rented rooms, the cheaper motels. Later, Kit heard it, too. From Chichi and Roman Slayter. Kit says Slayter is part of the gang."

"And Chichi, too." Wilma said. "Doing their surveillance."

Dulcie said, "If Chichi hadn't helped Clyde find us, we'd still be locked up. She didn't have to do that. And she was kind to Abuela." Hunching down in her chair, the little tabby sighed. "Even if Kit did see Chichi spying, and heard them talking about the burglaries . . . Chichi did help us."

"Chichi had a close friend in L.A.," Joe said. "Frank something. I guess he was part of the L.A. gang. He was killed during that bank job Harper was talking about." The tomcat scowled. "It's frustrating when all you can do is listen, and can't *ask* Harper or Dallas what you want to know. Sometimes . . ."

Clyde set down his drink. "If you two start asking questions! If you . . ."

Joe smiled. He loved steaming Clyde, he could always get a rise, even when Clyde knew he was only goading him.

Clyde poured himself another drink. Wilma shook her head. "No more, I won't sleep." She looked at the cats and thought about what they had told her and wondered if she'd sleep anyway. She wondered how much more they hadn't told her. Though Joe and Dulcie were seldom as secretive as her parolees, she was too often aware that the two cats did not share everything, that too often they kept their own counsel.

Or, she thought generously, maybe they just wanted to clarify unanswered questions before they shared their information.

She was certain that, first thing in the morning, the cats would show up in Harper's office, to try to fill in the facts. She imagined them crouching high in Max's bookcase, listening or reading over Max's shoulder. She said, "Where *is* the kit? You haven't told me, and I need to call Lucinda."

But immediately she saw the dismay on all three faces.

"She didn't . . . She didn't come back from that house with you," she said slowly. She looked intently at Dulcie. "She . . . she went away with the ferals? Oh, she didn't go off with the ferals, with the wild ones?"

"They wouldn't run far," Dulcie said. "Not tonight. Those three were exhausted. They wouldn't take off into the cold night and the dangers of the hills without rest and food and fresh water. Kit wouldn't let them do that, they can't be far away. They were weak with stress, from being in that cage." She put a soft paw on Wilma's hand. "She's just gone along for a little while, to take care of them, find them a safe place to rest. And maybe," she said, smiling, "maybe to Jolly's Deli?"

Wilma said, "Would she take them home to Lucinda? To her own safe haven, to eat and rest before they run again?" And before Dulcie could answer, Wilma picked up the phone.

Lucinda answered out of breath, as if she'd been hurrying. Wilma punched the speaker button as Lucinda was saying, ". . . out on the veranda calling Kit. I swear, that cat . . . Is she there, Wilma? Have you seen her? Have Joe and Dulcie . . . ?"

Immediately Wilma was sorry she'd called. What was she going to say? But now her foot was in it.

It took her a while to fill Lucinda in. Lucinda took it better than Wilma thought she might. The older woman was silent only a second. "The tree house," Lucinda said. "Our new house is empty, there's no one around. It would be safe there. Kit loves that tree house, she . . ."

Before Lucinda had finished, Clyde and the cats were out the door. "I'll call you," Clyde shouted back at Wilma; and they piled in the car and took off up the hills.

Wilma, alone in the house and strung with nerves, considered making herself another drink. Instead, she got a piece of cheesecake from the freezer and fixed herself a cup of cocoa. Sitting at the kitchen table waiting for Clyde's call, she could only think how incredible life was. Since Dulcie and Joe discovered their latent talents, and Kit appeared out of the wild, life was more amazing than she had ever dreamed.

She thought, amused, that one way or another, those three cats with their keen intelligence and insatiable hunger for criminal investigation would destroy the last of her sanity. Drive them all mad, either with the stress of keeping their secret, or with worry and fear for them.

But she couldn't be angry. She could only shake her head and smile.

33

From her wheelchair, Abuela stared defiantly up at Luis, her angry scowl matching his own. "They're gone! What could we do? We could do nothing. The man broke in, came through the window bold as brass and started sawing at the lock. When Maria tried to get out the door to get help, he swore and tied us up. Where was Tommie? Why didn't he hear us! *He* didn't come to help! That man threatened to kill us, and no one to help us. All that, over your mangy stray cats!"

"You're lying, old woman!"

"Who then tied us up? We didn't tie each other. And what do you think that is?" Abuela pointed at the severed padlock that lay on the floor among a scatter of cat litter. "Pulled those cats out, stuffed them in a bag and hauled them out the window. Said if we yelled or tried to use the phone, he'd do us, whatever that means. What did he want with cats? Why would he break in here, for cats? What did *you* want with them? Even you don't know!"

Behind Abuela, Maria remained silent. She was very pale, rubbing her arms where the belts had bound her. Luis stared at his sister and at his grandmother, picked up the lock and studied the severed pieces. "Where's the saw, Maria? What did you do with the saw! Why would you do this thing! You threw a fortune out the window! I swear, *I* should kill you both."

"I didn't cut the lock! Where would I get a saw! What did I do, cut the lock and then tie myself up?" Maria glared at Luis until she saw a spark of uncertainty. "Get out of here, Luis! Give us some peace! That was not a pleasant experience. There's not an ounce of sympathy in you." Putting her arm around Estrella, she peered down into the old woman's face as if afraid her abuela would collapse from fear and shock. "Go away, Luis, and leave her alone. You've done enough harm."

Luis turned away, muttering, and left them. Maria shut the bedroom door and leaned against it. She was amazed that she'd stood up to Luis.

It was the man who had come in the window and freed the cats, it was his boldness that had given her the strength to face Luis like that. Imagine, that man going to so much trouble to save a cage full of cats. Why would he do that? Maybe, Maria thought, there *was* something valuable about those cats. Or could it be, she wondered, that there really was such gentle goodness in the world that a man would risk his own safety to free the miserable beasts?

She could hear Luis and Tommie arguing out in the hall, then the front door slammed. She heard them tramping around the house through the bushes as the beams of their flashlights careened across the blinds. "Run, cats!" Maria whispered. "Run!"

At last they heard Luis's defeated swearing, heard his car doors slam, heard the car start and peel out into the street. As if they'd gone to search elsewhere. That made them both laugh, that Luis thought they could find terrified cats running scared out in the night.

But Abuela touched her rosary and closed her eyes, her lips moving. And Maria prayed, too, prayed for that good man. Then she crawled back into bed and lay imagining those cats racing free, far away from Luis. And she smiled.

"*My* tree house," Kit said, scorching up the thick trunk of the oak tree ahead of the three ragged-looking escapees. "My house, where you can hide and rest."

Willow and Coyote paused on the threshold, looking in at Kit, taking in the snug shelter. But Cotton pushed right in past them, bold and curious.

There were no cushions yet on the cedar floor, but the pile of dry oak leaves that had drifted into the corner of the cozy, square room provided a soft, warm bed. There was no ladder leading up the thick trunk of the oak to alert a human to the presence of the little house hidden high among the leaves. And though the cedar walls broke the wind, providing welcome warmth, there was nothing to confine them. The three open windows and open door offered easy escape in all directions.

Yawning, their stomachs full of kippers and smoked salmon, of imported cheeses, shrimp salad, and rare roast beef from the alley behind George Jolly's Deli, the three escapees curled up among the leaves in purring contentment. They were deep down into the most welcome sleep when a lone car woke them, slowing on the street below and pulling to the curb.

"Clyde's car!" Kit hissed, peering out the door as Dulcie and Joe leaped out and looked immediately up into the tree. "Wake up," she hissed. "Run!" This was not the time to be found though the three ferals so badly needed rest. Kit, herself, did not want to be found; but she didn't want to think about why she didn't. Clyde was getting out.

Swiftly she led the ferals out the window and into the next oak tree, and the next and the next until at last far away they scrambled down to a distant yard. And they ran.

Maybe Joe and Dulcie didn't hear us, Kit thought. When they go up in the tree house — which they would surely do — maybe they won't smell us. The ferals, coming through the village gardens, had rubbed against and rolled on every strongly scented bush they could find, to hide their own scent that was so strong and ugly after that stinking cage. So maybe Joe and Dulcie would discover only a windy miasma of garden smells that could easily have blown in from the surrounding yards, and no smell at all of cats.

Maybe.

But now they were safely away, hiding among the far houses, and Kit looked back to her treetop.

There was Dulcie looking out.

But with the tree house empty, surely they would leave soon. She thought she would make up to them later, for their useless search.

And it was there in her heart, what she meant to do. The thrill had been there all along, waiting inside her. The wild free days from her kittenhood. Forgetting all the hunger and cold and pain of that time, she remembered only that unfettered running, traveling on and on across the empty hills running with the ferals. Those wild and giddy feelings filled her right up; and with her little entourage, Kit leaped away through the dark gardens mad with pleasure, heading for the far hills.

In the tree house, though Joe and Dulcie could smell the medley of scents the cats had collected on their fur, those aromas did not hide completely the sour stink of caged cats. They could smell, too, that Kit had led the cats here by way of Jolly's alley, could detect a faint but delectable melange of salmon and fine cheeses. Dulcie, looking down into the dark gardens, felt incredibly hurt. "Why did she leave? Why did she lead them away?" She looked at Joe, sad and worried.

"They'll be watching us," Joe said.

"But why . . . ?"

"Kit doesn't want to be found, Dulcie. Kit is having a lark."

"But she knows we would worry."

"Best thing we can do is leave her alone, let those cats get on with their escape and their own lives. Then," he said, "Kit will come home." He wished he believed that.

"Will she? She isn't . . . She won't . . ."

"The kit," Joe said, "will do exactly what she wants to do. We can't change her. She's crazy with the excitement of the rescue, she feels big and powerful, invincible. These are her old clowder mates, Dulcie." His yellow eyes burned. "We can't run her life. Let her be, and she'll come home." But he looked away and licked his paw, hoping he was right.

"If she doesn't . . ." Dulcie said miserably, "if she goes off with them . . ."

Joe just looked at her. "There is nothing we can do. The kit must decide this for herself." And he turned away and left the tree house, backing swiftly down the oak with clinging claws and leaping into Clyde's car.

Reluctantly Dulcie followed, silent and worrying. What would they tell Lucinda, tell Pedric? That Kit had been there and gone again, that she didn't want to be found? What could they tell the old couple that would not break their hearts?

Dulcie knew that Joe was right. Kit had a powerful wild streak, a crazy headlong hunger for freedom, and they could only let her be.

But Kit had *chosen* to live with Lucinda and Pedric because she loved them. Now, would she at last return to them?

I'm worrying too soon. She isn't gone yet, not for good. She's only leading the ferals through the village, showing them the best way, how to avoid heavy traffic. If Joe and I try to force her back now, we would only bully her. We can't force her to be safe and loved, we can only trust in her judgment. And miserably Dulcie curled up on the cold seat of the car, ignoring Joe and Clyde. She remained lost and sad as Clyde carried her into Wilma's house and put her in Wilma's arms.

For a long time after Dulcie went to sleep beside Wilma, beneath the flowered quilt, Wilma lay in the warm glow from the bedroom fire, not reading the book she held but seeing the ferals and Kit racing away through the chill wind.

"Something in Kit's eyes," Dulcie had said. "When Clyde freed us and Kit went out that window, when she turned and looked back at me, something so wild — that look she gets . . ." And Dulcie had sighed, and hidden her face in the crook of

Wilma's elbow. Then later, just before she slept, Dulcie had roused and looked up at her. "I would miss her so. I don't want her to go back." And long after Dulcie did sleep, long after Wilma put her book on the night table and switched off the lamp and curled up around Dulcie, still she kept seeing Kit out there running in the night beside those untamed, joyous cats.

When Clyde and Dulcie and Joe had gone, the car gone, the street empty and the night silent again, Kit and the ferals returned to the tree house. There the ferals curled up once more, deep within the pile of oak leaves, and they slept. They needed to rest, needed to heal, before they made that last frenzied dash up into the open hills. For the first time in weeks they truly did rest; no crowding against each other and into a dirty sandbox, no shouting human voices to alarm them, no bars, no padlock. It was well past midnight when they left Kit's sanctuary, moving swiftly through the village shying away from the glow of shop windows, the fleeing cats no more than shadows. Above them behind reflecting glass golden light illuminated worlds of human artifacts, Gucci handbags, Western boots, red satin nighties and candied cactus, items of which these cats knew nothing. With the cats' shadows flashing across pale walls like the ghosts of long-dead cougars, Kit led them on a circuitous route avoiding the brighter streets. Surely Luis and Tommie wouldn't come looking, but still she was nervous. She guided them up to the rooftops among the chimneys and penthouses where they glanced into high windows and down through skylights into strange human worlds. They left the roofs at the little park that crossed over Highway One.

Racing up through tame residential gardens, they at last fled beneath fences into pastures where cattle slept. The full moon was setting when they bolted across Highway One and into the tall forests of grass that blew across Hellhag Hill.

Up through the windy grass racing and leaping, the ferals knew their way here; but still they followed Kit. They heard no threatening sounds, and no swift shadows paced them. Above them the sky grew darker as the moon set, and far below, the silver sea darkened. They were back in their own wild world, and still Kit ran with them. No one asked her why. Cotton, white as a ghost in the dark night, bolted ahead of the others wild for the far, empty reaches. Coyote waited for Willow; his long ears and encircled eyes, in the darkness, making him look indeed like a strange and uncatlike predator. It was Willow who kept glancing at Kit, wondering. Wondering if Kit meant to stay with them or go back. Willow thought that even Kit didn't know the answer. High on Hellhag Hill, the four cats paused.

Below them gleamed the endless sea with its drowned mountains. Kit said, "Does the sea run on to eternity? Humans don't think so. What *is* eternity?" But then she looked up at Hellhag Cave, looming black, high above them. If that was eternity, she didn't want any part of it. Cotton and Coyote were staring as if they wanted to go in there, but Kit pushed quickly on. "I don't like it there, it's all elder there." She made a flehmen face and they galloped away to a happier verge where they rolled on gentler turf and groomed themselves. There Kit curled up to rest against a boulder watching the others, her thoughts teeming with daydreams and uncertainties.

We could have our own clowder, we don't have to go back to Stone Eye. The four of us, off on our own. We don't need Stone Eye.

The night's siren song of freedom sang loud in her heart, running unfettered beneath the moon and wind turning her drunk with excitement. They would have their own clowder, beyond Stone Eye and beyond the world of humans.

But then she curled smaller against the boulder. I would never again see Lucinda and Pedric. I would never again be loved like they love me. Like Joe and Dulcie love me and all my human friends. Pressed tight against the boulder, steeped in a fugue of uncertainty, Kit did not know what she wanted.

A thin, dawn fog began to rise hiding the sea; lights appeared on the road far below, careening around the verge of the hill: two cars with spotlights blazing out of their windows to sweep the hill — the kind of spots a hunter would use to shine and confuse a deer, freeze it in its tracks before he shot it. The four cats closed their eyes and melted away up the hill where a stand of boulders offered shelter.

Kit thought of hiding in Hellhag Cave where they would never be found, slip deep into the earth where no human would ever see them. Yes, so deep they might never get out again. Lucinda, who knew so well the world of Celtic myth, thought Hellhag Cave might lead to places where no sensible cat would want to go. The idea that

Hellhag Cave's fissures might drop away forever had once thrilled Kit. Not anymore.

The two cars had pulled onto the shoulder. The headlights went out. The doors opened and five men emerged. As they crossed the road and began to run up the hill swinging their searching beams, the gusting sea wind carried the faint scent of Luis and of Tommie McCord.

The cats fled up the high precipice that rose above Hellhag's grassy slopes, up into steep rocky verges that would slow or stop a man. Up cliffs that could, on this dark night, be dangerously deceptive to a human. Kit was drunk with excitement — she was feral, born to fear and escape. Heady memories filled her as the spotlights gained on them, violent bright shafts knifing close. She scrambled up the cliffs panting so hard she could hardly breathe; and on they raced, drawing away at last to lose their pursuers in steep, rocky blackness.

Three of the men stopped and stood arguing and at last turned back, heading down toward their cars. Only Luis still climbed. Behind him Tommie McCord stood halfway up the hill shouting, "Enough! Not chasing cats anymore." They heard a tiny scratch as Tommie stopped to light a cigarette; they saw the flame and smelled the smoke. Luis pushed on, grunting.

"Don't care what kind of money they're worth!" Tommie yelled. "I'm not climbing any more hills."

"Do what you want!"

But Tommie raced up at him suddenly, lunged and grabbed Luis by the shoulders. "This crazy idea of Hernando's! Get your mind on business." Pulling Luis close, Tommie stared into his face. "I don't care what they're worth, to the movies, to God Himself. I don't care what they know. I'm not messing with any more cats!"

Luis hit him, hard. They fought across the hill pounding each other, reeling and punching until Luis sent Tommie sprawling. And Luis raced on uphill, leaving McCord groaning on the ground. The cats fled up the stony crest and skidded and tumbled into a rocky canyon too steep for any man; loose gravel scudded down around them.

But the danger didn't stop Luis. He came crashing down between the boulders sliding so precipitously the cats were certain he'd fall; they prayed he would fall, that they'd be done with him. As he came sliding down like an avalanche they leaped to the narrow rocky bottom of the ravine and up the other side, scrabbled up between hanging rocks and over the next crest into deep woods.

Swiftly they climbed a tall pine up into dense foliage. From among the concealing branches they watched Luis circle below them until at last he turned away and, swearing, started his slow progress back down the cliffs.

Exhausted, the cats curled among the branches and closed their eyes. They slept so deeply they hardly heard, far away, Luis's car start and head, alone, back toward the village.

was amazing. And it and the illustrations totally absorbed her. Turning onto the main road, he looked off across the pasture again where Bucky and Redwing had begun to play, chasing the two dogs.

Charlie's project had started out as a short, children's book, but was turning into a much longer and more complicated story, into a book for all ages; it reminded him of the horse and dog stories he'd read as a boy. He wouldn't have chosen cats to write about, but Charlie understood them amazingly well, her words rang so true that he had begun, himself, to understand the small felines better. As he reached the end of the drive he was surprised to glimpse a cat tearing across the pasture as if terrified, as if racing for its life. Stopping the truck, he tried to see what was chasing it, half expecting a coyote or bobcat. It must be a cat from one of the small ranches. Swinging the door open he stepped out thinking to turn the predator aside. Or, if it was a cougar, he'd run it off and go back to tell Charlie and to shut the horses and dogs in the barn.

But behind the fleeing cat, nothing else moved in the green grass; and suddenly the preoccupied cat saw him. It disappeared at once. It would be crouching low in the grass — yes, he could just make out its dark shape, deadly still; as if it was more afraid of him than of whatever chased it. He watched until he was certain nothing approached it, then headed on down to the village. Maybe the cat had, like the horses and the two pups on this chill morning, only been playing — running for pure joy in the cold, early dawn.

Parking near the Swiss Café he moved in across the patio to the back table to join Dallas and Juana Davis. Clyde was there this morning, too. Stopping to give the waiter his order, he sat down with his back to the wall; he reflexively glanced above him.

From within the thick jasmine vine Clyde's gray tomcat peered down at him, his yellow eyes returning his stare as bold as some skilled confidence man.

Clyde grinned. "He was hungry. I get tired of cooking for him."

Max looked at the cat, and looked at Clyde. "You order yet? I'm surprised the cat doesn't order for himself."

"He orders too much. Gets expensive."

Dallas laughed, then went silent while their orders were served. Max thought the cook must have seen him walk in the door; he nearly always ordered pancakes. He watched Clyde set a small plate up on the wall. Clyde said, "Slayter called Ryan again last night, wanted her to meet him again, was really pushy. She turned the speaker on so I could listen, told him she was busy. He said he desperately needed her help." Clyde grinned. "She told him to call 911." He glanced at the other tables, but the people around them were deep into their own conversations, a bunch of guys arguing about baseball, one couple so involved with each other they wouldn't have known if an earthquake hit the restaurant. "He told Ryan he's up here looking into a shooting in L.A., that he followed the suspect up here, that he's working as a private investigator."

Davis said, "Did he tell her what shooting?"

"Something that happened during a bank robbery. Said the case is still open."

"If he's legitimate," Davis said, "he'd have come to us, share information."

"She told him that. Slayter told her LAPD was accused of killing the guy. Unnecessary force during a bank holdup. Said there'd been an investigation and two officers had been suspended — that it was those officers who hired him to find out who did kill him."

"Who was the victim?" Max said. "Did Slayter mention a name?"

"A Frank something."

426

"Frank Cozzino," Dallas said.

Clyde nodded.

Davis spread marmalade on her toast. "Slayter wanted Ryan to pass him departmental information. Wanted her to pump us. Interesting."

"Sleazebag," Dallas said casually.

Clyde was silent, looking from one to another. Above him, Joe Grey belched. Everyone laughed. Clyde looked up at the tomcat, scowling. He couldn't mouth off to Joe — with sufficient prodding, who knew what the tomcat might do. Joe looked back at him, smug as cream.

Max said, "Frank Cozzino was a snitch for LAPD. He worked for several gangs, gathering intelligence for them on some high-powered burglaries. Then he started passing the information on to L.A. Looks like that got him dead.

"He and the DA managed the cases so smoothly that it was a long time before anyone caught on that he'd furnished the information. When one of the gangs made him on it, someone took him out and tried to make it look like the uniforms did it. Of course L.A. got the blame." Harper finished his coffee and set down his cup. "L.A. has the bullet but they've never come up with the gun."

Dallas finished his breakfast and laid half a slice of bacon up on the wall, making Clyde smile. "Maybe those two guys did hire Slayter. But if he's up here for that, why hasn't he come to us? Why try to go through Ryan to find out what we have?"

Davis finished her coffee, wiped her hands on her napkin, and straightened her uniform jacket. Tucking a five and some ones under the ketchup bottle, she rose. "You want to go over that matter you mentioned, Max?"

Harper nodded, reaching for her money to add to his own.

"I'll make a pot of coffee," Juana said. "I made empanadas last night, we can warm them up later."

Dallas rose, too, handed Harper a ten, and he and Juana headed back to the station. From atop the wall, Joe Grey watched them as he dispatched Garza's bacon. He liked and respected Juana Davis; she was a thorough, no-nonsense detective, yet with a frightened victim or with a wrongfully accused arrestee she was warm and understanding. Juana's proper, dark uniform and regulation dark stockings and black Oxfords contrasted sharply with Garza's faded jeans and old tweed sport coat, and Harper's jeans and boots and Western shirt. In this casual village, it was Juana Davis who stood out. Wondering what "matter" Harper and the two detectives meant to discuss, Joe slipped off the wall into the alley and headed for the station.

By the time Clyde and Harper rose, and Clyde turned to speak to the tomcat, Joe was long gone. Not a leaf stirred atop the wall where the gray cat had crouched. He'd vanished like the Cheshire cat. Only the empty plate remained, tucked among the leaves and licked to a fine polish.

Juana Davis's office was down the central hall, past Harper's and Garza's offices and past the staff room. If Joe had continued on, he could have entered the large report-writing room with its individual cubicles and latest electronic equipment, or the interrogation room. At the end of the hall was the locked, metal-plated door leading to the officers' parking area, and the jail. Having slipped in through the glass doors at the front of the station on the heels of a hurrying rookie, he double-timed back to Davis's office, hoping she wouldn't wonder why he'd shown up there so soon. But he might as well put a bold face on it. Strolling on in, he made himself comfortable atop her coffee table and stretched out, licking bacon grease from a front paw. Coming in behind him, Davis gave him a stunned look.

"You little freeloader. You spend all morning stuffing yourself, and now you think I have something to feed you?" She looked up as Garza entered. "Talk about pigs!"

Garza picked Joe up off the table and laid a stack of papers down in his place. Setting Joe on the couch, the detective made himself comfortable beside the tomcat. This kind of behavior never ceased to amaze Joe. All his life Garza had raised and trained gun dogs, their pictures were all over his office. Garza was not a cat person.

"There was a time," Juana said, "when you wouldn't be caught dead petting a cat."

"He's getting soft," Harper said, coming in. "You behave like this around those two old pointers of yours, they'll pack up and move out."

On the center cushion of the leather couch, Joe Grey washed his shoulder with deep concentration. He had to admit, he'd done a number on Garza. The guy was becoming almost civilized, turning into a regular cat fancier. For this, the tomcat had to congratulate himself. He had, very smoothly, charmed the department's upper echelon, while all the time maintaining a persona of simple-minded feline innocence. And as he lay purring and dozing beside Detective Garza, Joe realized he was smack in the middle of a major departmental planning session.

The confidential discussion he was witnessing was a brainstorming, nuts-and-bolts logistical plan of action, as the three officers laid out departmental strategy for handling a really big jewel heist — maybe the biggest jewel burglary this village had ever witnessed.

If their information was good. This wasn't intelligence that Joe or Dulcie had provided; Joe listened with curiosity and with rising anger. Why was it that the small, lovely village attracted these hoods? Why couldn't they leave Molena Point alone, go somewhere else to make trouble!

Well, but there was money here. Plenty of money. Movie stars; executive types coming down for conferences and for their brainstorming getaways; upscale tourists. And when the Colombian gangs in L.A. had discovered Molena Point and put the village on their thieving roster, every crook in California tried to copycat them. Didn't matter that Molena Point had one of the finest small departments in the country — with a little help undercover, Joe thought modestly

— every sleazy no-good thought he could beat the odds.

Davis said, "Doesn't seem possible that L.A. bunch would undertake this kind of operation, after they messed up so badly down there."

Dallas shrugged.

"Maybe not possible they can *do* it," Harper said. "But given their past attempts, I'd say it's way possible they'll try, that they think they can pull it off."

"Big dreams, short on brains," Davis said.

"I wouldn't bet on it," Max said. "They've pulled a few good ones. And with Dufio out of the way . . ."

They were quiet a moment. "You think they killed him?" Davis said.

Max refilled his coffee cup from the pot Davis had set on the coffee table. "We should have the ballistics, end of the week. I'd give a month's salary to get my hands on the gun."

"One thing sure," Dallas said. "The oak tree bark, outside his cell window, doesn't pick up prints worth a damn. But we have a nice collection of fibers."

In spite of himself, Joe felt his ears go rigid with interest. It took all his effort to keep his head down and appear to doze. With Garza on his right and Harper on his left and Juana looking straight at him from behind her desk, it was almost impossible not to stare from one speaker to the other like a spectator at a tennis match.

He could see Harper's notes, though. He was only a foot from the clipboard that Max balanced against his crossed leg, from the chief's bold handwriting. And he had a front-row view of the map that Dallas had laid out on the coffee table. Rising to rub against Harper's knee, he took a closer look at the map, getting a strong, pleasant whiff of Harper's horses.

Harper had marked twelve jewelry stores on the map, and five other upscale shops. He had noted, beside each, the store name, the opening and closing times and the names of the owners. Every officer, even the rookies, would have all the information at hand — every officer and one tomcat. Joe concentrated as hard as he could to set the layout clearly in mind. He wished Kit were there; with her photographic memory, she'd have the diagram down cold.

Through narrowly shuttered eyes, he studied Harper's notes, which included hidden video cameras both inside and outside the targeted stores, several still photographers and a team of officers hidden near each location — in one huge departmental sting. A sting that would employ not only every officer in the department — no one off duty or on leave — but a dozen or more men Harper would borrow from surrounding districts up and down the coast.

"Have them down here in time to get familiar with the layout. Billet them among us."

Dallas said, "I can take four comfortably, more if needed."

"Two, maximum," Davis said. She had, a little over a year ago, sold her house and moved into a small condo. Harper said he and Charlie could take the rest. "Ryan should have the upstairs finished by then — finished enough."

"Maybe not a shot fired," Garza said hopefully. "Not a piece of jewelry unaccounted for."

"If we're lucky," Harper said tightly. "Don't count your chickens."

"Jewelry stores still happy with their plan?" Juana asked.

Max nodded. "They've already collected every piece of faux jewelry they could lay hands on. This whole thing makes me edgy, it's too pat. The fact that we have a specific date, specific hits . . . If our intelligence is valid."

Joe closed his eyes so he wouldn't stare at

the chief. What intelligence? These guys were talking about things that neither he nor Dulcie were aware of. Nor the Kit, surely. Who was passing information to the department? And *was* it good information?

Or was someone playing snitch, meaning to double-cross the cops? His anger at that made his claws want to knead into the leather cushion. Hastily he shifted position, scratching a nonexistent flea. These officers thought their information was coming from their regular snitches, and they could be walking into a trap, being set up big-time. Joe's heart was pounding so hard he thought Harper and Dallas must hear it or notice its hammering blows right through his fur. He closed his eyes, trying to get a grip.

Juana said, "This snitch has never let us down. Without her, we wouldn't have a clue. If she's setting us up . . ."

She? She, who? Dulcie hadn't made those calls. Kit had made a couple of calls when she spotted Chichi spying. But did she have all this other information, that Luis planned to hit all the stores at once? As far as Joe knew, Kit hadn't been privy to any one specified time and date. Unless she hadn't told them — hadn't had time to tell them?

Had Kit learned this and called Harper

0435

while they were locked up? And in her panic to save them and to help the ferals escape, she hadn't thought to tell them?

It was earlier that morning, long before dawn, when Kit woke in the dark in the branches of the pine tree and thought about Luis chasing them and about his dead brother Hernando. She looked over at her three sleeping companions and shivered and was hungry again and lonely and didn't know whether to go home or to keep running with them, didn't know what she wanted. Didn't know if they would search for their clowder and their cold-hearted leader and return to that miserable life, or if they would go off on their own, as *she* wanted, just the four of them, and start their own clowder and be free of Stone Eye? Or defy him, battle him, run from him forever?

Was that what she wanted? This morning she wasn't sure, she didn't know. But a voice inside whispered, "Lucinda and Pedric love you. You will hurt them terribly if you don't go back."

Crouching in the pine boughs shivering from exhaustion and cold and the effects of fear, Kit wanted to run on across the open hills forever and she wanted to return to Lucinda and Pedric, to her human friends, to human civilization with all its faults and goodness. To her own dear Dulcie and Joe, to Wilma and Clyde and Charlie and all her human family, to a life so layered in richness and the mysteries of humankind that she would never truly learn it all.

She wanted both. Wanted everything. Crouched miserably among the branches, she might never have known what she wanted if she hadn't grown thirsty and backed down the tall trunk to find a drink of water — and come face to face with Stone Eye.

She dropped the last six feet into the soft cover of pine needles smelling the scent of water on the wind and there he stood on a fallen log. Watching her. Stone Eye. Broad of head and shoulder, heavy of muscle, ragged of ear. His eyes blazed with rage, his fangs were bared. He looked up into the pines where Willow and Coyote and Cotton slept, and he snarled with fury. As if they had purposely escaped him, had defied him and intentionally run away. And as he closed on Kit lifting his knifelike claws to strike, Kit ran.

35

When Charlie looked up from her computer, she was surprised to see that the pre-dawn dark had brightened into morning. She glanced at her watch. Max had been gone for nearly an hour. He'd been quiet this morning, solemn and distracted as he often was when police business presented a knotty problem. Breakfast in the village with his officers was good for him, he hadn't done that in a long while; and it lent her some extra time, which she appreciated right now.

She had wondered, slipping out of bed at four a.m., if she was raving mad to be getting up at that hour. She'd eaten yogurt and fruit at the computer, and now she was ravenous. But she was so into the world of the book that it was hard to leave — hard to leave the kit, cold and shunned by the older cats, wandering the winter hills alone. The story was so real to her that sometimes she *was* the homeless tortoiseshell, feeling sharply the terror of the thin, frightened

438

creature creeping through the night, hiding from the clowder leader among jungles of dense, tall grass. Charlie's rough sketches for the book marched across the cork wall behind her, sketches for which Kit had been the model. At first Charlie had meant the story for young children, but it had grown of its own accord, enriching and complicating itself until it had become a far more involving novel.

Rising from her desk she headed for the kitchen, her thoughts partly on her empty stomach but mostly still on the book. While the cat in the story looked and acted like Kit, the real challenge was that this fictional cat *was* an ordinary feral, and she must show the cat's life from that aspect. No speaking, no uncatly notions. The fictional cat's vocabulary was limited to mewls and caterwauling, to growls and hisses and body language. She had no name, there was no human to give her a name. Charlie called her, simply, the cat. But the details of a feral cat's life were as real as she could make them — facts right from the cat's mouth, Charlie thought, smiling. Immersed in Kit's story, the words flowed out in a rush, all the joys and terrors of that feral cat's perilous existence.

She was standing at the kitchen table

making a peanut-butter-on-whole-wheat sandwich when she heard rustling and scrabbling outside, beneath the bay window. Crossing to the window seat to kneel on the scattered cushions, she looked down into the bushes.

Within the tangle of geraniums and camellias and ferns, she could see nothing. Looking up across the yard, she saw nothing unusual around Ryan's truck where it stood beside Scotty's car in front of the barn. Rock was out in the pasture playing with their own two dogs. Turning away, she spun around again when a thud hit the window behind her.

A dark shape clung to the sill. The kit stared in at her, pressing so hard against the glass that her whiskers were flat; her round yellow eyes were huge with fear.

Hurrying to open the door, Charlie was nearly bowled over as Kit flew into her arms. The little cat clung against her, shivering, her heart pounding so hard that Charlie feared for her. Holding Kit close, she returned to the window seat and sat down to cuddle her. Kit's coat was matted and wet from the early morning dew, and full of trash and leaves. Her paws were ice-cold. She stared, terrified, into Charlie's face, but she said no word.

"It's all right," Charlie said softly. "We can talk, Ryan and Scotty are both on the roof, I can see them. No one else is here." Tucking Kit warm among the pillows, she rose long enough to snatch up the milk bottle, pour some in a bowl, and nuke it for half a minute. Setting it down, watching Kit inhale it, she opened a can of chicken, which Kit gobbled.

Sitting down beside her again, Charlie rubbed her ears. "What happened? What happened? What chased you? Where have you been? We thought . . ."

Kit looked up at her tiredly, still shivering.

"Worn out," Charlie said, hoping that was all. "You're exhausted. Oh, Kit, you mustn't be sick!" Picking Kit up and hugging her close, Charlie carried her to the table. She was reaching for the phone, to call Lucinda or the vet, when the phone rang. Charlie snatched it up with a shaking hand.

Lucinda's voice, agitated, cutting in and out. "Have you seen her? Have you seen Kit? Is she there with you? She hasn't come home at all."

"She . . ."

Lucinda pressed on, giving her no chance to speak. "I thought she might come there to you because you're closer to Hellhag Hill. We've walked all over the hills and down into Hellhag Cave . . ."

"You're in Hellhag Cave? Oh, Lucinda, come out of there. She's . . ."

"We're out now, you can't use a phone in there. But if the ferals didn't go down into the caves," Lucinda blurted breathlessly, "then they've headed back where they came from to their clowder, and the kit . . ."

"Lucinda! She's here!"

"There? Oh, my dear . . ."

"Kit's here! Right here beside me. Safe in my arms. What in the world happened?"

"You didn't know? Is she all right?"

"She's fine! Hungry, but that's nothing new. Didn't know what?"

"Clyde found three ferals from Kit's clowder, locked cruelly in a cage. Kit led him there, and he freed them — but she ran off with them. We thought . . . Pedric and I thought . . ."

Kit had her face in the phone. "I'm here, Lucinda! I'm fine. I'm right here with Charlie and I'm fine!"

Lucinda sighed, then was silent. Charlie pushed Kit away. "I didn't know," she said in a small voice, looking sternly at the kit.

"We thought she was just leading them away through the village and that she'd be back. When she didn't come home, we thought . . . No one told you? Wilma didn't call?"

Kit looked up at Charlie. Charlie looked at Kit. A little smile touched the kit's darkly mottled face, the first smile Charlie had seen. Pulling the wet, dirty cat warm against her, Charlie imagined Lucinda and Pedric tramping up Hellhag Hill in the dark, imagined those two old people going down into Hellhag Cave, calling and calling the kit, and she shuddered.

"When she didn't come home," Lucinda said, "we were terrified she'd gone forever."

Kit scrambled back to Charlie's shoulder, nearly shouting into the phone. "I didn't . . . I didn't mean to worry you, Lucinda. I love you!"

"We'll be there," Lucinda said. "Ten minutes, as soon as we can get down the hill, we'll be there to get you."

When they'd hung up, Charlie gave Kit some more chicken, and finished making her own sandwich. "Those caves go on forever, Kit! They could have been lost down there!" Though it was hard to be mad at the kit. Charlie had never been able to find anything written, and had found no person who could tell her, where those black fissures ended; but the tales about Hellhag Cave

443

were not pleasant. Carrying her sandwich and Kit back to her studio, she tucked the little cat into an easy chair, in a warm blanket, and sat down at her computer. Already Kit was nodding off.

But she couldn't work, she sat watching Kit sleep, watching the nervous twitch of Kit's paws, as if she was still running; and Charlie's heart twisted at Kit's occasional sharp mewls of fear.

As Charlie waited for Lucinda and Pedric to come for their lost kit, Joe Grey and Dulcie were preparing to search for Roman Slayter's gun, relying on Kit's information. They were flying blind, not at all sure what finding a gun would prove — unless it was the gun that killed Dufio. Or, if Chichi was looking for a gun, and if Chichi had been so pushy trying to learn where Slayter was staying . . . Though that didn't add up to much, it was enough to put them on Slayter's case. Cop sense or cat sense, Joe had the gut feeling this was worth a shot.

If they did find a gun in Slayter's room, and could hide it where the cops could find it, they might fit together a couple more pieces of the puzzle — a puzzle that seemed as nebulous as smoke on the wind.

They knew that Lucinda and Pedric were searching for Kit, that the old couple had been out since before daylight, and Dulcie was frantic for the kit; she alternated between feeling bad that she and Joe weren't searching, and sensibly admitting that Joe was right, that this was Kit's call, Kit's responsibility. Though Joe had, Dulcie noticed, glanced up to the southerly hills several times with a listening and worried frown.

Now the two cats lay comfortably on a warm, tarred rooftop across the street from the Gardenview Inn, scanning the windows and balconies hoping to spot Slayter. Kit had not heard which room. They knew better than to call and ask for a guest's room number; no respectable hotel would divulge that information. The building was a creamy stucco of Mediterranean style, three stories high, topped by a low, red clay roof and a dozen chimneys, implying that each large room boasted a fireplace. In the center of the long building three steps led up to an entry that opened directly into a small, bright lobby — they could see through it to glass doors at the back, opening out again to a garden and terrace between beds of roses. "You want to do the diversion?" Joe said. "Or shall I?"

Dulcie sighed. "You do it. I'll slip up on the desk, see if I can find the room number."

"Dulcie, if you don't quit worrying about the kit, I swear . . ."

"She *could* be in trouble."

"And if she is? How do you propose we find her out on a thousand acres of open land?"

"Lucinda and Pedric have gone looking."

"Lucinda and Pedric have a car."

"We could . . ."

Joe sat back down on the warming black rooftop, looking hard at her. "She's a big cat now. She is not a kitten anymore."

"But that Stone Eye . . . If she . . . I'm sorry, Joe. I just can't get it out of my mind that she needs us."

"That's the mothering instinct. If you want to go look for her, fine. Maybe you can find Lucinda and Pedric, join up with them. I'm going to find that gun or whatever Chichi's looking for."

Dulcie sighed again, and followed Joe as he dropped down onto a copper awning, then to a raised planter, and to the street and across on the heels of a half dozen tourists.

Earlier this morning, coming from home, she had detoured by the Greenlaws' second-floor terrace, had stood pressed against the glass door, looking in. The old couple's apartment had been dark and empty. Wilma had *said* they were out searching. And Wilma would be, too, Dulcie thought, except that she was the only reference librarian on duty this morning. Trotting with Joe across the street, she paused beneath a little bench. She watched him strut into the lobby and on through, bold as brass, and out the back to the patio. In a moment, his tomcat yells and blood-curdling screams filled the hotel, the street, the block.

Joe himself couldn't be seen among the roses; but with creative mimicking and plenty of pizzazz, he produced a fight between two tomcats that was so real, it was all she could do not to run before the two beasts found her. Gathering her wits, she watched the clerk and two more women hurry out into the patio with rolled-up newspapers, and one with a plastic wastebasket, which she filled with water at an outdoor tap.

The minute the lobby was empty she raced in and leaped to the desk, landing practically on top the guest register. She was pawing through, wondering how long ago Slayter had registered, how far back she'd have to turn the pages — and was keeping an eye on Joe in case those three women grabbed him — when Slayter himself appeared in the doorway, coming in from the street. Swallowing a hiss, Dulcie dropped behind the desk, then wondered why she'd done that. She was a cat, a dumb and simple cat!

In a moment she hopped casually up onto a file cabinet among untidy stacks of papers and books. Crouching where she could see through the window to the back garden, she pretended to pay no attention to Slayter. How could someone so handsome make her so uneasy?

He was dressed in pale slacks, sleek dark loafers, a dark shirt and a tan suede blazer. Pausing in the small lobby, looking out the window, he watched with amusement the scene in the garden. The three women had chased Joe up out of their reach onto a high wall. There the tomcat crouched among a tangle of ivy, licking angrily at his drenched coat. Slayter's grin had turned sly and, she thought, cruel — his amusement made Dulcie's fur crawl.

She hadn't yet found his room number; as Slayter moved on toward the hall, she came out from behind the desk and sat down where she could see the elevator. She watched him enter, then watched the dial; when its swinging arm stopped on three, she fled for the stairs that peeked out from behind the elevator's confining walls.

Racing up the two carpeted flights, she heard the elevator stop above her, heard the door open and close. As she hit the last step panting, she heard a door slam down the hall to her left. Peering around the corner, she scanned the hall in both directions.

Empty to her left, a maid's cart far down to her right. No maid in sight, but near it the door to one room stood open. Turning away toward the sound of Slayter's slamming door, she scented along the thick carpet, her nose and taste filled with the freshly laid smell of good leather and expensive, musky aftershave, the same aroma that had accompanied Slayter through the lobby. The trail ended at 307. On down the hall a narrow, carved table supported a potted plant beneath a large mirror with an old, hand-carved frame such as she had seen in the expensive antiques shops. Padding into the shadow beneath the table, she sat down, considering Slayter's closed door.

The room was on the west, so would overlook the garden. She wondered if Slayter had been sufficiently entertained by the tomcat's plight to be standing at the window now, looking down with that unpleasant smile. She hoped, if that was the case, that

Joe got the hell out of there. How long would Slayter be in his room? If she waited until he left, and she was quick, could she slip in behind his heels?

If she failed at that, surely she could get in when the maid came to do up the room — but who knew how soon that would be?

Kit's notion that there was something in his room that Chichi wanted might be all wild imagination. Except that Chichi *had* searched Abuela's house. *Was* the object of her search the gun she hadn't found? Whatever, there was surely something definitely "off" about Chichi's behavior — fawning all over Clyde, her dislike and aggression toward Joe, her surveillance and partner status in Luis's crime plans. Her appearance running from the jewelry store with the black bag that later showed up in Luis's pocket, then her search of Abuela's house.

But then she had helped Clyde to free them all from the cage, and that puzzled Dulcie; except maybe Clyde had really forced her to do that. Edging deeper into the shadows beneath the little table, she curled down, waiting for Slayter, intent on getting into his room — and hoping Joe had made his sodden escape.

36

Half an hour after Dulcie settled among the shadows to watch Roman Slayter's door, Joe found her there asleep on the hall carpet beneath the little table. Having waited for her in the garden as he cleaned himself up, after that fool woman threw water on him, he had at last gone looking for her. If she'd gotten into Slayter's room, she'd better be well hidden. From the garden wall, he'd seen Slayter up at a third-floor window, sitting as if at a table. Then when he'd tracked Dulcie through the lobby and up the stairs, there she was asleep in the hall. He nudged her.

She woke at once. "Where have you been? He's in there."

"I know, I saw him from the garden, sitting by the window with the TV on. What's to watch, in the daytime? The soaps? He made two phone calls, and answered three; I could just hear the phone ringing, and saw him pick up. Could you hear anything? But you were asleep."

"I . . ."

451

"I wish you'd stayed awake. I'd give a case of caviar to know what those calls were. So many pieces that don't add up."

"They never add up until the last shoe drops, the last mouse runs out of the hole."

Joe settled down beside her. They were softly whispering, patiently watching Slayter's door, when a door just beyond them flew open and a second maid came out, wheeling her squeaky cart. She passed by three closed doors with DO NOT DISTURB signs on them, and knocked at 307.

"Housekeeping."

"Come in," Slayter called. She used her passkey, then flipped down the little door-stop to hold the door open. The cats, scrunching down beside the cleaning cart, were ready to make a dash inside when they heard the elevator humming, heard it stop at the third floor. Heard its door slide open and soft footsteps coming their way along the carpet, and they smelled the sweet, flowery scent of Chichi Barbi's perfume. Hunching smaller, they stared at each other. Joe ducked his head down to hide his white nose and chest and paws.

Chichi hesitated beside the maid's cart; then everything happened at once: They heard Slayter inside talking with the maid, heard the closet door slide open, heard him coming. Swift as a cat herself, Chichi drew back into the recess of the door to the ice machine. She watched, unseen, as Slayter left his room and went on down the hall, carrying a newspaper. The minute he stepped into the elevator and the door closed, Chichi came out and stood listening.

The maid was in Slayter's bathroom, running the water as she cleaned. Chichi slipped quickly in. Joe and Dulcie followed, strolling in behind her between the cart and the door. They stood watching as Chichi tossed the room. She checked beneath the mattress, which was on a solid platform, shook out the tangled bedding to glance underneath, then dropped it in a heap. Stepping to the open closet she did a thorough job on his suitcase that stood inside on a stand, and on the hanging clothes. Fast and efficient, she was heading across to the windows when the maid came out of the bathroom.

"Hi!" Chichi said brightly, not missing a beat. "Roman sent me back up to find his jacket, he's waiting in the lobby. The blue one, but it isn't here. Could it be in the bathroom?"

"There's no jacket in there," the Latino maid said suspiciously, moving toward the phone. Quickly she picked it up, but before she could call security, Chichi was gone — and so were Joe and Dulcie. Chichi out the door, the cats behind the open draperies.

It was there they found the gun, in a hiding place so efficient that no maid would be apt to look. Maybe no one would discover it unless they were doing electrical repairs — or had their nose to the carpet.

Except a cop. Any cop would spot the loose carpet in the corner behind the draperies — but the cats were aware of more than that. They crouched in the corner excitedly sniffing the faint, distinctive scent, trying to close their ears against the violent roar of the maid's vacuum cleaner. They stared down at the loose carpet beneath their paws; Dulcie patted at it, her green eyes wide. Joe nosed at the crack where the carpet met the wall, where the rug did not lie snugly — where it had been lifted, then secured back in place. He clawed it back to get his teeth in, and pulled with a ripping sound.

"Double-sided tape," Dulcie whispered, and they pulled back the carpet to look at the floor beneath.

The plywood floor had been cut into a six-inch square, as if removed and then replaced. The wall at the corner was lumpy, too, as if it had also been cut, then repaired and replastered. "Old building," Dulcie said. "Older than the wing that goes along the end of the garden. Maybe when it was built, they had to make some changes here in the wiring?"

Together they clawed the plywood up. It fitted so snugly it was hard to remove without ripping out a claw. Beneath it, a black hole gaped, filled with wiring and with a plastic pipe running through. Concealed back beneath the old part of the floor, half hidden by wiring, lay a dark handgun, a plain blue semi-automatic with a dark grip. They could see that the clip was in. As their eyes adjusted, they could see the round silver S-and-W logo of Smith and Wesson on the grip. The cats looked at each other and smiled. Slayter had discovered an excellent hiding place — except for the nosiness of cats.

They had no way of knowing if the gun was loaded without removing the clip, and neither was about to try that. "I told you there was a gun," Dulcie said. "That Chichi was searching for a gun. What do we do now?"

Before Joe could answer, the loud, brassy blast of a jazz trumpet drowned even the roar of the vacuum, bursting up from the courtyard.

"It's starting," Dulcie said. "The first bands must be set up."

"The streets will be wall-to-wall traffic, the sidewalks a forest of feet."

"But it's only just past noon. Luis wouldn't hit those shops this time of day?" She stared down into the hole, at the gun. "What'll we do with it? Leave it here or . . . ?"

"We're not handling that thing. You want to haul that over the roofs? Besides, we can't move evidence. You know that."

"Was evidence what Chichi was looking for?"

"Whatever, the cops need to find it right here." Slipping the plywood back into place, he pressed the carpet flat over it. Sudden silence beyond the drapery, then little rustles of fabric told them the maid was making the bed. They listened as she plumped the pillows and moved around as if straightening the folders on desk and table. At last they heard the welcome squeak of wheels as she moved the cart, the click as she snapped the doorstop up, then the door slammed closed. They heard her turn the handle, testing the lock, then blessed silence. They'd have the room to themselves until Slayter returned.

Slipping out from behind the drapery, Joe leaped to the nightstand, pressed the phone for an outside line, and punched in Harper's private number. Quickly he gave Harper the location and told him where the gun was hidden. He wished he understood Chichi's role in this. If she was working with Luis, and apparently with Slayter, then why was she snooping? The only answer that came to mind was far too simple, and didn't seem to fit Chichi. Sure didn't fit her past behavior, ripping Clyde off. Across the room, Dulcie reared up against the door, working at the knob.

She had turned it and was swinging on it, ready to kick it open, when the door flew violently open. Joe thought she was crushed as Slayter hurried in; but she twisted and leaped out behind him, and was gone. Joe had time only to drop into the thin space between the bed platform and the wall, a crack that had been left to allow the bedside lamps to be plugged in, a space so narrow he had to wriggle to get in at all, and then could hardly breathe. He felt trapped there, and he sure was trapped in the room with Slayter. He hoped Dulcie wouldn't linger out in the hall or try to get him out. At least he wasn't crouched in the corner on top of the gun, in case Slayter went for it.

And Slayter did just that. Joe heard him pull the drapery back, heard the ripping sound as he pulled the carpet up, a screech as he lifted the plywood. To the accompaniment of the welcome noise, Joe slid on through to the far side of the bed nearest the door, and reared up to peer up over the bed.

He watched Slayter remove the clip and check it, replace it, and jack one into the chamber. Watched him slide the gun into a body holster beneath his jacket. As he turned, Joe dropped down again, backing deeper into the space between bed and wall.

This time when Slayter left the room the man moved so swiftly, barely cracking the door open, that Joe almost didn't make it. Scorching out behind Slayter's ankles without brushing against his leg, Joe followed on his heels. He meant to streak across the hall and in through the open door of the room that was marked ICE MACHINE — but Slayter headed that way, moving directly into the soft-drink room and through it, and through a door marked MAINTENANCE. He heard Slayter's hard shoes climbing the concrete stairs that would be used by maintenance to access all floors, stairs that probably led to the roof, to the vents and heating equipment. Had Dulcie gone that way? He heard the heavy door at the top slam, a door that sounded too heavy for Dulcie to have opened.

Joe didn't like going up on the roof with Slayter, even if he could get the door open. But if Dulcie was there . . .

And, he had told Harper where the gun was hidden, but now it wasn't there. Slayter was wearing it, and if an officer approached him . . .

Had he seen a house phone on top of the little table in the hall? But you couldn't call out on a house phone. Slipping back into the hall, he could see the cleaning cart down at the far end. Racing down, he paused by the open door, listening to water running and the TV tuned into a Spanish station. Before he could think better of it, he was inside the room and on the desk, punching in Harper's number. It crackled when Harper answered.

"He retrieved the gun. Wearing it in a shoulder holster, left side. He's gone up on the roof." He waited to be sure Harper wouldn't ask him to repeat, then hung up and was gone, out into the hall again, his nose filled with the stink of disinfectant — and he headed fast for the roof.

37

Cars lined the curbs and filled the streets, creeping slower than a cat would walk. Dulcie sat on the roof of the Gardenview Inn waiting for Joe and beginning to worry. She grew more certain each minute that she should go back, that Slayter had caught him. Below her in the street, drivers held up the single lines of traffic to let people out onto crowded sidewalks. The cacophony of a dozen jazz bands made her ears ache. Any sensible cat would be home, hiding under the bed among the dust mice.

Dulcie loved the beat of the old classic jazz — she'd just like it not all mixed together. She was so awash in Dixieland that she felt giddy. Where was Joe? At last, losing patience, she spun around and raced back across the hotel's tile roof to the little raised portion of the building that housed the stairwell — but before she could try to fight the door open, she heard footsteps coming up the stairs.

Fleeing away among the shadows of the

chimneys, she watched the door swing in, and Roman Slayter emerge. He left the door cracked, did not let the latch click. Moving to the edge of the roof, he stood considering the street below.

Had Slayter locked Joe in his room? But Joe could get out, he could turn the knob just as she had — if he hadn't hurt Joe. In a sudden panic, she crouched to leap for the door; she drew back when it began to swing open again, this time without sound.

Joe Grey emerged silently behind Slayter, glancing across the roof to Dulcie.

Slayter had a cell phone in his hand, and was looking away to the center of the village, across several blocks of rooftops. The cats could see, beyond an open lot where an ancient cottage had been torn down, that he had a clear view of the courthouse and PD. He could see the front of the station, and the back area beside the jail where the patrol units parked. They watched him punch in a preprogrammed call. He spoke softly.

"Looks like the expected number of patrols are cruising. Hardly moving, in the crush. Half a dozen uniforms on foot, mixing with the crowd. Four CHP units up along the highway. I think we're . . . Wait . . ."

Slayter was quiet as two men emerged

from the back door of the station and quickly crossed the police parking lot. When they hit the side street they moved off in different directions. Slayter described them; dressed as civilians, they wore faded shirts, worn jeans, the kind of clothes favored by many locals, comfortable and innocuous.

"Not sure," Slayter said, in answer to a question. As the men moved into the center of the village where the music was loudest, Slayter relayed their positions. "You have someone on them?" Dulcie glanced across at Joe. Had Roman Slayter figured out Harper's carefully planned sting? If there *was* another snitch working, she'd hate to think it was someone in the department.

Or was Slayter simply covering all bases? Whatever the case, from this vantage he could see every officer who left the station, uniformed or wearing street clothes. He could track every cop Harper assigned, see where they went, which mark they observed, and pass it on to Luis. She looked frantically across at Joe; the tomcat looked furious, his eyes blazing with a challenge so predatory that Dulcie felt her fur stand up. They had to stop Slayter before he ruined the carefully laid sting, before cops were attacked, civilians caught in possible gunfire.

Crouching, every muscle at ready, she

took her cue from Joe, praying they didn't kill themselves. A blaze of fire in Joe's yellow eyes, and a twitch of his ear, and she raced across the roof beside him . . .

". . . brown leather jacket," Slayter was saying, "tan Chinos, long blond hair and. . . ."

Together they leaped, hitting Slayter's back with all the power they had and all claws digging.

The force of their assault sent him to his knees, scrambling at the edge of the roof, gurgling a scream. The phone went flying. Like a streak Joe snatched it and was gone again, the phone sticking out both sides of his mouth like a dog bone; he vanished behind a chimney.

Before Slayter could get to his knees, shaking his head and twisting unsteadily around to see what had hit him, Dulcie landed on his back and struck him in the face. He screamed, twisting away, pulling loose the frail metal gutter as he tried to steady himself. He lost his grip and went over, snatching at air. Dulcie raked him again and leaped free; with a twisting grab she snagged the edge of the roof with her claws. She was swinging helplessly, trying to pull herself up, when Joe grabbed the side of her neck in his teeth and jerked her back to the roof. They heard Slayter hit the balcony below with a dull thud. They ran, stopping only for Joe to snatch up the phone again.

Scorching away across the rooftop and among some heating equipment, they paused at last, panting; and Joe punched in Harper's number.

Dulcie watched the roof behind them, but there was no sign of Slayter trying to climb up. She was a bundle of nerves at how close she'd come to falling maybe the whole three stories; she'd counted on Slayter cushioning her fall, and she guessed Joe had thought that, too. Beside her, he had Harper on the line.

He told the chief what they'd seen. "Slayter made three of your men." Joe described the three. "Gave directions to where the first two were headed. And then, I don't know exactly what happened, but he fell. It was pretty confused, I guess he might be hurt, though he only fell to the second-floor balcony."

"Where the hell are you?" Harper's voice was ragged. "If you saw him fall, you *know* what happened."

Harper didn't ask who this was; he knew the snitch's voice. "*How* did he fall?"

"His cell phone's lying on the roof where he fell." Joe hit end call and flipped the phone closed. Quickly carrying it back where he'd snatched it, he laid it in the gutter. Cautiously peering over, he smiled.

He returned to Dulcie, still smiling. "He's down there curled up and groaning, holding himself like he hurts bad." He glanced back with longing at the abandoned phone. He'd always wanted his own cell phone; but sensibly he turned away. "Let's get out of here." They headed away fast, before the cops arrived. Maybe the department could trace the numbers Slayter had called; most likely it was Luis's cell number.

"What will happen," Dulcie said, "when the cops see those scratches on his back and face? What will they think? What will Harper and the detectives think?"

"What can they think? Come on, Dulcie, it's getting late." The sun, in its low southerly journey, reflected a last path of flame over the western sea. It would be gone in a minute, and the winter sky would darken fast. And as evening fell, so would Luis's marks fall.

And so will Luis's men, Joe thought, smiling. If our luck holds. But behind him, Dulcie hadn't moved. He turned to look at her. "Come on!"

She stood staring down at the street, her tail lashing. "Chichi! It's Chichi. She's headed for the Gardenview, fast. She . . ." The tabby's eyes widened. "She knows something happened to Slayter!" She looked up at Joe, wide-eyed. "Was it Chichi he was talking to? Or was she with Luis when Slayter cut out, did Luis send *her* to find out what happened?"

Paws in the gutter, Joe watched Chichi, torn between following her and hurrying on toward the blasting music and crowded streets where the action would be coming down.

"Go on," Dulcie said. "You know those officers better than I do, you can spot them easier. I'll follow Chichi."

"Too dangerous. You . . ."

"I'm not a kitten, I'll stay out of the way. Go on." And before he could argue she spun away, heading back for the Gardenview — but when she passed the place where Slayter fell, and looked over, he was gone.

She watched Chichi hurrying in through the front door, and heard the distant whirring of the elevator. Before Chichi could reach the third floor, Dulcie slipped into the rooftop stairwell and flew down — she hadn't reached the bottom when she heard from below a soft banging as someone knocked on a door. Again, harder, a fist pounding. Dulcie paused in the small utility

466

room. Insistent banging, just outside. And Dallas Garza's voice.

"Police. Open up. We need to talk with you, Slayter."

With a shaking paw she pulled the door open a crack. Three uniformed cops stood in the hall with Garza, to either side of Slayter's door. With them was a pale, lean man in a suit, maybe the hotel manager. There was no sign of Chichi. She must have fled the minute she saw the law enter the building. Maybe she doubled back to tell Luis?

Would Luis call off the operation? Oh, that would be too bad, after all Harper's planning, after bringing men in from other districts. If Luis and his men left town and no arrests were made . . .

Dallas pounded again and shouted. When there was only silence, the hotel man handed him a passkey. Standing against the wall, Dallas unlocked the door and kicked it open.

Crouched between the ice dispenser and a soft drink machine, Dulcie watched the detective and one uniform enter, leaving the other two standing guard. From down the hall, she heard the elevator descend. Someone else would be coming. . . .

The elevator did not return. But suddenly

Chichi came hurrying around the corner from the stairs — maybe she rang for it, then ran up, too impatient to wait. She paused at the open door, watching Dallas and the uniforms.

Frightened that she might be armed, Dulcie was about to shout a warning and then run, when she heard Captain Harper's voice coming up the stairs behind Chichi. Dulcie caught her breath, shocked, as the two came along the hall together, talking softly like a couple of old friends.

They entered Slayter's room, pushing the door nearly closed. Now, with the beat of jazz filling the street outside, she could barely hear them. Dallas was saying ". . . found him lying on the bed, curled up on his side like that, moaning like a stuck pig. He may have broken ribs. The shoulder looks dislocated."

Dulcie crept nearer, peering through the crack into Slayter's room. "Those scratches on his face and back," Dallas said. "Exactly like Hernando." The detective looked at Chichi. But when he said, "You have any idea what could have made them?" Dulcie lost her nerve and fled again, back up the stairs to the roof.

38

On the rooftops, Joe was awash in Tiger Rag and then Tailgate Ramble; if Dulcie were there, her paws would be twitching. He was edgy with worry about her. As he approached the leather shop, he spotted one of Harper's stakeouts, and drew back. But when he saw no action he moved on to the first jewelry store on Harper's list. Molena Point had as many jewelry stores as art galleries, both important elements in the village economy. Tourists loved going home with a painting or a bracelet or necklace to remind them of their bright vacation.

Lingering near the jewelry store was a pair of cops dressed as carefree tourists, mingling with the crowd. No one would notice their sidearms beneath those loose shirts. Most of the officers on loan from other towns had been paired with Harper's men, who knew the streets. He saw Officer Cameron, just up the street, dressed in ragged jeans and a long, loose sweater, her straight blond hair kinked into a curly mop.

She limped only slightly from her gunshot wound. Beside her, Officer Crowley tried to ease Cameron's way through the crowd, his big bony hands and the thrust of his muscled shoulders slow and deliberate. His loose denim jacket might hide any sort of weapon, and very likely his camera. The two officers wandered among the crowd, brandishing big paper cups, half dancing to the jazz beat; they paused near two of the selected shops. Above them Joe Grey paced the roof.

He was edgy for the action to begin — and for Dulcie to catch up with him. He missed Kit, too, even though she would be sure to complicate matters. Lucinda was trying to keep her in, said she wanted Kit tucked up safe tonight. Who knew how long that would last? Though in truth, the little cat had seemed worn out, hardly objecting to Lucinda's bullying — grieving over the departure of her clowder. He was thinking hard of the kit, hoping she was all right, when something nudged his shoulder and a dark shape emerged from the shadows, her eyes wide.

"What are you doing, Joe? No one told me! Where's Dulcie? It's happening! Why didn't you tell me! It's coming down," she whispered boldly. "The st . . ."

Hushing her, Joe shouldered her away from the roof's edge. "Don't even say the word. Come on." He led her into a crevice between two peaks where they could talk. It took him some time to fill her in, twice that to appease her.

"But why didn't you tell me? I could help, I can . . ."

"That's just it. There's nothing more to do. *You've* already done more than your share. Without your information, Kit, this would never have happened. If it wasn't for you, the cops wouldn't have a clue! You're already a hero."

"But . . ."

"We thought you'd like to rest."

She looked at him as if he was crazy; she wasn't buying this. He licked her ear, explaining how worried they'd been about her, how glad that she was safe, that she'd escaped Stone Eye. It took a long time of coddling before she smiled again and made up, and followed him silently across the roofs. They were approaching another of the targeted jewelry stores when they spotted Officer Brennan wandering through the crowd, eating an ice-cream cone.

How different a man could look with a simple change of clothes. Instead of his dark uniform, Brennan wore a flowered shirt and a slouch hat. He looked thinner in the bright, loose shirt, but more florid. Half a block behind Brennan, rookie Jimmie McFarland wandered and gawked; he was dressed in a bright plaid sport coat and carrying a clarinet case, a big grin on his face. The two officers paused half a block apart, Brennan looking in the window of a golf shop, McFarland idly striking up a conversation with a pretty young tourist.

All over the village Harper's men were in place among the crush of civilians and with strict instructions not to fire their weapons, to use only a taser if such force was absolutely needed. That had to be stressful. And surely they'd got the word that three of their group had been spotted.

As the two cats crouched on the veranda of a penthouse above a leather shop, they saw tall, beanpole Officer Blake come around the corner, carrying a trombone case and a clarinet case. He'd have camera stuff in the trombone case; but Blake did play a mean clarinet. Joe watched three women in short skirts with amazement. Officer Davis was hardly recognizable out of her dark, severe uniform. In a miniskirt over those pale, stocky legs, Davis was not an appealing sight. All three women wore boots that could hide a weapon. He glanced at Kit.

"What are you grinning about. You're not laughing at Davis."

She shook her head. "I wouldn't. It just seems so strange. Disguised cops, disguised crooks, and civilians mingling all together in the bars and restaurants. Like a story . . ."

"Luis won't think it's a story," Joe said darkly. They heard, in the distance, a Count Basie number echoing out from the Molena Point little theater where there was a Basie concert, his music copied by a new generation of jazzmen. It was perhaps six-thirty when, quietly among the crowds, the crooks began to move.

Slayter lay uncomfortably on a stretcher, staring up at Garza as the detective read him his rights. Captain Harper and Chichi Barbi stood near the door. From across the hall, Dulcie watched, drawing back behind the ice machine only as Garza finished and the two paramedics carried the stretcher out, accompanied by two armed officers. Harper and Chichi stepped out behind them and stood in the hall, talking. Behind them in the room, Garza was collecting evidence. Dulcie still hadn't figured it all out, except that Chichi didn't seem to be under suspicion for anything. That, while she was passing her snoop lists to Luis, Chichi had given copies to Harper.

Dulcie had watched Garza drop Slayter's cell phone into an evidence bag, and then Slayter's gun. She had watched the two officers search the hole in the corner, removing the plywood, shining their flashlights down into it and feeling back underneath the wiring, then dusting the plywood and wiring for prints. As happened so many times, she could only pray there were no paw prints or cat hairs.

Dallas had already printed the room before Chichi entered, and had bagged Slayter's clothing and personal items. He had photographed the scratch wounds on Slayter's face and back, and that was stressful for Dulcie. What did he think? What did he wonder? Now, in the hall, he asked Chichi, "You said you know nothing about how he fell? And about how he got those scratches?"

Chichi shook her head. "I didn't see it, I was in the village with Luis. He was talking with Slayter, on his cell. Slayter was describing one of your men. He . . . then he screamed, then a bang as if he'd dropped the phone, and Luis couldn't rouse him. The line was dead, Luis dialed him back and got the message recording. That's when he sent me to see what happened. How *did* he fall?"

"You heard him." Harper shook his head. "Says he was pushed from behind, that he didn't see anything. That someone hit him hard between the shoulders and when he fell, they hit him again — some kind of weapon with sharp prongs." The captain frowned. "Crazy. Said it felt like he was raked with metal spikes, like an old-style golf shoe — he glimpsed something dark, the size of a golf shoe."

"Attacked with a golf shoe?" Chichi giggled.

Harper gave her a lopsided grin. "Weird kind of weapon. Why would someone . . . Well, maybe it was handy . . . You hit a guy with one of those old, metal-spiked golf shoes you could do that kind of damage."

"I'm glad it's over," she said, smiling up at him. "Or nearly so. If that turns out to be the gun that killed Frank, I'll be forever indebted to you, Captain."

"Thank you for your help, Chichi. We should know about the gun tomorrow, if the DA has Frank Cozzino's records in order."

"I hope he does. It's been a hard time." She started to turn away. "I'll call you in the morning then?"

Harper took her hand. "Call me, or Garza or Davis. We'll see what we get."

As Chichi headed down the hall and Harper returned to Slayter's room, behind the ice machine Dulcie sat putting the pieces together.

If Frank Cozzino ran with Luis's gang, but somewhere along the line he began feeding information to LAPD, then Luis might well want him dead. Slayter was part of the gang — Luis could have assigned Slayter to do the deed. Slayter had told Ryan he'd come up here to find out who killed Cozzino; but maybe Slayter had done it.

So who, Dulcie thought, killed Dufio? And why? She watched Dallas seal the door to 307 with evidence tape, watched the detective and captain head for the elevator. Then she fled up the stairs and through the heavy door, leaving it ajar, and away across the rooftops to find Joe. She longed to see Luis and his men arrested, see every last one of them jailed.

She spotted Joe and Kit on the roof of Molena Point Inn — you might know Kit would have slipped out and found him. The two cats, crouched at the edge of the shingles, peered over into the inn's secluded patio; when Dulcie pushed in between them, she saw that the crowds hadn't yet discovered the small hidden garden. Only one tourist couple was there, strolling hand in hand, smiling as if glad to have found some privacy: a plainly dressed, thirtyish man and woman with simple, neat haircuts, out-of-style starched shirts that branded them as being from a small midwestern town, and loving expressions.

The patio was enclosed on one side by the hotel, on the other three by rows of exclusive shops. There were no alleys between the shops. The couple seemed to have no interest in the fine china and silver and designer gowns, seemed aware only of each other. They sat down close together on a bench facing Emerson's Jewelry, their backs to the small pepper tree and lush flowers. The woman, fishing around in her large handbag, handed her partner a small, high-powered gas torch.

Moving quickly into a narrow walkway between the hotel and the jewelry store, he lit the torch and turned to face the wall where a locked, foot-square metal door closed off the electric meter. Burning quickly through the padlock, he opened the little door and turned off the power for that building.

With nothing to activate the security alarm, he stepped around into the patio again and used the torch to destroy the deadbolt lock on the jewelry store's glass door. Silently swinging the door open, he and his lady friend entered. Within two minutes they had breached seven jewelry cases, dropping the contents — diamonds, emeralds, heavy gold and pearl chokers — into her handbag and into his pockets. Leaving the shop, they closed the door quietly behind them.

Strolling away, they joined a crowd gathered around the Blue Gull Café, where they stood listening to a jazz trio that owed its style and funky beat to the legacy of Louis Armstrong. The trumpet player didn't sound as good as Satchmo. No one could. But he had a nice riff and a sure beat, and the crowd was rocking. The couple moved with the beat, then strolled on up the sidewalk, keeping time to Back 'O Town Blues.

Half a block behind them a pair of young men followed: muscular, skinny guys with sun-bleached hair, dressed in faded jeans and worn sweatshirts.

"Nice," Dulcie said. "They look like surfers."

"Let's make sure," Joe said, moving on quickly until he could look back and get a glimpse of the officers' faces; turning back, he grinned at Dulcie and narrowed his eyes with satisfaction. He'd seen the two men earlier, entering the station with Dallas Garza. Confident that in a few minutes, and when their quarry had moved away from the crowds, the officers would quietly make their arrests, the cats trotted on across the roofs where they could see the Oak Tree Café. Crouched between the two older cats, Kit was unusually quiet. Dulcie glanced at her several times. Was she mad because they hadn't told her the sting would be tonight? Or was she missing her feral friends? Was she wondering if she should have stayed with them, wild and free with no one to keep secrets from her and to boss her?

The Oak Tree, crowded with jazz buffs, vibrated with a throaty sax and bass and piano where a small stage had been set up inside. Next to the café was a small independent bookstore, then a shop featuring handmade children's clothes, then Karen Jenkins' Jewelry. All three were closed. From the rooftop the cats watched an elderly, gray-haired couple pause to look in the jewelry store window. They watched the portly man quickly diffuse the store's burglar alarm with a small electronic device the size of a pack of cigarettes.

"What *is* that?" Dulcie said.

"I don't know, but I mean to find out," Joe said irritably. He didn't like not knowing about such a useful invention.

"But they're elderly," Dulcie said. "They look like someone's grandparents."

"Maybe they are someone's grandparents." Joe gave her a wide-eyed look. "Does that make them law-abiding and honest?"

Dulcie preferred to think of criminals as young and rough, crude humans without any hint of gentleness. "And where are the cops? I thought they were all to have tails, I thought . . . Have they missed this one?"

Joe studied the crowd until he spotted a frail-looking young woman, slim as a model in her flowered skirt, boots, and suede jacket. "There. Eleanor Sand." Sand was Harper's newest rookie. Her companion was a clean-cut young man in jeans, with short hair and brown turtleneck sweater, on loan from up the coast. Standing in front of the café, glued to the music, they seemed unaware of the elderly burglars just three doors down. Fascinated, the cats watched Gramps and Granny within the dark store move directly to the inside meter box, where they threw the breaker, perhaps so that other alarms, within the store, wouldn't be triggered.

"These old stores!" Joe said. "These old simple alarm systems."

"You think the owners deliberately made it simple tonight? Deactivated some more sophisticated warning device? The whole idea is to let the perps get in and out again."

The tomcat smiled. "Maybe." He watched the old couple, working together, jimmy and empty nine glass showcases. "Those two might be grandparents, but they're skilled at their trade."

Leaving the store, the gray-haired couple wandered away into the crowd apparently confident they hadn't been noticed. A half block behind them, Eleanor Sand and her companion wandered aimlessly in the same direction. All around the village, similar break-ins were occurring in small, unnoticed corners, and similar teams of officers followed their progress, then made their arrests in other isolated retreats. The cats missed the action at Marineau's Jewelry.

So did the Greenlaws, though Lucinda and Pedric were sitting on their terrace enjoying the tangled mélange of music and watching the crowds below. Neither noticed a darkly dressed Latino man slip down the alley next to Marineau's, open the shop's metal-sheathed side door with a key, and slip inside. No smallest light shone. Nothing could be seen through the boarded-up windows. The Greenlaws did not see him leave, five minutes later, the pockets of his trench coat bulging with items taken from the safe for which he also had keys. Neither Lucinda nor Pedric was aware that, while the jazz group down the street at Bailey's Fish House played the gutteral, funky music of the old Preservation Hall group, Marineau's was being cleaned out a second time, with keys whose patterns had been taken the first time around. And meanwhile, four blocks away, the cats were intent on redheaded Tommie McCord and his Latino partner, as they strolled away from the last jewelry store on the list, walking along laughing and swilling cans of beer.

Neither man realized that Officers Brennan, who had already made one arrest, and Julie Wade, dressed as a frowzy pair of tourists, followed half a block behind, pawing each other and peering into shop windows, Brennan's big belly and firearm covered by his loose shirt printed with palm trees. Wade was on loan from Santa Cruz PD. She wore a long, smock-like blouse and long, full skirt; very likely the officers' garments concealed not only regulation automatics but radios, cell phones, handcuffs, and belly chains.

As Tommie McCord and his friend turned away into a dark residential street, leaving the scene, and headed up toward the crowded hillside cottages, the cats followed them over the rooftops. The cats watched as they were arrested. No shot was fired. Tommie tried to run, and got pepper spray in his face, which made him double up, choking. His friend got a dose of the taser that put him on the sidewalk, for trying to take down Officer Wade. Cuffed and helped into a squad car, they would be, as Kit said, "Locked in a cage themselves. Let's see how they like that." This kit was not big on forgiveness.

39

The cells of Molena Point jail were indeed satisfyingly overcrowded. Men were stacked in the bunks and sleeping on pads on the concrete floor. The department's evidence room was equally full, its safe filled with sufficient small, sealed bags of jewelry and valuables to convict an army of thieves. The detectives' reports had gone to the DA. All arrestees had been denied bail. It would be some weeks after the Greenlaws moved into their new house before the town would be treated to the full details of the sting — or to that part of the story that could be told, and that those in the department knew. Some facts would remain unrevealed even to the chief — forever, the three cats hoped.

The Greenlaws' housewarming was impromptu but satisfying in its camaraderie and good cheer. The hodgepodge of treasures with which the old couple had furnished their new home formed an amazing collection, gleaned from used-furniture stores, garage sales, and the most exclusive shops. On a three-day shopping trip to the city with Hanni Coon, to the exclusive designer showrooms, they had purchased the last pieces; except for the bright primitive rugs, which had come from Hanni's own showroom. Among their purchases was a large box marked "Kit," destined for the tree house.

The night after the last deliveries were made and in place, George Jolly's team arrived bearing trays of delicious selections; the Greenlaws' front door was propped open, the department brought the wine and beer, and cops and civilians crowded the bright rooms. While out in the tree house, Dulcie and Joe and Kit reclined among a tangle of exotic new pillows.

Lori Reed and Dillon Thurwell had been eager to carry the pillows and the cats' loaded plates up a ladder. The girls had wanted to have their own supper there, but Lucinda made it clear this was Kit's exclusive property. Both girls had, however, begun dreaming of tree houses of their own, plotting how to accomplish that endeavor.

The cats, full of delicacies, sleepily watched the party from their cushions, through Kit's open window, and listened to conversations and laughter too tangled together to make sense. Cop talk; woman talk;

talk of children and clothes and cooking; cop jokes and excessive high spirits. The Rivas trial was scheduled for two days hence. The eighteen prisoners had decided on one group trial, perhaps because their sleazy L.A. attorney might charge them less — if they were paying him at all. Who knew what kind of favors Luis was calling in? Certainly the single trial would cost the county far less. Though Roman Slayter would stand trial alone for the murders of Frank Cozzino and Delfino Rivas. The evidence in both cases was solid. Ballistics showed that one of Slayter's several guns had killed both men. Three other firearms were found in the trunk of his car, including a .22 revolver. Chichi thought Slayter had killed Dufio because Dufio alone had seen Slayter kill Frank. Certainly Dufio had been near when Frank went down.

"And the gun that I found under Abuela's dryer," Dulcie said, "that didn't kill anyone."

Joe shrugged. "Not that they know of. But it was stolen. Who knows what might turn up later, in some other case."

"There she is," Dulcie said, peering out the treehouse window. "Chichi. Just coming in." The tabby cat stared, her green eyes wide. "How different she looks!"

Chichi stepped across the tile entry beside Detective Davis and Dallas Garza, just behind Ryan and Clyde. Since the department knew the whole story, since Chichi had furnished a preponderance of evidence, she was more than comfortable with the officers. She did not look hard now, not like the brittle Chichi Barbi the cats knew. She was dressed in a soft, pale, loose-fitting blouse belted over a gathered skirt, and sandals. Her pale hair was pulled back and caught at the neck with a simple clip. She wore little makeup, just a touch of lipstick.

"She's really pretty," Joe said, gawking. "Who would have thought?"

Dulcie and Kit smiled. All females like to see a successful makeover; unless of course they are jealous.

"She told Clyde she might stay here," Joe said, "after the trial. Look for a real job and a small apartment. Says she likes the village." He watched her with interest. "Since the sting, since they arrested Slayter, she hasn't come on to Clyde at all." He yawned, full of Jolly's delicacies, and sinfully comfortable among the cushions; and for a little while, the gray tomcat dozed.

He woke when Dulcie nudged him. "Come on, people are leaving, we can clean up the plates."

He stared at her. "You can't be serious. After what we just had to eat?" But Dulcie spun away through the window, Kit followed her, and the three cats headed across the oak branch and in through the dining-room window. They paused on the wide sill. People were shrugging on coats, carrying away little paper plates filled with leftovers. Charlie beckoned to them and as she cleared the long table, she filled clean paper plates for them.

"I don't know how you can eat so much." She set their suppers down on the window-sill, and stroked and hugged them. "Such good work," she whispered. Though they didn't dare answer, they let their looks warm her. From the kitchen door, Wilma watched them, smiling.

At the dining table, Pedric was saying, ". . . the faux jewelry, every gleaming diamond and emerald as fake as Grandma's teeth." The thin old man laughed with pleasure.

"Yes, it was," Harper said, sitting down across from Pedric, patting Charlie on the behind as she passed. "Even the key-locked safe at Marineau's was a set-up. We got some nice fingerprints off of it, and off the fake jewelry — some of those guys weren't a bit careful." Harper's long, weathered face looked happier tonight than the cats had seen in a long time. "Store owners polished the jewelry all up before it went in the cases, not a trace of their own prints."

Wilma and Lucinda came in from the kitchen and sat down. Lori and Dillon heaped their plates for the third time, and retired to the far corner of the living room, beside the tall bookcases. At the table, Detective Davis, who had resisted earlier and had eaten little, now filled her plate. If Davis was dieting, she'd lost the battle, this night.

"And all your reports are in, to the DA," Pedric said.

Harper nodded. "Two weeks ago. We're pleased that Judge Anderson denied all bail. And with this sleazy attorney Luis brought up from L.A. . . . They don't have much of a case."

Lucinda said, "And not a civilian hurt, by the grace of God and the skilled way the department handled it."

"Mostly by the grace of God," Harper said. "And the information Chichi and a couple of snitches provided."

Davis said, "We didn't have enough on Luis or Tommie to lock them up before the sting. They'd have been right out on bail . . . only circumstantial evidence to the first jewelry store burglary."

"What you did," Lucinda said, "was amazing." She looked at Chichi, who had come out of the kitchen with Charlie. "What Chichi did was very brave."

"Not brave at all," Chichi said, sitting down. "I was so angry, and hurting. I never believed the cops killed Frank, they knew he was on their side. But no one . . . Who was going to believe me? Luis swore at the hearing that he *saw* a cop shoot Frank. He did that for Slayter, lied for Slayter." She looked up at Lucinda, a hurt, naked look. "I did the only thing I could think of, hang in with Luis until I had the evidence. I hated that, hated being nice to them. I was hoping to find the gun." She looked at Harper. "But that turned out fine, that you found it.

"In L.A., when Luis ran out of the bank right behind Frank that night, I didn't see Slayter at all." She had balled up her fist, gripping her wadded napkin. "Slayter *was* there, in the shadows. Dufio told me, a couple of days before he . . . Before Slayter shot him." She shivered. "Shot him in that cell like an animal in a trap! Poor Dufio. He told me he'd seen Slayter in the shadows near the bank, but that's all he said. If he'd told me all of it, and sooner, you'd been able to arrest Slayter, and Dufio would be alive."

Wilma glanced across to Dulcie. No one

had mentioned Slayter's scratch wounds; but the subject *had* been discussed earlier, more than Wilma and the cats cared to think about . . . As had the remarkably similar wounds on Hernando Rivas's body. Wilma had been in favor of the golf-shoe theory. No shoe had been found.

It seemed more than strange, to those who knew the truth, that in neither case had the coroner found any cat hairs. Surely there must have been a few. Wilma wouldn't think of broaching that subject to John Bern, though they had been friends for many years. If Bern did not care to mention cat hairs, that was fine with her. If he knew more than he should and was keeping it to himself, that was fine, too. She wasn't going to rock the boat.

Pedric looked at Chichi. "And there's no doubt that Frank Cozzino *was* furnishing information to LAPD?" Leaning forward, his elbows on the table, the thin old man looked very frail between the harder, young officers and Clyde.

Chichi nodded. "He informed LAPD for a long time." She said no more. She did not offer an explanation as to why Frank had turned to helping the police, what had made him change his thinking, any more than she explained why she had changed.

The cats, cleaning their plates, were again so sated they could hardly keep their eyes open. Any normal cat would have been sick. Joe sat nodding on the windowsill until Clyde gathered him up, and Wilma picked up Dulcie. Kit had only to trot into the master bedroom and tuck down among the quilts — or leap out across the oak branch to slumber the night away high in her tree house.

But Kit thought it best to stay inside at night, for a while, best that the old couple would not awaken in the small hours to search among the blankets for her, then wonder if she had gone off with the wild ones again, perhaps this time forever.

I'm done with that, Kit thought. *This* is my home, with Lucinda and Pedric. Willow and Cotton and Coyote have chosen their way, they didn't want what I want. She hoped they were safe, that they'd found a place of their own far away from Stone Eye.

She thought about her three wild friends the next morning when she woke before dawn to hear the first birds chirping, and when she went to sleep the next night and heard an owl hoot outside the window. She worried about them, as Lucinda and Pedric worried about her. And then, on the night of the next full moon, she dreamed so vividly about the ferals that the following morning, when she went with Lucinda to see the finished pictures for Charlie's book, she asked Charlie. The minute she and Lucinda were in the door, Kit asked her.

"Will you take me there? On horseback, up in the hills? I don't want to go alone. Stone Eye . . . I want . . ."

But Charlie interrupted her. "I've seen them, Kit. Not up on Hellhag Hill at all, and not off beyond it. Right up there," she said, pointing up toward the hills that rose away behind the house and barn. "Up beyond our own pastures, where that little brook comes down. I saw them there. Ten cats, and I'm sure your three friends were among them. A dark-striped fellow with long ears, creamy circles around his eyes and a face like a coyote? A pure-white cat with long hair and blue eyes? And a lovely bleached calico, sleek and creamy?"

Kit nodded to all three descriptions; and Charlie rose, reaching for her jacket. "Come on, Kit. I'll take you, while Lucinda makes herself a nice cup of tea."

Lucinda nodded. "I can look at the drawings again? And read a bit of the manuscript over again?"

"Of course you can." Charlie hugged Lucinda and went to saddle her mare.

Folding a saddle blanket across the pommel of the saddle and strapping it securely, she made a comfortable perch where Kit could ride. And they were off into the hills, the mare twitching her ear as she looked around at the kit. Charlie said, "Your friends could have a home with Estrella Nava — with Maria's abuela. She might welcome a little cat, maybe all three."

"They would never go back to that house, even if Abuela did try to help them."

"Luis should be gone a long time," Charlie said. "Maria is going to stay there with Abuela. She's determined he won't come back there. She means to clean up the house and paint it, and get a job in the village. Maybe rent out the downstairs, for some income." They rode for a long time, but saw no cats. Softly, Kit called to them. They rode up in the direction of the old ruined mansion, searching for the small clowder that the three must have gathered around them. Kit called and called, but no one showed themselves. It was growing late when they turned back, the kit bitterly disappointed. And suddenly there they were, crouched on the trail before them. Charlie pulled up the mare, and sat still.

Maybe they had been following them all along, maybe afraid of Charlie. Maybe taking some time to decide about her. Perhaps they decided that if she was treating Kit so well, then she, like the man who had cut the lock off, must be a friend. As the ten cats stood watching them Kit leaped from the saddle.

Three cats came to her; and slowly, one by one, the rest of their little clowder gathered around Kit. She said, "Stone Eye hasn't bothered you?"

"You know that old mansion to the north of here?" Coyote said. "That huge stone place, all fallen down?"

"The Pamillon mansion," Kit said.

Coyote smiled. "Stone Eye is afraid to go there."

"You made a home *there?* Where the cougar . . . Where I saw a cougar once?"

"We smelled the cougar," Cotton said. "An old smell. We made a home, for now. Those cellars are full of rats. Look how fat we've grown."

Kit laughed. They were fat. She licked the cats' ears, and they talked for a long while. Their conversation, about all manner of cattish concerns, so fascinated Charlie that she began thinking of a second book. Kit told them that Abuela would give them a home, but of course that did not appeal. "No," Coyote said, looking away toward the wild hills, and toward the fallen mansion. "We would not do that. This is our life."

Charlie said, "You will come to me, if you are in need?"

They looked up at Charlie a long time. They did not seem afraid of the mare, but they were wary of the human. At last Willow said, "We will come." And as the afternoon drifted toward the hour when larger predators would come out to hunt, Kit's wild friends left her. With a last whisker rub for Kit, and a flick of ears and tail for Charlie, gestures that Charlie would not forget, the wild clowder was gone into the falling evening. And Charlie and Kit turned for home, both content, both smiling.

About the Author

Shirley Rousseau Murphy has received six national Cat Writers' Association Awards for the best novel of the year for the Joe Grey books and five Council of Authors and Journalists Awards for previous books. She and her husband live in Carmel, California, where they serve as full-time household help for two demanding feline ladies.

www.joegrey.com

The employees of Thorndike Press hope you have enjoyed this Large Print book. All our Thorndike and Wheeler Large Print titles are designed for easy reading, and all our books are made to last. Other Thorndike Press Large Print books are available at your library, through selected bookstores, or directly from us.

For information about titles, please call:

(800) 223-1244

or visit our Web site at:

www.gale.com/thorndike
www.gale.com/wheeler

To share your comments, please write:

Publisher
Thorndike Press
295 Kennedy Memorial Drive
Waterville, ME 04901